What was it tha

He forced himself to look s... and days of his own likely e... the longest possible lifetime ... and twenty years during which he could be active and useful. What a drop that still was in the ocean of time that was the history of human race itself.

He did not want to be just a drop in the ocean of past history . . . His whole self rebelled against the idea that he could live and die without having had any important impact on the rest of humanity . . . He must find some greater value for himself than the millions of others had . . .

He tried to picture the human race. There was much, very much, that was good about them . . . they had spread out from their original home to fifteen other worlds. But what they were on all those worlds now was largely what they had been when they first began to stand upright and think on Old Earth. They were still the same people.

Perhaps there was some way in which he could help them up the stairs, even one step toward being something better. Something more capable—as he was capable.

The moment that thought occurred to him, he knew that the had found it. *That was what he wanted to do.*

Tor books by Gordon R. Dickson

GORDON R. DICKSON

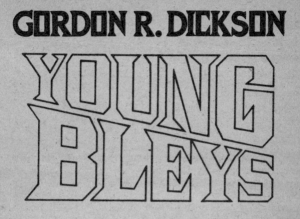

YOUNG BLEYS

A TOM DOHERTY ASSOCIATES BOOK
NEW YORK

YOUNG BLEYS

Copyright © 1991 by Gordon R. Dickson

Cover art by Royo

A Tor Book
Published by Tom Doherty Associates, Inc.
49 West 24th Street
New York, N.Y. 10010

Tor® is a registered trademark of Tom Doherty Associates, Inc.

ISBN: 0-812-50947-1
Library of Congress Catalog Card Number: 90-48781

First edition: April 1991
First mass market printing: February 1992

Printed in the United States of America

0 9 8 7 6 5 4 3 2 1

ACKNOWLEDGMENT

The author wishes to express his appreciation to Professor O. J. Harvey of the University of Colorado. The main themes of Bleys Ahrens' psychological development were based on the theory of belief systems, first published by Professor Harvey, David Hunt and Harry Schroder in 1961 and further refined by Professor Harvey, his students, and his colleagues in the intervening years. The discovery of the theory at a time when I was casting about for a scientific model that would tie my conception of Bleys Ahrens' early life to the man he would eventually become is one of those happy little accidents that has made my career as a writer so interesting.

YOUNG BLEYS is dedicated to two old friends who have shared fifty years of this twentieth century with it—Marvin and Jean Larson.

CHAPTER

1

THE WOMAN SAT on the pink fabric of the softly padded float, combing her hair before the oval mirror and murmuring to herself. Those murmurings were all repetitions of the compliments paid her by her latest lover, who had just left her.

The unbreakable but translucent brown comb slipped smoothly through the shining strands of her auburn hair. It was not in need of combing; but she enjoyed this little private ritual of her own, after the men who kept her in such surroundings as this had gone. Her shoulders were bare and delicate, with smoothly pale flesh; and the equally pale column of her neck was hidden from behind by the strands which fell clear to the float. A faint odor, as of musk and perfume mingled, came from her—so light as to make it uncertain whether she had actually touched herself with perfume, or whether it was a natural scent, one that the nostrils of another person could barely catch.

The boy stood behind her and watched, his reflection hidden from the mirror by her own image in the shimmering electronic surface. He was listening to the words she repeated, waiting for a particular phrase to come from her lips.

It would come eventually, he knew, because it was part of the litany she taught all her men, without their really knowing that she had trained them to say these things to her, during and after the time of their love-making.

He was a tall, thin boy, halfway only on his way to adulthood, and his narrow face had almost unnaturally regular features that would grow and firm into a startling handsomeness with maturity, just strong enough to be beyond all delicacy. At the same time they resembled those of the woman gazing into the mirror.

He knew this to be true, although at the moment he could not see her face. He knew it because he had heard many people say it; and had eventually come to recognize what it was to which they referred. It did not matter to him now, except in his rare encounters with other boys his own age, who, glancing at him, assumed he could be easily dominated—and found out differently. On his own, and watching the woman over his limited years, he had learned many ways of defending himself.

—Now. She was coming close to the phrase he waited for. He held his breath a little. He could not help holding it, in spite of his determination not to.

". . . *how beautiful you are,*" the woman was saying now to her image in the screen, "*never was anyone so beautiful . . .*"

It was time to speak.

"But we know different, don't we, Mother?" the boy said, with a clear calmness in his voice that only an adult should have been able to achieve—and only hours of rehearsal had made possible even for him, intelligent beyond his years as he was.

Her voice stopped.

She turned about on the float, which spun unsupported in the air to the movement of her body; and her face stared back into his from hardly a handsbreadth away.

In that moment her green eyes blazed at him. Her knuckles clenched about the comb were bloodless, holding it now like a weapon—as if she would rake its teeth across his throat to open both windpipe and carotid artery. She had not known, she had not thought—and he had planned on that—of the possibility that he might be standing behind her at one of these times.

For a long moment the boy looked at death; and if the expression of his own face did not change, it was not because the great fear of extinction was not on him, at last. It was because he was frozen, as if hypnotized, in no expression at all. He had finally taken this risk, knowing that his words might actually drive her to kill him. Because he had at last reached the point where he knew he could only survive away from her. And in the young the urge to survive is strong, even at the cost of risking death.

A few years from now and he would have known what she would do when he said what he had just said; but he could not wait to know. In a few years it would be too late.

He was eleven years old.

So he waited . . . for her to follow the impulse to kill that blazed in her eyes. For the cruelty of his words—even to her—was the utmost he could use against her. For what he had just said was true. A truth never mentioned.

They knew. They two—mother and son—knew. The woman was not bad looking, except for the heavy, squarish boning of her face. With the almost magical art of makeup she controlled, she could be taken for attractive—perhaps very attractive.

But she was not beautiful. She had never been beautiful and never would be; and it was to give her that word for which her soul hungered that she had used the great weapon of her mind, to teach those men she chose to parrot it to her at the right moments.

It was her lack of beauty, in spite of all else she had, that she could not bear. The fact that all her power of intelligence and will, that could give her everything else, could not give her this, too. And Bleys, at eleven years, had just forced her to face it. The comb, tines outward, rose in her trembling hand.

He watched the points of it approach. He felt the fear. It was a fear he had known he would feel; even as he knew he had no choice, for survival's sake, but to speak.

The comb, shaking, rose like a weapon unconsciously

driven. He watched it come, and come, and come . . . until, inches from his throat, it stopped.

The fear did not go. It was only held, like a beast on a chain; though now he knew he would live, at least. In the end, what he had gambled on—her heritage and training as an Exotic, one of a people socially incapable of any violence—was making it impossible for her to do what her torn ego urged her to do. She had left the twin worlds of the Exotics, and all their teachings and beliefs, as far behind her as she could; but she could not, even now, go against the training and conditioning they had given her, even before she had been able to walk.

The blood returned to her knuckles. The comb slowly lowered. She laid it carefully down on the table of honey-colored wood below the mirror behind her; setting it down carefully, as if it was fragile and would break at a touch, instead of being tough as steel. She was once more her controlled and certain self.

"Well, Bleys," she said, in perfectly calm tones, "I think the time has come for you and I to go different ways."

CHAPTER

2

≡≡≡

BLEYS HUNG IN space, solitary and completely isolated, light-years from the nearest stars, let alone from any world holding even one of the human race. Cold, apart, and alone, but forever free . . .

Only, his imagination would not hold. Abruptly, he lost it. It was only a private screen in the ship's lounge that he stared into—and it was full of star-points of varying brightness.

He was alone; but back with the cold, scared feeling that had never left him since he boarded, seated in one of the great, green, over-padded swivel chairs in the ship taking him from New Earth, where he had left his mother two days earlier, to the "Friendly" planet of Association, which was to be his home from now on.

One more day and he would be there.

Somehow he had not thought about the future in any detail beyond the moment when he would confront his mother. Somehow he had expected that once he had won free of her, and his legion of ever changing caretakers who kept him encased in an iron routine of study, practice, and all else, things would automatically become better. But now that he was actually in the future there was no evidence that it was going to be so.

His docking place on Association was to be the large spaceport at Ecumeny. This city had one of only twelve such spaceports on that whole world; for it was a poor planet, poor in natural resources, like its brother "Friendly" world of Harmony.

Most of the religious colonists who had settled both worlds made their living from the land, with tools and machines that were made on the planet where they lived. For there were almost no interstellar credits to pay for imported devices; except when a draft of young men would be sold off on a term contract, as mercenaries to one of the other worlds where military disputes were still going on between colonies.

Bleys had been pretending to be absorbed in that destination on his starscreen. Particularly the star of the destination, Epsilon Eridani, around which circled both Association and Harmony. As Kultis and Mara circled the star of Alpha Procyon—the twin Exotic worlds on which Bleys' mother had been born and brought up; and which she had left forever in fury and disgust at her people, the Exotics, who would not give her the privileges and liberties to which she was sure her own specialness entitled her.

Association was only eight phase-shifts from New Earth—as restatements of the ship's position in the universe were ordinarily, but not correctly, called.

If it had been only a matter of making each phase-shift in turn, Bleys was already aware, they would have been at Association in a matter of hours after leaving New Earth. But there was a problem built into phase-shifting. It was that the longer the ordinary space-time distance that was disregarded by an individual restatement, the more uncertain became the point at which the ship would return to ordinary space-time existence after making a shift. That meant recalculation of the ship's position, every time a shift was made.

Consequently, to be extra-safe for the paying passengers, this trip was being made in small shifts of position, taking a full three days. He would be met on landing at Association by the man who would take care of him from now on; the older brother of Ezekiel MacLean, one of the earlier men in his mother's life. Also, the only other permanent individual in Bleys' life along with her, for as far back as he could remember.

It was Ezekiel who had been the only bright spot in Bleys' existence. It was Ezekiel who had chosen to accept the blame not only for being the father of Bleys, but of Bleys' older half-brother, Dahno. Dahno, who had, like Bleys, been sent off to Henry MacLean and his farm on Association, some years back. It was like Ezekiel to do so.

In a strange way Ezekiel was both like and unlike Bleys' mother. She had left the Exotic worlds. He, born a Friendly on Association, had left that world as if he fled from it, rather than with the disdain and fury with which she had shaken the dust of her native world of Kultis from her feet. Ezekiel MacLean was the exact opposite of what those on other worlds imagined Friendlies to be. He was gentle, warm, easygoing—and somehow so good at all these things that he had been suffered to continue to hang around Bleys' mother and Bleys himself, through the succession of lovers that Bleys' mother had taken since.

Normally, Bleys' mother drove her former paramours from her, once she had chosen a new one. But Ezekiel seemed willing to take on a position that was half-friend, half-servant. His round, freckled face always cheerful, always obliging, he raised the spirits of Bleys' mother—and they were usually not high spirits. Ezekiel was useful to her, although he had long since been shut out of her bedroom.

An example of this convenience—for Bleys' mother had no idea of who his real father was—had been Ezekiel's contacting Henry on Association, two weeks back, to see if he would take in yet one more supposed bastard child of his wandering and irreligious brother.

Bleys had always suspected that Henry had a soft spot for Ezekiel, although Ezekiel had pictured his brother as hard as flint. Certainly, Henry had not turned Dahno, Bleys' 10-year-older half-brother down, earlier; and he had not turned Bleys down now. It had been Ezekiel, with his never-failing good humor and kindness, who had offered Bleys some relief from the iron discipline of the caretakers and his unpredictable mother. And now Ezekiel was left behind also.

Dahno, in his time, she had kept with her, on the basis that only she could control him. But this had not worked after all; and Dahno, at only a couple of years older than Bleys was now, had literally tried to run away from her. As a result she had shipped him off to Henry, and determined that she would not make the same error again.

Nor had she. She herself was completely willful and undependable. But Bleys had been put under the control of caretakers, changed as each new lover moved them to a different location and hired a different set. They guarded and ordered him at all times, letting him out only to show off to his mother's guests. At which times she basked in the reflected glory of having a genius child.

A genius he was, legitimately. But that accident of birth had been supplemented by long hours of study, under the caretakers' discipline.

Actually, the study was the last thing he minded. All things fascinated him. His mother, unable to escape her Exotic upbringing, would never, for example, have punished him physically. But the rules of an environment she laid out for him, making sure he would be under the supervision of caretakers at all times, were as rigid as those in a prison.

So it was little help that punishment was non-physical, a room to which he would be sent to "think over what he had done."

This would be a room, not unpleasant in itself, but with the only furniture in it a force-field bed, that needed no bedcoverings. It was merely a field in which the body sank until it was enwrapped by the field itself and kept at a desirable warmth and softness according to the wishes of its occupant.

It had been a room which enforced idleness. There were not even books; not merely in the archaic sense of bound cardboard and paper, but in the modern sense of spindles or disks inserted into a reading machine. So he did there what any lonely child would do; and let his imagination take him places.

He had dreamed of a land where there were no caretakers, there was no mother, and he had a wand with ultimate power that gave him unlimited authority and freedom. It had been a land where there was absolutely no changing of the people about him. That was one thing that, as absolute ruler, he insisted upon.

It was a land where he lived in sharp contrast to his real life.

He sat now, remembering all this on the spaceship to Association. He had been ecstatic at first at the idea of escaping. But gradually it had dawned on him, during these days on shipboard, that he might be going merely to the equivalent of yet another set of caretakers.

As he had used his quick, childish memory, schooled and trained until it was almost eidetic, to memorize stock tables and current news, so now he studied religious materials he had brought along to prepare himself and shield him in this new encounter—with this "uncle," and his two sons, whose names Bleys did not even yet know.

In between the times when he merely sat staring at the stars, feeling himself not so much enclosed by the warmth of the spaceship but as someone apart and isolated from the human race, placed light-years from anything human or any human world. In solitude, he had studied the material brought with him, committing long passages to memory until he had all of it tucked away to the point where he could parrot it back.

—As he had parroted back the stock tables, real estate prices, and current political actions of the world his mother was on, to make himself sound knowledgeable to her guests. When, indeed, most of the time he had no idea of the meanings of many of the words he said to them.

It was on the second day of spaceship travel that, all unprepared, he suddenly became aware of someone at his side.

Unaware of it, Bleys had been a subject of discussion in the lounge for some time now.

"I think he's lonely," one of the two uniformed women on lounge duty had been saying to the other. "Most children move around. They want soft drinks from the bar. They get bored and pester you. He just sits and isn't any trouble at all."

"Be thankful, then, and leave him to go on doing it," said the other attendant.

"No, I think he's lonely," the first attendant had insisted. "Something serious must have happened where he came from, and he's lonely and upset. That's why he's keeping to himself this way."

The other lounge attendant was skeptical. She was the senior of the two in job experience and had been on many more flights than the concerned one, who was a young, pert-faced redhead, with a small, neat body that complemented her blue and silver uniform. Finally, in spite of the strong suggestions by her co-worker that she simply leave the boy alone, the redhead approached Bleys, sitting down on the seat closest to his and swiveling it so that she could look at him from the side.

"Are you getting acquainted with the stars?" she asked.

Bleys was instantly on guard. His life had taught him to be wary of any seemingly friendly approaches. In spite of how she looked and spoke, here was most probably another caretaker come to pretend friendship as a preliminary to controlling him. It had become a reflex in him to reject any sudden attempt at friendship by people hitherto unknown; experience had too often taught him it was a false front.

"Yes," he said, hoping that the pretense of being immersed in star study would cut short the overtures of the other. Perhaps she was only going to offer to show him how to handle some of the controls—though he had already worked these out for himself. Then she would go away and leave him alone.

"You're getting off on Association, aren't you?" she persisted. "Somebody's meeting you there, of course—at the spaceport?"

"Yes," answered Bleys, "my uncle."

"Is he fairly young, your uncle?"

Bleys had no idea how old his uncle was supposed to be. But then he decided that it really made no difference how he answered.

"He's twenty-eight years old," said Bleys. "He's a farmer in a little town some distance from the spaceport and his name is Henry."

"Henry! That's a nice name," said the attendant. "Do you know his last name too, and his address?"

"His last name's 'McClain.' Actually, it's spelled 'M-a-c-L-e-a-n.' I don't know his address——"

This much was a lie. Bleys had read the address, and his memory, which now forgot almost nothing, had stored it away. But he hid that fact, just as he had learned to hide his own intelligence and skills, except in those cases where he was called upon by his mother to show them off, or the situation was such that it looked as if he could gain by performing.

"But I've got it right here at my feet," he said, and reached down toward the little bag that he kept with him at the foot of the chair, that had his identification and his letters of credit.

"Oh, you don't need to show me," said the attendant, "I'm sure you're all set. But wouldn't you like to do something else for a change, instead of just sitting here and watching your star-screen? Wouldn't you like some kind of soft drink from the bar?"

"No, thank you," said Bleys. "Watching the star-screen is part of my studies. I'm missing some school because of this vacation with Uncle Henry; so I've got to keep up on my studies as much as possible. I thought I'd do most of my space-watching on the way there, so that I wouldn't have to spend any time doing it on the way back."

"Oh. I understand," said the attendant.

It was not so much Bleys' words, as the confidence he was able to put into his voice, alert and vital, that reassured the cabin attendant. She was beginning to rethink her original guess that his trip was the result of some death or other crisis in his family, and that he had needed to be brought out of himself.

Actually, she also knew the name and address of the Association man who was to meet Bleys. It was required on all regularly-scheduled spaceliners for the cabin attendants to take on certain responsibilities toward any passenger twelve years of age and under, traveling alone.

"In fact," said Bleys, "I really should be getting to my studying right now, if you don't mind. I've got a book and reader I ought to be checking the stars with."

"Oh. Well, I'm sure we don't want you disturbed. But if you want anything, you just press the buzzer and I'll be right over. All right?"

"All right. Thank you," answered Bleys, already reaching over to get into his carry-bag, "I will."

She got up and left. She did not bother to glance at the reader now on his knees, slightly bigger than a slim box that could be held conveniently within Bleys' two hands. So she did not notice that the page of the first book revealed on the electronic screen of the reader was entitled in large letters, *The Bible*. Nor could she have guessed that underneath that book were stored others by some writers of the Muslim and other faiths.

Having taken out the reader, Bleys sat with it on his knees. He was experienced at appearing to do something, while leaving his mind free to occupy itself otherwise.

He actually still had some reading to do in the Bible, which had been Ezekiel's, and given to him when he left, with a strange sadness. Bleys had long since memorized the names of the prophets; but he had also been reading through it for what he thought of as stories, little bits of histories and adventures, like the account of David's encounter with Goliath, that were more interesting, and stuck better, if anything, in his memory with one reading.

But the attendant had gone now; and in this particular moment he was feeling more lost and abandoned than ever. It was a strange thing. He would have liked to have trusted her and welcomed the warm emotional offering she was making to him, but he could not trust her. He could trust nobody.

He did not think of his feeling about the attendant as a sign he was lonely. He did not, in one sense, really know what "loneliness" was. He felt it, strongly; but he had never had the opportunity to measure its dimensions. He only knew that when he had been very young he had been under the impression that his mother loved him. Then, sometime very early, he had become aware that she did not. She either ignored him, or was briefly pleased with him, when he was able to do something that reflected well upon her.

Now he should carry through what he said he would do, and read. But the will to do it failed him, foundering in his even deeper fears of the future which had been triggered off by his turning away the attendant's attempt to reach him.

The reader with its Bible, its Koran, and the other religious books which the library to which he had gone on New Earth had listed for him as being the most likely ones that might be used in worship on the Friendlies, lay forgotten in his lap.

Once more, he felt the terrible separateness, the feeling of being off in space from all the other human worlds and human people; and to combat it he dredged up his old dream of a magic wand that would give him exactly the kind of people around him and the kind of life he yearned for.

But even this would not work, now. The passages he had memorized from the books in the reader he now held on his knees seemed like fragile, almost useless, things to make friends for him with whoever he might encounter on Association. The ways he had learned to amuse and impress grown-ups like his mother's guests, would not work on a farm on an ultra-religious world like Association.

All sorts of things could be required and expected of him by Henry and his two sons, beyond the matter of being clever or learned.

He had never felt so helpless. He had really nothing to offer them, Henry MacLean and his family, beyond these memorized words from the Bible and the other books he had brought. What was he, after all, but a monkey with a bag of tricks—?

The memory came grimly back to him, of where he had heard that phrase. Shortly before he had left his mother, a friend of Ezekiel's had come around—obviously with his mother's indifferent permission but at Ezekiel's invitation—and talked to him.

The friend had been a slightly overweight, gray-haired man, with a touch of accent. There had been something different about his talk that Bleys could not put his finger on exactly. Like the cabin attendant just now, he had tried to be friendly.

Bleys had been tempted to like him, but those he had dared to let himself like had been taken from him so many times before that he held his feelings in check automatically. The man had asked a great many questions and Bleys had answered truthfully those he felt safe answering truthfully; otherwise he pretended he did not understand their real meaning.

After a couple of meetings with him, he did not see the gray-haired man again for several days. Then on the day just before the one on which Bleys left, he was coming into a side sitting room of the main lounge of the enormous hotel suite that his mother was now occupying, and heard Ezekiel's voice from the next room. Answering him was the voice of the gray-haired man. But the gray-haired man was now talking much differently, with different words and cadences to his speech; and Bleys realized suddenly that he was hearing the type of Basic affected by some of the ultra-religious Friendlies—called "cant."

Bleys had checked, hidden in the side room and listening. The gray-haired man was talking about him.

"—A monkey with a bag of tricks," the gray-haired man was saying, "thou knowest it as well as I do, Ezekiel. That was all the need his mother ever has had of him, and all the use she ever made of him. It was wise of thee to call me in to observe the boy. There are no lack of good psychomedicians in this city; but none who, like myself, grew up in the same district as Henry and yourself on Association. For I can indeed tell you something about the boy. For one thing, he's not another Dahno."

"I know that," said Ezekiel, "Dahno was very intelligent too; but he was as big as a grown man at twelve years old and easily as powerful as a grown man. The Lord only knows what size he is now."

"That, I don't know," said the gray-haired man, "but I have heard he is as a giant nowadays, and probably it has been the will of the Lord that he have a giant's strength."

"But you say Bleys is different," said Ezekiel's voice. "How can that be? His mother kept him if anything, more under control than she did Dahno. You're the psychomedician.

You actually saw and met Dahno when he was still kept on a string by his mother."

"But this difference is enormous, I tell thee," said the gray-haired man's voice. "Dahno grew up with their mother, for she trusted no one else to control him; and he is another like her, in every way. He even has the ability she had, to charm a snake into choking itself to death by swallowing its own tail. But this boy, Bleys, even though he hath been under the same roof, hath been raised entirely differently."

"Oh, I know," Ezekiel said. "You're thinking of the caretakers. It's true that he's been tied down much more tightly than Dahno was. But—"

"Nay, but the difference goeth far beyond that," interrupted the gray-haired man. "He hath been given a totally different upbringing. Dahno was part of his mother's life. This little fellow hath had no part of it. As I say, to her he hath been only a monkey with a bag of tricks. Something to show off to other people and preen herself about. But think thee now of Bleys' life as it must be and hath been, from the inside. He was like unto a soldier, under strict discipline at all times. A child less intelligent would have been ruined by this time. He is not ruined, the Lord be thanked for that; but he is put on a totally different path. Hast thou marked the boy's isolation? Hast thou noticed that he trusts no one—unless it is yourself?"

Bleys could hear Ezekiel's sigh.

"Yes," he said, "that much is true. When I've had a chance to, I've tried to get him out of his shell. But all the rest of the time, and everything else's he's had to do, put him in it too tightly. Anyway, that wasn't the point. I wanted you to give me an idea of whether he would be all right with Henry, back on Association."

"Thy brother, Henry," said the gray-haired man's voice, "was someone I grew up with. I may not know him as well as yourself, but I know him very well indeed. Yes, whether for good or ill, Bleys will survive and grow along the path he hath been already started on, once he gets to Association. What has been nurtured in him is far closer to that of our people—that which thou ran away from, thyself, Ezekiel—than it is to this world we're on, or even the world of Exotics. Yet, he is Exotic also; and what will come of the blend I do not know. But, he will get along with Henry. Dost thou suppose I could see him again for a short time?"

"Certainly, certainly," said Ezekiel, "I'll just go and have a word with the chief caretaker and then I'll come back and get you. Do you want to wait here?"

"As well here, as any place in this over-pillowed suite," said the gray-haired man.

"I'll be right back," said Ezekiel, his voice receding.

Bleys turned and hurried back into his own quarters. He was apparently deep in reading a book on ancient languages of Old Earth, when Ezekiel came and got him.

"Medician James Selfort would like to speak to you again," said Ezekiel, when he found Bleys, "would you like that?"

"Yes," Bleys had said, putting down his reader with the book still in it, "I like him."

The last few words, like so many that Bleys uttered, were not strictly true. But it was a fact that he did not dislike the man; and now, having overheard part of their conversation, he was warming to James Selfort, who seemed to be on his side, with Ezekiel, in spite of his "*monkey with a bag of tricks* . . . " statement. So Bleys found himself wanting to talk to Selfort again, in hopes of hearing more hopeful things about himself.

As it turned out, he did not. But he had clung tightly all through this trip to the fact that in the overheard conversation Selfort had said to Ezekiel that he, Bleys, would survive on Association. Remembering it now, he found himself warmed by that opinion, and his current depression lifted.

One thing in favor of the people and the place he was going to. They and it would not change on him within weeks, or a few months, as the caretakers had and everything else about his life with his mother. He could learn the rules there once; and then be sure of them.

He was nothing right now but that monkey Selfort had called him. Certainly he was no Exotic, twice removed from that identity by his Mother's denial of it; and the fact that she had kept all things Exotic—except herself—from him. Consequently, he could be anything, in pursuit of the dream he had dreamed so many times when he had been in the caretakers' "thinking room," with himself in a solid, fixed universe, holding the magic wand to keep all of it the way he wanted it.

There was no reason he could not reach that dream also by becoming a Friendly first. It would mean everything would have to be learned all over again—all of it different from anything he had ever known before. But he would be able to belong to other people and still make his own freedom.

It was even possible that Uncle Henry could be a rock against which he could lean—Henry and the probably stable, dependable people who were his neighbors and attended the same church. It was just barely possible that Bleys might find them understanding of him, accepting him, and offering him a place to belong.

It all depended on his being able to become a Friendly. Maybe then, in time, he could actually go on to become what he pretended; and there would be no doubt in anyone, no doubt in himself. . . .

He sat in the big chair, staring at the screen with eyes that did not see it, but instead seeing a future that might be what he had always wanted. The warmth of the possibility carried him back into his dream, in which he hung in space, solitary, completely isolated from the rest of the race—but master, at last of himself and his universe.

He looked at all the suns with planets where the human race had settled. But it was the planets he gazed on, not their suns. The time would come, he told himself, the time would inevitably come, when nowhere on any of them was anyone who could order his life.

Rather he would order theirs.

That last thought was so exciting as to verge on frightening him. He pulled back from it. But he lingered a moment longer. . . .

"—Do you see that?" the young, red-haired cabin attendant said to the older one.

"No, what?" asked the older one.

"The boy. The look on his face. Look!"

The older was busily inventorying the liquor. She did not look up right away.

"What look?" she asked, when she finally lifted her head.

"It's gone now," the younger said. "But he was looking so strange for a moment, there. So strange. . . ."

CHAPTER

3

═══════════════

BEFORE THE SHIP entered the atmosphere of the planet of its destination, it switched from phase-shifting to its ordinary engines. Within the hour it landed at Ecumeny; and its passengers were escorted from the lounge into a deceptively small terminal—that was actually only one of many terminals scattered over a large plain near that city. All senses alert, like some small, wary animal, Bleys carried his personal case off with him, hidden from his surroundings by the tall adult bodies that joined him in thronging the disembarking passage.

He was tight as a bowstring. Now that he had arrived, his plans, the Bible and other books he had studied on the way, seemed like fragile things for his hopes of making new friends to depend upon. The reality of finally being here was like stepping into a new universe.

The terminal waiting room was a large, circular place with light silver carpeting, as opposed to the familiar dark green of the upholstery on the overstuffed chairs of the lounge; and a number of people were standing there waiting for those who were landing. The red-haired cabin attendant went with him, saying she would point out his uncle to him when they got there. She had, herself, been provided with a picture of Henry.

He was standing a little aside from the others who were waiting when they found him; and Bleys' hopes sank a little at the sight of him. He had none of Ezekiel's open face and engaging smile. This was a man of surprisingly indeterminate age, whose hair had not so much grayed as become drab with approaching middle age. Certainly he was more than twenty-eight years old.

He was tall, thin almost to the point of emaciation, with a narrow, potentially unyielding face, and an impatient air about him.

His clothes were universal working clothes—rough dark pants, and rough dark shirt, under a leather-like jacket of some black material. The bones of his face were so narrow that the features of it seemed pinched to a sharpness like that of an ax-blade. He had dark eyes which focused like twin weapon barrels on the attendant and Bleys as they came up to him.

"Bleys," said the cabin attendant, stooping down a little to speak into Bleys' ear, "this is your uncle, Henry MacLean. Mr. MacLean?"

"The same," answered the man. His voice was somewhere between rusty and harsh in an otherwise light baritone. "I thank the Lord for your kindness, attendant. I'll take care of him, now."

"Honored to meet you at last, sir," said Bleys.

"No need for frills, boy," said Henry MacLean. "Come with me."

He turned around and led the way out of the terminal waiting room with such briskness that, although his height was only a few inches greater than the average, he set a pace that had Bleys trotting to keep up with him.

Outside the terminal, they went down a slope into a long underground tunnel and stepped onto a floating strip that moved them along; at first, slowly, then at faster and faster speeds, apparently accompanied by a flow of air that moved with them, since there was no feeling of a breeze in their face.

Still, so swiftly did they end up moving that Bleys guessed they had covered a number of kilometers within several minutes by the time the strip slowed again and they were let off at the far end before wide, glass doors that opened automatically. They stepped out into a gray, cool day with a stiff breeze moving damp air under low-hanging clouds that threatened rain.

"Sir! Uncle! said Bleys, trotting beside him, "I have luggage—"

"That will already have been delivered to me," answered Henry, without looking down at him, "and let me hear no more 'sirs' from you, boy—Bleys. 'Sir' implies rank; and there's no rank, in our church."

"Yes, Uncle," said Bleys.

They continued for some distance, until the parked vehicles thinned out. At last they came to a number of other vehicles, motorized, but with wheels, rather than the skirts around their bottom edges that marked the hovercraft or magnetic-field style of transport which made up most of the ranks they had passed through so far.

Eventually, beyond these, they came at last to unmotorized transports. These varied from carts to wagons, and finally to something that was neither cart nor wagon, but something of both, but which like the rest had a team of goats harnessed to it and tethered in place. Beside it stood Bleys' single small bag.

"How did they get it here so quickly, Uncle?" asked Bleys, fascinated to see the expensive case glittering beside the unpainted, goat-driven cart.

"They drop off a luggage container on landing, before taxiing to the terminal," answered his uncle, shortly. "It's done automatically. Put your bag in the back and we'll cover it with a tarp. It'll likely rain before we're home. You and I sit in the cab, up front."

Bleys moved to help; but his uncle was too quick for him. The bag was loaded and covered before Bleys had done more than begin trying to help.

"In the other door with you, boy," said Henry, opening the left side door of the wooden cab for himself. Bleys ran around and let himself in on the right side, closing the door behind him and securing it with a loop of rope that seemed to act as a door-lock.

Within, the cab was much more obviously home-built than it had appeared to be, looked at from the outside. It was like a closed wagon on the inside, with cut-out holes for the reins in a dashboard below a windscreen made of some transparent material—not glass, for it was bent and creased in places.

Reins to the goats ran through the holes. He and his uncle were seated on what seemed like an old bench, thinly covered with something like the tarp they had used to cover the luggage in the open back of the vehicle, and padded underneath the tarp-material with straw or dried grass, of which ends stuck out. The back, where there was a backrest to their seat, was similarly padded.

Bleys had been eager to get into the cab. He was dressed for shipboard. In fact, he had never owned anything but warm-weather clothes in his life, since his whole life had been spent either inside buildings or at places that were at a season of summer temperatures. But the cab, aside from the fact that no wind blew through it, was just as damp and cold as it had been outside.

He was shivering.

"Here!" said Henry MacLean, gruffly. He picked up what turned out to be a jacket, not unlike his own, but smaller—though still too long in the sleeves and wide in the shoulders for Bleys. He helped Bleys into it with one arm. Bleys gratefully closed it about him, buttoning the front up tightly, with its row of awkward, primitive buttons.

"Thought you wouldn't have anything to wear," said Henry. For a moment there was a blunting of the edge to his harsh voice. "Think you'll be warm enough, now?"

"Yes, Uncle," said Bleys; and with the warmth to prompt him, his mind began to work again. A lifetime of surviving by giving grown-ups the responses they thought proper and correct brought the answer to Bleys' lips without conscious thought. "I thank God for your kindness, Uncle."

Henry, who had picked up the reins and looked ahead again, stopped abruptly. His head snapped around to stare at Bleys.

"Who told you to say that?" His voice was totally harsh again, and threatening.

Bleys stared back at him with a look of utter innocence. Actually Henry himself had given him the words, with Henry's opening speech to the lounge attendant. But the question triggered a panic in him. How could he ever explain to this almost-stranger how he had learned to pick up phrases from adults and use them back to the same people?

"The woman," he lied, "the woman who took care of me said that that was the proper thing to say, here."

"What woman?" demanded Henry.

"The woman who took care of me," said Bleys. "She took care of me, arranged for my meals and my clothes and everything. She was from Harmony. She'd married somebody on New Earth, I guess. Her name was Laura."

Henry stared hard at him, as if his eyes were searchlights which would illuminate and uncover any lie. But Bleys had had too much experience at looking completely blank, misunderstood, and innocent. He stared back.

"Well," said Henry, turning back his head once more toward the front of the cart. He gave the reins a shake that started the goats to moving. There were eight of them, harnessed in pairs, pulling the cart; and they moved it, it seemed, with comparative ease. But it was strange to Bleys to feel the jolting of the wheels of the vehicle on the surface over which they were passing, used as he was to hovercraft and magnetic-floatcraft.

"We'll talk more about this woman, then," said Henry.

In spite of his last words, however, Henry MacLean said no more for a long time, merely concentrating on guiding his goat team and the goat cart along various roads leading away from the spaceport.

At first the road was like a massive ribbon of half a dozen colors, draped over the surface of the ground. All around the land was bare, not even trees showing; only in the distance, occasionally, they would see one of the landing terminals.

All Bleys' senses were alert, his eyes, his ears, his nose

recorded the sights, sounds and smells of the goat-cart, the road surface beneath their wheels and the day outside the windscreen and cab of the cart.

They were traveling in the lane on the far left of the highway, the darkest colored of all the stripes that made up a number of different parallel roadways leading away from the spaceport and obviously designed for different vehicles.

At the far right, the striped road was so wide that Bleys was not able to see clearly the vehicles on it. But at its further edge must be the near-white surface, seamless and almost electronically smooth, above which Bleys could almost see magnetic float vehicles traveling. These were disk-shaped. They moved, by contrast with the goat-cart, at blinding speed; so that in any case it would have been hard to get a good look at them.

Not that Bleys needed to know what they looked like, since he had traveled in many such during the earlier years of his life, going with his mother from one hotel to another, or from a hotel to some palatial private home.

Just in from the strip for float vehicles was the one for hovercraft. Next was the strip for small passenger-carrying, wheeled vehicles that were also motorized, and then, next closest, the one for large, motorized transport-carrying wheeled vehicles.

Last of all was their strip, the one for unmotorized wheeled vehicles, with the slowest, like the goat cart, at the extreme edge.

In between the goat-cart and the wheeled vehicle strips were a number of other unmotorized vehicles of varying types. They ranged from other versions of goat wagons like Henry MacLean's to odd vehicles, such as one whose wheels were moved by two men pumping a horizontal lever, see-saw fashion, between them. In among all the rest, in and out, were bicycles, some of them with carts pulled behind them.

As their own cart moved along, strip after strip peeled off from the roadway. First to go was the near-white strip above which the magnetic vehicles moved. It headed off over the horizon to their right. Shortly thereafter, the strip for hovercraft also parted company with them. It was some longer time—whether it was a longer distance or not, Bleys was in no position to judge—before the two strips carrying motorized vehicles also left them. They were at last traveling on a single strip for unmotorized traffic, though this was still at least five vehicles wide.

Finally, however, even this strip also began to narrow, as the carts and wagons on it turned down side roads. A few trees were beginning to appear on the horizon now; and Bleys, who in his omnivorous reading had also gotten into books on trees, recognized most of these as variforms of earth flora—mainly the softwoods and conifers. Only occasionally was a variform hardwood maple, elm, oak, or ironwood tree seen growing among them.

Now as the traffic dwindled down to almost nothing, the trees moved in, and soon they were passing through what seemed to be almost solid forest with only an occasional open area of grassy meadow, or an occasional valley with a small river. Now they were headed uphill; although the goats pulling Henry's goat-cart showed no sign of the extra effort this must require.

It was only when they had the road almost completely to themselves, that Henry MacLean spoke again.

"This woman," he said, glancing briefly down at Bleys and then back at the road, "what else did she tell you?"

"Stories mainly, Uncle," said Bleys, "about David and Goliath. About Moses and the Ten Commandments. Stories about the kings and prophets."

"Do you remember any of this?" demanded Henry. "What do you remember of the story of David and Goliath?"

Bleys took a deep breath and began to talk in the tone of voice with which he had kept visitors to his mother entertained. Hope rose in him at the chance to show off this early to this new uncle. He spoke in a solemn, steady utterance that made every word plain.

The words flowed freely from his memory:

"*—And there went out a champion out of the camp of the Philistines,*" said Bleys, "*named Goliath, of Gath, whose height was six cubits and a span . . .*"

He was aware of Henry's eyes on him—but they gave him no clue. Bleys went on.

"... And he had an helmet of brass upon his head, and he was armed with a coat of mail; and the weight of the coat was five thousand shekels of brass.

"And he had greaves of brass upon his legs, and a target of brass between his shoulders.

"And the staff of his spear was like a weaver's beam; and his spear's head weighed six hundred shekels of iron: and one bearing a shield went before him."

Out of the corners of his eyes, Bleys could still see Henry's face, unchanged. Bleys felt his heart sink. But he kept his voice confident and went on.

"... And he stood and cried unto the armies of Israel, and said unto them, Why are ye come out to set your battle in array? am not I a Philistine, and ye servants to Saul? choose you a man for you, and let him come down to me.

"If he be able to fight with me, and to kill me; then will we be your servants: but if I prevail against him, and kill him, then shall ye be our servants, and serve us.

"And the Philistine said, I defy the armies of Israel this day; give me a man, that we may fight together.

"When Saul and all Israel heard those words of the Philistine, they were dismayed, and greatly afraid ..."

Henry MacLean was staring fixedly at Bleys, who continued to watch the man out of the corners of his eyes while pretending to gaze ahead out through the windshield. The reins hung lax in Henry's hands, but the goats continued, keeping directly down the road as they had been doing. Bleys went on:

"... Now David was the son of that Ephrathite of Bethlehem-judah, whose name was Jesse ..."

He continued quoting. Henry continued to listen without a change of expression; and the cart continued without direction directly down the road under the lowering gray sky, the clouds of which were now darkening and threatening rain.

Bleys had had experience in holding an audience, and he knew how with tone and voice to work up to the climax of a story. Now he was getting to the climax of the account of the combat between David and Goliath, the Philistine. Henry should be showing some reaction now if he was ever going to; but he showed none. Bleys' voice changed accordingly, rising a bit in tone and the words speeding up:

> ". . . *Then said David to the Philistine, Thou comest to me with a sword, and with a spear, and with a shield: but I come to thee in the name of the Lord of hosts, the God of the armies of Israel, who thou hast defied.*
>
> *"This day will the Lord deliver thee into mine hand; and I will smite thee, and take thine head from thee; and I will give the carcases of the host of the Philistines this day unto the fowls of the air, and to the wild beasts of the earth; that all the earth may know that there is a God in Israel.*
>
> *"And all this assembly shall know that the Lord saveth not with sword and spear: for the battle is the Lord's, and he will give you into our hands."*

Henry's face had not changed.

> *"And it came to pass, when the Philistine arose, and came and drew nigh to meet David, that David hasted, and ran toward the army to meet the Philistine.*
>
> *"And David put his hand in his bag, and took thence a stone, and slang it, and smote the Philistine in his forehead, that the stone sunk into his forehead; and he fell upon his face to the earth.*
>
> *"So David prevailed over the Philistine with a sling and with a stone, and smote the Philistine, and slew him; but there was no sword in the hand of David.*

"Therefore David ran, and stood upon the Philistine, and took his sword, and drew it out of the sheath thereof, and slew him, and cut off his head therewith. And when the Philistines saw their champion was dead, they fled."

Bleys was openly watching Henry now, but Henry's face was as unchanged as the cart around them.

". . . And the men of Israel and of Judah arose, and shouted, and pursued the Philistines, until thou come to the valley, and to the gates of Ekron. And the wounded of the Philistines fell down by the way to Shaaraim, even unto Gath, and unto Ekron.

"And the children of Israel returned from chasing after the Philistines, and they spoiled their tents . . . "

Bleys stopped reciting. He turned and looked directly at Henry. For a long moment the other merely stared back at him. Then, as if suddenly waking up, he jerked his head, gathered up the goat reins and turned his attention to the road before them, chucking the reins to urge the goats temporarily to a trot, which gradually dwindled as they went on, until they were back in their walking pace again.

Meanwhile he continued to stare straight ahead and say nothing.

"Was that the way it actually was, Uncle?" asked Bleys at last, out of a desperate need to break the silence.

For a moment it seemed that Henry had not heard him. Then he drew a deep breath.

"There are no miracles nowadays!" he said violently to the windscreen, as if Bleys was not even there. "No! No miracles!"

But then he turned and looked at Bleys.

"Yes, boy," he said, "that's how it was. As it is written, in the First Book of Samuel in the seventeenth chapter."

"I thought so," said Bleys softly, for now the time for histrionics was past. He had had some success, after all. All this, and all that was yet to come from him, was simply a basis upon which perhaps he could build a better relationship. "I knew you'd be able to tell me for certain."

But Henry said nothing, driving the goat cart ahead.

Bleys let the silence continue again for a good time. Finally, he ventured another timid feeler.

"Would you like me to tell you what I know about Moses and the Ten Commandments?" he asked.

"No!" Henry stared unchanged of face through the windscreen. "No more! No more of that, for now!"

They drove on in silence. The skies had lowered and darkened; and Bleys was beginning to feel weary. He had been doing his best to use his trick of sitting unnaturally still. But his natural fund of eleven-year-old energy was threatening to explode inside him. He wondered how much further they would go before they got to their destination.

Desperately, he went on waiting. Sometimes that was the only way, to let the other person lead the talking. Then you could answer with some certainty; and with a reply tailored to what was said.

"What was her church?" demanded Henry, suddenly.

"Her church?" said Bleys. "Oh, you mean Laura? I can't remember."

"What were some of the prophets she taught you the names of?" demanded Henry.

"Moses and Isaiah, Daniel, Obadiah, Malachi, John and Jesus—" On sudden impulse, on the chance that Henry's church had other prophets, Bleys threw in a couple of extra names—" 'Ali and Mohammed Ahmad—"

"I knew it!" Henry interrupted him fiercely, striking his fist on his knee. "She was of a Bridging church!"

"I don't know what a Bridging church is," Bleys said. "She never mentioned anything like that."

"Well," Henry's voice had dropped to a satisfied mutter, "it will have been one like it, it will be one of them. She taught you wrongly, boy! 'Ali and Mohammed Ahmad are not among the prophets. They are false, and those are false who name them so!"

He sat back in the cart, more relaxed than Bleys had seen

him since Bleys had first used the phrase in which he thanked God for Henry's kindness.

"I'm glad you told me, Uncle," he said. "I wouldn't have known if you hadn't."

Henry threw an approving glance at him.

"Yes," he said, "you're young. But you'll learn. Though it's surprising you memorized so much from the Bible. Bleys . . . what else from that Book can you tell me?"

"There's Moses and The Ten Commandments—" Bleys began.

"Yes," interrupted Henry, "recite that to me."

Bleys took a deep breath.

> "*And Moses called all Israel, and said unto them, Hear, O Israel, the statutes and judgments which I speak in your ears this day, that ye may learn them, and keep, and do them.*
> "*The Lord our God made a covenant with us in Horeb . . .*"

Bleys went on reciting Chapter Five of Deuteronomy. Henry listened. His face seemed incapable of smiling, but there was a satisfied look on his face, as if he was someone listening to music well known and loved.

While Bleys was still talking, the first few drops of rain began to strike the windscreen before them and ran down it, like drops of oil. Henry ignored it, and Bleys went on talking, even as the rain increased and thunder crackled overhead while occasionally flashes of lightning could be seen off toward the right horizon.

Henry was no longer watching Bleys. His attention was all concentrated on what Bleys was saying. Bleys allowed himself to twitch and move on the seat, which had become very hard with its thin covering of straw and tarpaulin.

At Henry's urging Bleys went forward from the Ten Commandments, to recite part of Chapter Thirty-eight of the Book of Job, where the Lord answered Job out of the whirlwind; and from there to the Psalms. He was still reciting Psalms—in fact he was on Psalm One Hundred and Twenty, when he felt the cart lurch, and realized they had turned off the road onto a dirt track which led them off among the trees.

The dirt road led them only a short way before coming out in the open farmyard before a one-story building of logs and a few outbuildings, also made of logs.

"Here we are," said Henry, interrupting the Psalm.

The rain was now coming down heavily. Through its curtain and the windscreen Bleys saw a boy a little younger than himself who ran out ahead of the goats and took hold of their reins. Meanwhile the door on Henry's side was opened and a boy a year or two older than Bleys, more heavily built and looking a great deal stronger, jerked it open.

"Father—" he began, and then stopped, seeing Bleys beyond him.

"This is your cousin Bleys, Joshua," said Henry stepping out into the rain as if it did not exist at all. He looked back into the cab. "Bleys, you'll have to make a run for the front door."

Bleys stared at Joshua keenly for a second. An older, larger boy like this might offer physical aggression. Then he opened his door and stepped out into a veritable downpour of cold rain. The jacket Henry had given him seemed to be waterproof, but the rest of his clothing was soaked in an instant. Dimly he saw that the large log building, which was obviously a dwelling, had a door in its middle right ahead of him up three steps from the miry yard in which he was now standing. He ran for it, got up the three steps, took hold of a block of wood which seemed to do for a knob, and pushed. The door did not open.

"You'll have to turn it," said a voice behind him, and he looked back to see the older boy, Joshua, standing just behind him. He turned it and went inside, grateful to be out of the rain and for the warmer interior of the building.

"Stand there," said the voice of Joshua, as Bleys heard the door close behind him. "Stay on the entry rug. If you get the floor all wet Father won't like it at all."

His voice took for granted the right to give orders.

Bleys stood where he was, dripping onto and over the roughly woven rug, which seemed to absorb the water without

too much problem. The room he had stepped into was clearly
a large part of the house's interior. It had a rough ceiling made
by lengths of saplings laid side by side, and the partitions that
took the place of walls on the two sides of it that were not the
exposed logs of the building's exterior were made of medium-
sized logs standing upright between the floor and ceiling of
saplings.

In the far wall of the house, the other outside wall that would
face backward, there was a large, stone fireplace—like everything else around the house, obviously homemade—that had a
good fire going in it which accounted for the warmth, and with
a rack that stretched out across the flames to hold a large metal
pot above them. The furniture in the room consisted of a
couple of chairs with straw-stuffed tarpaulin cushions on their
seats, and a rectangular table with upright chairs having no
padding whatsoever. The single exception was one enormous
chair, strongly built, which was pushed back into a corner.
Surprisingly, the floor, which was made of split logs, had been
planed almost level and had apparently been scrubbed might-
ily, for it was as clean as the rest of the interior and the
furniture, itself.

The door opened and shut again behind him. He turned
around to see Henry and the younger boy.

Henry stood aside, stepping onto the thick entry rug as did
the boy, so that they were all crowded together.

"Will, meet your cousin, Bleys. Bleys, this is Will, my
younger son."

"Hello," said Will, offering a smile. He looked something
like Joshua, built on a more flimsy and smaller scale.

"Honored to make your acquaintance," said Bleys.

"Never mind being formal!" said Henry. "Bleys, this family
doesn't speak cant and it also doesn't go in for high manners.
Say hello to your cousin."

"Hello, Will," said Bleys.

Will blushed, evidently at simply being directly addressed
and called by name. He said nothing.

"All right now," Henry was saying above Bleys' head,
"Joshua, take Bleys to your room and find some clothes for

him besides this old jacket of yours he's wearing. They'll have
to be your clothes, and there's no reason he shouldn't get the
older ones, since he's come later to the house. They'll be too
big, but that's all right—he'll grow into them. Go along with
Joshua, Bleys. Never mind about the floor. You're pretty well
dripped off by this time."

Bleys followed Joshua through an entrance in a wall on their
left and directly into a relatively small room that had two chairs
and three bunkbeds in it, the bunkbeds fixed to the wall. The
last of these was obviously freshly carpentered, but had
nothing but a mattress so far. This could only be the one
intended for him.

"Here," said Joshua, holding out some pants and a shirt to
Bleys. He was on his knees, rooting around in a chest that he
had pulled from under the bottom one of the other two bunks,
attached to the outer wall of the room. He went on, still in a
commanding but, Bleys thought, not really a bullying tone.
"As Father says, they'll be too big; but you can roll the sleeves
and pant-cuffs back, and make do. I'll have some socks for you
in a second and maybe we ought to give you a different pair of
shoes. They'll be old ones of mine, which means they'll be too
big but we can stuff them with some cloth. Your shoes won't
stand up for five days out here. Hurry now, it's almost dinner
time."

CHAPTER
4

THE CLOTHES FELT strange, heavy and stiff upon Bleys, even though the elbows of the shirt and the knees of the pants had been worn smooth by use. Happily the pants had belt loops.

"You'll need a belt—oh, you've got one," said Joshua, digging further into the chest.

Bleys indeed had a belt. This was by deliberate intent, since such things were ornaments nowadays, worn with the type of clothes he usually wore. But, even though he was still young, he had read a great many stories in which the hero, about to go into strange territory, worries about having enough funds with him to buy whatever he might turn out to need. He had been hoarding all the money he could get his hands on since his decision to challenge his mother; and in that profligate household had gathered together a surprising amount.

He had used it all to buy interstellar credits—good anywhere. The belt he now wore had a magnetic seal along the inside that opened up into a long thin envelope, in which he had folded bearer certificates for about fifteen hundred interstellar units—enough to buy him passage on a spaceship off this world, if it came to that.

Also, in the two weeks it had taken his mother to arrange for his being sent to where he was now, he had managed to get a bank to supply him with some small denomination Association currency, most of which he kept with the bonds. Now, he threaded the belt through the loops of the pants he had just been given, and pulled the oversize waist tight around him, before latching the buckle.

"You'll find a chest under your bunk, too," said Joshua, nodding at the single bunk on the wall opposite to the two beside which he knelt. "You can keep these spare socks and underwear there. I'll show you how to fold them. Father likes things neat."

He was about to close the chest and shove it back under the bed when he saw that Bleys was still standing, now dressed in the new clothes and shoes, but with his arms wrapped around him.

"You're cold?" asked Joshua. He reached into the chest and threw something dark and soft into Bleys' hands. "Here, you can have this sweater. It's a little worn out at the elbows, but I'll help you patch that. Do you knit? You don't? We all knit here, in the wintertime when there's nothing else to do and we're rained in. I'll teach you how."

He closed the chest and pushed it back under the bunk out of sight. Bleys had struggled into the sweater, finding it, as he had expected, too large for him, so that he had to roll back the sleeves from both wrists. It was a pullover sweater that clung to him fairly well, in spite of the fact that it was large for him; its knitted fabric fitting itself to his slim body. It was a dark blue in color.

"Now, we'd better be getting out to the dinner table," said Joshua. "Will is going to have it set and ready to dish up by now; and Father will have finished his prayers. He went into his room to pray when we came here, because he had to miss a couple of prayer times going in to get you."

"Prayer times?" asked Bleys.

"Yes." Joshua stared at him, almost as much at a loss as Bleys.

"Didn't they call them that, where you come from?" Joshua asked. "We pray four times a day. Morning, at getting up, at our midmorning break, just before lunch, and at bedtime. Some churches have their people praying six or even seven times a day; but that's not what our church is like. It's terrible how many apostate churches there are, Father says. But it can't be helped. We stick to the true gospel and the true way."

For a moment Joshua's last words echoed in Bleys' mind. ". . . *True* gospel . . ."—"*true* way." His heart bounded at the prospect of possibly finding something for which he had longed. To believe in a single truth for each and every thing—and all the stability that promised . . .

But even as he was thinking this, he was following Joshua and they were back, outside the bedroom. As Joshua had predicted, the table was already set.

Its scrubbed surface was now covered with a cloth that had originally been checkered red and white, but now had been washed so many times that it was almost all white. This cloth was laid with wooden forks and spoons; and homemade knives that were sharp enough, Bleys discovered by accident during the meal, to shave with.

"What kept you?" demanded Henry as they emerged from the boys' bedroom. "Well, never mind. Sit yourself down, sit yourself down. Will, you can serve us now."

Bleys found put before him a large wooden bowl that contained a dark-looking stew, from the iron pot that had been hanging over the fire in the fireplace. It had an odd smell, mainly of vegetables, but it was an appetizing one; and Bleys found himself suddenly weak with hunger. He realized then that it had been a long day since they had left the ship and he had last eaten.

He was about to pick up his wooden spoon and dig into the stew, when he saw that no one else at the table had done so. They were waiting with their hands in their laps looking expectantly at Henry. Finally, when everyone had been served and Will himself had climbed into a chair opposite his own bowl of stew, Henry spoke.

"Grace, Will," he said.

"*Lord we thank thee and thee alone, always for the food that thou has supplied us. For all things are supplied by thee, in thy name . . .*" Will's young, clear, high voice began immediately and continued for some time, the extreme earnestness of it giving a special intensity to what he said.

Bleys, looking at him, thought that the other boy could not be more than a year younger than he was; but in some ways he was much more childish. It was obvious, now, that in this moment Will was not just thanking a deity in whom he believed. He was speaking directly to an invisible, all-powerful presence that stood just behind his father at the foot of the table; and weighed every word the boy said for correctness and sincerity.

The result upon Bleys was impressive. For the first time, he appreciated emotionally how deep the dark river of believed truth in their religion and all its observation ran, in the three people with him here.

At last, Will came to an end. Still, none of the family moved until Henry took up his own spoon.

"Now we will eat," he said. "Joshua, pass your cousin the cheese and the bread."

Bleys had scarcely noticed that also on the table were two platters, one holding thick-cut slices of dark, rough-looking bread, the other a whitish cheese cut into two-inch cubes. He accepted the plates from Joshua.

"Thank you, Joshua," he said.

"Here, we say thank the Lord," said Henry. "Remember that, Bleys."

"Yes, Uncle," said Bleys. "Thank the Lord for these foods."

He waited until he had spoken before he helped himself both to the bread and a couple of cubes of the cheese and then he passed the platter back to Joshua himself, who swiftly, without taking anything, passed it to Henry.

For the first time a wintry smile showed on Henry's features, a smile directed at his oldest son.

"Bleys is just come among us, Joshua," Henry said, "and it was because you were eldest I asked you to serve him first. It was polite of you to remember not to help yourself before passing the platters to me."

Having taken what he wanted, he passed the platters back by way of Joshua down to Will; who both, at last, got to help themselves.

Bleys was busily searching for an understanding of the people around him—but particularly an understanding of Henry. It would be Henry he wanted to understand and bring to a liking for him. Henry, from whom in the end he could win the most in freedom and favors.

Indeed, in the long run, he had some hope—but it was faint—of eventually being able to in a small way, at least, influence the man, as he had literally controlled some few of the adults he had known around his mother. Nearly all of these he had been able to take some advantage of, first by the method of getting into their good graces, and then by playing on their own likes and dislikes to make them give him what he wanted. But only a few of them had become so amenable that he had been able to get anything at all he wanted from them.

Henry did not look like an easy man from whom to get anything at all.

Luckily, at the present moment, Bleys had time to think about it. There was no conversation; since mouths were full and jaws were busy with the stew, the cheese and the bread.

There were also large cups full of dark liquid standing by each plate. Bleys tasted it and discovered that it was the brew of some local herb, probably considered the equivalent of coffee. Its taste was bitter and unpleasant to him, but he drank some of it anyway, not only because he wanted to seem to like everything and be as much one of them as possible, but because he needed some kind of liquid to wash down the food he was busily eating.

Curiously, otherwise everything at the table tasted good to him. The stew was indeed mainly vegetable. But it had been enriched by small threads and chunks of fattish meat. Goat probably, Bleys guessed, since there would be no native animals here; and if there were, they would be indigestible by human digestive systems. Also he had seen no sign of other domestic animals about the place.

Later he found out that he was wrong. The planet had almost a plague of wild rabbits; and the meat in the stew had been from one of these.

The goats, he told himself now, must mean everything to this farm. Not only as draft animals to pull the cart; but to pull other things such as plows, to supply leather, hides, meat, and even the milk from which this cheese was made.

For the cheese alone was the one thing that had at least a slightly familiar flavor. It was not quite the same as the goat cheese he had eaten on occasions with his mother, but it was close enough to be identified as basically that, and not something else.

As far as making an attempt to ingratiate himself with Henry . . . clearly Henry's religion was everything to him and his family. Bleys had been informed by Ezekiel that things were like this with all those who lived on Harmony and Association, and belonged to one of the innumerable churches there—which were at the same time always at each other's throats over religious ritual and doctrine.

He felt instinctively that he had scored a strong point with Henry, by his quotations from the Bible on the trip home. But, where to go from there was a question. Here, in his own house, on his own land, Henry seemed complete and invulnerable to persuasion, except along religious lines; and those lines were the only route now to the kind of freedom that Bleys wished and needed to gain for himself.

Basically, he wanted escape from all people and all restrictions, as he had wanted escape from his mother; and the chance to find a life for himself, in surroundings much more like those he had been used to during his first eleven years. The thought of living out his life in the surroundings of this rough cabin, with its rough table and homemade food, repelled him. But he had been ready to risk his life to escape from his mother; and he would not shrink from anything that turned out to be necessary.

There was a deep hunger in him for something he could not

even put into words, but which he knew he would finally recognize when he found it—if he simply kept searching for it and working to understand it. This he knew: it was bigger than what anyone else he had known—including his mother—had ever dreamed of having.

Now, for the first time, he could feel a solid hope that he could find it here, on Association. But first and foremost, it must mean freedom for him, in all respects . . .

The voice of Henry jarred him out of his thoughts.

"Bleys," his uncle was saying, "what schooling have you had?"

Bleys' mind leaped to find answers to that question. In effect, he had had no real schooling. From time to time, there had been tutors in one subject or another when his mother thought of it. But, since he and she were generally on the move, it was troublesome and time-consuming to find someone for a short period. Anything else, from his mother's point of view, was unthinkable. As a result Bleys had educated himself, more than been educated; and his education had been oriented toward those things that interested him, or would impress the people before whom he showed off for her approval.

Now he tried to think of things in which his own reading might have trained him enough so that he could get by with giving the impression he had a knowledge of them; as he had hastily pretended to have a knowledge of the Bible. Mentally, he scrambled for subjects that would make him valuable to Henry.

"I can read and write, of course," he said, reaching for the most obvious topics first, "and of course I know arithmetic, up into algebra and geometry. I know a little bit of practical mathematics, like the basics of surveying, and figuring how tall a tree is from its shadow and so forth. There's a formula—if your house was built of boards instead of logs, Uncle, I could probably make an estimate of how many board feet of lumber there were in it. Then I know something about chemistry, too, and mechanics—"

"What do you mean by mechanics?" interrupted Henry.

"Oh, how engines and things like that are put together." He took a chance on an outright lie. "I had some training in shop too, which helped."

"Shop?" demanded Henry.

"That's where they show you how to take apart and put together motors and things. It teaches you how to make them," said Bleys.

"Is that so?" said Henry; and Bleys thought that for the first time he heard interest in his voice. "What other things have you learned?"

Bleys found himself running out of ideas and educational topics, particularly any that might interest Henry. Henry would clearly not be interested in music, literature, or ancient Earth history, and such things.

"I was taught something about first aid, and medicines," said Bleys, "but not much. But I really am quite good at arithmetic, Uncle. I can add up figures without making mistakes, and keep records."

"Can you now?" said Henry.

He sat for a minute, obviously thinking. Then he went on.

"We're not a bunch of storekeepers here," he said finally, "but there are some records that could be kept. I've kept them myself, but if you're capable of helping me with that, Bleys, it'd be a good use for you to put yourself to, as well as your other duties"—Bleys' hopes sank fearfully at the thought of what "other duties" might be—"I'll think about this; and we may talk some more about it. Is there anything else you've got to tell me about subjects you've been schooled in?"

It occurred to Bleys it was best not to claim to know too much.

"Maybe, Uncle," he said, "but I can't think of any more, right now. If I remember I'll tell you."

"I'll say one thing for you, Bleys—and your cousins"—he looked from Joshua to Will—"should take note. You're willing to be helpful. And this is the right attitude."

"Thank you, Uncle," said Bleys, with relief.

He had been unsure whether an emphasis on a sense of duty would necessarily recommend him to Henry. But from what he had learned about the Friendlies beforehand and from what he had seen of Henry himself, it seemed possible. The thought occurred to him, abruptly, that Henry might want to send him off to some local school; and that would be the last thing Bleys wanted.

Any time spent in local schooling by him would be a waste of time; and, beyond that, pure misery, since he would almost surely know more about many things than those already there. Even if he did not, he would learn all they had to teach children of his age in a few weeks; and he cringed at the thought of trying to fit in with the other students.

"Very well, then," said Henry, shoving back his chair and standing up. "Will, Joshua—get to your evening chores. Bleys, come along with me."

He headed out the front door. Bleys, following him, snatched off a peg the jacket Henry had given him earlier. Henry smiled his wintry smile again, watching Bleys struggle into it as they went down the front steps together.

Henry led him to one of the outbuildings, unlatched the rope loop that held the door, and let them inside, carefully closing the door behind them as if on something precious.

The room was dimly lit and about big enough to hold two of the goat-carts they had ridden out in, without the goats. Henry reached up on a shelf, took down a lamp with a tall glass chimney, its transparent base three-quarters full of a pale, oily liquid, and with a wick extending upward into the chimney. He removed the chimney and set the wick alight before replacing the chimney.

The glow it cast was yellow but bright. Bleys saw that they had stepped into some kind of workshop. In the center of the floor was the engine block of an internal combustion engine. Bleys recognized it from a history book as one of the simplified varieties that had been especially designed for the Younger Worlds when colonization was first started. It had three cylinders and according to what Bleys had read about it, had been designed to run on just about anything combustible that had been made into a liquid. Even wood and ordinary weeds, ground powder-fine, could be utilized by it as fuel.

This particular block had a lubrication pan below, but no head above it. Its three cylinders gaped empty. On a shelf to one side sat the three pistons that would fit into the holes, and some other parts. Bleys stared at it all, puzzled; then suddenly understood.

Henry, like a great many of the poor colonists Bleys had read about, was gradually building an engine that could be used to drive a homemade tractor or car, buying it part by part as he could squeeze out the funds for it.

"Do you recognize this from that class of yours? What did you call it—'Shop'?" Henry asked him.

"I—think so. Yes, Uncle, I do," said Bleys. "There're different models of course. To know which one this is I'd need to look at its plans."

"I've got those here," said Henry. He reached to the back of the shelf behind where the pistons were standing on end, and came up with a sheaf of working plans printed on sheets of plastic, two by three feet in size. He spread them out on an empty section of the bench and put the lantern down beside him. "Here they are. Look at them and tell me if you know this particular model of engine."

Bleys looked. The closest he had come to any plans like this had been to see reproductions of them in a book on mechanics. He had been attracted by what he saw then, as he was by everything, but particularly stories and mathematics.

Still, anything new fascinated him. All that was new showed him things, proved things to him. The stories reported and informed. So did the plans. So did the mathematics.

But the mathematics had the additional attraction of proving something. He had been particularly delighted with a volume on solid geometry. He had seen a beauty between the solid, three-dimensional shape, represented on the screen of his reader, and the proof for that shape being as it was.

Now, he looked at the plans for the motor with interest. They were not the plans he had seen in the book on mechanics; but they were close enough so that he could make a ready identification between them and those he had looked at before. Essentially, the engine had been designed so that it could be put together by anyone with a minimum of intelligence and the patience to work with his or her hands. The instruction lists were simple and clear as far as the assembly of the motor went.

"Yes, I think I recognize it, Uncle," he said again. He looked once more over the parts that were arrayed on the bench. "You aren't missing too much from what's needed to put it all the way together and get it working. The largest piece missing is the head for the block and the bolts to put it down on the gasket. Or do you already have the gasket here—?" He began searching among the parts on the bench top.

"No," said Henry, "heads, bolts and gaskets are all in short supply. There're a few, but the price is high, particularly for gaskets. I'll get one yet before the year is out, one way or another."

"With that, and just a few more smaller parts," said Bleys, half to himself, "the engine can go together and run." He looked up at Henry. "Can I help you put it together, Uncle?"

"Yes," said Henry, "I think you can. I think you know enough so that your help will be useful, Bleys. But that's something for the future."

He turned away from the block, blew down the chimney to blow out the flame of the lantern, and put the lantern itself back up on the shelf. They stood in the shed, lit now only by the last of the twilight that was glimmering through its windows. Henry led the way back to the house.

When they had stepped inside, the table had been cleared and Will was busily washing the dishes.

"Bleys, help your cousin Will wipe those dishes," said Henry, "then the both of you—to bed."

He turned and left them, going in through the doorway on the other end of the wall from the entrance that led to their bedroom. Obviously that end, Bleys thought, must lead to his personal bedroom.

Bleys walked over to the bench with the washbasin where Will was working, and Will handed him both a dish holding soap and a towel.

"Josh will be in shortly," he said, "he's busy settling down the stock."

"The stock—they're the goats, like the ones pulling the cart?" Bleys asked, as he took dish and towel and began to dry the dish.

"Oh yes," said Will, "but the ones that Father uses to pull the cart and other things like that have to be specially trained. The rest are just for milk and cheese; and meat for us when we can spare one to slaughter for food."

Bleys nodded.

With Will he finished cleaning up the dishes, washing the pan they had washed the dishes in, drying it, and hanging it up on a peg on the wall. Together they carried out the slop water, which was the dishwater poured out into a bucket, plus whatever other water had been used in making the dinner and cleaning the table both before and after the meal.

"You'd better learn all this," Will said, "because you'll be doing it from now on, I think. Now that you're here, Father will want me outside helping with the rest of the place."

He showed Bleys where the wash water could be dumped, pointed out the privy, and brought Bleys back inside to their bedroom. The single bunk on the wall that must be the separating wall between their room and Henry's still held only the bare mattress. But some blankets, sheets and a pillow had been neatly piled in the center of this.

"Joshua will be in, in just a bit, and show you how to make the bed," Will said, climbing up into his own bunk and beginning to undress. He dropped his shoes from the height of the bunk; clearly, it seemed to Bleys, enjoying the large thump they made as each hit the floor. The rest of his clothes Will put into a net that was suspended from two pegs on the inner wall of his bunk. When he was done he climbed back down onto the floor again, knelt beside Joshua's bunk, and began to pray.

Bleys stood beside the one that was to be his own, uncertain as to whether he should start to try making the bed by himself. Everything he had met in his life had fascinated him; and the activities of the chambermaids cleaning the hotel rooms they had been in had been equally interesting. He had had one of them teach him how to make a bed and he thought he could duplicate that process now without Joshua's help.

But at that moment Joshua did come in, taking off his heavy outer jacket and hanging it on a peg just inside the wall of the bedroom, rather than one of the pegs by the door.

"Did you ever make a bed before?" he asked Bleys, coming over to join him.

"Yes, I have," said Bleys.

"Well I'd like you to watch me closely anyway," said Joshua. His voice was gentle; and in general since Bleys had first met him, he had seemed pleasant and unusually considerate. "Father wants things done just so. We wash our bedding on Saturday and hang it inside the house to dry, if it's raining outside like it is today. You'll have to take care of your own bedding, usually, but sometimes you'll be washing everybody's bedding. It just depends. Now as far as making it goes, watch me."

Bleys watched. There were apparently no springs to the bed, only the mattress, which was of a heavy cloth stuffed with something that he hoped was soft. Joshua began by first covering this with a sort of bag, which he referred to as the mattress cover, then put on the bottom sheet.

"This is God's corner," Joshua said, folding the end of the overhang from the sheet neatly and tucking it in under the bed so that it made a right angle triangle where the side turned into the end. "You'll make God's corners on all four corners of the bed with everything that needs to be tucked in."

He went on to put down and tuck in a top sheet, fold it back, lay the pillow on top and then cover it with several thick blankets, that looked as if they might have been home-knitted. They were all of a dark gray-black color. On these, too, he made God's corners. Bleys looked at them with pleasure. Their neatness and regularity appealed to him, and the hint of a solid, makable thing through which their God could be touched struck a resonant note in him.

"The first two or three days for sure," said Joshua, "Father'll be in to see whether you made your bed properly. After that he may just look in at any time. So you want to make sure that the bed is properly made, always."

CHAPTER

5

═══════

THE DAY AFTER his arrival, when Bleys woke up, he saw everyone else getting into what were better clothes—and could well be their best clothes. By the time Bleys was awake enough to fully understand the situation, Will was already dressed, his bunk made, and he was out of the room. Joshua, looking remarkably adult in black jacket and trousers made of rather stiff, but obviously not very expensive material, was finishing up his own bed-making.

Bleys clambered out of his own bunk, still wearing his pajamas (the other two boys had worn nightshirts) and went over to Joshua.

"What is it?" Bleys asked, "what's going on?"

"It's church day," said Joshua briefly.

"I don't have anything black with me," said Bleys. "What should I wear? I'm supposed to come with you too, aren't I?"

Joshua paused, straightened up from his bed and looked at him with a strange look that matched his clothes.

"That isn't for me to say," he answered, briefly; and,

turning away, pulled the top blanket of his bed tight, then went out the door.

Not for Joshua to say? Bleys could only guess that must mean it was for Henry alone to say. Hurriedly he put on the darkest trousers, shirt and jacket he owned, in equal haste went outside. Henry and the others were already climbing into the goat cart, which had its animals already waiting in harness.

Bleys came up to the cart and stood waiting to get Henry's attention. But Henry merely glanced at him briefly, walked around the cart, and got in. The reins flipped and the goat cart turned out of the yard heading for the road and leaving Bleys behind.

He stood, watching them go. He had expected that if there was to be any going to church, he would automatically be taken along—commanded to go with them, if anything. But instead they had left him behind without explanation.

He felt curiously ignored. The last thing he had thought of wanting to do was endure a service in a Friendly church. But at the same time, it was almost as if he had been rejected by Henry and his family.

It made no sense. Plainly, Henry was the one to give him an explanation. But also, Henry had made no effort to do so and Bleys had no idea of whether he had been supposed to ask his uncle or not.

He turned slowly back into the house and found some porridge had been left in the all-purpose cooking pot, set to one side of the morning fire to keep warm. There was one place still set at the table. He sat down at it to eat his porridge, wonderingly.

What should he do? He could simply ask Henry, or he could wait for some cue from the other before asking; or he could wait until Henry chose to tell him in a time of Henry's own choosing. The more he thought about it, the more he thought that in his situation it was best to do nothing but wait and see what would develop. Even the boys, clearly, did not want to be asked.

He cleaned up after his breakfast, washed his dishes and the pot and did whatever other things seemed to need doing about the main room of the house. In the process he managed, finally, to put the whole matter out of his mind. A little more than three hours later, Henry and the boys returned and life took up as if this day was no different from any other.

During the next few days Bleys came as close to liking Joshua and making a friend of him as he ever had with anyone in his life. The older boy was always pleasant, certain but easygoing. He apparently knew his way about the various tasks and duties of the farm as Henry did himself; and he never seemed to get impatient or tired of explaining these to Bleys. For that matter Joshua never seemed to get upset over anything.

Bleys had had almost no acquaintance with other children his own age. What few he had met from time to time were so inferior to him in knowledge and intelligence that he had nothing in common with them; and they soon perceived this difference and resented it.

On the other hand, the few older children he had run into, were from Bleys' point of view apparently cut-down adults. They were neither as bright nor as knowledgeable as the adults that Bleys had to do with generally; and it seemed that he could not even try to talk about the things in which they were interested without somehow making it plain to them that although he was younger he was far more capable than they were. They, too, were quick to sense this difference, and resent it.

The result was that Bleys had never actually had a friend, in the ordinary sense in which youngsters have them. He was conscious of this as he was conscious of the fact that he was different from the adults; even though they might be entertained by him, and consent to give him at least a little of their time. There was a phrase he only chanced to come across in his reading; but it fitted so well he thought of it frequently. He felt like "neither fish nor fowl."

He was condemned by being unique, and off by himself at a distance where no one else seemed to have any real reason to be concerned with him. The single person who might have been concerned had been the very one who was so glaringly not—his mother.

Therefore, Joshua's acceptance of him and lack of jealousy

or resentment took Bleys unawares. It was a little while before he figured out that from Joshua's point of view there was no competition between them because Joshua's place in the family was already fixed—he was the oldest, and certain things came to him by right.

Bleys, also from Joshua's point of view, was fixed. He was the cousin who had been taken into the family, and placed in a sort of probationary position between Joshua and Will. In short, there was no way that Bleys could supplant him, or infringe on Joshua's territory, because God had ordained that their respective spheres should be separate ones; and Joshua's father, as God's nearest representative, would enforce that separateness.

To his own surprise, Bleys found a measure of contentment in this fixed order, that tied in with his appreciation of the general order he had found here. From only being determined to become a Friendly to reach his own goal, he found he was beginning to desire to be one for the way it fitted with his own dreams. Now, it was even a certain type of Friendly he wished to be. It seemed that those much admired by other Friendlies were called by them "True Faith-holders." A True Faith-holder was supposed to have given all of himself totally to his religious beliefs, setting them above all things, even life itself.

As Will had predicted, Bleys was given the duties of taking care of the inside of the house. This involved making the meals—which were almost invariably the same simple stew, only varying in ingredients as these became available—and cleaning everything in the house that was not the responsibility of some other individual to keep clean.

This meant that the table, the benches, the chairs, the floor, the walls and floors in both the boys' bedroom and in Henry's, were to be scrubbed daily. The windows were also to be kept clean, and all the tableware and household tools.

In spite of these chores, Bleys had free time on his hands; and in that free time, both Will and Joshua introduced him to the duties that they, themselves, were concerned with outside. Will, now freed from the house, had been given the responsibility of the farmyard itself. This included the cleaning of the goat barn, the daily examination of the goats for signs of skin diseases, illness, or hurt that might be affecting them; and the minor repairs that needed to be done to any of the buildings.

Joshua had the responsibility for everything beyond Will's area. This included taking the goats out to pasture each day, the milking, the cheese-making, and the repair and upkeep of the split-rail fences that enclosed outside areas on the farm, such as the pasture. The heavier maintenance and repair of all structures was his responsibility.

Over and above all this, Joshua had a general responsibility to pitch in and help or substitute for any of the two younger ones, if they needed help or ran into difficulties with the work they were doing.

Altogether, he put in a long, hard day, every day.

Henry spent his time checking to make sure everything was right about the farm, and doing the things that could only be done with a man's strength. For example, they cultivated several acres; and while goat teams pulled the plow or the harrow, it was Henry who muscled the implement itself, and made sure the work was done. He also made almost daily trips in to the small, nearby store where necessities could be bought; and, occasionally, day-long trips to Ecumeny for more important and rarer things, such as added parts for the motor.

Through all this daily pattern of existence ran a thread of extreme regularity. They got up at daybreak, prayed and had breakfast; as soon as their beds were made and their rooms were cleaned they went about their daily duties until prayers at ten; then again about eleven-thirty in the morning, which was lunch time and prayer time once more, and the largest meal of the day.

Following lunch they went back to work and worked until near sundown, when Henry would go around and call a halt to everybody's labors. Bleys was quick to join in the motions of kneeling where he happened to be, and praying. But although he tried desperately, he could not seem to manage to bring either his mind or his heart to accept the idea of religion or any belief in the idea of a deity.

On the fourth day they were eating lunch, when over their

conversation, a roaring sound could be heard approaching closer and closer to the farm.

"It'll be your brother," said Henry, looking at Bleys.

Bleys felt a coldness in him, suddenly, that was almost panic. He had forgotten entirely about this older sibling, who had been sent away by his mother to Henry, years ago—in fact, shortly after Bleys' birth. Not seeing or hearing anything of him around the farm, Bleys had assumed that the other was either dead or gone. He had ceased to think of the possibility of an older half-brother; as if no such possibility had ever existed.

Now, suddenly the possibility was reality, and the reality was approaching—obviously by hovercar, to judge by the roaring sound of the fans that would be holding it off the unpaved road that led to the farm. That road must be barely wide enough for it to slide through.

A current of excitement seemed to have run through the two other boys. Henry looked at them reprovingly.

"Your older cousin has come during meal time," he said pointedly. "He may join us, or he may wait until we are done and everything is taken care of. There will be no changes simply because we have a visitor."

The roaring sound grew very loud, moved into the yard and stopped. Lunch was almost over. But Will and Joshua were eating a little faster than normal—not enough to earn their father's reproach—but as fast as possible without doing so. Bleys, as usual, had taken less than any of the rest, and his bowl was nearly empty anyway, as a result.

But, he reflected, he was the one who would have to clean up and wash up after the meal.

There had been silence outside for a few moments. Now came the sound of heavy steps mounting the three stairs outside, the door opened, and Bleys' older half-brother, Dahno, came in.

Bleys had heard Dahno, as a boy, described to him by various friends of his mother's; but mostly by Ezekiel, Henry's older brother. He had heard it from Ezekiel, who had taken responsibility for the fathering of both boys and arranged to have Dahno—and Bleys later—sent off to Henry.

Bleys, therefore, had expected someone outsized in the way of height and width. Somebody with large bones and a great deal of muscle. But he was not expecting what came in the door.

Dahno had to duck his head to get through the doorway itself; and, standing just inside, it seemed that his head was within a few inches of touching the saplings that made the ceiling. He was dressed in a black business suit of soft cloth, and ankle-high black boots brightly polished, except where the mud from the yard had splashed on them. He bulked to the point where he seemed to overshadow all of them, dominating the room.

He was like a thick-set man of ordinary height, blown up to half again his original size. His arms and legs bulged the clothes that covered them. His face was round and cheerful under a cap of curly, jet-black hair; and he had a merry, warm smile for them all.

"Don't let me disturb your lunch," he said in a voice as warm as his smile, a light baritone that did not echo the outsize elements of the rest of him.

"You would not in any case," said Henry.

But Henry, Bleys noticed, was smiling back at Dahno, that wintry smile that was the most Henry could achieve. "You know our customs. You'll wait until we're done."

"Fair enough," said Dahno, with a wave of one large hand. "By the way, I brought you some parts for your motor."

"I thank God for your kindness," said Henry formally. "If you will sit, that chair of yours is there in the corner."

Bleys had wondered about that one extra-large chair; but assumed it was for Henry on special occasions.

"Thanks. But I'd just as soon stand," said Dahno.

Whether it was intentional or not, his looming over them had the tendency of speeding up the lunch. Even Henry, indifferent as he appeared to be to Dahno's size and presence, seemed to finish his bowl of stew faster.

"I came to see my little brother, actually," said Dahno, looking at Bleys.

"Did you so?" said Henry, laying his spoon down at last beside his empty bowl. "In that case, Bleys, you are excused from the normal cleaning up after lunch. Will, you take over for your cousin."

Bleys sat staring at the large man.

"Bleys,"—there was a slight edge to Henry's voice— "you're free to go. Rise, therefore, and go with your brother."

Bleys pushed back his chair, stood up and then pushed it back into position again at the table. He walked around it, approaching Dahno, feeling smaller with every step, by contrast with the enormous bulk he was approaching.

"Come on then, Little Brother," said Dahno.

He turned and opened the door leading outside. Bleys followed, carefully closing the door behind him, as even the few days he had spent here had taught him to do.

"We'll walk off a ways," said Dahno. He took the strides of his long legs slowly, so that Bleys did not have to run to keep up with him. They walked around the now dirt-spattered white body of the brand-new looking hovercar squatting on the muddy ground; and Dahno led the way off and around the goat barn, so that they were out of sight of the house. Once behind the barn, he turned and faced Bleys.

He gazed down for a long moment, the smile on his face gradually broadening until he finally burst into full-throated laughter.

"I knew she'd send you eventually!" he said.

He was still laughing, when, with a casual flip of the back of one of his massive hands, he knocked Bleys clear off his feet and against the wall of the barn. Bleys, dazed, slid down it to the ground below.

Bleys lay where he had fallen, in the rank grass by the goat barn. He was barely conscious, half-knocked out from even the light blow of that massive hand; and it took him several moments for his senses to come back. For a minute after they did return he felt merely odd, lying on the ground; and then a sharp headache burst into life behind his temples.

"Up with you," said Dahno. Bleys felt his wrist and right hand enclosed in a massive fist; and he was hauled to his feet.

Bleys was still not sensible enough, not enough fully recovered from the blow, to guard his tongue as he usually did.

"Why did you do that?" he asked.

Dahno laughed again.

"Because you had to learn, Little Brother," he said, "you're very fortunate to have me for a half-brother—you know that? But if you're really going to be fortunate, and I'm really going to find a use for you, you're going to have to start out understanding what I'm really like."

The first fierce burst of pain was receding from Bleys' head and his mind was beginning to work.

"I'd have found out shortly, anyway," he said.

"Ah, the little brother has teeth," said Dahno, "but they're milk-teeth, young Bleys. Don't try to use them on me. Yes, you'd have found out. But I decided I wanted you to find out right away. Now you know. I'm not exactly the laughing boy that everybody takes me for."

"You're like our mother then," said Bleys.

"Ah, quick. Even quicker than I'd thought!" said Dahno. "Yes, that's exactly it. I am like mother in that particular; but that and one other are the only ways. The other is that I always get my way. That means I'm going to get my way with you, too. I want you to get that straight, right from the beginning. Have you gotten it straight?"

"Yes," said Bleys. He put a hand to the side of his head briefly. "I have it very straight."

"Good," said Dahno, "because what I just did to you is nothing to what I'll do to you if I have to. There's no limit to what I'll do to you if it's necessary. But I don't expect to. I think we're going to work together, hand in glove. Like brothers indeed, Little Brother. But we won't come to it quickly. There's a few things I have to do first; and it won't hurt you to have a little seasoning here on the farm of our 'Uncle' Henry."

Bleys' mind was finally fully back in working order. He recognized that what Dahno said was true. This man was one person he was not going to be able to control—at least, not for a long time. He retreated behind the barrier of childhood.

"What are you going to do with me?" he asked.

Dahno did not answer directly. Instead, he looked at Bleys for several long moments, thoughtfully. Even his smile was gone.

"You know," he said, "I was just like you when I came here. Oh, there was the difference that I was as big as Henry himself, even then, even though I wasn't much older than you are—and twice as strong as Henry, if it came to that. But it was still my intelligence I used to protect myself from him, and this whole way of life of his. You'll already have started to do that. Haven't you?"

"Yes," said Bleys. There was no point in trying to explain himself to someone like this.

"Yes, you would've," said Dahno, thoughtfully, "and we'll put that mind and those abilities to good use eventually, you and I, Little Brother. But not just yet. You still have a lot to learn. So far, by and large you've been working only on people who were halfway ready to be agreeable to you in the first place. The test comes when you work on somebody who is ready to disagree with you at the very sight of you. That's the real test. So, as I say, you stay with Uncle Henry."

"And finally? Someday?" asked Bleys. "What happens then?"

"Then you move to where I am, in Ecumeny—in the city," said Dahno. "By that time I'll have a place ready for you in what I'm doing."

"What are you doing?" Bleys asked.

"That, you're going to have to wait to learn," said Dahno. He turned away.

"We probably ought to be getting back to our relatives," he said.

"Wait—" said Bleys. "How long do I stay here?"

"Some weeks? Some months? Maybe even a few years," said Dahno, looking over his shoulder back at him, "it all depends."

"On me?"

Bleys had to follow him to ask the question, because Dahno was already walking toward the end of the goat barn.

"On you to a certain extent, yes," said Dahno, "but on other things as well. Don't worry. I'll come and see you from time to time. Meanwhile, you can be finding out what you can do in the way of handling the relatives."

Dahno led the way back around the barn. Henry and Joshua were out in the yard. Will, presumably, was inside, still doing the cleaning up after lunch. Bleys hardly saw the two in the yard, for the hard knot of emotion that was in him at the moment. In his mind there was just a single thought. *Never again!* Never again would Dahno hit him!

Then the knot dissolved, and his mind was clear once more—and he understood. He realized that of course Dahno would never hit him again. His older brother had no intention of it, knowing it would never be necessary.

The blow was not a blow in the ordinary sense of the word, as much as a signal. Bleys was being notified that Dahno was taking over the role that their mother had played in Bleys' life.

Delivered in that heavy-handed slap from Dahno, the message was unmistakable. Dahno now owned him. Nor was there anything that Bleys was in a condition to do about it now. As Dahno had said, only too truly, Bleys still only had his milk-teeth, compared to the weapons of his older brother. But time would change things. Bleys tucked the whole episode away in the back of his mind for future study.

Dahno waved his hand at Henry.

"If you don't mind, Henry," he said, "I'll take my little brother here into town and buy him some clothes. Now, if you'll come around to the trunk of the car, I'll give you those engine parts I brought you."

"That'll be quite all right, Dahno," said Henry. "Bleys and I thank God for your generosity."

As he spoke he was coming to meet them at the back of the hovercar. Dahno sprang open the trunk and took out a couple of paper-wrapped packages, each one of which filled one of his large hands. He handed them to Henry, who received them in his arms.

"And I thank the Lord for your generosity to me in this," said Henry.

CHAPTER

6

≡≡≡

HENRY STOOD BACK and Dahno went around one side of the hovercar, while Bleys went around to the other and opened the door there. The two seats inside were separate and swiveled. There was a control stick in front of each chair, and Dahno took hold of his as the two doors were closed.

"You know enough not to touch the spare control rod while I'm driving the car, don't you?" he said to Bleys.

"Of course," said Bleys.

Dahno laughed.

Below them the under-fans roared to life. The hovercar lifted, spun about, and began to go back between the trees toward the highway, along the dirt road from the farm.

Dahno, Bleys saw, as they left the farm behind, was a fast and excellent driver. By the time he hit the main highway and had found a strip for hovercars where he could let the vehicle out at full speed, the meter on the dashboard showed that they were doing over two hundred fifty kilometers an hour.

Bleys had assumed that they were just going to the local

store. But Dahno took him clear into Ecumeny. Once there they shopped in some of the larger stores for various kinds of work clothes, jackets, and boots for Bleys—and one formal suit of soft, black material like that Dahno himself was currently wearing.

"That'll be for Sundays," Dahno said, speaking of the suit. "It won't hurt if you outshine Uncle Henry and his two boys a little bit. Not too much—but a little bit. And that suit should do just that, as well, to anything the others at the church'll be wearing."

They stopped for a snack at a restaurant, and Bleys found himself enjoying the day. Dahno was a different person, now. He was a warm and friendly companion; and he poured out information about Ecumeny, about Henry's church, and a hundred other things that would be useful to Bleys. It was clear he knew that it was information Bleys would need; and therefore it was information he supplied.

By the time they had eaten, it had reached late afternoon. They left the restaurant, found the hovercar and headed back out toward the farm. As they went, Bleys' spirits sank in spite of himself.

Today had been the sort of day he would like to have always. Comfort, pleasant company—and an unending spate of interesting information to be gathered up and stored away for future use in the back of his mind. Now he was going back to where the rooms were cold at night, the bed was hard under the stuffed mattress, and with the next daybreak there would be household duties to do; but there would be no conversation of any worth.

Dahno was no longer talking, finally, and Bleys did not feel like talking himself. He stared out the windshield ahead; and the silence lasted between them until they drove at last up the dirt road to the farmyard.

"Don't look so down, Little Brother," said Dahno. The half-mocking note that had been in his voice when he first spoke to Bleys was back there again. "There'll be other days and I'll make other visits; and we'll go into town again. Just do what you have to, here, and learn as much as you can."

He reached across and opened the door on Bleys' side.

Slowly Bleys got out, reached back in for his purchases, and looked back at him for a moment through the open door.

"I had a good time," said Bleys.

"Good," answered Dahno; and there seemed to be a note of real approval in his voice.

Then he shut the door in Bleys' face, and the hovercar rose again on its fans, spun about and disappeared away down the road from the farm to the highway. Bleys found himself standing alone in the farmyard with his hands full of boxes and bundles that were the fruit of their shopping.

He turned numbly to the house to take these things inside. But before he could reach it Will came out rather hurriedly, stopped very briefly to close the door softly behind him and then came swiftly down the steps.

Will would have dashed on past Bleys without even looking at him, if Bleys had not stopped him. The younger boy's face was white, so that here and there a freckle that Bleys had not noticed before stood out against the paleness of his skin.

"What is it?" asked Bleys, catching Will's arm with one hand and holding him.

"One of the goats got its head caught between a fallen fence bar and the bar below, and strangled," said Will. He wrenched himself loose from the grip of Bleys' hand and left at a run, disappearing around a corner of the barn.

Wondering, Bleys went up the steps and in through the door.

Henry was seated in a chair half-turned from the table, and standing before him was Joshua. Joshua's face was not pale but his expression was solemn and still.

"—You didn't see it die then," Henry was asking Joshua.

"No, Father."

"That means you didn't see the rail come loose and fall down to trap her?"

"No, Father."

"One of our best milk goats." There was a regretful note in Henry's voice; and he seemed to be speaking more to himself than to Joshua. He looked up at his son.

"Well," he said, "you won't let a loose rail like that happen again, will you?"

"No, Father."

"Yes. Well, see me after dinner then." Henry got to his feet. "You can go back to work, son."

Joshua turned and went out the door without looking at Bleys. Henry caught sight of him and beckoned him over to the table where, Bleys saw, there were a number of slips of paper spread out.

"Bleys," said Henry, then interrupted himself, "—take those things your brother must have bought you into your own room and leave them on your bunk. Then come back here. I've got some questions I want to ask you."

Bleys did as he was told. When he got back, Henry was seated in the chair again, apparently sorting the slips which he had laid out in rows stretching away from him, like the cards in a game of solitaire.

"Bleys," said Henry, looking up as Bleys appeared, "these are the records each day for each milk goat as to how much milk they gave. They vary in amount, but also in quality. Is there anything in the mathematics you say you learned in school that would help me figure out which are the most profitable of my milk goats?"

Bleys looked at the slips. Each was simply a small piece of paper with a date, a name—which he assumed was the name of the goat—and a figure that must be for the amount of milk that animal had produced.

"Are those figures volume or weight, Uncle?" he asked.

"Volume—oh, I see," said Henry, "yes, they're the number of liters and part-liters we got from each one. Why?"

"I just thought . . ." Bleys hesitated. He was raking through the back of his mind, putting together several things picked up from different people at different places and different times. "If you weighed the milk they gave each morning, instead of just measuring it, you might be able to get an idea of how rich it was. I think the richer the milk the more fat there is in it. So kilogram for kilogram the goat giving richer milk should be worth more."

He hesitated again.

"I think that's right, Uncle," he said, "I can't be sure.

Maybe there're other ways, other things that have to do with whether it makes more cheese or not—the milk I mean."

"Hmmm . . ." said Henry, "it's a possibility. I can go to the district library and ask them if weight is a measure of whether goat milk makes better cheese, or not. But there's still the problem of comparing goat to goat."

"You could make a spreadsheet for that, Uncle," said Bleys, a little more boldly. One of the men who had lived with his mother for a while had shown him how to make a spreadsheet. But it had been done on a screen, working with a keyboard.

Still, possibly the same thing could be done simply with a pencil and a piece of paper.

"You put all the names of the goats across the top of a sheet," said Bleys, "then you put the dates down in the left-hand column and list the amount of milk each day under each goat that gives it, so that at the end of the year you can get totals. Maybe even just the totals could tell you something."

"Yes," said Henry, still looking at the slips of paper, "I can ask about that, too. You may have been very helpful, Bleys. I thank the Lord for your trying, however."

"I thank the Lord you have found me useful, Uncle," said Bleys. Henry looked at him; and Bleys found himself on the receiving end of one of the wintry smiles. But it only lasted for a few seconds.

"Well, that's enough of that," Henry said, abruptly. "Will cleaned up after lunch; but there must be a good deal of other work around the house that wasn't done because you left so early and just now got back. You should get busy at it right now."

"Yes, Uncle," said Bleys and went off toward the closet where the cleaning tools were kept.

"Oh, you can take time out to unpack those packages you brought in first, if you want," said Henry.

Bleys unpacked the packages, put the clothes away in the trunk underneath his bunk and stood, unsure of what to do with the boxes; finally he took them out and put them in one of the sheds where extra bits and pieces of equipment and worn-out items were kept. Few things were thrown away around the farm, he had noticed.

He had no idea if the boxes would be useful; but he did not want to risk disposing of them. Henry had gone, or else he would have asked his uncle what to do with them. He went back in and gave the house a cleaning. Since it was scrubbed every day, it hardly needed even that much attention. Meanwhile, he had started the evening stew in the pot over the fire; and in due time everyone came in and ate.

Henry announced the end of the meal as usual by putting down his eating utensils and standing up.

"Will," he said, "since you cleaned up after lunch you're free now. You can go to bed early or do anything you want until regular bed hour; and then you better be in your bunk. Bleys, you clean up everything and then it'll be bedtime for you. Joshua, in my room after your prayers."

Bleys noticed that as he went through the doorway of his room Henry lifted from a nail in the wall a long strap and took it in with him.

Bleys found the action puzzling. He could think of no reason for Henry to be bundling up things in his own room. As far as he knew, none of them were going on a trip, and it was the kind of strap that would reinforce a suitcase or other piece of luggage. However, there was no obvious answer. He put it out of his mind for the present, going to work at the business of cleaning up after the dinner and washing the dishes.

It did not take long to do the washing and clean up, now that he was experienced at it. He finished up and went to the bedroom he shared with the other two boys.

Will was still on his knees when Bleys came in, which meant he had been praying for an unusually long time. But at Bleys' entrance he scrambled to his feet, climbed up into his upper bunk, undressed hurriedly and wrapped himself in his blanket, turning his face to the wall. He had not looked at Bleys since Bleys entered.

Further puzzled by this, but only slightly, Bleys went about his own business of undressing and getting into his own bunk. After the first few days of being awakened at dawn, he had adjusted to the idea of going to sleep early to make sure he got a full night's rest. It was only when he was pulling the covers up over him, that he looked across the room at the upper bunk, clinging to the outside log wall, where Will lay; and saw that the other boy had his head completely buried under his pillow.

Bleys had learned when he was a good deal younger not to chase after mysteries, but to lie in wait for them, adding up evidence until at last the mystery revealed itself. He told himself that this odd behavior of Will's would explain itself in the long run, turned over in his bunk so that he faced the wall to Henry's bedroom and dug his own head comfortably into his pillow.

It took him a few moments to doze off. He was vaguely aware of the sound of voices from Henry's room, but they were too low-pitched for him to understand anything. He was just starting to drift off when the voices ceased. There was a long moment of silence in which he hovered on the very edge of sleep, and then he heard an odd sound that he could not identify. There was a pause, then it was repeated. Then another pause and another repetition . . . and then he began to hear Joshua's voice . . .

Horror flooded through him, leaving him cold as an icicle. Suddenly, clearly and unmistakably, he identified the sounds from Joshua as sounds of pain; and the rhythmic repetition of the first sound he had heard he now recognized as the kind of sound made by a leather strap hitting a human body.

To someone like himself, born to an Exotic who, whatever else she was, was incapable of violence, raised completely apart from anything physically violent except in an occasional interaction with children his own age, the idea of a man beating a boy was frightening beyond conception.

He threw a quick glance over his shoulder back up at Will. The younger boy not only had his pillow over his head but both hands on top of that holding it down. At the sight, Bleys felt Will's reaction become his reaction. He huddled in his bunk pulling his own pillow over his head to block his ears, lying there and shivering. But the sound still came through.

Try as he would, he could not shut out of his imagination the image of Joshua being beaten by his father. A terrible fear possessed him, a fear so great that he felt hollowed out inside. Never could he endure such a thing himself. Never!

The sound ceased at last; or at least the sound of the strap ceased and Joshua's crying soon dropped below a level that could be heard through the wall. Bleys lay, trembling in his fear, but filled at the same time with a sort of terrible curiosity—the same kind of curiosity someone might feel to look upon the place and machine of his own execution.

He thought of Joshua, and his mind was torn, like an open wound. At all costs, he thought, he must go to the older boy. Now.

Shakily, he got up from the bunk. The air was already cold; and automatically he put his jacket on over his pajamas. Will was still huddled against the wall with the pillow over his head, motionless.

Bleys went out into the main room, and almost bumped into Henry. A Henry carrying no strap, and looking no different than at any other time.

Bleys was not thinking. He simply headed toward the entrance to Henry's bedroom. The man intercepted and caught him.

"Bleys!" said Henry, sharply, catching him by one shoulder. "What are you doing up? Where are you going?"

"Joshua," said Bleys, still with his eyes fastened on the doorway, "I've got to go to Joshua."

He tried to pull away, but Henry put his other hand on the shoulder that he was not holding already, and stopped him.

"*No!*" he said. "You shall not!"

His voice softened, for the first time since Bleys had heard it.

"Joshua won't want to see you now," he said. "Go back to bed."

Bleys looked up at the man. It was the same stern face. There was no change in it. Only the face of a man, not of a monster.

"You—" Bleys could not find the words he wanted to say what was in him.

"I am God's instrument, nothing more," said Henry. But there was still that unusual softness in his voice. He turned Bleys around with his hands and his superior strength, so that against his will, Bleys found himself facing in the opposite direction.

"Go to bed now. You'll learn, boy. You'll learn."

Numbly, Bleys stumbled back to the door of his room, into it and into his bunk. He covered himself completely with the covers, as if he would shut out everything, and waited. After a while, there in the darkness, sleep finally came.

CHAPTER
7

THE NEXT MORNING was no different from any of the other mornings Bleys had seen in that house; except that he was drugged with sleep. Will literally had to pull him out of his bunk.

When he was able to stand up and start dressing, he saw that Joshua was already dressed and leaving, and Will was right behind him. He hurried to finish getting into his clothes and went into the main rooms to begin bringing the embers of last night's fire to a fresh blaze that would heat the coffee—as they did indeed call the dark liquid he had been given on his first meal here.

He shivered in the sweater Joshua had given him as the little flames came alive among the tinder he had carefully laid on the still glowing coals. The fire grew as he added more fuel to it; until its strong flames licked at the blackened bottom of the coffeepot.

He was all alone in the house. Henry, Joshua and Will had gone outside to their pre-breakfast chores. He continued making breakfast, starting the water boiling for the porridge-

like cereal that they made from a powdered form of the local,
oat-like grain. Like the coffee, its taste at first had been strange
in his mouth; but now hunger and familiarity were overcoming
that difference. He found he was as eager for it this morning as
his two cousins and his uncle.

After about twenty minutes they were all back inside and by
that time both coffee and porridge were ready for them. He
served it on the table and they all ate, in the silence of early
morning when there was nothing much to be said and not much
point in saying anything anyway. Plainly, it was a customary
silence. Bleys stole glances at Joshua, but the other boy
appeared no different than he had the day before. This thing
that had happened to him seemed not to have touched or
changed him in any way.

"Joshua," said Henry, at last, pushing his empty bowl away
from him, "you'll see that that fence is fixed, first thing."

"I already have, Father," said Joshua, finishing his last
spoonful of porridge. "I did it late yesterday afternoon."

"Good," said Henry. He looked at Bleys. "Bleys, I'm going
to the store this morning; and as soon as you clean up here I
want you to come with me. The storekeeper needs to get to
know you; and you should get to know him, in case I have to
send you alone for supplies."

He stood up; and at that signal that breakfast was over they
all stood up with him, pushing their chairs back into place at
the table.

Henry and the boys went out. Bleys busied himself collect-
ing the porridge bowls and cups and washing them. Practice
had begun to make him swift at this, also. It was not long
before he was through and outside, looking for Henry.

Henry was in the yard with the goat team harnessed beside
him. As Bleys came out, he was examining the feet of the
goats he had harnessed to the cart. At Bleys' approach, he
looked up and spoke.

"It did them no good, that traveling on surfaced roads," he
said, "remember that, boy. These creatures don't take having
metal shoes fixed to their hooves, the way horses do, back on
Old Earth. Now, in the cart with you. We'll get going."

By goat-cart, it was about half an hour's ride over country roads to the small local store. Bleys found it a strange, small place crowded with things. From Joshua, Bleys had learned that it both bought and sold; acting as a market for things like the goat cheese that Henry's farm produced, shipping some of it on to Ecumeny, but keeping most of it for resale, locally. It also sold the local people all types of farm equipment and supplies, including the ground meal from which they made their cereal and other dry goods.

"James Broeder," Henry introduced Bleys to the store-keeper, "this is my nephew, who's living with us now. His name is Bleys Ahrens. Bleys, this is Mr. Broeder."

"Honored to make your acquaintance, sir," said Bleys.

Broeder, a short, squat, dark man, frowned slightly. "Pleased to meet you too, Bleys," he said, "as for that 'honored' way of speaking—I don't go much for that."

"I think I told you, Bleys," said Henry, sharply, "we don't use formal speech in our church; and Mr. Broeder is a fellow member."

"May the Lord forgive me," said Bleys, quickly, "I won't forget again, Uncle."

But Broeder had failed to smile; and Bleys, sensitive as a leaf to the lightest breeze, could feel that the store owner still had not accepted him into the community of which he and Henry's family were a part.

Without hesitation, Bleys turned to Henry and leaned close to him, lowering his voice as if to speak confidentially into Henry's ear alone.

"Uncle," he almost whispered, "how does Mr. Broeder keep track of all these things he buys and sells, as well as how much we and other people buy on credit?"

Henry turned his dark eyes slowly and terribly at Bleys; and Bleys felt as if a protecting curtain had been ripped away from between them.

"Bleys," said Henry, icily, "you are to tell the truth at all times!"

Somehow, he had read Bleys' purpose in the tone of his

voice. But now Broeder was smiling and the feeling Bleys got from him was tinged with warmth.

"Well now, there's truth enough in that, Henry," Broeder said, "you've got a sharp understanding, boy. It's not everybody who can keep track of everything that goes into running a store like this."

Bleys felt the success of his flattery; but at the same time fear had shot through Bleys suddenly, like an icy spasm. Henry had become an incalculable quantity to him. He had no idea what might trigger the man to beat him as he had beaten Joshua. Certainly, if a fence rail fell on a goat and strangled it, it was at least partly the goat's fault, and probably the result of the goat trying to push through the fence or do something unusual with it. But Henry had acted as if there was no blame to be attached to anyone but Joshua. So there was no telling what might make him choose to punish.

Bleys told himself that he must find out what was safe to say and do with Henry and what was not. It was not enough, just to say what he thought Henry wanted to hear all the time. He would need to know certainly what his limits were; and what were the lines that should not be crossed, the taboo subjects not to be mentioned. It could have been that using the polite form of address he had been taught since he had first been able to talk to people was enough to cause Henry to turn on him with the strap.

Henry had suddenly become dangerous. But, Bleys told himself, there must be a pattern. There had been a pattern to everything Bleys had ever known. He must talk to Joshua. Joshua would tell him.

At the same time, right now, something inside him shrank from approaching Joshua. Surely undergoing the sort of torture the older boy had endured the night before would have done something to him. Possibly changed him in some way. Bleys could not imagine any result in himself but a violent change, as a result of such an experience. So he could not imagine it otherwise in Joshua.

The business Henry had with the storekeeper turned out brief enough. It was merely disposing of some few wheels of cheese that he had brought along, buying some more of the cereal, and dickering over the cost of a pound of nails, the price of which, it developed, had been raised by a small amount since Henry was in last.

Henry finally got his nails at the old price; but with a flat statement from Broeder that from now on he would have to pay the new and higher price.

Bleys and Henry headed back to the farm. On the way, Henry was silent, evidently busy with his own thoughts. Bleys appreciated his uncle's silence for two reasons. If Henry did not talk to him, there was less chance Bleys might make a mistake in the way he answered, and get himself in trouble as a result.

Secondly, Bleys needed to do some thinking himself. He could not imagine living with someone who would beat him as if he were an animal.

Just what he, himself, would or could do to avoid it happening to him, he did not know. And that frightened him. He spent the morning worrying about it.

Lunch went off as usual. Again, Bleys watched Joshua—more openly now—for any sign of change in the other boy; and found none. Joshua was still his ordinary, quiet-voiced, friendly self. It was as if what had been done to him had not touched him internally—and that Bleys found inconceivable. Bleys could not imagine torture doing anything but destroying the innate pattern of the individual. Bleys had to know; and only Joshua could tell him. He summoned up his nerve and spoke to Henry.

"Uncle," asked Bleys, while they were eating lunch, "I don't know much about goats; and something might come up where I needed to know about them. After I finish cleaning up here this afternoon, could I go and help Joshua with the goats and their milking?"

Henry looked at him.

"That's a sensible request, Bleys," he said. "Yes, I think you may. Joshua—"

"Yes, Father?" responded Joshua, looking up from his bowl.

"Let Bleys be with you as he says," said Henry. "Afterwards be sure to tell me how quick he was to pick things up; and how useful he might be, if for some reason he had to take care of the goats by himself."

"Yes, Father," said Joshua agreeably.

As a result, in late afternoon sunlight—for the weather had been good that day—Bleys found himself out in an enclosed field with Joshua. Joshua had taken seriously the injunction of his father to teach Bleys about the goats. He did so now, conscientiously, telling Bleys the name of each one, and showing him little differences in hair color, action or size, by which that goat could be identified.

". . . We have one billy goat to about every ten nannies," Joshua explained. "That's because it's the females that pay their way in milk and cheese and kids. All these goats you see here are variforms, genetically tailored to this world. They're the descendants of a dozen frozen variform embryos shipped out from Old Earth while they were still tiny; then raised to birthing age in the plant in Ecumeny."

He looked at Bleys.

"You understand?"

"Yes," said Bleys.

Joshua went on.

"Because the kids of most goats are deformed when they're born and don't live, we have to buy new embryos every so often to avoid inbreeding. That's awfully expensive, but there's no help for it. Anyway, now we have over forty of the animals; and most of those are good-producing nannies. The billies—the male goats—are good for hides. We get a slightly stronger leather from them; and they're also better for pulling the goat-cart and plowing, and such things like that. We'll use up to a dozen billies to pull the plow. But they're hard to work with. We'll all be glad when Father gets the motor put together; and we can build a motorized vehicle that can pull the plow, the harrow, and other things."

He stopped and looked at Bleys.

Bleys nodded. He understood about the goats not reproducing on most New Worlds, along with many other species of animals; a fact that continued to puzzle biologists. The rest was new to him; but he stored it in his memory.

"Is there some particular question you've got?" Joshua asked. "You're looking at me as if you wanted to ask something. Go ahead. That's the whole point. I can tell you what I know, but I don't know what you need to know, unless you tell me."

Bleys felt as if he were standing on the brink of a cliff. Nonetheless, everything he knew about people told him that now was the moment for him to speak, and so he spoke.

"It's just—" He hesitated. "Are you all right?"

Joshua looked puzzled.

"All right?" he echoed. "Of course. I haven't been sick for six months or more, not since last winter, and even that was only a bit of an upset stomach I got from something I ate. Though we were all surprised, because neither Will nor Father got sick. What makes you think I might not be all right?"

Joshua had been so open and certain in his answer that Bleys found himself for a moment without the words he needed to say what he wanted to say. He hesitated again.

"It's just that . . . last night . . ." he said, and ran out of words again.

"Oh!" said Joshua, "you mean the beating Father gave me because that goat got killed? Is that it? You must come from very strange people, Bleys, to be wondering about that. It was nothing—just a beating."

"But—" Bleys still found himself at a loss. "I just didn't understand why your father took it out on you. I mean, it was an accident that the goat got killed, wasn't it?"

"Yes," said Joshua, "but it was my fault for not making sure the fence was secure, so that a loose rail fell or got pushed down and pinned the nanny's neck between that rail and the one below it. So the nanny strangled and we lost a valuable goat; and I was responsible for the fence not being safe. Who else could be responsible but me?"

"But it was an accident," said Bleys.

"No, Bleys," said Joshua seriously, "nothing is ever an accident. God made it happen because I was careless, to show me the results of my carelessness. That's why Father beat me. So I'll remember and never be careless that way again. And I won't."

"But it's so . . . hard on you," said Bleys.

"Hard?" Joshua shook his head. "But the way of God is always hard. It was as hard on Father as it was on me. But it was his God-given duty to see I was punished for being careless."

Bleys became silent. Somehow, according to the thinking of Joshua and his father—and probably of Will as well and all the other members of their church in addition—there was a pattern and meaning to all this that justified what had happened to Joshua.

He remembered the touch of gentleness he thought he had sensed in his uncle; when he had tried to go to Joshua afterwards, and Henry had stopped him in the main room of the house, to send him back to bed. Here, even Joshua was agreeing that what had happened to him was the right thing; and at the same time it was more horrible than Bleys could imagine.

"When I have a family, finally," said Joshua, "I'll have to beat my own son when he deserves punishment. To do otherwise would not be to bring him up in the way of the Lord."

Bleys nodded, hoping that Joshua would take this as a sign that he had understood. But he had not understood. His own newly kindled fear of Henry was still there and he still had to learn what he must do to feel safe in that household.

He was left still uncertain, still insecure. But he stayed with Joshua, learning what Joshua had to tell him about the goats, as they rounded them up and took them in at the end of the afternoon to the barn.

A part of his mind kept searching for an answer. There must be someone from whom he could get information. The pattern had to be there but questioning Henry to find it was unthinkable; and Joshua was evidently so deeply caught up in his faith already, that he could not describe what he took for granted, as he took gravity and the oxygen in the air for granted.

Bleys also considered asking Will. But it struck him that between the younger boy's own terror at the time of Joshua's beating, and Will's youth, plus his immersion in the religious aspect of the household, that Will would not be useful either.

Still, the pattern had to be there.

On the way back to the barn, an idea came to him.

"Who is the—" For one of the few times in his life, Bleys found himself searching for the proper word. He had no idea what these people called the leader of their religious practices. "Who's the pastor of your church?"

"Pastor?" Joshua turned to stare at him, switching his attention off the goat he had just driven back in with the rest of the herd as they mobbed their way toward the stable.

"Whoever's in charge of your religious services," said Bleys. His mind hesitated over the word *priest* and a strong instinct made him reject it. "The religious leader at your church."

"Oh, you mean the Teacher," said Joshua. "Yes, he lives about two miles from here, right next to the church itself. His name's Gregg—it was something longer than that, but none of us could pronounce it properly, so he shortened it to Gregg."

"I see," said Bleys, nodding.

They took the goats the rest of the way into the barn and saw each of them stalled, each in its proper place. That night, just as they were finishing dinner, Bleys spoke to Henry.

"Uncle," he said, "do you think it would be a good idea if I talked to the Teacher of your church? I need to learn from him."

Henry put down his spoon and looked at Bleys. His eyes were once more the fierce eyes Bleys had first seen on meeting him at the spaceship terminal.

"I am a Member of the Church; and I belong to God, myself. What questions do you need answered that I can't answer for you?"

Bleys thought swiftly.

"I want to understand—all about your church," he answered.

Henry's gaze lost its terrifying intensity.

"I see," he said. "If it's all about the church, then indeed you should talk to the Teacher. Understand me, Bleys—and my sons have heard this before but it will do them no harm to hear it again—"

Joshua and Will's spoons went down flat on the table.

"—As I just said, I belong to God—and He is all I require. There are no lack of those, even in our Church, who would go forth to proselyte, or missionary, and strive to convert people from other churches. But I have never done this, nor would I. For I need only God. I have no need for other worshipers about me to warm my faith. If it should happen that I stood alone in what I believe, that would not change me—nor should it, any Godly man or woman."

He paused to look directly from Joshua to Will.

"Children may need counsel or guidance in their search of the Lord, while growing up," he said, "but when my two sons become men I will expect them to choose for themselves; and if their choice is a different church than mine, I will be sad to see them go, but honor their going. For God is always there and no one need be helped to Him. Those with faith will find Him where they look for Him. Those without faith must do without a Lord."

He stopped speaking and Bleys found that, with the other two boys, he had actually been holding his breath.

"Therefore," Henry looked back at Bleys and his voice gentled, "you should indeed speak to the Teacher. You have been with us now through three church-days, Bleys; and not once yet have you asked to come with us to Service. Talk to Gregg and decide how you wish. No decision you ever make about God will alter by so much as a hair the way any of us feel or act toward you."

He paused.

"His name is Albert Gregg; and his house is just down the road from ours, here," he said. "It is too late tonight, but tomorrow after lunch, Will can take over the cleanup from the meal, and you can go down and see him. He's always at home there; and if he isn't, there'll be a message tacked to the door to say where he is. Yes, Bleys, you must thank God you thought of that."

CHAPTER

8

═══════════

THE NEXT DAY after lunch, Bleys walked down the road in the direction that, ironically, led back toward Ecumeny. The rain had let up for some days now, it was already hot and the road was getting dry and even a little dusty. The summer was beginning to move toward them.

"You can't miss it," Will had said, "it's a little brown house next to the church. The Teacher said it wouldn't be right to paint his house the same color as the church. But there's no trees in the way; and anyway, if you did miss it, you couldn't miss the church, because its steeple is higher than the tops of the trees in any direction."

Bleys spent the walk wondering how he would go about questioning the Teacher. He had never been more aware that he was completely out of his depth. He had not realized it before; but all the men and women he had known until now had a pattern of behavior and attitude that came from a very different life than this, but one with which Bleys had been familiar since birth. Here the imperatives were all different. People would not be responding to the stimuli that he had been able to use when trying to get anything from them, back when he had been with his mother.

The church steeple showed itself, and shortly after that both the church and the small brown house beside it came into view. Bleys walked up the road to them; and in a short distance saw them clearly, since house and church alike did not sit back far from the road, being separated from each other only by what evidently was some sort of parking lot.

The small, brown house had a tiny porch on it and behind the porch a door. Bleys mounted to the door and knocked on it.

There was no answer. He looked at the door but there was no message fixed to it. He tried knocking at the door a little harder.

This time, after a moment, he heard shuffling steps inside and the door was opened. What he took at first to be a rather small man, even shorter than Bleys himself, peered out, looked at him and smiled.

"Ah," he said, "you must be Henry's new nephew. Come on in."

He stood aside, opening the door wider for Bleys to enter a dark little hall. The door was shut behind Bleys and his host shuffled ahead of him down the hall and through a door to the left into what seemed to be a sort of parlor or sitting room, although it too was tiny. Bleys saw that the man was almost bent double, so that he had to crane his head back on his neck to look up and see who he was talking to.

In the room, he took one of the chairs that was apparently adjusted to him; because once he was fitted into it he was able to look straight across at Bleys, whom he waved into an opposing chair. Both chairs were fairly small, but overstuffed and comfortable, if a little in need of dusting. Bleys' last few days at Henry's house had made him unusually conscious of cleanliness; and he was conscious of the fact that not only was the house far from being as clean as Henry's was kept, but the man himself smelled a little musty, as if he had not bathed recently. But Gregg smiled at him.

"So you came to see me," he said. "I'm Albert Gregg. But

you know that. Church members generally just call me Gregg outside the church. In the church I'm 'Teacher.' If there're any adults around"—his eyes almost twinkled—"you should probably call me Teacher. But since there're just the two of us, Gregg will do. Don't be startled at the way I look. It's arthritis. Yes, I know it's curable—but the cost is more than we can afford here. Now, you're—Bleys Ahrens, aren't you?"

"That's right, Teacher—I mean, Gregg," said Bleys.

He found himself even more at sea than he had expected. He had assumed he would be meeting someone cast in the mold of Henry. Someone direct, decisive, and more than a little intolerant. This man seemed none of these; and yet he was head of their local church. Bleys was puzzled.

"Would you like some coffee?" asked Gregg. "The kettle's hot in the kitchen, and the makings are there. I'll ask you to make it for both of us, if you do want some, because it's a little hard for me to get around."

"No thank you, Gregg." Bleys found the name awkward in his mouth. "I just finished lunch."

"Not only that," said Gregg with something very close to a chuckle, "but you haven't adjusted to the taste of what we call coffee here yet, I'd guess. What brings you to see me?"

"I need"—this time Bleys had the word ready prepared— "instruction in the religion of your church, since I'm going to be a member."

"Instruction? You're sure you don't just mean information?" Gregg eyed him shrewdly. "In the first place, there is no formal instruction in our church; and, in the second place, you don't strike me as someone particularly in need of instruction—particularly if you're here at your own wishes. Or did Henry send you?"

"No," answered Bleys, "it was my idea to come and see you. You're right, I wanted to ask some questions."

"Good," said Gregg, wriggling himself a little more deeply and more comfortably into his chair, "that's much more to the point, and much more to be desired. I'd rather have somebody asking me questions of their own, and for their own reasons, than a hundred people sent to me to be taught."

"I lived with my mother all of my life until just now," said Bleys. "She was born and raised an Exotic; so I suppose I grew up an Exotic, too. I never knew any people from Harmony or Association until now—except one, and he—"

Bleys found himself hesitating.

"—He wasn't like what people said about people from your two worlds."

"In other words," said Gregg, "he was probably somebody like Henry's brother Ezekiel, if he wasn't Ezekiel himself. And Ezekiel was someone who simply ran away from the whole question of faith—left these two worlds where faith flourishes and changed his way of life completely. Was it Ezekiel?"

"Yes—Gregg," answered Bleys, "we all liked him."

"Yes. Oh, yes." Gregg's voice was thoughtful. "Ezekiel was one of the most likable human beings I ever knew. He still would be now, no doubt. But go on," he said, "you were telling me that your mother was an Exotic and you were raised an Exotic. I take it from the fact that you're here now, that for some reason you couldn't stay with your mother anymore. She's all right, isn't she?"

"Oh, she's fine," said Bleys; "it just wasn't—well, practical, for me to stay with her and travel around with her the way I was doing. She thought I'd be better off with Henry."

"Yes," said Gregg, "I can imagine. Just like your older brother."

"You know Dahno?" asked Bleys. For some reason it had not occurred to him that this man might.

"Oh, yes. I was Teacher here when your brother first came, too," said Gregg. "I think what you're leading up to is the fact that you don't know how you should act as a member of our church, because you've never had any experience with anything like it. Is that it?"

"That's it," said Bleys, relieved.

"Any more than that?" asked Gregg.

Bleys hesitated.

"It wouldn't be," said Gregg, "part of what you mentioned, about your having trouble fitting reality to what you've always heard about the people that call themselves Friendlies? Would it be that, too?"

Bleys nodded.

"I—" A rush of honesty suddenly brought words from him that he had not intended to say. "I'd always heard of Friendlies as sorts of fanatics. Oh, I also heard about them as being called true faith-holders or true believers. Is either name true, or are both? If both names are true, what's the difference?"

Gregg smiled. He had a small, round face, now marked with the wrinkles of fairly advanced age, but which still showed elements of extreme youthfulness buried under the wrinkles.

"Of course," he answered, "we all like to think of ourselves as true believers. True Faith-holders is what we usually call ourselves. We have to think that way; otherwise we couldn't live with ourself and God. But yes, some of us are what's called Fanatics. And yes, there is a difference between Fanatics and True Faith-holders."

"That's what I want to understand, then," said Bleys. "Which are which, and how do I tell who is what?"

"Actually," said Gregg, "the distinction is very simple. *'By their fruits ye shall know them'*—which is a quotation from the New Testament of the Bible—"

"I know," said Bleys, eagerly. He was feeling quite comfortable with this bent little man. "Matthew; Chapter Seven, verse twenty, I think."

"You know the Bible?" said Gregg looking at him penetratingly.

Bleys felt suddenly embarrassed.

"I learned to read very early," he said. "I've done a lot of reading and usually anything I read sticks in my mind. But you mean, that the Fanatic distinguishes himself from the True Faith-holder by what he does?"

"Exactly," murmured Gregg, "you are very like Dahno, you know? At the same time, you're very different. But you're right in what you just said. The distinction is simple. The True Faith-holder lives to serve God. The Fanatic, whether he's conscious of it himself, or not, makes God and God's worship a tool to serve his own ends."

"I see," said Bleys, thoughtfully.

There was a small silence.

"Something in particular recently has you concerned about this?" asked Gregg.

Bleys started to shake his head, then stopped the impulse.

"Yes," he said, and the words came out almost painfully. He felt a tremendous need to trust the bent, small Teacher. "As I said, my mother was an Exotic. I think I grew up like an Exotic. The whole idea of violence is something we simply don't entertain if we think like Exotics."

"And you've witnessed an act of violence recently, then?" asked Gregg.

"Yes," said Bleys slowly, "I—"

Suddenly it all came out with a rush, about Henry's beating of Joshua for the dead goat, and how Will had reacted and how Bleys himself had felt, both at the time and afterward.

"I see," said Gregg at last when he was finished. For another moment again there was nothing said between them; then Gregg went on.

"I can see how it would be hard for you," he said at last, slowly. "What you witnessed is tied to the very structure of Henry's belief, and the beliefs of most of us. Did you realize, at the time or afterwards, that Henry wasn't taking any pleasure in punishing his son?"

Bleys nodded.

"I found that out," he said. "Henry stopped me when I tried to go to Joshua afterwards; and he was almost—kind about it. And from what Joshua said when I talked to him about it, the next day. He said that when he was grown up he would beat his own son for the same reason."

"And so he will," said Gregg, "when the time comes; and yet, he'll be a good and loving father."

He broke off, almost abruptly.

"I'm going to have to leave you fairly shortly," he said. He shifted slightly in his specially built chair. "One of my church-members is going to drop by in his motorized car to take me out to his place. His grandmother's very old and close to dying. She'd said she'd appreciate a visit from me; and right at the moment she needs me more than you do."

"I see," said Bleys. He felt dismissed, pushed off to one side as unimportant.

"Don't look like that," said Gregg. "I don't think you do see. It's just that, I'm sorry to say, the truth of the matter is that I can't be very much help to you. I think I know what you want; and what that is, is an understanding of why we are as we are, here in this church, on this planet of Association. I don't think I can help you, because for you really to understand, you'd have to be capable of a belief in God. And I'm certain that, just like your older brother, you simply don't have that in you."

He smiled.

"Thirty years ago when I was a younger Teacher," he said, "I would have felt it my duty to try to hammer the concept of God into you. I now know that such things never work. God in any true sense will never come to you unless you find him on your own; and from what I've seen of Exotics, of your brother and even of you, I think that's going to be very hard, if not impossible."

He paused and looked at Bleys sympathetically.

"It can enrich your life, however, if you merely embrace the path a Friendly must tread," he went on. "In fact, I would advise you to try for that, rather than a belief that is beyond your reach."

"I see," said Bleys again. "But what if what I want's the belief?"

"You still have to find Him yourself," said Gregg. He looked sympathetically at Bleys. "You're disappointed, and I don't blame you. I am, in a way, too. Because it would mean a great deal to me if you were able to discover God or understand what makes Henry what he is and the rest of us what we are. Possibly, if you stayed here a very long time . . . but that's as God wills it. As I say, in any case, unless you find him on your own, you never will."

"But how can I at least try to do it?" asked Bleys.

"Take for granted there's a fabric of reason behind everything we do here," said Gregg. "You seem to be almost unbelievably intelligent for your age; and maybe you can come to have the comfort of seeing at least the framework of that fabric, even without belief. I don't know. I hope so."

He paused and sighed.

"For what it's worth," he went on, "I can tell you that Henry's not a Fanatic. He's a man of true faith. Perhaps, if you start out from that point, you can begin to understand."

He stopped speaking and smiled sadly at Bleys.

"Now," he said, "if you'll give me a hand up out of this chair—I could get out by myself with some struggling, but it's much easier if somebody helps me—I'll appreciate it. I want to get a coat before I go out to visit. Once I wouldn't have needed a coat. But now, as I get older, I find the cold gets to me, even mild cold gets to me; and since many of us believe that it is wrong to pamper ourselves with undue heat, among other comforts, I find myself in some cold places."

Bleys got up from his chair and stepped over to give the old man his hand. As he lifted Gregg out of the chair, the musty odor of the old man filled his nostrils.

Gregg smiled at him.

"I should apologize for that, too," he said. "You find I smell, don't you? I'm afraid it's the result of a foolish vow I took many years ago when I was young and strong. I vowed I'd never bathe in artificially warmed water. But the years have made it not only uncomfortable, but dangerous, for me to bathe in water that's at the temperature of the outdoors."

He smiled at Bleys again.

"That means that, while I can bathe in the summer, the winter months make it difficult—and we're just now finishing our winter as you know. When summer comes, my water tank outside will be warmed enough by the sun to deliver water safe for me to wash in. Until then, I try to stand at least at arm's length from people."

"I don't mind," said Bleys, "particularly, I don't mind most things once they're explained."

Gregg smiled again.

"You know," he said, "I think I may have hopes for you after all."

He began to shuffle out of the room. Then he paused and turned back.

"Oh, by the way, I'd suggest you wait here until Walser Doyle has picked me up and taken me off. It'll be easier for you if the rest of the congregation doesn't know for a while you felt the need to have a talk with me. Oh, and by the way, when you tell Henry about our talk, it'll do no harm if you refer to what I told you as *instruction*. It's a word that'll make Henry more comfortable."

"I'll remember," said Bleys, "and I'll wait here until you're gone—oh, excuse me. There's one more thing. Do I go to church with the others?"

"If you wish to, of course. Now just let yourself out after I'm gone," said Gregg, disappearing slowly through the doorway. "This house is never locked night or day. It hasn't been for more than forty years."

Bleys sat back down in his chair and waited. It was not more than two minutes later by his watch that he heard a motorized vehicle pull up to the front of the parking lot, close to the small brown house. The front door opened and a voice called.

"Gregg!"

"Coming, Walser!" Bleys heard Gregg's voice answer.

There was the sound of Gregg's shuffling footsteps heard faintly in the distance, a word or two spoken too low for Bleys to understand. Then the front door opened and closed, shutting off the voices entirely. A moment later Bleys heard the vehicle start up again and leave the area.

He waited a few moments more until it should be out of sight, then went out himself by the front door.

He did not go immediately back toward Henry's farm, however. Instead he made a tour of the house from the outside and located the black-painted tank fastened high on one outer wall by a rear corner. It was in shade at this time of day, for the house was so placed that that wall was more east-facing than anything else.

Bleys went back into the house. It took him some searching, but eventually he uncovered a hammer, a screwdriver and some other tools. A little more searching down in the basement discovered a stepladder, which he brought up and carried outside.

Mounted on the stepladder, he found that the tank, pretty much as he had guessed, was fastened to the house by a couple of straps, each one secured at each end by a screw, and the pipe running to it up and along the outside of the wall was the usual flexible plastic used for plumbing connections.

He was starting to unscrew the first of the eight screws that held the straps, when he realized that with the tank full of water, he could probably not lift it. He searched and found both an intake valve and a drain valve on the bottom of the tank. He closed the intake and let the water out, before finishing the unscrewing of the screws.

With the empty tank in his arms, he loosened the flexible pipe and bent it around the corner of the building just to see if it would reach. It would.

He fastened the water tank in place temporarily with one screw. Then he climbed down, moved the stepladder around the corner of the building and climbed it again. Reaching around the corner of the building, he took out the single screw and shifted the tank to the south-facing side of the building.

The sun would not only hit it more strongly now, but would hit it most of the day, both winter and summer. He fixed it firmly in place, closed the drain valve and turned the intake valve to refill the tank. Once he heard the water reach the top and stop automatically—it must have, he thought, some kind of float inside to warn it when it was nearly full—he went back down the ladder.

He folded up the ladder and, carrying it and the tools, went back to look at the side from which he had taken the tank, originally. The holes made by the screws that had held both tank and pipe there were visible—but only if you looked closely for them from the ground and knew where to look. Satisfied, he took tools and ladder back into the house, replaced them where he had found them, and turned back down the road to Henry's.

CHAPTER

9

BLEYS WALKED BACK toward Henry's farm from Gregg's small house by the church. The late winter day had turned out cloudless, with a touch of the first fierce heat of the short summer to come.

Bleys seemed to find it kindling a matching fierceness in him. Gregg had as good as told him that he could never be a Friendly because he could not believe in a God; and it would follow, therefore, that there was no use in his trying to become one of them.

There was more to his need to be a Friendly than a wish to prove Gregg wrong. He had already felt strongly that there was something he wanted to make out of his life—and would make, even though everybody on all the inhabited worlds told him it wasn't possible.

His future simply had to be something far greater than someone like Gregg, or even Henry or Dahno, could imagine. If it was necessary for him to be a Friendly to reach it, then he would be a Friendly. But he would also find a way to God, or find a God, if necessary to do that.

That much was settled. He deliberately set it aside as a thing fixed and done with. He made himself think back instead to his talk with Gregg, and what he might be able to use from it that would help him to his goal.

Now that he thought about it, the bent and crippled man had told him almost more by his personality and attitude than he had in what he had said. An important point was the difference between him and Henry, considering they belonged to the same church—which had led Bleys to believe earlier that they would think exactly alike.

This one discovery had opened up for Bleys a whole new picture of the people here. It had triggered off an understanding that they all were prisoners of what they believed in. It was not a case, as he had first thought, from Henry's actions, of those same beliefs letting them do things that otherwise would be unacceptable. That was evidently what Fanatics did that was wrong.

This changed everything. It made people like Henry and Gregg simply a different kind of the same sort of grown-up Bleys had dealt with all his life.

In each case, each person was a prisoner of what he had chosen to be. Once you understood what that was, it was simply a matter of finding out what let each one do what he did and kept him from doing other things. Then, once you knew, you could use your knowledge of this to understand them on a much deeper level.

Even Bleys' mother, with all her denial of her Exotic background, had been an Exotic in every way she lived and acted.

In Henry's case, Bleys would have to learn all about his way of life; and in the church community's case, what it was they all agreed on.

All this was undoubtedly true as well of Joshua and Will; though at this point they did not seem to pose Bleys any particular problems. Just the opposite. They were a comfort and a help, both of them.

Whether Dahno had done what Bleys planned to do in becoming a Friendly was still hidden from him. But it, too, would be discoverable eventually. Dahno himself would know this, of course, and Dahno himself would be on guard against Bleys finding out about it. But in the long run, if Dahno allowed a close association between himself and his younger half-brother, he could not help giving away what both moved him and limited him.

Since Dahno had once been in Bleys' situation, probably he in turn would be trying to search out the pattern to Bleys. Whatever happened, Bleys must not let him know that he had planned to use being a Friendly as a means to some larger end. It would be a chess match between them, with Dahno's age and experience giving him a large advantage.

Bleys got back to the farm in time to take over the cleaning and beyond that the disposing of the noon meal; and then set himself to concentrating on the two things that he already knew had a strong influence over Henry. One was a matter of the motor he was trying to build. Another was clearly an intention on his part to bring up not only his sons, but Bleys, within the same way that he approved of himself.

Bleys went about the rest of his day's work back at the house with his mind considering idea after idea.

"Did you learn a great deal from Teacher Gregg?" asked Henry that night at dinner.

"Yes, Uncle," said Bleys, "I thank God for your sending me to receive instruction from him."

In that moment Bleys decided to take a chance. It was doubtful that Henry would check with Gregg as to exactly what he said to Bleys and what Bleys said to him.

"I must begin going to church with you, next church-day," Bleys said, "and when convenient I'd like to talk to him again. He said it would be all right."

"In that case, you shall," said Henry. "We can always make time for that."

Bleys had already learned enough about his uncle to know that a statement like the one Henry had just made was not likely to be forgotten, or as a promise, broken. Bleys let himself fall, accordingly, into the daily routine of the farm, ready to wait for the right moment in which to suggest to Henry that the time might be right for another visit by him to Gregg.

However, before the next church-day came around, a day or so later Dahno came again on one of his visits, once more carrying small gifts of engine parts for Henry. Once more he took Bleys off on a trip into Ecumeny; and they had the afternoon together in which to talk.

Bleys was happy to see him. There was one thing that he had felt he must speak to Dahno fairly quickly about. School would be opening soon, and he did not want to be crowded in with the other local youths. He waited until they were settled at an eating place in Ecumeny, before bringing up the subject.

"We're only a few weeks away from full summer now," he said to Dahno, "and you know that the only thing that keeps Joshua and Will and me out of the local school, is the fact that in winter things can be grown and other things done around the farm. I think it would be a lot better if I wasn't sent to that school. For one thing it's probably a little school that doesn't go very high in the grades. For another thing, even the best I could do to hide it, they'd catch on very quickly to the fact that I wasn't like the rest of them."

"Good thinking," said Dahno, thoughtfully.

"I think," said Bleys, choosing his words as carefully as he would place his feet in trying to cross a room floored with eggs, "the idea of my being different is bound to come out sooner or later; but it would be better if they just thought that I had some sort of quirk. Don't you think so?"

"Yes," said Dahno slowly, "I do think so. Not that I can see any immediate problems coming from it, but it's always better not to take chances if you don't have to. Particularly, if you're going to have to stay there for another three or four years."

Bleys felt a cold thrill run through him at the thought of three or four years. He was still young enough so that three or four years sounded like a lifetime sentence.

"I'll be going to the church on Sundays with Henry, Joshua and Will," Bleys went on. "But if, aside from that, I had to leave the farm as little as possible, then things would be disturbed as little as possible, wouldn't they?"

"Don't go assuming I'll agree with you, like that," said

Dahno. "You know, I just might disagree with you. However, in this case I think you're right. The less Uncle Henry's foreign nephew is found to be different, the better. Also it means that you'll be following a schedule different from that of the other two boys, and that'll give us more and more opportunity for me to bring you into the city and get you trained in, when the time comes."

"I was thinking of that too," said Bleys. "Also, there's the fact that I probably know more than anyone else who'll be a student there—probably more than the teacher himself."

"As far as book learning goes," said Dahno, "that, anyway, is probably true enough."

He thrummed his fingertips on the table for a moment, thoughtfully.

"Yes, you're right," he said, "you'd stand out like the ugly duckling in the barnyard; and there's nothing to be gained by that; and possibly something to lose. But there's two things to deal with if you don't go to their school. One is, you'll need to continue your education some other way. The second thing is, and more important, there'll have to be an excuse for your staying home."

"I could be a sort of *idiot savant*," suggested Bleys eagerly, "you know what I mean. Someone with one talent, but otherwise not too bright—"

"I know what you mean," said Dahno. "Have you forgotten who I am? All right, we'll handle the first problem of your education at long distance. I'll get hold of a tutor for you, here in Ecumeny, and have him lay out a course of study for you. I can bring you the study materials, the books for your reader and anything else that's needed when I come out on these visits. That takes care of that—"

"Just one other thing," interrupted Bleys quickly, "in addition to the reader with the books and the other study materials, could I have any books I ask for myself? And Henry mentioned something about there being a place called a District Library—"

"Oh yes," Dahno interrupted in his turn, "when these two worlds were first settled, the corporation paying for transpor-

tation and the terraforming and everything else, set up free
District Libraries. The local people were to go to them for
information on how to raise their crops, breed their animals
and build things right on up through large construction; and
city- and even country-wide finance. You'd like access to that
too?"

"If you don't mind," said Bleys, with quick diffidence.

"Why should I mind?" Dahno said. "The more you prepare
yourself, the better use you'll be to me when the time comes.
By all means study everything under the stars, Little Brother.
I'll only approve."

"Thank you, Dahno," said Bleys.

"Never thank me," said Dahno. "Anything I do for you I do
as much for my own benefit as for yours—in fact I do it more
for my own benefit than for yours. Now, as regards coming up
with a good reason for Henry to keep you home, and let you
study instead of helping around the farm. That may take some
thought."

He sat silent for a moment, and Bleys sat in silence also, to
let him think. Then a smile spread across Dahno's face again.
He looked at Bleys.

"How do you feel about being sick for a day or two?" he
said.

"You mean, pretend to be sick?" said Bleys.

He felt a very similar chill to the one he had felt earlier. He
was sure that if Henry discovered that his sickness was not
real, it might be something that would justify the strap being
brought into play again, this time against him.

"Certainly not," said Dahno, still smiling. "We'll locate
something to make you literally sick; with a high temperature
and an upset stomach for a couple of days. Wait until someday
on the farm where you either work very hard, or spend a lot of
time outdoors in the sun, then take the medication. At the very
least Henry'll have definite proof you're sick. Tell him that it's
something that happens to you often; and that I can explain it.
That I told you that if it ever happened to you to have him call
me collect here in Ecumeny and I'd tell him what to do."

Bleys curled up a little inside at the thought—not so much at running a temperature—but of being nauseated. He hated it when his body was anything but a fully obedient and unconscious servant of his. Above all he hated throwing up.

"Does it have to be that kind of sickness?" he asked. "Can't I just run a fever?"

"No," said Dahno, decisively, "you need more than that. Enough to make Henry call me, instead of the local medician they've got out there. Tell him no local medicine there'll fix you. Tell him you can't take it; it'd be dangerous to you. Tell him that I'm the only one who can bring out the proper kind of medicine for you."

"All right," said Bleys.

As he had confronted the problem of facing up to his mother, Bleys faced the fact that the business of taking the medication was inescapable. He had his own way of doing this. He simply placed the necessity of taking the medicine in the category of things unavoidable, and put it out of his mind.

"In fact," Dahno was saying, "we can pick up the stuff I want you to take, yet today, so you can carry it back with you when you go."

Even as he spoke, he was turning to his wrist monitor, to use it as a phone. He had its mute on, so Bleys could not hear what he said into it; but after a few moments he dropped his wrist and turned back to Bleys.

"We'll go now," he announced, getting up from the table. "We have to cross to the other side of the city to pick it up. Then it'll be time to take you back to the farm."

The pills turned out to be three small brownish things, so small that it was hard for Bleys to believe that they would have much effect on him. He was to take only one at any time. Nonetheless, the day came, a little less than a week later, when he had been told to leave the cleaning up to Will and go out with Joshua early in the afternoon to move the goats from their winter to their summer pasture some two thousand feet up the side of a nearby small mountain. He took advantage of the opportunity, waiting until he was almost back at the farm before he surreptitiously swallowed one of the pills.

It went down with no trouble; and for about half an hour he

felt no different and was beginning to wonder if perhaps he should not take a second pill. Then he began to feel the first flush of heat in his body; and within fifteen minutes after that came the first slight twinge of nausea.

Within the hour, he had vomited several times. Henry was away from the farm with the goat-cart on business of his own; but Joshua, taking charge, ordered Bleys to bed, and told Will to put cool cloths on his head until their father could get home and arrive at a more definite decision of what was to be done for Bleys.

Bleys ended up that night by being very sick indeed. Henry had arrived home just before dinner, and been surprised to find Bleys in bed.

Joshua was outside working, out of sight, so the first person to tell Henry about things was Will. Henry was puzzled. Sickness was uncommon among their people.

He took a look at Bleys, produced a medical thermometer from some storage place and took Bleys' temperature. It was two and a half degrees above normal and seemed to be climbing.

"We'll have to get in Medician Kris Roderick," Henry said, looking at the thermometer. "It may be nothing, but on the other hand I'll feel better if Roderick's looked at him."

Bleys protested feebly, stammering out the story that Dahno had said he should tell his uncle.

"Well, all right," Henry said at last, "I can call the city from the local store. I'll be back just as soon as I can."

When he returned after talking to Dahno, he was clearly resigned to waiting for Dahno's arrival—which might be late that night, or might not be until the following morning.

He questioned Bleys again about this sickness of his, and its history. But Bleys only repeated that it was something that hit him occasionally when he overexerted himself. Henry finally gave up and left him to himself, except for the ministrations of Will and Joshua, who were taking turns putting cold cloths on his head.

Eventually, the boys went to bed, and Henry took over the business of putting the cool cloths on Bleys' head and also helping him to a sort of chamber pot in which he could vomit, when the waves of nausea got too bad. He stayed up with Bleys all night long, and was surprisingly gentle in his ministrations to him.

Bleys was vomited empty early in the evening, and continued to retch without being able to bring anything more up through the rest of the dark hours. Altogether he spent a miserable night. But with the morning, fairly early—in fact not much later than a couple of hours after sunrise—there was the roaring of the hovercar coming up the road to the farm, and a little while later Dahno was with him.

"Well, well, got it again, have you?" Dahno said gently, coming up to his bunk. "Well, this won't cure it right away, but it'll make you feel better and let you get some sleep."

He produced three more white pills not much larger than the ones that he had originally given Bleys to make him sick; and he held Bleys' upper body upright in the bunk with one huge hand, so that the boy could wash one of the white pills down with a cup of water.

He laid Bleys easily back down on the bedcovers. Bleys lay there, hardly caring what had happened to him or what might happen next . . . but with surprising quickness, whatever Dahno had given him began to take effect. The nausea finally began to disappear from him; and he felt his body cooling.

He was obsessed with a desire for sleep—so exhausted, that he had not taken into account really how tired Henry must be from sitting up with him all night. Without even thanking Dahno or Henry, he closed his eyes; and sleep pulled him down into a very profound slumber.

He was much better the next day, but still got dizzy when he tried to sit up and he needed someone to help him walk even as far as the chamber pot. The day after that he no longer felt sick in any way, but was still very weak, so that he spent most of the day in bed.

He made a mental note that the next time he was involved with Dahno in any matter which required him to take drugs, he would try to find the source of the drug himself and make sure he knew what he was getting, or else insist on talking to whoever the supplier was and cross-examining that person to make sure he was not getting hit as hard as he had got hit this last time—which seemed to him to be much more than was necessary.

By the fourth day, however, he was well enough to be up and about, although his strength did not allow him to do too much in the way of cleaning, and the other two boys took care of this.

The day after that he was fine, and Dahno who had left after delivering the white pills and having a very short talk with Henry, returned, bringing a reader, books, and a schedule of studies that Bleys was to concern himself with.

"You'll take over the inside work again," Henry instructed him, "and such light jobs outside as I myself set you to. But the last four hours of every afternoon you'll devote to these studies that Dahno has brought you to do. And this will take the place of your regular schooling, when school opens."

Looking around at the three faces of Henry, Joshua and Will, Bleys could see no expression on the faces of the boys that showed envy or any thought of favoritism, nor any expression on Henry himself other than that he normally wore.

CHAPTER
10

"UNCLE," SAID BLEYS, "I thank God for your kindness and care of me, all that night when I was ill and you put cold cloths on my head and helped me."

It was two days after Dahno had shown up with the study materials and had a brief, private talk with Henry. This was the first chance that Bleys had had to be alone with his uncle in the house and speak to him. What he had to say would be more effective if the two were alone. He did not know exactly what Dahno had told Henry; but he did not need to know that precisely. Dahno would have stuck very closely to the story they had agreed on during their last visit to Ecumeny together.

At the moment, Henry was working at one end of the dining table, busy with accounts dealing with the goats; and at the other end Bleys was reading his calculus book. At Bleys' words, Henry looked up. His face had stiffened a little. It was close to, but not quite, a forbidding look.

"You need never thank God for that, boy," he said. "I did only my duty. *'Where there are sick, you shall minister to them'*—Teacher Gregg spoke a sermon on that topic not three months ago. But I need no sermon to remind me of my duty."

"Still," Bleys said, "I thank God for your kindness, Uncle. I've also thanked God, not once but more than once, for bringing me to live with you and Joshua and Will. Particularly, I'm thankful to know Joshua and Will. They've taught me all sorts of things that I needed to know. Things they probably learned from you; but I'd never had a chance to learn, before."

A faint shadow of difference disturbed the stiff look on Henry's face. After a moment it melted back to his ordinary expression.

"It's good of you to think well of your cousins," Henry said, dryly. "Perhaps it's prideful of me, but I think they're good boys, myself; and due to be good men in years to come. I'll be happy if it's so; and I'll be happy also if you grow to be like them."

He looked sharply back down at his slips of paper, arranged as usual in order before him.

"Now, back to your work, Bleys!" he said, "and I must get back to mine. Neither of us has time to chatter."

Bleys turned cheerfully to a book on wave-theory. As was his usual habit, he had first read through all his textbooks as if they were works of entertainment, merely letting himself be filled with the beauty of the things they proved and showed. Then he read through a second time, slowly, eager to stop and try his own hand at doing the things they explained.

But in this case, the lightheartedness inside him was for a different reason. He had just proved something he had suspected; and that was that Henry deeply loved his sons and was already becoming fond of Bleys himself—although he would never admit or show it. Bleys had never seen him hug, or even touch Will or Joshua. The most Bleys had seen any of the boys get from him had been a sparse word of approval; or that touch of a wintry smile which seemed the most Henry could do in showing an expression of pleasure.

But Bleys had also watched the boys, in those moments; and he knew they were not deceived. They read their father as clearly as Bleys was coming to do. They knew the affection was in him; and that the brief smile was the equivalent of exuberant praise from someone of a different nature.

Now Bleys felt he had finally broken through Henry's outer armor to his inner feelings.

It was a beginning. The fourth day after that was a church-day and they all went, Henry, Joshua, Will and Bleys, in the goat cart.

They were among the first few families to get there. Bleys noticed that Gregg stood at the entrance to the church, welcoming those who had come for the service. Bleys found, however, that the other families that were already there, and those that arrived after—for he, Henry and the boys stayed outside until the actual time for the services themselves— greeted Henry and the boys warmly, but were fairly cool to him, even after Henry had introduced him as his nephew.

Finally they all went into the church. Just inside the doorway, in a little anteroom with hooks on which to hang clothes—evidently a sort of cloakroom—Henry stopped Bleys while the boys went on down the center aisle of the church.

"We share the pew with the Howardson family," he explained to Bleys, "and there is room for no one else in it. I'm afraid you'll have to sit further back and by yourself, Bleys."

Bleys was not unhappy to do so. He preferred to be at the back where he could watch but not be watched by the rest of the congregation.

"That's quite all right, Uncle," he said, "anywhere in God's house is all the same, isn't it?"

"Yes," Henry said, looking at him keenly, "you're exactly right, Bleys."

The last few pews were completely vacant. Bleys sat down in the last one to the left of the aisle and watched the other families filing into the church and going to their pews farther up front. Finally, when the last of them seemed to have filed in, a middle-aged man with a gunbelt and empty power-pistol holster around his rather capacious belly came in and sat down beside him, giving Bleys a friendly smile.

"I'm Adrian Wiseman," he said in a whisper, offering his

hand. "I'm church constable. You'll be Bleys Ahrens, Henry MacLean's nephew who's just come to live with him."

"Yes," whispered Bleys back, taking the hand gratefully. "Why are you wearing a gunbelt—and where's the pistol that goes with it?"

"Shh," said Adrian, "service's starting. I'll explain it all to you afterwards."

After the church service, which lasted a little over two hours, Bleys got up and followed Adrian out to the cloakroom in time to see him lift a power pistol off a shelf and put it in the holster at his side. He turned, saw Bleys and took him by the sleeve, pulling him back into the church out of the way of the other church members who were filing out. He sat down, pulling Bleys down to join him in the pew they had both just left.

"The church constable," said Adrian, in a low voice, if no longer in a whisper, "has the duty of protecting the service from outside interruption."

"Who'd interrupt?" asked Bleys, fascinated.

"Members of other churches who don't like ours," explained Adrian. "It can be an actual attack by members of another church. But usually, it's just teen-age youngsters who might want to show off their bravery by disrupting our service. Even trouble like that doesn't happen often. But when it does I need to get to the gun quickly; probably not to use, but as a threat, to drive them off."

"Why don't you wear it all the time then?" asked Bleys, fascinated. "—Oh, I know—it's because you're not supposed to bring a gun into church."

Adrian smiled approvingly at him.

"You're right," he said, "for my purposes, the cloakroom is considered outside the church. At the same time I want to be able to get at the weapon quickly in case I need it."

"And that's why you don't take off the gunbelt itself?" Bleys asked.

"Yes," said Adrian.

At that moment, Henry and the boys came down the aisle and collected Bleys, after a few friendly words between Henry and Adrian. It was not until they were in the goat-cart on the way home, that Bleys had a chance to ask further questions of Henry.

"Uncle?" he said, "how often does one church actually ever attack another? I mean—with all the people in the church doing the attacking."

"Rarely, nowadays," said Henry. His mouth was suddenly a straight line in his face. "I've seen it and I hope none of you ever do. It's a cruel thing to see brothers and sisters in the Lord killing each other over the interpretation of a single line of scripture."

Bleys had not been so chilled by Henry's manner or tone of voice since he had first met him at the spaceport. As soon as possible, in the afternoon of the next day, he asked Joshua why his father was so grim on the subject of wars between churches.

Joshua hesitated.

"If he wants you to know, he'll tell you himself," Joshua said.

Bleys had never had Joshua evade a question of his before.

"You know he won't," Bleys said. "He never tells me anything."

Joshua still hesitated. Finally, with an effort he spoke.

"He told me to tell Will when Will was old enough. I guess he'd be agreeable to me telling you. You're family, too." Joshua hesitated again. "Bleys—he's been a Soldier of God!"

"A Soldier of God? You mean he was drafted on one of the levies you have here every so often, for young men to fight off-planet, so as to improve Association's interstellar income?"

"No, no," said Joshua, "—though he's been that, too. He can tell you about that when he wants. He's never really told me. No, a Soldier of God is—well, sometimes, Bleys, when a church gets attacked by some other church, the church that's attacked gets help from members of those fellow churches that're on friendly terms with it. I mean, it's up to the members. Father has fought for other churches than his own."

"Oh, I see," said Bleys. "He made money that way—"

"Money! Of course not!" Joshua was outraged. "Not even a

Fanatic would fight for money alone! No, he fought for the people of the church that was attacked—at first."

"But I don't understand," said Bleys. "You say 'at first.' What did he fight for after that?"

"No, you don't understand, Bleys," said Joshua, patiently. "To fight for God's people is all right. Most of those who offer their help this way, do it for the people of the church they're helping. But . . . sometimes, after a while they come to like it. The fighting, itself. The fighting, and—God help us—the killing. In the end they just go from church war to church war. Father found one day he . . . well, he didn't trust himself to fight with a pure heart any longer. The militia were finally called in on a war he was part of, and . . . but he'll have to tell you that part himself, Bleys. I can't."

Joshua was upset; and Bleys had never seen him upset before.

"Even when we need to shoot some rabbits for the evening stew," Joshua went on in an emotion-filled voice, "he has me do it. You've seen me take the gun and go out and bring the rabbits back, but you've never seen him, have you? That's because he doesn't like touching any kind of weapon, even today. I don't think he's laid hands on the needle gun more than two or three times that I can remember in my life; and then it was only to clean it in some special way or fix it for me."

"It's all right, Josh," Bleys said, hastily. "Never mind. You're right. He'll tell me himself when the time comes."

In the days and weeks and months that followed, Bleys worked to fit himself into the pattern of life that was Henry's, and that of the other members of his church. From time to time, understandings would come to him, even without conscious searching. He would suddenly realize that an action, one attitude, or a word by one of the other three had held a meaning he had not suspected before.

These bits of information he saved and fitted together. Little by little, he got to know each of them better. But particularly, he got to know Henry.

The brief fall came, followed by the long winter, a time of cold rains and blustery winds, here in these latitudes. He continued to study apart from those in the little school, that now daily took not only Joshua but Will from the farm. Aside from this one difference, however, he was part of their lives; and was beginning to find a peacefulness and a comfort in the regular patterns of them.

He went to the little church with them, and listened to Gregg preach. He joined with them in their hymns, that were sung, according to the conviction of their sect, without any musical accompaniment, and knelt also and prayed with them.

Struggle as he might, however, none of this brought him any closer to their belief in a God. But he began to feel a solidarity with them, that was like a warmth wrapping them all together in a single large blanket. There was a reassurance in being part of their small community; a stability that he had never felt with his mother and his mother's friends.

All this meant a great deal to Bleys, who had hungered for such stability. When he was with one of the other local people, he seemed to be liked and get along well. But little changes in the person's attitude, as he or she turned from him to give their attention to another member of the congregation, seemed to signal a lessening of this apparent liking for him. He feared that his old problem—that of being recognized as *different*— was affecting their attitudes, even if only unconsciously. It was as if they could smell his inability to believe in a God and be like them.

This was backed up one day when he was in the bedroom and he heard Will, who had just come in, speaking to Henry.

"Father—" Will's voice asked.

"Yes, Will," Henry's answered.

"Why don't the other church members like Bleys? He prays more than any of them; and he's always so good to everybody else. Joshua and I like him a lot!"

"Will," said Henry, "every person has a right to their own likes and dislikes. Pay no attention to how others feel toward your cousin. In time they may come to feel like you and Joshua toward him."

Here, the same things happened six days a week, all except the one church-day, and everyone was caught up in them together. The same rhythm of work and living possessed them all; and he was part of them in that. In a strange way, though it could never take the place of the love he had never had from his mother, it dulled the ache of that lack, which had never completely left him before this. But the source of their own comfort eluded him.

Yet, he came to understand how the effects of Henry's belief built a solid structure to the human race and the universe surrounding it. It was all ordered, planned, brought to a singleness and permanence for which Bleys found his inner self yearned. Surely, if there was a way to belief in God, it was through appreciating and understanding this single, orderly universe that centered around him.

He resolved to redouble his prayers and his efforts to find the deity.

If he could not have love, at least he could have this single, orderly universe. All he needed to do was accept the idea of an all-powerful, controlling God.

Meanwhile, his visits with Dahno had become more and more informative and interesting. Gradually, Dahno was introducing him to the life and structure of the city of Ecumeny.

He had begun taking Bleys about the city, showing him the various parts of it, and explaining how they worked, on this religiously-oriented New World. But he avoided any reference to, and stopped any questions about, his own goals in all this. Nor could Bleys find out from him what part he played, in the city and the world.

So it continued; until one weekend, when he talked Henry into letting him take Bleys for a four-day visit to Ecumeny, over Sunday.

"Of course," Henry frowned, "but the boy will miss church."

"No I won't, Uncle," said Bleys, "will I, Dahno?"

Dahno smiled.

"I don't know if your church has a place in Ecumeny," he said to Henry.

"It does," said Henry. "I'll write the address down for you."

He did so on one of his slips of paper; and—interestingly enough—handed it not to Dahno, but to Bleys. Bleys folded it and put it in his shirt pocket.

"Well," said Dahno, "that's taken care of, then. Is there any other reason why Bleys shouldn't go?"

"None," said Henry. He looked directly at Dahno. "You'll take good care of him, of course."

"Of course," answered Dahno.

"You understand me," Henry said, still directly to Dahno, "the boy has lived with us for some time now and in the way of the Lord. You'll not lead him anywhere he shouldn't go?"

"I won't, Uncle," said Dahno warmly, "I promise you."

So, it was settled. But in the hovercar, once Dahno had turned on to the highway, he burst into a sudden bellow of laughter. He turned his head to look at Bleys, momentarily, a broad smile on his face.

"Good old Uncle Henry!" he said, "making sure I won't lead you astray!"

"I wouldn't be led astray, in any case," answered Bleys, levelly, meeting his brother's eyes.

The smile did not leave Dahno's face as he glanced at Bleys again, but it was diminished and the expression of the face around it had altered.

"Don't forget those milk-teeth, Little Brother," he said, gently. "Wait until you've got some real tusks."

Bleys fell silent; and nothing more was said on the ride in until they were almost into the city. Then Bleys spoke again.

"Why did you want me for four days?" Bleys asked.

"Because it's time for you to start school," answered Dahno without looking at him, "a different sort of school, Little Brother. My school. It's a place where you teach yourself; and it's most important in this case that you teach yourself rather than anyone else teaching you—including me."

Bleys' question had come because Dahno was heading the hovercar in toward a different section of Ecumeny than they had gone into before. He tucked Dahno's answer in the back of his mind, to let it ferment and wait for other small items of information that might begin to translate it into something he could understand more.

Dahno had slowed, now, for they were in the city streets themselves; and the local speed law applied. The section they had entered was dingier than any one Bleys had ever seen in that city—or elsewhere for that matter. It was a section of office buildings, warehouses, and every so often an apartment building reaching as high as five or six stories—which for a city on this world was fairly extravagant.

It was before one of these apartment houses that Dahno finally pulled the hovercar to the curb.

"Out we get," he said, glancing over at Bleys.

CHAPTER

11

DAHNO LET HIMSELF out his side of the hovercar and Bleys opened the door on his side and also got out. As he turned to come around the car to the sidewalk where Dahno already stood, he heard the locks snick on the door of the hovercar.

He followed his older half-brother into the apartment building. There was a small, musty anteroom, long rather than wide and with its two long walls covered with postal boxes. An old man, one of the building attendants that were usually found on this world—but not in places as cheap-looking as this—sat at a desk.

His eyes met Dahno's. He did not say anything nor did Dahno. There was a moment of recognition between them and that was all. Dahno went over to three lift tubes along the wall, and pressed the stubby round cylinder of a key into the slot at the innermost one. Its doors slid open. They stepped in onto a disk; and the doors closed behind them.

The disk lifted them up the cylinder of the lift tube.

Bleys was watching Dahno closely. He was wondering why

they should come to a place like this. Such an apartment building, and the kind of an apartment it would probably have in it, was not his brother's style at all, on the basis of what he knew of the man so far.

He waited for Dahno to offer some sort of explanation, but his brother said nothing. The lift stopped at the top level of the building, its doors opening on a short hallway with faded carpet and wall decoration, and a single door in the wall before them.

Once more Dahno used a key. He took it from his pocket and Bleys could not tell whether it was the same key that had operated the elevator or not. At a guess, it was. In any case, at the touch of it in the lock socket, the door before them slid back; and they stepped through into a large lounge-style room; with at least a dozen men sitting about it in overstuffed chair-floats, some talking to each other, some reading, a few with partially-filled glasses beside them.

As the door closed and locked behind them, Bleys had a single glimpse of the men there relaxed in their chairs. A moment later, they had all scrambled to their feet.

"Well, good morning, Vice-Chairmen," said Dahno, genially, "Vice-Chairmen-in-training, I should probably say. Sit down, gentlemen, sit down."

They all took their seats again. This time Bleys got a longer and better look at them. They were all large, active-looking men; none younger than the mid-twenties, and none probably older than thirty, all of them exceedingly well-dressed, in a casual style. Their clothes were rich but not flamboyant. At the same time they were not the kind of clothes that Bleys had come to associate with this world and its people. For all their size, not one of them but looked like a stripling, compared to Dahno. Standing, as usual, he dominated the room.

"This is my brother, Bleys," said Dahno, waving a hand at Bleys. "I'd like you all to take a good look at him."

He paused; and the pause gave emphasis to his next words.

"I want you all to remember him," he went on slowly, "so that you'll know him anywhere. He'll grow up in the next few years, but you're always to recognize him at a glance. You're to take good care of him, future Vice-Chairmen. Unless I tell you otherwise, you're to guard him with your lives; at any time, in any place, under any situations you see him."

He paused to smile again. His voice lightened and became playful.

"That's because he's more valuable than any of you—or all of you, together," he said. "You'll remember that, as loyal trainees should. So, you'll guard him at all times, whenever it's necessary; and if I tell you to get him for me, you'll go get him. Is that understood?"

"Yes, Mr. Chairman." It was a chorus of voices from the men.

"Good," said Dahno. He turned to Bleys. "There should always be at least one of them here. There're others who aren't here now that you'll have to meet in the future. Meanwhile, we'll leave them to their well-earned relaxation; and I'll show you around the place."

He strode ahead through the room. Bleys went with him, feeling the eyes of all of the men in the room upon him. It was not a pleasant sensation. He had more the feeling of an enemy being pointed out as a possible target, than of a valuable friend to be taken care of, as Dahno had implied.

They passed through a further door that slid open as they approached, and slid shut again behind them. They were in a room which seemed to be a kitchen with an entrance to its left into what was either a large boardroom or a large dining room. Dahno paused to wave at the room with its long table through the open doorway.

"The room in which my future Vice-Chairmen practice being Vice-Chairmen," he said to Bleys, "we needn't spend any time there. Come along and I'll show you first through their private quarters. They've all got a room apiece, with private bath, back here. In fact, this arrangement takes up this whole top floor—"

As he talked, they were walking down a central corridor, with open doorways on either side showing rooms in which the bed had been made. Within each, things were more or less neatly arranged, but that was as much as Bleys could say for them.

In fact, trained now as he was by his cleanings and scrubbings at Henry's, Bleys found the place very shoddily housekept. There was no lack of dust in corners or on sills, which showed that cleaning was either careless or infrequent; and overall, although the rooms had the best of furniture and other appointments, they also had a slovenly look.

But Dahno was already leading them through a further door into a very large room indeed that rose up the height of at least another floor above their heads. This was clearly necessary, for it was set up like a gymnasium. It had exercise mats on the floors and several climbing ropes hung from the ceiling. One corner of the floor space was taken up by a swimming pool that was not as small as Bleys had first thought, judging it in relationship to the whole open area.

"Here my trainees exercise," said Dahno. He was still walking forward. "I've got a number of people coming in to train them in various skills. People from all the other worlds who're willing to teach."

He led the way along the length of the gymnasium and through a further sliding door into what was obviously a lecture hall or classroom. Here, at last, he stopped. Lights had gone on overhead and in the walls automatically when they had stepped through; although there was no one else there.

"Here," he said, "is where the other part of their education takes place. Primarily, there're several teachers from our mother's world, from the Exotics, to teach them. This is most necessary; because eventually, when they're full Vice-Chairmen, they're going to go out to other worlds and set up their own groups, in which each one of those you just saw will become a local Chairman and recruit his own Vice-Chairmen. What do you think of it all, Bleys?"

"Those men in the front room," said Bleys, "they're all from this world?"

"Oh yes, all but one or two of them," answered Dahno, "but you could hardly tell it on those who aren't now. In addition, they're all hand-picked, by me. You'll learn about that as the years go on. The great thing I want you to get from this little visit now, is that they're learning to be leaders. So they can spread the word—my word. Do you understand yet, Bleys?"

"Only partly," answered Bleys.

Dahno laughed.

"Good!" he said, and then his voice became unusually serious. "I want you to make up your own mind about this. Keep your eyes open and come to your own conclusions. And remember, you've got to grow up yet. That gives us a few years for you to mull things over."

He turned abruptly about.

"All right," he said, "I've shown you this place, let's get on to other things."

He led the way back out through the various rooms—the men in the front room were on their feet again as he came through, but he waved them back down. He led Bleys through the door and they descended in the elevator, back to the hovercar.

"Now," Dahno's voice was cheerful and openly friendly, "we'll go to my place. I think you'll find at least one thing there that suits you better than the place you were just in."

He drove out of the neighborhood they had been in and into another that was completely different. Here, it was all high-rise apartments, but these were obviously the kind of buildings that housed individuals and couples and families with wealth. The hovercar ducked down a ramp into a basement underneath one of them; and they took an elevator up several floors to a landing, richly carpeted in midnight blue; and with flowering plants around the walls everywhere but in front of a tall, church-like window. This gave on a small glimpse of a wooded area, so it seemed that they had left the city behind entirely and were looking out into open forest.

Once more Dahno used a key to let them into a different set of rooms. They stepped into a bright apartment, the entryway lit by a skylight right over its head. Windows, seen through the large lounge area straight ahead of them, completely filled one wall. To the right there seemed to be a sort of conservatory, filled with plants—and oddly enough, with chirping of birds coming cheerfully from it.

To their left was a hall that gave on a good-sized, although not enormous dining room that could possibly seat twelve people; and a glimpse of further rooms off the hallway beyond. The carpeting here was dull gold and unusually deep and soft, under a white ceiling, pierced here and there with skylights that let the sunlight in.

The walls were a sunlight yellow, with a picture of some outdoor scene hanging here and there. Listening closely, Bleys thought he could now pick up the tinkle of water, as of a stream or small waterfall from the conservatory area.

All in all, it was remarkably like the reproductions Bleys had seen of the sort of place that might be found on either of the two Exotic Worlds.

"Well?" demanded Dahno. "Do you see what I meant when I said there'd be at least one thing you'd like?"

Bleys knew instantly what he meant. It was not merely the Exotic flavor, even over and above the general luxury and good taste of the apartment. It was also the fact that it was spotlessly clean—the walls, floor, ceiling, every surface within sight. Everything gleamed as if it had been dusted or polished just a few moments before. Henry's house could have been no cleaner.

"Yes, I do," said Bleys.

He had come here, he realized now, with a chip on his shoulder, ready to resent whatever Dahno showed him. Now, that chip fell away. This was a pleasant and attractive place to live in; and there was no denying it. If it reflected the attitudes of its inhabitant, he had been more mistrustful of Dahno than he should have been.

"I like your apartment, Dahno," he told his massive brother.

He felt the light touch of one of the huge hands on his shoulder.

"I'm glad to hear you say that," said Dahno. His voice was serious again. "Come along, then, we'll have something to eat in someplace other than a restaurant."

Behind a false wall in the dining room that slipped into the floor at the touch of a marker was a small, neat, automatic kitchen that apparently seemed capable of providing just about

anything. In this case it provided sandwiches and drinks—a
very good imitation of the New Earth orange juice, to which
Bleys had become accustomed in the years he was there, and
some sort of dark ale for Dahno; plus a plate of little
sandwiches—all done within about three minutes.

"Here's to celebrate the gathering of the family," said
Dahno, lifting his glass. "If you were a little older, Bleys,
we'd both be having drinks on it. Not that I care whether you
drink now or later or whenever, but this week while you're
with me I want your wits about you and I don't want your brain
muddled with alcohol, even a little."

Bleys smiled internally but kept his face straight. He had
discovered, more than a few years back with his mother, that
for some reason he was particularly resistant to the alcohol in
most of the alcoholic liquors. Not that he couldn't get
drunk—he had experimented and done so; but it had taken a
remarkable amount for a boy who had then been barely six
years old. This was a piece of knowledge which it might be
advantageous to keep to himself.

"I just made us a snack," said Dahno, "because we'll be
eating dinner out later. This will just see us through until about
then."

They ate, Dahno dumped dishes and all down the disposal
slot and they left the apartment.

"I'll get a key for you at the office," Dahno said, as he
closed the door to the apartment behind them, "since you'll be
staying here the next few days. We're on our way to the office
now."

They went back to the hovercar.

Bleys had wondered about the source of Dahno's income;
but he was too wary of Dahno's ability to do any subtle probing
for clues. He had imagined a number of things; but none of
them had approached what they actually entered, which was a
suite in an office building. A bronze plaque simply said DAHNO
AHRENS, INVESTMENT COUNSELOR on the heavy, dark-wood
door.

They stepped into another office in which two women were

working behind automated desks with what seemed quite a stack of paperwork.

"Anything important?" Dahno asked them. They both shook their heads. He led Bleys on through a grass-green-carpeted room, which was evidently completely buried in the interior of the building, for it had no windows at all, and into a further room. This one was much larger, with a single large, black, wood desk; and some very comfortable padded float-chairs about it. One, built to Dahno's size and padded accordingly, sat behind the desk. This room by contrast had windows on two sides of it.

"What do you think, Bleys?" Dahno asked when they had stepped into it.

"You must be successful," Bleys said. "What's an investment counselor? I mean—what do *you* do as an investment counselor?"

Dahno laughed.

"I give good advice," he said. "And usually the reason is because I know the advice is correct. Oh, not all the time. Maybe twenty-five percent of it, I'm guessing or estimating. But otherwise I know. What would you do with an office like this, Bleys?"

Bleys looked around the huge office, which had more floor space than all of Henry's house.

"I'd turn it into a research center," he answered honestly.

Dahno smiled. He beckoned Bleys, led him across to one of the blank walls of the room, in which there was a door, which slid aside as they came to it. They stepped through it and Bleys, following him in, checked, disbelievingly.

There was a whole section of book readers and scanning devices; and the rest of the space was taken up in shelves and compartments to hold books, in both rod and disk form.

"You see what I mean, when I say that most of the time I know that the answer is right," said Dahno. "Here's where I find out the answers, a lot of the time. Maybe you can see now why I'm so interested in you, Little Brother."

Bleys hesitated. He was intrigued and his curiosity had him by the back of the neck. He was also aware that Dahno knew this, and that his older half-brother was deliberately withholding information to lead him on.

A hidden shiver passed for a second through Bleys. Dahno was laying down an attractive trail to follow; but most surely—and Dahno had all but admitted this himself—one that would lead to a situation from which the younger brother would have no escape. Still, the curiosity fought in Bleys—and won.

"What kind of people do you advise?" he asked.

Dahno's face broke into a broad smile.

"People in all walks of life," he said. He looked at a clock on the wall of the room they were in. "And it's just about time for us to start for where we can meet some of them, now."

CHAPTER

12

THEY WENT TO a restaurant.

But this was different from any of the restaurants Dahno had taken Bleys to before. The others had been comfortable to luxurious, but in all other ways, small, discreet and away from the general center of town.

This was a very large restaurant, expensive to the point of being ostentatious, with four-story-high windows along one side, framed by heavy swag drapes. A pool about half the size of an Olympic swimming pool, but divided into grottoes and other divisions by ornamental sculptures or architecture, held variform fish, the embryos of which must have been imported at very high cost indeed. They were up to a foot or more in length, of many different brilliant colors, and swam lazily among the rich surroundings.

It was the last sort of restaurant Bleys would have expected to find on one of the Friendly Worlds, according to his picture of what the Friendlies had been before he came here, and the point of view he had picked up during the last months out at Henry's farm.

Rather, it was the kind he would have expected on New Earth or Freiland, or one of the other, non-specialized worlds; where a great deal of commerce and manufacturing was done and there were a great many people with credits to throw around. People who enjoyed throwing it in places like this; where they could show off their ability to afford the high prices.

Dahno was recognized as they came up to the entrance of the dining room itself, and led without a word to a table; a round table with a clear, transparent top that could seat at least six people.

"Sit tight," said Dahno to Bleys, "order what you want from the waiter, but brace yourself for a long session. Eating and drinking here is just incidental."

The waiter was already with them and Dahno ordered another of the dark beers. But Bleys, to play safe, ordered another fruit juice. He was interested to find listed on the menu not only the local fruit juices but others listed as imported. They would not, of course, be imported. What they were, were clever imitations of imported fruit juices, like the New Earth orange juice he had drunk back at Dahno's apartment. For the moment he decided to be cautious, follow Dahno's lead, sit quiet and see what happened.

They were not alone more than five minutes before a tall, thin, rather elegantly-dressed man, in what looked like his late sixties, sat down at their table without asking for permission. A glass of some blue drink fizzed in his hand.

"Well, we're up against a brick wall," he said to Dahno, sipping at his drink. He paused to look doubtfully at Bleys.

"You know my rule," said Dahno. "Anyone sitting at this table is safe to talk in front of. If they weren't I'd have sent them away when you sat down."

"If you say so," said the elderly man, still doubtfully. "Well, I've worn my feet off and I've talked to every delegate in the Chamber and I don't think we're going to get 417B."

"Who's holding out?" Dahno asked.

"There's only five of them. The Five Sisters—you know them. And each one of them, on this subject, is simply a closed mind. They want off-world trade for Association and they're going to have off-world trade; no matter whose pocket it hurts here. They all want profits, every one of them, but they see a removal of restriction as God's intent—"

He shrugged helplessly.

"—I thought you might be able to think of something," he said.

"Such as?" Dahno asked him.

"I don't know," the elderly man shrugged again, "you're the Golden Ear . . ."

"All right," said Dahno, "I'll think about it. It's possible I can think of a way to swing them over. If I come up with anything I'll get in touch with you."

"Thank you," said the elderly man. He got up and left.

Almost immediately his place was taken by a short, solidly-bodied man in his thirties with black hair and a pugnacious face with bright, brown eyes. He was not carrying anything to drink and he stared hard at Bleys without saying a word.

"You know my rules," said Dahno.

The brown-eyed man turned his face abruptly back to Dahno.

"Yes, sure," he said jerkily; and it occurred to Bleys that he was possibly not so much pugnacious as unsure of himself. He continued in the same jerky speech.

"I think they're out to get me," he said to Dahno.

"Who?" asked Dahno.

"Bombay," he answered.

Bleys looked at the man with interest. The only Bombay he knew of was a city back on Old Earth. And he knew nothing more about that except that it was a port in the south of the East Indian peninsula. He assumed that it must be the name of someone local, or some local group or company.

"What makes you think so?" asked Dahno.

"Things have been happening," said the brown-eyed man. "Someone's been selling Core Tap shares heavily this last week."

"I can't stop that," Dahno grinned. "Nobody can."

"No, but you can find out who's behind it, can't you?" said the brown-eyed man.

"Perhaps," said Dahno, "if anyone is."

"Take my word for it," said the brown-eyed man, rising, "somebody is!"

He went off in turn.

There were a few moments of breathing space during which Bleys and Dahno had the table to themselves.

"Who are the Five Sisters?" Bleys asked his brother.

Dahno's face, which had sobered, got its large smile on as it turned back to look at him.

"Four old men and one woman," he said, "representatives of some of the larger church groups on Association."

"So that just now was a matter of politics, was it?" asked Bleys.

"Do you think so?" asked Dahno—and just at that moment, somebody else sat down. This time it was a woman in her forties, striking-looking if you did not—as Bleys did, having learned from his mother—know what high-priced skin management and makeup could do. She ignored Bleys completely.

"Dahno," she said, "you have to drop in this coming Saturday afternoon. I'm having just a few people in, but I'd like them to meet you; and I think you'd enjoy meeting them."

"Charmed," said Dahno.

She rose again and went off without another word. Dahno turned to find Bleys' eyes still upon him.

"And, before you ask," he said, "she is probably the second richest woman on this world. Can you believe that she's a True Faith-holder?"

Bleys felt shock.

"She doesn't look like she'd be one," he said.

"She is," said Dahno. "She's also one of the Five Sisters."

A few minutes later, two men who looked like brothers sat down at the table, said a few enigmatic words to Dahno and got back from him a few more monosyllables even more enigmatic, then left.

So the parade continued for several hours. Bleys at last began to get weary, and to fight off his weariness ordered food, which helped for a while. But within half an hour after he'd eaten, his full stomach began to leave him feeling more sleepy and worn out than before. Outside the tall windows, night was upon the city. Back at the farm about this time, he would be cleaning up after supper and getting ready for bed.

"Enough for today," said Dahno, who, he suddenly realized, had been watching him. Dahno got to his feet, and a groggy Bleys followed. Waving off a heavy-set young man who was just approaching, Dahno led Bleys through the crowded dining room, now noisy with conversation, and out the front door. He did not stop to pay for anything he or Bleys had eaten or drunk.

Bleys was too tired even to ask questions, he merely went with Dahno from the restaurant down the lift to the basement garage where their hovercar waited, got in it, and let himself be taken back to Dahno's apartment, where he was assigned a bedroom. He sleepily undressed and tumbled into a force-field bed, such as he had not slept in since he had left his mother. He fell asleep instantly.

The next day he woke to find Dahno already gone, and several hours of daylight already passed. From his experience of the years with his mother, he knew how to operate an automatic kitchen, and produce a breakfast for himself. Then, since apparently Dahno had left no message about when he would return, Bleys took advantage of the opportunity to key-in on the lounge monitor screen the day's newsfax sheets. He sat and read them in detail.

He tried to relate what he found in them with anything that he had seen or heard the day before; but no connection appeared. But it was a fact the newsprints held much more financial and business news than he had expected, from his early exposure to an Association which was supposed to be merely a planet of poor farms and poor farmers like Henry. Apparently, Ecumeny and a few other large cities like this were at their core very little different from cities just like them on the other New Worlds.

In particular, this seemed to be true of Ecumeny. It was, he learned, the seat of the planetary government, and a number of large local companies had their headquarters there. He had assumed, particularly after what he had heard the evening before, that the Friendly governments did not like lobbyists—or what passed for lobbyists here. But their first visitor at the restaurant table last night had certainly sounded like a lobbyist. Or at least like someone whose job it was to sway the representatives in the planetary government.

Dahno, evidently, was involved in this somehow. But how this tied in with his being a financial consultant, and particularly how it tied in with that crew of obviously intelligent musclemen Bleys had been taken to see first yesterday, Bleys could not figure out.

But he had learned not to worry about such things. He tucked the information in the back of his mind, waiting for more information to start to bridge the gaps and holes in its fabric until finally the whole picture should be revealed.

But the next three days were more of the same. Each day, they went around dinner time to the same restaurant and the same table and people came by. What Bleys overheard, however, was too fragmentary for him to understand most of it without interpretation. Beyond this, even if he had been able to understand the individual conversations, he would have been a long way from putting together a general picture of what Dahno was engaged in doing.

Riding home in the hovercar, back to Uncle Henry's, Bleys simply tucked the whole four days of question marks and unexplained data into the back of his head and left it there.

He had learned a long time ago that matters like this, dealing with what he privately had named "mass-questions," were much better solved by the unconscious than the conscious. If you applied the conscious mind to a situation in which you had only partial information, you ended up going around in circles, with guesses reinforcing guesses until you were further afield than when you started.

In spite of his sleep in the force-field bed at Dahno's the three nights, Bleys found himself feeling washed-out as the hovercar approached the farm. It was the tension of the three days, rather than any physical exertion, that had wound him up.

It was a curious idiosyncrasy of his that whenever he was concerned with a problem, his whole body seemed to be concerned with it, even though it was something that only the mind could handle. The only way of getting away from it was to push it into the back of his head, as he had done with the visit just over, and consciously try to forget it. Eventually, answers would begin to come and to erupt into his conscious mind; and then he could attack it.

He had argued with himself about asking Dahno just what the other had in mind for him. He did not want to ask too soon, or until he could at least come up with some knowledge of his own about his older brother.

But riding back now, without really knowing why, but trusting the instinct that he knew to be based upon at least some of the unresolved data in the back of his mind, he decided to ask. A sort of companionship had grown up between them in these last few days, and if he did not ask now, there was no telling when he would be able to ask again. By the time his next chance came, that present feeling of companionship might have evaporated.

"Dahno," he said, hastily, for the farm was getting close now, "why are you interested in me anyway?"

Dahno looked over at him, seemed to think a minute, then pulled the hovercar to the side of the road and cut the motor.

He looked back at Bleys.

His face was utterly serious.

"I know you," he said. "I'm the only person on sixteen worlds who does. I think I know what you're capable of. You're isolated by your ability. So was I. So am I—except that I've learned to live with it. Now, it's too late. We'll always be isolated, you and I, even from each other. But the point is I can use you, Bleys, in what I'm doing."

"And what's that?" asked Bleys.

Dahno ignored the question.

"You lived with Mother until you were old enough to know how you get what you want from someone else," Dahno went on. "It's a matter of looking ahead, planning ahead, and arranging a one-way path for that person that leads only to the end you want for him or her. You know it can be done and you know how it's done. I don't want you to think that I did that to you."

He stopped speaking. Bleys merely stared back at him.

"You follow me?" asked Dahno.

"Yes, I follow," said Bleys, "but you still didn't answer my question."

"I am," said Dahno. "What I'm telling you is that I need your help, but I only want it if you give it of your own free will. There's no way—and even young as you are you know this as well as I do, Little Brother—that either one of us can really force our will on the other. So I want you to *choose* to come in with me. So, I'm letting you take a look at everything I do, and we'll keep on letting you look until there's nothing more to look at, in the hopes that you'll see that it's something you want to be involved in as well. That's all there is to it."

"Are you sure?" said Bleys, a little bitterly.

"You're remembering our mother," said Dahno. "Don't. I'm not her! If nothing else, I want something much greater than she ever wanted. But what that is you're going to have to find out for yourself. Find out for yourself, and then decide if you want any part of it. That way I know you're coming in with me completely of your own free will. All right?"

"For now, anyway," answered Bleys, "all right."

One of the huge hands was extended. Bleys took it in his own narrow, now-twelve-year-old fingers and they grasped hands. Then Dahno let go, and without another word, restarted the hovercar, swung up on the road and they drove the rest of the way to the farm.

CHAPTER
13

BLEYS, CARRYING HIS suitcase and some parcels, trudged across the yard, up the steps and into the house, expecting to find it empty. But it was not. All three were there. Uncle Henry, Joshua and Will.

They were busy at the cheesemaking, which could be done with one or two persons, but went faster if more hands were available. Clearly, the fact that Henry was there with the boys had kept them from dashing out into the yard the moment they heard the hovercar coming up the road to the farm. They looked at him bright-eyed now; but Henry merely gave him a brief flash of his normal wintry smile of welcome and spoke.

"Put your things in the bedroom," he said, "then change into some clean work clothes and come out to help us, here."

Bleys obeyed. There was a strange, unreal quality to the tiny, spartan rooms of the farm after the ample, luxurious ones he had been used to over the weekend; and the whole smell and process of cheesemaking. He put his suitcase and packages on his bottom bunk and made the change into his work clothes, then returned to the kitchen and joined the work.

"You look well, Bleys," said Henry unexpectedly from the other end of the table where they were working. "Your weekend was good for you."

"Yes, Bleys, you're all bright an—"

"Will," said Henry, "my remark was not a signal for general chatter. Work mixed with conversation goes slowly."

His two sons became silent, but kept glancing at Bleys whenever they had a chance. He knew at once to what Henry had referred and what had caused it. He had felt a sudden sense of guilt at his uncle's words, which deepened now. For four days he had not thought about his effort to make himself into a Friendly. It was that mind of his which became captured by any new puzzle that presented itself.

But that, he told himself, was no excuse. Dahno's way of living was not his, Bleys' way. Not yet at any rate—and perhaps never. His home was here now. His struggle was a religious one. This cheesemaking was more important than all of Dahno's mysterious trainees and people interviewed in a restaurant.

Now that he thought of it, he had gradually let his prayers slide while he was in Ecumeny, until the last two days there had been none at all. He told himself he would pray extra hard and long tonight before bed.

Nonetheless, the sense of unreality he had felt, stepping into the house and the small rough bedroom he shared with Will and Joshua, stayed with him. The boys were obviously brimful of questions, which they would be asking as opportunity provided in the next few days.

But for now, under their father's eyes, they concentrated on their work without words. Bleys joined them, and the simple habitual actions of what they were doing reinforced his feeling of unreality; so that a transparent, invisible wall seemed to surround him and block him off from the rest of them, even as he worked side by side, occasionally touching the others in the process of his job.

Later on that evening, over the dinner table, the boys bombarded him with questions; and Henry permitted it.

The questions did something to thin the air of unreality that held him, but it was actually several days before it disappeared completely. Once it did, curiously, Ecumeny and the four-day weekend there began to seem unreal in turn. It was as if Henry's farm and Dahno's city were places in two different universes, and there was no way they could coexist in the same moment as realities.

However, from then on the daily activities went in pretty much their normal fashion.

Dahno dropped by at least a couple of times a month; and the trips on which he took Bleys gradually had a tendency to run longer and longer; until nearly every trip meant at least a four-day if not a six-day absence. At the farm, Bleys himself was both growing up and sorting matters out in his own mind.

It was not until Will mentioned it one day, that he realized he was now a good two inches taller than Joshua. Joshua himself had not made any reference to it; simply because Joshua was not at all concerned about whether Bleys was taller than he was or not—Josh's self-possession still remained unshakable—because in his view of the world their relative heights made no difference.

Nonetheless, Bleys was shooting up like a weed. He would soon be as tall as Henry himself, although he remained thin, and almost gawky-looking.

He was at home with the farm, now. By this time he knew more about what needed to be done about the place than anyone, possibly including Henry himself. Henry, finally asked directly by Bleys if Bleys could help with the motor, had let him do so. The truth of the matter was, Henry was no mechanic.

Bleys was not a mechanic, either; but he had a natural feeling, both for the logic of things and for how the parts of the real world fitted together—including the parts of an engine.

By the time he was thirteen years old, they had the engine running; and four months later, at Bleys' demand upon Dahno for the funds to do so, they had bought a used tractor into which it could fit.

Henry was overjoyed, but would not show it. He went to the

unheard-of extent of not merely thanking God for Bleys' help, but thanking Bleys personally.

At the same time, Bleys was beginning to realize that once again he was isolated. Henry and the two boys had accepted him. But the community—particularly that part of the community that clustered around the church most closely—still saw him as a complete outsider.

They had accepted Henry's explanation gained from Dahno, that Bleys was unusually intelligent and needed to study beyond what the local school could offer.

It was a convenient fiction, one the others could accept easily and so they did. Nonetheless, it was not something that, by itself, endeared them to Bleys. In addition, Bleys himself had found that no matter what he did, he tended to distance himself from other people.

He finally accepted that the truth of the matter was he simply did not want people emotionally close to him. He had accepted Henry and his two young cousins, simply because they were there and there was no way to live with them without being emotionally close to a certain extent.

In his own way he was fond of both his cousins. With the sensitivity of younger people, they felt this; and gave him back real affection, with which Bleys was at once uncomfortable and at a loss as to how to accept.

It was strange that all his life, from his earliest years with his mother, he had yearned for affection. But eventually, from her, he had learned to distrust it, and now he could not be at ease with it.

More attractive to him as the weeks, months, and years went on had been the rock-firm religious structure of which Henry was so settled a part. Bleys found a kind of cold but deeply comforting feeling in the idea of a perfectly ordered and controlled universe.

But he could not conceive in the face of all he knew about science and logic that there could be such a universe without anchor, a controlling and regulating part. That regulating part, for Henry and other Friendlies, he knew, was the concept of God. But he could not make himself believe in a supreme deity. For some reason his mind, his imagination, his faith—whatever operated to produce that—would not work for him. In the years that followed he tried everything, even secretly making himself a hair-shirt out of a piece of goat-hide—it was really a girdle rather than a shirt—under all his other clothing and with the hairy side next to his skin. But all this discomfort did was make it difficult for him to fall asleep at night.

As a last-ditch effort, in desperation he conceived of the idea of fasting. Prophets and hermits had fasted and been vouchsafed an awareness of the deity. Perhaps he could duplicate that. However, he would have to have Henry's permission for something like that.

"Uncle," he said, cornering the older man by himself in the goat shed one afternoon where he had been working with a billy goat who had somehow gotten his right front leg cut, and Henry was trying to clean the wound, "you know—I've never said anything, but I know you've noticed, Uncle, how unsuccessful I've been putting myself in touch with the Lord. I thought that maybe the way to do it would be the way Holy Men have done it for centuries. If it's all right with you, Uncle, I'd like to try fasting."

Henry was squatting on the floor of the goat shed before a basin brought from the house, holding some water and some of their homemade soap. He looked up as he finally rinsed his hands and wiped them on a clean cloth he had brought out in his hip pocket. He was not exactly frowning at Bleys, but there was a strong concern in his unflinching gaze.

"God himself knows I would never stand against anyone's search for a path to Him," he said, picking up the basin and standing. After stowing the towel back in his hip pocket, he went on. "But you're still a growing lad, Bleys. You need regular food for your health's sake."

He stopped speaking. Bleys stood watching him. It was unusual to see Henry indecisive about anything.

"I think," said Henry after a moment, "you had better go see Medician Roderick. If he says it's all right for you to fast, I'll agree you can do it."

"I can go on with my work here just as usual," said Bleys, "I'd just not eat."

"As to that, the details of it will be something that Roderick can decide," said Henry. "He's a good hour's walk from here, and another hour's walk back again. Why don't you clean up and get started right now? Then you can come home and tell me at dinner time, if you don't see me before, what his decision was."

Bleys, accordingly, left the farm for the long trudge down the dirt roads to the combined home and office of the medician.

The brief, very hot summer of Association, caused by its extreme tilt away from Epsilon Eridani, was with them once again. Bleys wore a wide-brimmed hat of plaited straw; and his lightest pair of pants and shirt, both of which had been lengthened in the sleeves and pant-legs until they came down and fastened to gloves and boots. They were clothes that had belonged to Joshua previously, and they were, if anything, too full in the waist, but a belt cinched that in.

Except for his face he was completely covered. Epsilon Eridani, at summer angle, was nothing to expose naked flesh to if it could possibly be avoided. This was one of the reasons all work outside on the farm ceased during the summer, and everything else went on inside—including the local school.

Bleys was lucky enough to find Medician Roderick at home when he got there. Even though travel outside in this season was nothing anyone wished to do, emergencies called Roderick out regardless. He was a heavy-set, dark-skinned man in his sixties, worn down by years of work at all hours, to save lives and deal with the many accidents that happened to farmers. He could be, Bleys knew, exceedingly gentle with his patients; but the years had also given him an explosive temper if his opinion was crossed.

Accordingly, all through his long walk, Bleys had been working out how best to suggest his fast.

Roderick set him down in a wooden chair with a slanted back, in the outside area that became his surgery in summer. After walking in the sun, the shade of the thatched roof high overhead made the area seem almost icy to Bleys.

"Well, Bleys?" said Roderick, once Bleys was settled, and with a glass of a cool summer version of the local coffee in his hand, "you said it was no emergency. Everyone's all right at the farm, I take it, then. So what is it?"

Bleys began by explaining his long struggle to see a deity. He ran it through the years, so that Roderick would understand that this was no sudden whim, but a desperate effort to solve an apparently unsolvable problem. But eventually it came down to stating what he wanted to do, in plain terms.

"—So I thought," Bleys wound up, "I could try fasting. We've got records of many people who've seen the Lord, once they've abstained from food for a while. I told Henry I could go right on working—"

"Out of the question!" said Roderick. "If you do any fasting, you don't want to be working at the same time. Oh, perhaps the first two or three days, but after that you'll want to take it easy. Moreover, youngster, if you want to have an experience where you come face to face with the Lord, it's best that you're away from familiar surroundings and all by yourself."

"That could be arranged," said Bleys. "We have a patch of woods near the back of the farm, with a stream running through it that has good water in it, even in this hot weather. I could build a sort of lean-to there, and just sit and pray and . . . fast."

"Not so quick," snapped Roderick, "I haven't agreed to your fasting yet. It depends on what kind of physical shape you're in. As I remember, you're prone to some sort of unusual sickness that your brother brings you medication for."

"Oh, but that never hits this time of year," said Bleys ingenuously.

"Well," said Roderick, "get those clothes off and let me give you a thorough examination. How old are you now?"

"I'll be seventeen in three months," said Bleys, as he stripped off his clothes.

"You're already a skyscraper," Roderick grunted, beginning to examine him with a listening instrument that clipped to his right ear. "You may grow out of sight before you're done . . ."

However, meanwhile he continued with the examination, thumping Bleys in various places, having him lie down, palpating his abdomen, and asking questions about his normal diet and how much he ate. He ended by taking a syringeful of blood from just below the inside of Bleys' elbow and put the blood into a little machine on a table nearby, which after a few seconds began to click out a number of figures on a strip of paper. It stopped eventually, and Roderick tore them off and studied them.

"Disgustingly healthy," he almost grumbled, "typical of one of Henry's boys; hard work, a simple but adequate diet—a good environment generally."

He sat down in a chair, waved Bleys into another one and laid the paper on a little table beside the chair.

"Tell me," he said, "how do you sleep?"

"Oh, pretty well," said Bleys.

"What does 'pretty well' mean?"

"I wake up now and then in the night," said Bleys, "then, after a while I go back to sleep again. I've always done it—as far back as I can remember."

"But perhaps a little more lately, since you've been struggling to see God?"

"Perhaps . . . a little more," said Bleys cautiously, "but you see, it's always the way I've handled problems—I think about them a bit during the night."

"I see," said Roderick. "So you've been thinking about these efforts of yours to see God, in these waking periods at night? And you've been waking more lately?"

"It's been harder and harder to find ways to try to approach Him," said Bleys, "so naturally He's been on my mind more and more; and so, naturally, I suppose, I've been waking more during the night, come to think of it."

"Yes," said Roderick. "Are you allergic to anything? You've got dark circles under your eyes."

"Oh, no! Genetically—well, my mother had me genetically tested and I was perfect in the autoimmune department."

"I see," said Roderick. "Well, as I say, you're disgustingly healthy—except for one thing. If you can't be allergic to anything, I'd have to guess you've been running a lot shorter on sleep than you make out."

"No, no! Absolutely," said Bleys, "I'm no different than I ever was."

Roderick looked at him grimly.

"I think you're depressed," he said.

"I promise you, I'm not depressed!" said Bleys with a rush. "This is a great adventure I'm on, trying to see God. I'd rather be doing this than anything."

"You're sure?"

"Yes, I am. Absolutely!"

There was a long pause while the two stared at each other.

"Well, I'm a church member myself," Roderick said, at last, "and a good one. In conscience, there's no way I can deny you the right to search for God. But the fact of the matter is you're still growing, you need an unusual amount of food, and you need adequate sleep. A depressed person shouldn't try going on a fast the way you want to do."

"I've been thinking about it for a very long time," said Bleys, "I've studied to find God very earnestly for all the years I've been here; and so far I've failed. This is pretty much a last attempt. I've got to do it!"

"All right then." Roderick got to his feet. "Put your clothes on, I'll be back in a moment."

By the time Bleys had dressed himself Roderick had stepped inside his combination house and clinic and come out again with a bottle holding perhaps a quarter-liter of dark brown liquid.

"This won't taste too pleasant," he said, "but it's absolutely necessary for your body, if you're going to deprive it of food. It contains vitamins and other essential minerals and elements that you need, plus a few other things that are particularly necessary to anyone on this planet—particularly someone still growing up. You take two teaspoonsful a day. Also, you're going to have to eat something. A large bowl of clear soup, twice a day. Also, I want you to let Henry see you at least once a day. Can I count on you to do that?"

"Yes," said Bleys.

Roderick passed the bottle to Bleys, who opened it up and sniffed at it tentatively. It did not smell any better than Roderick had promised it would taste.

"Tell Henry he can pay me for this the next time he butchers a goat and has some meat to spare," Roderick went on. "By the way, how are you making out there with your income against the need to buy new embryos all the time?"

"We're doing a little better than breaking even," Bleys said, "but just so."

"Well," Roderick dismissed him with a wave of his hand, "tell him he can pay me whenever he has goat meat literally to spare. I wouldn't charge at all, if it wasn't for the fact that bottle you're holding cost me a certain amount of money. And the supply store in Ecumeny is cash only."

"Thank you," said Bleys, "I thank the Lord you've been so kind to me."

"Maybe He'll consider I've been 'kind,' maybe He will . . ." said Roderick, turning away from him. "Now you'd better get started back if you want to have anything of the day left, once you're home."

CHAPTER

14

BLEYS SAT CROSS-LEGGED on a pile of springy fir boughs covered by an old blanket, in front of his lean-to.

The summer heat was unbelievable. At the same time, he told himself, he at least had water, even if it was warm enough to be hot, and the fir trees around him threw a dense shade that kept the sun off him directly.

He thought idly for a moment that it must have been a bad problem for the geneticists engaged in the terraforming of Association—breeding a variform of pine that could survive these hot, if very brief, summers, as well as flourishing in the more normal climate of wintertime.

He was in his twelfth day of idleness and fasting; and he found his mind had a tendency to wander, no matter how hard he tried to keep it to a specific subject. Finally, he had simply decided to let it wander. He had the feeling that his unconscious was deeply engaged in potentially useful considerations of many things.

It was a state almost like those moments before falling

asleep when inspiration was most likely to come to him—
except that he was not getting ready to go to sleep. Not that
sleep did not surprise him from time to time. That was
evidently part of the weakness that had come from fasting.

Finally he had reached the point where he really did not feel
hungry. The days from the second to the fifth day, he had been
tormented by his hunger. He had been very tempted to give up
the whole idea and go back up to the farm house. But while the
desire was strong in him, his body stayed where it was.
Something greater than his physical feelings kept him at his fast.

He had not discovered God. But his mind had, over the
days—over the latter days, particularly—put together a great
deal of the structure that must result from a God being at the
center of all things. His earlier idea that a universe could not
exist as a whole and single entity, without some massive,
controlling cog-wheel that was a deity, had gone beyond an
opinion into a belief.

There was no doubt about it; a God, even if he could not see
him, must exist.

In a sense this was an answer to his long search. Even if he
was blind to any direct feeling of God's existence, still he was
now positive that a deity had to be there. That, in its own way,
was finding It, or Him.

So, in one sense, he could break off this fast now, saying he
had accomplished what he wanted. No one would argue with
him. In fact the others would be glad to have him stop. Not
merely Henry, but the boys were obviously very deeply
worried about him. It was strange, because while he had lost a
little weight, he did not feel any real change in himself except
a sort of peacefulness that had come over him, and a feeling
that all other things were unimportant.

If it were not for outside reasons and the orders of Medician
Roderick, he would almost be willing to spend the rest of his
life this way; merely sleeping and sitting and letting his mind
roam. He could understand now how being a hermit could have
its attractions.

The universe he now felt was inside him as well as around
him. He did not even need to look in a starscreen—had there

been one available—to be conscious of the vast expanse of space that went outward from him, here, sitting cross-legged on his blanket, falling out to the limitless limits of eternity and infinity. He could not see these things, but he was now conscious of them; and he marveled that a perception of them had been waiting since before the human race was born, only to be revealed to him now.

The planet he was on had ceased to be an important, or even a relevant thing, to him. He was aware now that its fierce sun was westering and soon would be so low on the horizon that nearby hills would block it out. Then welcome shadow would cover all the farmland.

It was time to start up to the house where Henry and the boys would already be, to get his evening bowl of soup, and let them see him. He felt no real hunger for the soup now, and was only distantly concerned with his duty to let them have a look at him. But he had obeyed orders all his life. He made himself get to his feet and begin the walk to the house.

From the woods the ground sloped gradually up through pasture for the goats to the farm buildings. It was not a great distance and the slope was gentle, but it had become an effort for him to make the trek. He came at last to the house, mounted the steps with effort and opened the door. He stepped in to see the table already set and Henry, Will and Joshua already seated at it. A fourth place had been laid for him and as he came over and took his chair, Will jumped up to go after his bowl of soup.

He was conscious of them all looking at him very keenly, but once again it was something of small concern to him. It was as if all things were relatively unimportant at the moment. The soup came and he picked up a spoon and went to work on it slowly. The hot liquid felt comfortable in his mouth, but beyond that he was not too interested in it. By the time he was halfway through, he felt filled up. He laid the spoon down.

"What is it, Bleys?" asked Henry. "You haven't taken more than half your soup."

Bleys looked down at the bowl and saw that Henry was correct. He picked up the spoon again, but still without any real desire for the rest of the soup.

"Bleys?" said Henry again.

Bleys laid his spoon down once more and looked across the table at the older man.

"Yes, Uncle?" he asked.

"How do you feel, boy?" said Henry.

"All right," answered Bleys.

"Do you know your two weeks are almost up?" Henry said.

"Are they?" asked Bleys.

"And have you reached God as you wished you would?" Henry asked.

"No," said Bleys. He felt as if he ought to have been able to add something to that; but he could not think of anything. He had, in a sense, reached God, but not as he had planned. But it would be too much effort to try to explain this to Henry. He sat looking at his uncle.

"I think this has gone far enough, Bleys," said Henry decisively. "If you can't eat any more of your soup I want you to come with me."

"Where?" asked Bleys, mildly interested.

"I want you to talk to Gregg," said Henry. "You're in no condition to walk down to his house. We'll take the goat-cart. Joshua, Will—get the goat-cart harnessed up and ready."

A little bit of the indifference that had been cloaking Bleys like a mist began to thin and disappear. Why should he be taken to see Gregg, he wondered? Again, it was too much effort to ask. When the boys came in to announce that the goat-cart was ready, he pushed himself upright from the table, carefully placed his chair back where it belonged, and followed Henry out to the goat-cart.

He climbed in. Joshua closed the door for him from the outside. Henry lifted the reins and they started down the road.

"Uncle?" asked Bleys. "Why am I going to see Gregg?"

"Because I think you should talk to him," said Henry. "I think the time has come when you have to talk to him."

Bleys lost himself in wondering what the reason should be; and with that on his mind he paid no attention until the goat-cart drew up in front of Gregg's house. He fumbled with the latch of the door next to him, opened it and stepped out on the ground. Henry was already around the cart, to take him by an elbow and steady him as he led him up to the door. When they reached it, Henry opened it and, sticking his head in, called out.

"Gregg?"

"I'm in the sitting room, Henry," the voice of Gregg came back.

"I've brought Bleys," said Henry. With that he put a hand on Bleys' elbow again and guided him down the short hallway into the room where Bleys had sat and talked with Gregg, once, long ago.

"I'll leave you here with him," said Henry to Gregg. "I'll be outside with the goat-cart after you've talked."

"I thank God for your help, Henry," said Gregg. He was seated in that same specially built chair that allowed him to fit his arthritis-crooked body into it with comfort. He waved to a chair opposite him. Bleys sat down in it as Henry went back out. The chair, also, was the same padded one with armrests in which he had sat when he had first talked to Gregg.

"Why was it you wanted to see me, Gregg?" Bleys asked.

"I was only one of the people who wanted me to," answered Gregg. "Both Henry and Roderick wished it too. When I spoke to you before I don't believe I mentioned to you that, before I became a Teacher, I'd studied to become a psychomedician. I'd graduated and even put in my internship. But I felt the call of the Lord, and ended up being a Teacher, instead. I didn't tell you that before, did I?"

"No," said Bleys.

"Have you ever been seen by a psychomedician before, Bleys?" asked Gregg.

"Yes," said Bleys, "just before I came here to Association. Ezekiel brought around a man——" his memory, which never failed him, still had to search for a moment to come up with the name. "James Selfort. He said he was from around here. He said he'd known Henry; and, as I say, he was a friend of Ezekiel's. Ezekiel brought him to find out how I'd do, here on Association."

"James Selfort?" said Gregg. "So that's where that young

fellow got to. Well, it's true that to do any really advanced work as a psychomedician you have to leave our Friendly planets. We simply don't have the resources to supply the schools and clinics where learning can be extended into its higher levels. Do you know what his opinion of you was?"

"He thought," said Bleys, delving into his memory, "that considering the way I'd been brought up I might do quite well here."

"I see," said Gregg. He was silent for a moment, then went on. "At any rate, you know what a psychomedician is, then, and what he does. As a psychomedician, rather than a Teacher, I have to tell you something. I wouldn't have told you this, ordinarily, but both Henry and Roderick said—and I can almost see for myself right now—that you've pushed yourself to dangerous limits in your search for an understanding and knowledge of God. Bleys—"

He paused to shake his head.

"—You're going to have to face something. And that is that you never will see God, nor understand Him."

Gregg's voice was gentle, almost sorrowful.

"I don't understand," said Bleys. "Why tell me this? And if it's been true all along, why didn't you tell me before?"

"I'm afraid," said Gregg, "I was in error. I didn't think that you'd understand. Now I think you would. You're old enough, for one thing; and for another, by this relentless search you've made for understanding, I have to believe you won't give up until you have it. More is known about you than you think, you know."

He paused again, looking penetratingly at Bleys.

"Ezekiel wrote some long letters to Henry," he went on, "Henry showed them to me; and since, he's shown them to Roderick. The letters said what James Selfort had told Ezekiel; and it's what I have to tell you now from my own experience as a psychomedician. You'll never succeed in your search for God, simply because it's impossible for you."

"Why should it be impossible for me?" demanded Bleys. Suddenly, all his detachment from what was going on around him had evaporated, he was as clear-headed and as closely attentive to Gregg as if he had never begun his fast.

"You saw very little of your mother, as I remember, while you were growing up, isn't that correct?" said Gregg.

"Yes."

"But you remember only so far back. There's a period before that you were too young to remember. Then, when you were a very young child and a baby, and to some extent after that, you were still very much under your mother's influence, the way any child is under its mother's influence. In spite of yourself you picked up a lot of what made her what she was. And what made her what she was was her Exotic birth and upbringing."

"Are you saying I've something of the Exotic still in me and that's getting in my way?" asked Bleys.

"Yes, I'm afraid it'll always be in you," said Gregg; "at an early age, influences like that are never lost. One of the things you picked up from your mother was the innate Exotic skepticism; and you picked it up at a time when you worshiped your mother. Under all the surface feelings and the antagonism you came to feel against her later on, that early influence, that skepticism, still stands—and will always stand—like a block in your way. It'll always be there to prevent you from becoming a 'True Faith-holder.'"

"What makes you so sure?" demanded Bleys.

"As I say—all my studies and all my training, before I became a Teacher," answered Gregg. "I know this is an unpleasant fact for you to face; but, Bleys, you have to face it or else you'll destroy yourself trying to do the impossible. You can no more overrule this early-learned skepticism, than you can tear yourself apart into two people. Face it, believe it, and give yourself freedom from this desperate attempt you've been making."

"And if I don't?" challenged Bleys.

"You'll probably end up killing yourself," said Gregg in a flat, matter-of-fact voice.

"I see," said Bleys. He got to his feet. "Well, I thank God for your kindness, Teacher, in telling me this. I'll think about it seriously. Now, maybe I'd better be getting back to Henry so he can drive me home."

"Go with God, Bleys," said Gregg, not moving from his chair, "because He is there for you, even if you can never know Him or reach Him."

Bleys nodded stiffly and went out of the room, down the little hall and out of the house.

Outside, Henry was standing waiting beside the goat-cart, the reins of the goats loosely in his hands, to keep them from moving away from where they stood.

"You've talked to Gregg?" Henry asked.

"Yes, Uncle," said Bleys. He offered nothing further, but opened the door on his side. Henry helped him into the cart, then went around and got in the other side, passing the reins through the slot in the dashboard first. He picked them up again once he was inside; and they rode back to the house in silence.

Bleys knew Henry was waiting to let him, Bleys, speak first. But Bleys sat with his mind in a turmoil, caught between rage that he had not been told what Gregg had just told him, earlier; and the self-training that had taught him to consider everything he heard.

"I'll end the fast now, Uncle," he said, abruptly, as they turned into the farmyard.

"Boy, I'm very happy to hear you say that," said Henry with unusual feeling. "You've lost nothing, and possibly gained a great deal! Also, you've got us, your family, still with you and always will have."

The note of Henry's deep emotion penetrated into Bleys' thoughts.

"Thank you, Uncle," he said, looking at Henry, "I thank God for those words of yours."

They were home. Bleys got out of the cart as Will and Joshua came tumbling out of the door and took over disposal of the cart and goats from Henry. Henry steadied him as they went up the steps and inside.

"I think I'll lie down now, Uncle, if you don't mind," said Bleys.

"By all means," said Henry, "you'll need to rest now, and build yourself back up again."

Bleys fell asleep the moment he touched his bunk, for the first time in nearly two weeks. But he woke during the night; and lay staring at the darkness overhead. Gazing at it, he realized he had never given up on anything he had gone after; and this was to be no exception.

To become a True Faith-holder, no matter what was or was not, was still his goal. He would be a better Friendly than any of them from now on. He would live as if he walked hand in hand with God; and if the others remarked on this, it did not matter. He would not discuss it, he would merely be what he was going to be. And from that he would eventually build to the kind of society and the kind of human race and the kind of God-ordained universe that he had envisioned from the beginning.

CHAPTER

15

BLEYS WOKE LATE in the morning to an empty house. His first thought was that he had slept through breakfast and the cleanup afterwards; and that Henry and the two boys were already outside working. Then he remembered that today was a church-day. The other three had let him sleep past the time when he could have got up to go with them.

He started to get out of bed and was surprised at the effort it took. Still, he persisted; and, once out, dressed in his ordinary clothes—since it would now be too late for church for him—and went into the main room of the house. The table had one setting on it, and a bowl of porridge was being kept warm in the iron cooking utensil, by the side of the fire. On the table he found a note from Henry. Typical of Henry, it was short and to the point.

I thought it best that you should rest today and not go to church. You can go next week.

Henry

Bleys put the paper aside on the table. It was true that he was in no shape to go to church. He felt physically weaker now than he had at any time during his fasting. He went to the porridge and spooned it into a ceramic bowl of glazed, gray-white clay, then brought the bowl back to the table and collapsed in the chair before it.

He sat for a few moments, merely catching his breath. Then he took up a spoon and made an effort to eat the porridge. It tasted good, but as with the soup the day before, half of what was there more than filled him.

He told himself that he should scrape what was left of the porridge back into the pot to warm and drove himself to do so; then went back to his bunk; kicked off his boots and crawled once more under the covers with his clothes on.

He went to sleep immediately.

When he woke again, Henry and the boys were still not back from church. He went back to the dining room, put what remained of the porridge in a bowl, and this time managed to finish it. It felt good inside him, for all the reluctance his body had to accept it spoonful by spoonful.

Henry had been very right about the physical shape Bleys was in. It took him most of the next week to recover, although, once started, he came back fast.

In the middle of the week Joshua returned from a trip to the store having plainly been in a fight. But he refused to tell them with who or why.

"Father," he said to Henry, "haven't you always told us we must face and fight our own battles? Well, this was simply one of my battles and it's no one's business but my own."

Henry shook his head.

"Son," he said heavily, "when you quote my own words back to me I can't insist you tell me."

And that had been the last word said on the subject by any of them.

By the following Sunday Bleys felt as well as ever, although Henry still had him doing only light chores around the house. But he put on his best black suit that Dahno had got him and went with them when they left for church this time.

They were among the first few families to get there. Gregg stood at the entrance to the church, as he always did, welcoming those who had come for the service. His welcome to Bleys was no different. Bleys noticed, however, that the other families that were already there, and those that arrived after—for he, Henry and the boys stayed outside until the actual time for the services themselves—all greeted Henry and the boys but ignored him.

Both Joshua and Will were a little paler than usual. But Henry's face showed nothing. Bleys, on his part, was used to the fact that the rest of the church membership had not strongly taken to him, long before this. He left Henry and the boys outside and went into the church, toward the back of which he found one other person who did not seem to have changed at all, but welcomed Bleys in as kindly and as friendly a manner as he always had: Adrian Wiseman.

He spoke with Bleys for a little while, then went back through the cloakroom and out onto the porch where Gregg was standing, greeting people. Bleys sat where he was; and eventually the people in the churchyard began to file inside. Soon Gregg came in and mounted his pulpit and the service began.

But this particular service was to have the kind of interruption Adrian had described to Bleys a long time before, and which Bleys himself had seen at least a dozen times in the past few years. There was a sudden whooping and hollering outside; and the thud of some thrown rocks, or other missiles, hitting the side of the church. Adrian was immediately on his feet, moving out into the cloakroom to pick up his pistol and step outside. Bleys rose immediately and followed him; but as he approached the door, the constable pushed him back in.

"One of them's armed," said Adrian.

Behind Bleys, Gregg's voice sounded from the pulpit interrupting his sermon.

"Please leave the constable to his duty," he heard Gregg say, "and return to your seat, Bleys. There's nothing you can do out there."

Bleys turned back and reseated himself in the final pew.

"I ask God's pardon and yours, Teacher," he said.

It was the sort of apology that was standard for such occasions as this. But Bleys was suddenly alerted by the fact that murmurs were running through the congregation; and members among it were casting hostile glances at him. From being an object generally ignored, he seemed to have suddenly become one who was actively a target for general criticism; and his last attempt to join Adrian had triggered off that attitude.

The glances he saw occasionally directed back at him from the pews further front were looks of pure enmity.

He puzzled over this, now more concerned rather with what this would all mean to Henry and the two boys, than how it would affect him. It all turned upon whatever had made the sudden change in community feeling. He decided, finally, that he would try to talk to Gregg after church.

If anyone, Gregg would tell him straight out what was wrong; or what had caused the congregation to start to feel this way about him. It could not be his relationship to Dahno, because that had been an established fact for years. Moreover, far from being disliked locally, Dahno was generally admired.

How much of that admiration was due to the fact that he seemed to have been someone who had gone to the city and gotten rich, Bleys had no idea. But it was a fact. And if they liked Dahno, why should they have anything against him?

At the end of the service, Bleys slipped quickly from his bench and tried to get up to Gregg. However, the mass of congregation, now leaving, were a human tide running against him and Bleys gave up the idea of pushing through them, particularly under the present conditions of the way they were feeling toward him.

He shrugged his shoulders, turned and went outside to wait for Henry and the two boys, who had been seated, as usual, together at the very front of the church.

The rest of the congregation poured out and began to sort themselves out around their various vehicles. Outside of a few unfriendly glances, none of them looked his way. He was continuing to stand by himself when something hit him from behind on his left shoulder.

He reached up automatically to feel it and brought his fingers away grimy with dirt. Looking down, he saw simply a clod of earth with some variform grass attached, that had evidently been thrown at him. Experience had taught Bleys, even back in the years when he was with his mother, that there were times to confront things, and times not to. Now was clearly a time to confront. He turned about and walked toward the people by the carts standing almost directly behind him.

In front of them was a group of boys about Joshua's age. They all had two or three years of age on Bleys, but none of them was his height. It might have been any one of them who had thrown the clod; but Bleys had learned as a young child that the thing to do was to pick out the most worthy opponent in the group and confront him. He would either take the responsibility, on being challenged, or indicate the person who was guilty of throwing.

In this case, the one most likely to be the leader, and to have thrown the clod himself, was Isaiah Lerner, a tall, somewhat swarthy boy going on seventeen years old. He was one who had had a fight or two with Joshua in the past; and Joshua had lost. Not, reflected Bleys, that that would ever save Joshua from having to fight him again. Henry's teaching was deeply ingrained in his oldest son. If you felt that right was on your side, the only way to go was forward.

The group of boys seemed to be waiting for Bleys. He came up to them, face to face with Isaiah, and looked a little down into his eyes. This, he knew, would additionally annoy the other. Isaiah outweighed Bleys by a good twenty pounds or more, beginning already to have the musculature of a man, but to be looked down on was always an affront. Still, in the case of any physical conflict between the two of them, there was little doubt among the locals who would be the winner.

Isaiah met his gaze boldly and did not move.

"You threw that, Isaiah?" asked Bleys.

"That's right," answered Isaiah. He stood with his arms

dangling loosely at his sides, square on to Bleys. "Something about that bother you?"

"Only when you do it," said Bleys.

Isaiah laughed and half turned away; and as if it was a signal the rest of the boys around him also laughed.

"You haven't got an answer?" said Bleys, "I thought as much."

He turned his back on them and began to walk away again and a voice spoke behind him.

"Whore's baby!" It was Isaiah's voice, and it sounded almost in his ear. "You don't belong in our church, whore's baby!"

Bleys swung back to face him. Isaiah was already getting ready to hit him, his right fist starting from low by his thigh and back a ways. Bleys had had training, on and off, while he was with his mother, both from hired instructors in the martial arts, and some unofficial tutoring by friends of his mother's. He waited until the hand began to move, and then he swayed aside gently. Isaiah's punch shot past his jaw and hit empty air.

Bleys' own bony right fist struck Isaiah's throat. The other boy fell to the ground, choking and breathing in great whooping gasps, trying to get air into his lungs. Looking at him, Bleys hoped that he was more frightened than hurt.

Behind him the other boys stared; and there was a dead silence from most of the adults, who by this time had also turned their attention to what was going on. It was a silence for a moment only. Then a low, building roar of anger grew among them; and the adults moved forward as a body, and the boys with them.

"Hold it! Just as you are!"

Henry's voice came from the entrance of the church. The moving crowd checked suddenly. Henry had just come out of the church onto its small front porch where Adrian stood, pistol in his holster. Henry had emerged on the side of the constable where the holster hung. He reached down now and closed his hand around the butt of the weapon, but without withdrawing it from its holster.

There was a coldness and a finality to Henry's voice, that

Bleys had never heard before. It was a voice that could and did stop the crowd. The combination of it with his hand on the power pistol that could incinerate them all in seconds, on wide aperture, was more than enough to bring them all to stillness and to silence.

His eyes swept the crowd from side to side, missing no one. *"You all know me!"* The slow, hard words dropped like stones, one by one, upon them.

He paused for a moment.

"No one touches any of my family without dealing with me, first." Once more his eyes swept over them and stopped on a heavy, round-faced man. "Carter Lerner, your boy started that fight. Now, pick him up. He's not hurt."

Indeed, Isaiah, still on the ground, had stopped choking; but he was still breathing in great whooping gasps and holding his throat with one hand.

"Joshua, Will," Henry went on in the continuing silence, as Carter Lerner bent to lift his son to his feet, "get in the goat-cart. You too, Bleys. Adrian—"

He turned to the constable.

"—You can pick your pistol up again at the storekeeper's."

With that, he took the pistol from the holster; and, holding it in his hand with the muzzle down, descended the steps and joined Bleys, Joshua and Will in their movement toward their own goat-cart. In the absence of any sound from the crowd, they got into the cart and drove away down the road.

Henry handled the reins without a word, the pistol in his lap. His sons were equally silent, though both of them threw glances at Bleys, in the back seat of the goat cart, that were clearly intended to be comforting. Henry drove on until he came to the store. Here, finally, he stopped, got out, and spoke to the three boys.

"I'm going to use the storekeeper's phone," he said. "The three of you stay here. I'll be right back."

He went up to the store, which was unlocked. The storekeeper himself had been at the church and was left behind them; but as with everything in this community, no doors were locked. Henry disappeared inside.

The three of them in the cart looked at each other.

"It's not true, is it, Bleys?" asked Will, timidly.

"Shut up, Will," said Joshua, "we don't pay any attention to what people like Isaiah Lerner say."

"They've all always thought you were stuck up, studying by yourself and everything," Will said in a low voice to Bleys, beside him. "They thought you were showing off by fasting. And then—"

"Will," said Joshua, sharply, "you heard me. Let it be."

After that they sat in silence until Henry returned. He got in the goat-cart quite as if it was an ordinary day and an ordinary trip to the storekeeper's.

"We'll go home," Henry announced. "Bleys, I've called Dahno. He'll be here in less than an hour, to pick you up. Get your things ready—everything you want to take with you."

Henry had not said that the packing should be for a permanent parting; but it was easy for Bleys to know this from the tone of his voice. After that one short speech he said nothing more; and none of the boys talked. They returned to the farm as silently as they had left the church.

Bleys packed, also in silence. Joshua and Will perched on Joshua's bunk and watched him; and silently offered a hand to help where it was useful. Joshua also produced another suitcase, for Bleys' possessions had grown over the years. It was with these two suitcases packed that he finally went out the door into the front yard, as the hovercraft came roaring up the road to the farm.

Henry and the two boys followed him out. He turned to them, unsure as to how he should say good-bye. Henry stood a few paces from him, as cold and self-contained as usual.

"Well, Bleys," he said, "your brother will take good care of you, I'm sure. You're always welcome here, in spite of the attitude of our fellow communicants in the church. You've done well and been a big help; and I appreciate it."

"I've liked being here, Uncle Henry," said Bleys.

Joshua hesitated, then stepped forward and offered his hand. Bleys took it; and they held for a long moment, somewhat stiffly but gripping each other strongly.

"Good-bye, Bleys," said Joshua, "come back from time to time."

"I will," said Bleys; and meant it.

He turned to Will. But Will dashed forward at the last moment, threw his arms around him, and hugged him. Bleys hugged him back. It was the first time he could remember ever hugging anyone in his life, with real emotion behind the action. He let go at last and had literally to push Will back from him.

"Good-bye, Will," he said.

"The Lord be with you in all things," said Henry, and the two boys echoed him.

"May the Lord bless you all, also," said Bleys.

It was the ritual answer to what Henry had just said; but Bleys found himself, God or no God, saying it for once with all the fervor with which he had heard the rest of them utter the words. He turned and got into the hovercar, the door of which Dahno was already holding open.

"I'll bring him back from time to time, or see he comes back," Dahno told the three. He walked around the hovercar and got in on his own side. The engines roared to life, the car lifted from the ground to the extent of its skirts; spun, and they drove off down the farm road, onto the highway and away.

They traveled for some distance in silence. They were off the back-country highway and out onto the multi-highway trip before Bleys spoke.

"Interesting that someone should've found out about Mother just now," said Bleys.

"I suppose so," said Dahno, his eyes on the road ahead of him.

There was another pause.

"Only one person could have told them," said Bleys. "Why did you let the word out, Dahno?"

Dahno slowly put the hovercar on autopilot, then turned to look at him for a long moment.

"I had to be sure," he said, "that once you left for good you couldn't go back there again. What else did you expect?"

Their gazes met.

"You're quite right," said Bleys, "I should've expected this."

They looked at each other with naked eyes.

CHAPTER

16

NEITHER OF THEM spoke again on the ride into Ecumeny and even in the elevator up to the suite of rooms that Dahno owned. They acted, it crossed Bleys' mind curiously, like two people who were entirely unconnected with what had brought them together just now.

Dahno left Bleys in the bedroom he always had in Dahno's suite, his suitcases looking strange in their shabbiness among the luxurious surroundings, and went out. Still, neither had said anything more.

Bleys began to unpack. When he was done he lay down on the bed with his hands locked behind his head, staring at the white, arched ceiling.

He was at a breakpoint in his life. It was really not like the breakpoint he had encountered when he had faced up to his mother and been sent away to Henry's farm. Now he was older, more experienced, more capable of controlling any situation in which he found himself. It was a time to think.

He let his mind run. It had always been, for him, best to let the engine that he carried in his head find its own way to its own answers, rather than try to force it in one direction or another.

He had not expected this, of all things. Though he should have, he reproached himself again. Knowing Dahno, he should have known that his older brother would want to assure himself that Bleys' change from the farm to Ecumeny was permanent; and that Bleys would be completely under Dahno's control when the change came.

But Bleys had not known. Unthinkingly, he had expected that the visits to Ecumeny would grow longer and longer; so that, as he grew older, he would gradually break away from Henry and the boys at the farm. But it had not gone that way—and now it was too late to do anything about it.

He was here, and he was—at least for the present—completely dependent upon Dahno.

To this day, he had never identified Dahno's real aim in life; and what end it was toward which his older brother was working. Without knowing these things, he had no way of guessing what part Dahno expected Bleys to play in it.

His mind veered, as minds do. He had never come so close to an outright display of emotion as in that moment in which Will had run forward and thrown his arms around him, as if to keep him at the farm. A long time since, Bleys had asked himself if he was simply cold by nature. But he had watched himself and kept track of his own feelings, and knew now he was not.

Only, by the very nature of being the person he was, he was set off, apart from the rest of the human race; able to see its other members only as something outside and beyond him.

—And he still did not know what Dahno's goal was.

He did know now that his older brother actually did a great deal of actual counseling; and that much of this was, indeed, financial. But it was also political, and personal—and covered half a dozen other areas of commerce as well. Essentially, Dahno seemed to act like nothing so much as an adviser in general.

"The Golden Ear," one of his clients had told Bleys, a little drunkenly, one evening, as the two of them were seated at the table in the restaurant where Dahno always held court. It was at a moment when Dahno had stepped away from them and the table to talk privately with somebody else. "That's what your brother's known as, did you know that? The Golden Ear!"

"Why Golden?" asked Bleys.

The other winked. He was a fat man with a face much thinner than his body, so that seated he did not seem to be the unwieldly person he showed himself to be once he got to his feet and his potbelly became visible. A few remnants of hair were carefully arranged on his balding head.

"Golden—because what he tells you pays off," said the man. "Oh, I don't mean to say he doesn't make a mistake now and then. But he's right most of the time—and more important than that—the most important thing is he usually thinks of a way to do something you wouldn't have thought of yourself. A way in, or a way out—"

He winked again.

"—Know what I mean?"

The return of Dahno to the table put an end to this conversation. But Bleys had stored it away in his head over a year ago, for future reference. It backed up what he had suspected from the minute he had seen the room with the scanning machines and the books. Dahno dealt in information. But the surprising thing was, he did not seem to sell that information, but simply to give it away.

Undoubtedly, Bleys told himself now, lying on the bed, as he had told himself many times before, there must be a payment for each piece of advice given, somehow. He must also have to pay for things, himself. But so far neither of these transactions had been visible—to Bleys at least.

The payments to Dahno must come in unorthodox ways, Bleys told himself now. But the payments the big man made—these also had been invisible. Dahno might very well get or make some payments in the ordinary way at his office, for most of the things he did. On the other hand, in the restaurant, no one seemed even to keep track of what was

ordered at his table, let alone present him with a check or bill
for it.

The suggestion that came to Bleys now was that the pay
could be in something other than money . . . something that
was capable of satisfying the kind of bills that were usually
answered with money.

Bleys had never seen his older brother handle anything in the
form of cash. Perhaps he did not handle cash at all. That would
account for the fact that his presents to Henry were always in
the shape of things that Henry could use; rather than outright
currency, local or interstellar, which Bleys had come to know
his uncle could have found much more useful—if, of course,
he was willing to accept it. Henry was just as likely to be
stiff-necked enough to refuse.

Lying on the bed, Bleys came to the conclusion that he was
not going to solve that problem here and now. What he would
need to do in the days to come was to keep his eyes open and
collect information until he was able to come to some more
solid conclusions. Above all, he must not underestimate Dahno
himself.

He had only one thing to go on as far as a hope that he might
beat Dahno in whatever game of wits into which his older
brother had drawn him. It was his innate belief in his own
superiority; and a strange sort of certainty in him that his view
was wider and deeper, his dreams were larger, than any Dahno
would have.

This conclusion was based not on any solid evidence, but
simply on his general experience with his older brother.
Somehow Dahno was much closer to the ordinary mass of
humanity; from which Bleys, like it or not, was so distant and
apart. That extra distance could give Bleys an edge when the
time came.

He forced his mind off the subject. A little more, and he
would be running around in circles. He recognized the symp-
toms of just such circular thoughts in himself now. It was as he
had told himself before. Nothing could be really decided until
he had more evidence.

He turned his mind deliberately to another subject. It was

only in these past few years that he had begun to notice time. Up until then he had assumed that he had an infinity of time in which to work; and that most of his larger questions would find their answers automatically as he grew older. But a lot of them had not.

For one thing, what was it he, Bleys, wanted from life?

He forced himself to look squarely at the limited years, months and days of his own likely existence. Suppose he gave himself the longest possible lifetime—say a hundred and twenty years during which he could be active and useful. What a drop that still was in the ocean of time that was the history of the human race itself.

He did not want to be just a drop in the ocean of past history, his ripples spreading out and affecting the rest for a moment, and then gone. With his abilities, he should not be. His whole self rebelled against the idea that he could live and die without having had any important impact upon the rest of humanity.

He had never thought about this before. His hands pulled out from behind his head and clenched themselves into fists. He must find some greater value for himself than the millions of others had, who made up this teeming mass called the human race.

He must do something the rest could not do. Some one thing only, maybe, but a single thing that would change the race itself for all time into the future—or at least as far as his mind could envision.

To do that he must touch them all; and at present he had only touched a few dozen. At most a hundred. And they had been glancing touches. In no way had he altered what they were or where they were going.

For the first time in his life, he felt the moments of his lifetime slipping away from him, like sand from the top of an hourglass to the bottom—grain by grain only, but in a steady succession that would eventually leave the top of the hourglass empty. There must be something he could do with his life. But he must identify it before he could start to work at it; and right now he had no idea what it could be.

He thought of himself again as standing light-years out and

away, from the sixteen worlds on which the individuals of the human race were born, lived and died. He imagined looking at them from that great distance. They were an unorganized mass, changing even as he watched them. What good to affect any one, or any number of them, if those he affected would die and his affect on them be buried with them?

There must be something bigger, something permanent, he could do.

He tried to picture them as a race, apart. There was much, very much, that was good about them. There was much that was bad. They had spread out from their original home to fifteen other worlds. But what they were on all those worlds now was largely what they had been when they first began to stand upright and think on Old Earth. They were still the same people.

Perhaps there was some way in which he could help them up the stairs, even one step toward being something better. Something more capable—as he was capable.

The moment that thought occurred to him, he knew that he had found it. *That* was what he wanted to do. He wanted to help humanity up—just one step forward. Just one. Hopefully, then, with momentum helping them, they would keep climbing. But at least that one, first step should be taken; and he should bring about the taking of it. How?

That question stood like a living thing before his eyes in the pleasant dimness of the artificially-lighted bedroom. But it was not a question to be answered in this instant, or even in the next few weeks, months or even years. But it must be answered soon, so that he could be about the business of accomplishing it—

The door of his bedroom swung open suddenly and the huge frame of Dahno filled it. His smile and his voice were no different than they had been hundreds of times before when Bleys had been in visiting. It was as if what had happened at Henry's had never taken place.

"All right, now! Let's get to the business of planning what you're going to be doing from now on."

Bleys made up his mind. He took his hands from behind his

head, swung himself to his feet and walked out through the doorway, as Dahno stood aside to let him through it. He went into the lounge and sat down in one of the huge chairs, his long forearms extended along the tops of the massive armrests of the over-padded piece of furniture.

"No," he said.

Dahno came over from near the doorway where he had been standing and sat down in one of the big chairs opposite him. His face was puzzled and concerned.

"What's this?" he asked. "I don't understand, Bleys."

"I'm sorry," Bleys said, "but that's the way it is. I'm not going along with you any further until you tell me exactly what you've got in mind for me."

Dahno leaned forward with his elbows on his knees. His face was more concerned than ever.

"But I told you," he said. His voice was warm and worried. "Remember—the first time I took you to my regular restaurant. On the way home from that visit I told you when we stopped just before getting back to the farm. I said *'you're remembering our mother. Don't. I'm not her. If nothing else, I want something much greater than she ever wanted. But what that is you're going to have to find out for yourself. Find out for yourself, and then decide if you want any part of it. That way I know you're coming in with me completely of your own free will. All right?'*—and you told me it was all right."

Dahno had recited what he had said then, almost word for word. Bleys was not particularly impressed by this, since he could do the same thing himself. In fact, he did so, now.

"*'For now, anyway,'* was what I told you then," answered Bleys. "Well, this is nearly five years later. Now I need something more than that. Look at me, Dahno. I'll be twenty before very long. I'm a different person and this is a different world for both of us, than when you told me what you just said and I agreed to it—for then."

"Do you remember," said Dahno, "asking me a few moments before that why I was interested in you?"

"I remember exactly—as you do," Bleys said.

"Remember then," said Dahno, "what I told you. In brief,

I said I was the only other person on all the sixteen worlds, including Old Earth, who knew and understood you, and understood what you were capable of. I also knew about your isolation—because I'm isolated the same way. But I pointed out that even if neither of us could do anything about our isolations, we could at least have a connection, a friendship, a joint endeavor between the two of us, you and I."

"You also said you could use me," Bleys answered, "but when I asked you how you didn't tell me. Well, the time has come when I've got to know how. It's as simple as that."

"Little Brother," said Dahno, almost sadly, "do you know what it means for you if you cut yourself off from me? I'm not universally loved, you know. You may not be aware of it but there are a few people who don't like me and who I have to be on guard against. You'd be easy pickings for them, since you know nothing about them or why they'd want you. But they'd think if they took you they'd have a card to use against me."

"And would they?" Bleys asked.

"Unfortunately," Dahno's face hardened for just a second, "they wouldn't. The one thing I can't ever afford to give in to is any kind of blackmail. Which would mean the end of you, Little Brother. You need me to stay alive."

"Maybe," said Bleys, "on the other hand—maybe not. You see, I don't really know these enemies you tell me about exist. The people who might come after me, who'd kidnap me, or whatever you were referring to, may be just your own people, putting pressure on me to get me back in line. Perhaps, if I'm not with you, you're safer off with me dead. Could that be so—Big Brother?"

"Ah," said Dahno softly, and once more sadly, "the milk-teeth have begun to fall out."

His face became very serious indeed.

"Bleys," he said, slowly and with emphasis, "I don't know whether it would be safe for me with you alive and not working with me."

"Explain," said Bleys.

"Because it depends on you," Dahno said. "Would you take it into your head to become a threat to me? Would I get in the way eventually of whatever you were doing on your own? The possibility of both things are there. That's why I don't know. But I do know that the safe way is for us to stay together, and keep working together. I think you need me."

"I do need you," said Bleys; and the back of his mind held an entirely different meaning to those words than the one he knew he was giving Dahno. "The trouble is, that doesn't change things. Even if everything you've said to me is true, it doesn't change things. I've outgrown being a pawn of yours. If I'm to be a partner, it's time that I started being admitted to the inner rooms of what's going on. Otherwise, I'm going to have to assume there's no real partnership there. I'll have to assume you're planning to use me for a pawn all my life. I can't live like that, Dahno."

Their eyes met.

"Believe me," said Bleys, "I can't live like that. You know I can't, being who and what I am."

Dahno sighed, a little bitterly.

"You're remembering our mother," he said. "Please don't. I told you I'm not her. As I told you, if nothing else I want something much greater than she ever wanted, but while I can open things up a little bit for you I can't, I daren't for my own safety, let you know everything that I'm doing right now. If I can see—if I know—what you said just now I had to know, then you have to see and know that. I'll tell you what I'll do. I'll tell you my goal for you is to be my right-hand man."

He paused, waiting for Bleys to speak. But Bleys stayed silent.

"Of course," he said, "you won't have as large a share as I will. No one ever will. But you'll have the next largest share after me. Now that's as much as I can tell you. For the rest, what I said in the first place is still true. What I'm doing, how I'm doing it, are things you're going to have to find out for yourself. *Then* come and tell me if you want any part of it as my right-hand man. Will that do you?"

Bleys sat in silence for a moment, turning his brother's words over.

"For now, anyway," he answered finally, "all right."

One of the huge hands was extended toward him. Bleys took it in his own narrow, long fingers.

For a moment their grasp held firmly, and a current of truth and real feeling ran between them that Bleys could feel. Then the grip broke, the feeling was gone; and the arms fell apart.

"Now!" Dahno stood up, his voice brisk, and the smile back on his face. "As I said some minutes back, let's get to the business of introducing you to what you're going to be doing from now on."

CHAPTER

17

THE VISITORS' GALLERY of the Room of Speakers, that assemblage of concentric arcs of desks mounting, amphitheater style, from the center of the room which was the center also of the government of the world of Association, was not open to ordinary visitors.

Bleys had seen Dahno pin a green and white badge on his jacket as they came down the corridor toward the gallery's entrance; and after doing this he handed a similar badge to Bleys.

"Stick it to your jacket where I did," Dahno said.

Bleys complied. By the time he had it hooked they were at the entrance, guarded by a black-uniformed, military-looking guard with a power pistol in an open holster at his side. This man smiled genially at Dahno as the two came up; but frowned at Bleys and raised a hand palm outward in front of him, stepping in front of him to examine his badge closely.

Dahno and Bleys both stopped.

"My partner in the firm," said Dahno, "also my younger brother. Tom, I'd like to have you meet Bleys Ahrens."

The guard dropped his hand.

"You're welcome to the visitors' gallery, Bleys Ahrens," he said.

It was an answer, Bleys noticed, that avoided both the "honored . . ." salutation common on the worlds generally on any formal occasion, and at the same time skirted any of the special forms of address used by the various churches.

"Thank you," said Dahno before Bleys could answer, smiling genially at the guard. He and Bleys went inside to the gallery.

"Never forget the little people," Dahno said to Bleys softly, as they left the guard behind, "they can be useful when you want an exception to a rule."

At the moment the gallery seemed empty of other watchers. There were a dozen rows of seats, capable of holding perhaps fifty observers, ranked in three tiers down to the balcony edge itself, and split by an aisle. Dahno descended the aisle just ahead of Bleys, and stepped into a seat in the front row, to his left. He sat down, and gestured to Bleys to take the seat beside him, which Bleys did.

The balcony before them was low enough so that they could see most of the space below, with its semicircle of desks for the representatives elected to the chamber. The walls were of dark stone, mounting to a high-domed inner ceiling, also of the same stone; the lighting was below the level of the balcony around the room and mainly directed downward for the use of the representatives.

The color of the dark stone drank up that light; and this, together with the somber blacks and grays of the representatives' clothes, gave the whole place a cave-like appearance, as if it had been some chamber hollowed out of rock.

At the flat end where the semicircles of seats ceased, there was a raised dais and a pulpit in which a speaker could stand with straight lines of other seats behind it arranged in two ranks. There was space for perhaps twenty-four people behind whoever was speaking.

Only one of the seats there was occupied right now, by a man who sat rather carelessly in one of the places off to the left of the speaker, with his legs crossed and no desk surface raised in front of him. He seemed more a casual watcher, than a member of the assembly itself. This puzzled Bleys, since the assembly appeared fairly full of people listening to the speaker currently in the pulpit.

"Someday," said Dahno, "I'll probably be sending you here to listen to the debates and votes on some propositions. That's the Chief Speaker with his legs crossed, sitting behind the speaker who's talking now. The Chief Speaker's name is Shin Lee. He polled enough votes in our last election to have taken the title of Eldest from the chief representative on Harmony; but until Harmony has another election, he remains simply Chief Speaker. His church is The Repentance Church."

"How much power has he, compared to the rest of them?" asked Bleys, fascinated by the whole situation—the cave-like chamber, the empty seats behind the pulpit and full ones before it, and the odd names.

"Less, in some ways, officially," said Dahno; "he can cast a tie-breaking vote, but otherwise he's got no vote at all. On the other hand, outside this chamber he has enormous power. He controls the militia and the governmental apparatus all over the world, plus having the right to step in on any deadlocked dispute within one of the other churches, or between churches, and cast a deciding vote. But his great advantage is his prestige. He's responsible, ultimately responsible, for defense of this planet; and if he ever acquires the title of Eldest, he'll be responsible for the defense of both planets."

Bleys took his eyes momentarily off the scene below, to look at Dahno.

"Why," he said, "nobody's ever attacked a whole world, let alone two of them, since Donal Graeme attacked Newton—and that was—it must be nearly a hundred years ago."

"I know," said Dahno, without taking his gaze from the scene below, "but whoever is Eldest still has the power, just the same. He can also legislate, or even initiate legislation for both planets' chambers to consider. Watch what's going on."

Bleys looked back down into the room of speakers.

"The one talking right now," Dahno said, "is Svarnam Helt.

What he's saying isn't too important. It's a speech he makes every so often." He keyed the control panel on the top rail of the balcony before each of the seats, and the voice of the speaker came clearly to their ears.

"—*And these temples must be cleansed. They must be cleansed now*—"

"No point in listening to all of it," said Dahno, "it's a piece of general legislation, designed to deliberately attack a couple of the churches that his church doesn't like—a lot. The measure he's proposing'll go nowhere. Otherwise, though, Helt swings a lot of weight, politically. He's consulted me from time to time. In fact, probably most of the rank and file Speakers here have, one time or another. You won't remember them from my table at the restaurant, because they don't like to be seen talking to me in public—"

Bleys stored that particular, last piece of information for future use.

"—But a lot of them consult," Dahno was going on, "and a lot of them are important. Now, if you'll look over near the end of the eighth row up, there's a man with reddish-gray hair, a rather full, red beard, and wearing a turban, seated near the end of the row. That's Harold Harold, of the Church of the Understanding. He's powerful. So is the woman you saw at my consulting restaurant, that time, sitting in the seat beyond the empty seat to Harold's right . . ."

Dahno went on identifying various members of the chamber, and telling Bleys what churches they represented.

Bleys sat, absorbing the information Dahno was giving him and storing it away. This was the first time that his brother had made any move that resembled directly helping Bleys to understand what the other did.

Instinctively, Bleys felt the importance of everything being said to him. Even if he never had anything to do with the particular person being identified, knowing would help to fill in the matrix of understanding he was gradually building about his older half-brother.

"Which ones are the Five Sisters?" Bleys asked, when Dahno at last stopped talking.

Dahno looked at him curiously.

"That's stuck in your memory, has it?" Dahno said. "Well, outside of the woman I just pointed out, they aren't all five together here, all the time, like a matched set of spoons. But there's one of them down there now, if you'll look in almost the very back row, over to the right, the man wearing a business suit with a bald head and large, bushy beard that looks completely white from here but is actually sort of gray going on white. That's Brother Williams of the Faithful Church. The only time you'll see all five together will be when a particularly important bit of lawmaking is going on in which they're all united, strongly trying to swing the room to vote the way they want."

Bleys searched that part of the floor below, squinting his eyes against the way the lighting was set up, and finally identified the man that Dahno was talking about. He would have gone on to ask more questions, but at that moment somebody else walked down the gallery aisle, looking at them, and moved over into the tier of seats across the aisle from them to its very end.

"We better get going," said Dahno, in a low voice.

They got up and went out. Outside, the corridor that led to the visitors' gallery was of the same dark stone, but less oddly lit than the gallery and the room itself had been, so that it seemed almost like an ordinary corridor anywhere. Right now it was empty; except for one short, rather fat man who was passing just as they came out. They had only taken half a dozen steps when a voice behind them called out.

"Ahrens! You there! Just a minute! I want a word with you!"

Dahno sighed a little under his breath and turned. Bleys turned with him. Approaching them was the rather plump man who had just passed them in the corridor. He was wearing something between a kilt and a skirt, below which his puffy knees looked ridiculous. A regular shirt and jacket clothed his upper body. And on his head he wore a black beret. Red hair peeped out in untidy swatches from around the edges of the beret.

When Dahno and Bleys turned, they stood where they were

and the man walked back up to them. He ignored Bleys and spoke directly and fiercely to Dahno.

"You shouldn't even be in this building!" the man snapped.

Close up, Bleys saw that it was his extra weight that had made him look no more than middle age. Actually, he must be at least high in his fifties or even older.

"It's just a matter of time! We'll get you ruled out of here!"

"I'm sorry I'm in the way," said Dahno.

"You're not sorry at all. You're one of God's outcasts and incapable of feeling sorry!" retorted the fat man. His gaze switched suddenly to Bleys.

"Who's this?"

"My brother, Bleys Ahrens. And partner," said Dahno.

"He'll be kept out too! Anyone connected with you or knows you, shouldn't be here!"

He turned about and stamped off once more in the direction in which he had been headed when they had emerged from the gallery.

Dahno looked down at Bleys and smiled a little.

"A few enemies are inevitable," he said softly. "Now, we'll swing by the office; and I'll see what's going on there."

So they went to Dahno's office. It was the first time Bleys had been in the place since that long-ago first long weekend with Dahno. But it was as if he had stepped out only five minutes before. The same two women were at the same two desks working through reams of paper, reading them, making notes and dropping the pieces of paper they had read, which Bleys now saw were message transcripts, into a flare box beside their desks, so that they were instantly converted to ash.

Dahno led the way toward the further door to his interior office, but Bleys turned abruptly, walked over to the nearest desk and began examining the pile of so-far unread messages there.

"Dahno Ahrens!" shouted the woman behind the desk, reaching out to cover the two piles with her hands.

Bleys looked over at Dahno, who smiled a little wickedly.

"That's all right, Arah," he said, "this is my half-brother and partner, remember? Let him look."

Reluctantly, and still looking shocked, the woman withdrew her hands from the piles of messages. Intrigued, Bleys paged through them. They were all in code. He studied every one he came to for a moment. Then he let go, nodded and smiled at Arah, and went back to Dahno, who led him into the further office.

Dahno sat down behind the large desk which was now piled with neat stacks of paper, nowhere near as high or as loose as the ones on the desks of the two women outside. Bleys took one of the overstuffed armchairs.

"Be with you in a moment," said Dahno.

Bleys watched as Dahno rapidly read through the stacks of paper on his desk. Dahno did not read, Bleys noticed, quite as quickly as he himself did—but then the material might be something that required more minute attention. Dahno sat back and punched a button on his desk control pad.

"All right," he said, "you can come in and collect everything now, Arah."

The woman who had been behind the desk where Bleys had examined the pictures came in and gathered up the papers from Dahno's desk. She gave Bleys a tentative smile, and carried the papers out. Dahno rose.

"And now," he said to Bleys, "I want to get you enrolled with the rest of my executives-in-training."

He led the way out as he had led it in. In the white hovercar they moved through the streets again, streets now beginning to fill with traffic as the afternoon grew late, and drove until they came to a place that Bleys remembered—the apartment building in the rather run-down district.

This time there were none of the trainees in the front room relaxing, with drinks or otherwise. Dahno led the way on through and they came at last on the inhabitants of this place in the gym, clearly undergoing martial arts training under the eye of a brown, quiet man about five feet nine or ten, who in spite of his unremarkable size radiated a remarkable air of physical competence.

"Sit down," Dahno said to Bleys, himself taking a seat in

the first tier of benches against the wall. Bleys sat down beside him.

They sat for a short while, watching. Bleys had had brief periods of instruction from various instructors in combative sports, Earth-traditional martial arts, and combat systems that had grown up on several worlds. If the ongoing session was typical, the instruction here tended toward Earth-traditional systems. Right at the moment, the students were practicing one of the more basic judo hip throws, while the instructor walked among them offering encouragement or criticism or demonstrating some fine detail that defied verbal explanation. Bleys couldn't recall the name of the technique, if he had ever known it.

After a few moments, the instructor clapped his hands and the students separated and lined up along the edge of the practice surface.

"*Randori*. Fifteen minutes. *Hajime!*"

So, thought Bleys, remembering the judo training he had had while still with his mother. This *sensei* was a traditionalist. Old-Earth Japanese.

The students paired off and began their free-exercise session. Bleys liked this aspect of the training less. From the one or two vid-tapes he had seen, he suspected that the exacting discipline of the formal *kata* led to deeper understanding and mastery. There was a beauty to a *kata*, properly done, like the beauty he had found in a mathematical proof.

The instructor detached himself from the class and walked over to where Dahno and Bleys were.

Dahno had risen to his feet as the other approached and Bleys followed his example. As the instructor came up to stop before them, Dahno inclined his head briefly and the instructor did the same. Bleys, aware at least of this much of ordinary *dojo* courtesy, bent his own head more deeply.

"*Sensei*," Dahno said, "this is my brother, Bleys Ahrens. I would appreciate his being trained up to the level of these others, or beyond if he wishes."

The dark brown eyes of the *sensei* turned on Bleys.

"He's had some bits and pieces of instruction in martial

arts," said Dahno—surprising Bleys, who had no idea of how Dahno could have discovered that.

"Tell me," said the *sensei* to Bleys, "in your own words, what have you been taught?"

Bleys thought it politic to identify only the traditional systems to which he had been exposed. Most traditional instructors had a rather parochial contempt for the eclectic and synthetic combat systems that had sprouted in such profusion on the New Worlds. Apart from this judicious editing, Bleys told him as concisely as possible that he had had several periods of training not more than three months at the longest, two periods concerned with judo, one in karate and about three weeks in an *aikido dojo*, which he greatly preferred.

"What I teach in these classes," the *sensei* told him, speaking as if Dahno were not there at all, directly to Bleys, "is the three disciplines you've encountered, and one or two that are more obscure. It is regrettable that your learning has been so unsystematic, but it is good that you began young. Students who begin early have fewer bad habits to overcome when they take up serious training. Do you have a *do-gi*?"

"He has," spoke Dahno from the sidelines as it were, "I had one put in a locker for him here. Locker number forty-two."

"Put it on," said the *sensei*, "and we'll see if you remember how to fall."

Bleys found the training uniform and put it on. The trousers tied at the waist with a drawstring and were cut from an unbleached white cloth that was as heavy and stiff as the work pants he'd worn on Uncle Henry's farm. The jacket was a loose white robe that fell about the middle of his thigh. It was sewn from a coarsely woven fabric and was heavily reinforced around the collar and lapels with a wide strip of the same cloth as the trousers. He was pleased that he recalled how to tie the long, quilted belt that held the jacket from hanging open. He was not surprised that the belt was a plain, unbroken white, although those on the practice floor wore belts of various colors, but none black. Only the *sensei* himself wore, not only a black belt, but a black *do-gi* that was otherwise of the same pattern and dimensions as Bleys' own.

Bleys came back and stood on the sidelines where he had stood before. Dahno had disappeared and Bleys stood waiting, feeling a little overwhelmed—almost a little shy in the presence of this group.

The *sensei* paid no attention to him for a short while. The other students were going through a grappling *kata* that Bleys did not recognize, working in pairs. Most of them were down on the mats after taking a formal, stylized throw and struggling there for an advantage. None of them seemed to look at him directly, but Bleys caught momentary glimpses directed at him; and he felt very strongly the feeling he had felt when he had first stepped into the front room of this establishment. Those in training here felt no kindness toward him. There was an obvious aura of resentment from them.

If the *sensei* felt this too, he completely ignored it. After a while he called a halt to what was going on and beckoned Bleys toward him. When Bleys came up to him he led him to one of the men wearing a brown belt, a tall man not quite Bleys' height but clearly in his early twenties at least and obviously outweighing Bleys by something upwards of twenty pounds.

"This is James," said the *sensei* to Bleys, "and, James—this is Bleys. I want you to work with him for a while."

James was a broad-shouldered man with a shock of blond hair and a square face. He did not smile at Bleys, but inclined his head in a bow. Bleys matched the bow.

The *sensei* went back and addressed the class.

"We'll work on combinations now. Easy throws followed by either *katame-waza*, joint-lock technique, or *shime-waza*, strangle technique. Don't fight your partner's throws. The throw is just an entry into the arm-bar or the choke."

"*Hajime!*" It was the command to begin.

James smiled at Bleys and bowed. It was not a particularly welcoming or friendly smile.

Bleys remembered to return the bow before reaching for James' sleeve and lapel. The fundamentals came back naturally. Don't grip the lapel too tightly; don't pick up your feet, slide them—but not too close together. It was almost a dance.

Tentatively, Bleys stepped into position for a basic hip throw. James' arm on his lapel suddenly became rigid, and Bleys stumbled backward, momentarily off balance. He looked at his partner inquiringly. The *sensei* had said not to fight the throw. James' face was innocently impassive.

Bleys relaxed. All right, he, Bleys, would take the first fall. James made no attempt to throw him, but worked his right hand up Bleys' lapel so that he now gripped the collar behind Bleys' neck. Bleys could feel the knuckle of his partner's thumb against the base of his skull. With his own hand no longer snugged against James' chest, he could not stiff-arm the other and keep him away. Once again Bleys twisted his body sideways and slid forward to attempt a throw.

As he did, James shifted his left hand from Bleys' sleeve to the left lapel of his *do-gi* and snaked his right forearm over Bleys' head, while keeping his grip on the collar. The brown belt scissored his crossed forearms, pressing them against Bleys' carotid arteries. Bleys remembered the technique— *gyaku-juji-shime*, reverse cross strangle.

Bleys was turned away from James and half bent over. When he jerked to straighten up he felt his legs swept out from under him. He was too startled to remember to slap the mat to break his fall, and the painful impact knocked the last of his air out of his lungs.

Bleys made up his mind to hang on for as long as possible in hopes that he might at least make a good impression upon the other trainees and the *sensei*.

Very swiftly, however, he felt his senses leaving him. His peripheral vision clouded with a red haze as his brain, deprived of blood through its two main arteries, became starved for oxygen. At the edge of unconsciousness, he released James' sleeve and tapped lightly on the other's arm, the signal of surrender.

But the pressure was not relaxed. He tapped again, more urgently. But still the pressure remained.

Then, as he began to slide completely into unconsciousness, Bleys found awareness coming back to him. James had released the hold momentarily. Bleys was just beginning to feel a sense of relief when the pressure was resumed; and once more he began to slip into unconsciousness.

Again, he went almost into, if not completely into it before James let him up. This time, as soon as Bleys was able to do so he gasped out one word.

"Dahno."

Almost magically, it was so instantaneous, the hold was relaxed completely.

Bleys lay where he was for a moment, simply recovering. His mind had saved him from what promised to be a very rough initiation indeed. James had been taking this opportunity to express the group's resentment against Bleys' supposedly favored status. But he had obviously not thought it through that Bleys had Dahno's ear; and might tell the huge man of what had been done to him. In which case, James himself might suffer.

After a bit Bleys stirred, pushed himself up on one elbow and then got to his feet. James rose with him.

Following that, James offered only token resistance to Bleys' throws and performed his own throws with suitable restraint, following them with grappling techniques that were quickly applied and released on Bleys' signal. At all times now, James' handling of him was considerate, not to say delicate. This went on for another fifteen minutes or so, when the exercise class was at last dismissed by the *sensei*.

Bleys walked over to his locker to hang up his *do-gi* and change back into his ordinary clothes. He was a little disappointed that the *sensei* had shown no sign of seeing what had happened. He felt sure that if he had, he would have put a stop to it right at the very beginning. On the other hand, perhaps his treatment had actually been instigated by the *sensei* to test him.

In either case, the episode would have to go unreported. It went against Bleys' grain to actually complain to Dahno. Besides, Bleys was sure doing so would not raise him in his brother's eyes. And it was not beyond possibility that the incident had been Dahno's idea. Plainly, he would have to conquer the trainees' dislike of him on his own.

Dahno had reappeared by this time, as if he knew—which

probably he did—when the class was due to end. He led Bleys back out.

"Tomorrow, you'll start joining them not only in the exercise classes but in the classroom sessions," he told Bleys as they walked toward the front of the building and the door that would let them out to the elevator.

"You'll find that the sort of thing they're being taught is something you could learn on your own in a fraction of the time, given someone experienced to work with and the necessary books. But I want you to spend some time with them anyway and get to know them. Above all, they've got to get to know you. We aren't going to emphasize from the first that you're destined for a higher position with me than any of them are. They've probably guessed it; but I want it to sink in as a fact on them gradually."

He smiled at Bleys; and Bleys heard the unspoken order. He would have to dominate these men before Dahno would publicly acknowledge any superiority in him.

He had begun talking as soon as they were outside the apartment and beyond the earshot of anyone within. They had taken the lift down and were back in the car before he spoke again.

"I've got things to do," he said, "but I'll drop you off at home. Undoubtedly, you'll find something there to amuse yourself with."

"Yes," said Bleys.

Dahno smiled again, looking at the road ahead. Curiously, Bleys thought, in his smile this time there was something like a touch of genuine pleasure.

CHAPTER

18

DAHNO DID NOT even come up to the apartment with Bleys; he merely reached across, opened the door and said, "I've got to get going." He drove off.

Bleys rode up on the elevator, his mind still full of the problem of settling in with the other trainees at the *dojo*. He had considered the possibility, in fact the certainty, that sooner or later he would have to arrange to dominate in his own right all those whom Dahno could dominate. This, before he could think of possibly coming to any kind of a conclusion with Dahno himself. He had not thought confrontation with one of the trainees would come quite so soon.

There was a classic Exotic pattern for this sort of situation normally. It consisted first of making friends individually with everybody concerned; and then gradually allowing his natural superiority to show until he was accepted by all in a leadership position. A problem in this instance would be the fact that he could not start making friends until he had first mended matters between himself and James. Otherwise with each new friend

he made James would be pushed further and further into dislike
and enmity.

Dislike could be a reaction, not only toward those who had
acted unfairly toward you, but those to whom you had acted
unfairly. In the latter case, dislike served as an excuse to
yourself for what you had done. What James would need
would be some excuse for what he had done that would remove
his need to personally dislike Bleys.

By the time he had reached this point in his thoughts, Bleys
had also let himself into the apartment. He put the whole
matter of James, the *dojo* and the rest of the trainees out of his
mind. He had learned early that one of the most valuable
abilities to cultivate was that of being able to concentrate
exclusively on any problem he wanted to solve. To put out of
his mind absolutely what he did not want to intrude on his
thoughts. It was the habit of dividing different problems into
compartments where they could be forgotten while others were
attended to.

Now there was other work to be done.

He searched around the apartment until he found in a writing
desk a pile of sheets with Dahno's letterhead on them,
obviously there for correspondence purposes. They were of a
plastic so well made that it had the very feel of paper itself, an
expensive version of such to find on one of the Younger
Worlds.

He took a stack of these back to the dining table with him
and sat down, placing the stack upside down so that he had the
blank back of each sheet to work on. With this and the desk pen
in hand, he concentrated on the blank sheets; and began to key
in his memory of the messages he had looked at in Dahno's
office.

Bleys did not have a natural eidetic memory. But both of his
own intention, and with Exotic techniques he had been taught
at his mother's insistence, he had cultivated into permanence
the extremely tenacious memory of early childhood; and
supplemented that with a version of autohypnosis, so that in
nearly all cases he was able to summon up a visual picture in
his mind of what he wanted to remember.

He envisioned the first message he had scanned in Dahno's office and copied down the symbols and letters that had been there. Then he put that message from his mind and went on to copy the next, until all were written out.

He ended up with some twenty sheets of coded messages. He compared these and made counts of the number of times of reappearances of the same symbols, and particularly the same symbols in conjunction with other symbols, and began to try breaking the code.

It turned out not to be extremely difficult. Bleys liked doing puzzles; and the code was a simple commercial one, not meant to stand up under intensive decoding efforts. Within a little more than a couple of hours he had reduced all the messages to plain ordinary Basic, the language spoken on all the Younger Worlds; and understood, if not spoken by, a majority of the people on Old Earth.

He took a break, made himself a sandwich, got a glass of juice and brought these back to the table where he could eat and drink while studying the messages.

The interesting thing was that the messages were cryptic in themselves. They were all very short. Their contents meant nothing to Bleys in most cases because he did not know what use Dahno had for the information in them.

He could make guesses and that was all. For example, the first one he looked at said briefly:

"*V.* (That could stand for *variform*—there were almost none of the New Worlds on which an edible plant, fish or animal existed that was not originally of Old Earth and had needed to have been genetically tailored to the planet's non-Earth environment) *winter wheat up twelve points.*"

It was very obviously a bit of news that Dahno could somehow put to use in counseling one of the people he advised here on Association. It was also obviously a quotation from a commodities market report of the world it came from.

Bleys looked at the point of sending, printed at the top of the letter; which, uncoded, now read "*New Earth.*" He could think of nothing in common between the climates and growing conditions of New Earth under the star of Sirius A, and

Association under Epsilon Eridani, that would make agricultural information from one valuable on the other—but undoubtedly there was a reason that lay beyond the area of his present knowledge.

It was the same with the rest of the messages. They were all now comprehensible; but they were also obscure. None of them asked questions, all of them reported facts. Facts which Dahno would certainly be putting to use in the sorting and computing equipment of that research-equipped room off his own personal office, that he had shown Bleys on their first trip to that location.

Struck by a sudden thought, Bleys went through the pile again, this time paying attention to the places from which the messages had been sent.

He found the result interesting.

Of the fifteen New Worlds over half were represented as sources from which Dahno was getting mail. Mentally Bleys compiled a list of Newton, Cassida, New Earth, Freiland, Harmony, Ste. Marie and Ceta. That made, with the addition of Association, the world he was on right now, and which was obviously Dahno's headquarters, a total of eight of the fifteen Younger Worlds, on which Dahno had connections.

This plainly revealed a much larger organization than Bleys had imagined his brother to control. It was also pretty good evidence that this set of trainees was not the first that had been sent out.

Bleys decided that the whole intent of Dahno's activities called for further investigation.

He did not have a key to the office as he had one to the apartment. He glanced at the wrist monitor that Dahno had given him, and asked it for the time. The answer came back—twenty-seven minutes after three of the afternoon. Provided Dahno himself was not using his office right now, there should only be the two women on duty; and Dahno had already established Bleys' right of entry and action to them.

Accordingly, Bleys called an autocar service and thirty minutes later an automatically programmed hovercar delivered him to the front door of the building in which Dahno's office was located.

He went up to the office and entered, smiling, through the door, waving at the two women at their desks as he passed and heading for the entrance to Dahno's private office.

"We're closing up in about five minutes, Bleys Ahrens," the one called Arah called after him. He checked and turned about, still with his smile.

"You go right ahead," he said, "I'll wait for Dahno in his office."

Turning, he went on through the door into Dahno's office and closed it behind him.

It was not at all the office he was interested in, however, but the equipment room beyond its one wall. He let himself into this, and went about examining the various computing and other equipment that was there. Sitting down before a screen, he pressed the button that summoned the machine's attention and began asking questions.

It was not a quick process. It took him nearly an hour merely to establish the limits of the area in which Dahno had stored sensitive information. But there remained available a wealth of information that was peripheral to what was held secret, and from which Bleys' quick brain could deduce much.

In the next three hours he was able to establish that the organization Dahno controlled called itself the *"Others."* It had apparently grown spontaneously out of an essentially social association among people who were the result of intermarriage between individuals from the three largest Splinter Cultures in the New Worlds—the Friendlies, the Exotics, and the Dorsai. Dahno had joined this organization and effectively taken it over, turning it into a business tool.

Following that, he had begun gathering more recruits from the mixed-breeds, although non-mixed were by no means excluded if they were useful; and started educating class after class of these, like the group of trainees Bleys had already had to do with. On graduation, these were then sent to one or other of the New Worlds, to spread out individually to the larger cities of these worlds and set up their own satellite organizations which now sought influence there and useful information to channel back to him.

The organization had something of the old-fashioned information network about it. The sort of pattern that had allowed eighteenth and nineteenth century banks to make fortunes by communicating special information before it was received by other, slower routes. Also, it had something in common with the networks of spy cells during the turbulent times of the twentieth century when the large nations of Old Earth struggled and fought with each other on a massive basis. However, they were in fact much more tightly organized than either of these prototypes; kept tightly in Dahno's grasp by the fact that the organization's aim and purpose was to make use of, not wealth, but information—information that would give the organization—and particularly Dahno—power on these worlds.

It was Dahno's thesis, which he always announced to the graduating members of his group just before they left for the worlds of their destination, that wealth and power would come automatically if the information was first found. He further emphasized the point that the information would be useless unless it was processed by a central mind of unusual quality—which was his.

The structure would not have worked, Bleys thought, if anyone with abilities less than Dahno's had tried to run it.

In fact, his abilities made possible something otherwise impossible for more than a single world—a network that potentially allowed him to simultaneously influence the leadership of Association, as well as other Younger Worlds.

This had only been made possible by Donal Graeme, a century before, forcing these worlds to join peacefully in a community with a common economic base. This allowed the individual world to specialize safely in the type of specialists it trained; and trade these for the other specially trained people they needed from other worlds.

This in turn was possible because it was cheaper than trading anything else, given the high cost of interstellar travel. Also it allowed a world, by specializing, to devote only a small proportion of its population to high levels of training, leaving the rest to make use of the fruits of the labors of the experts imported in return. In sum, this was what made possible the worlds as not merely surviving, but progressing social entities.

Otherwise, an overwhelming majority of their populations would have had to have been assigned to training in a multitude of necessary areas; so that the world would struggle merely to maintain itself.

It also allowed civilization to develop—and develop at more or less a common level on the fifteen Younger Worlds. Only one of those worlds—Coby—traded anything of importance in addition to experts. That was simply because it happened to be a planet of great interior riches in the form of metals and other substances badly needed on worlds which were naturally poor in their own supplies of these things.

But it was time to return to the apartment. Bleys closed up and left, after calling for an autocar.

Bleys' monitor spoke up just as he entered the apartment, to warn him that it was getting close to dinner time. It was possible that Dahno might swing by the apartment to pick him up and take him out to that favorite restaurant of his for dinner. All the time he had been working, Bleys had kept an ear cocked, metaphorically speaking, against the unexpected entrance of Dahno.

It had started to rain outside, and Bleys watched the day fade on the rain-blurred vegetation beyond the large windows of the outer wall of the main room. The planet Association was both close to its primary and strongly inclined to its ecliptic, and therefore had a short year—of about eighty days—which included a very hot summer of a couple of weeks' duration, and a longer winter.

Outside of the sheltered cities, nobody really attempted much in the summer. Farmers worked to grow and harvest their genetically-tailored crops in the remaining days of the year. Most of the planet's land-mass was in the temperate or tropical zones, the poles having little land, and that usually lying under sheets of ice or standing water, depending on the season.

Winter, where Bleys now was, therefore, was a time of long twilights and a good deal of rain like that which was now falling. He waited it out, however, until it was dark. It was obvious by that time that Dahno was not coming. Bleys made himself a meal from the kitchen equipment in the apartment; and then, for the day had been long, he took himself to bed. Experience had taught him that he would gain as much by sleeping on the information he had acquired and letting his unconscious sort it out, as he would by staying awake and trying to puzzle it.

He slept heavily. When he woke, there was a message for him on the screen of his bedside phone. It was from Dahno.

If you'd asked me, it read, *I'd have given you a key to the office. You'll find it at the base of the phone here.*

—Bleys looked, and indeed the key was there.

I've taken the liberty of setting your alarm. You've got a couple of hours, then at nine o'clock each day like this during the five weekdays, you're due to join the trainees for all the various phases of their education.

As far as their classroom work is concerned, I've left copies of the books they are studying with your reader on the dining table.

> *Dahno* ›

Showered and dressed, Bleys made himself breakfast and sat in the dining room, eating and scanning the books that had been left for him, in the reader Dahno had laid out for him—although he could have used his own reader in his bedroom, if necessary. But this was closest.

He was able to get through most of them by the time he decided he had to call the driverless taxi to take him to the building that housed the trainees.

The morning, he discovered, was devoted to book work in the classroom. The books he had been given, he had been surprised to see, had been concerned almost exclusively with information about the various worlds that would be the destination of this particular class.

It seemed to him that that was rather one-sided preparation for the kind of work that he had expected would occupy most of those in Dahno's network eventually. But he discovered what made up the difference. There were specialized teachers for those subjects he had assumed they would need to know.

When they came to the final hour of the morning the instructor that had been dealing with them left and* was replaced by another, a pleasant-faced man in his sixties, who had something of the Exotic about him but was—Bleys was ready to swear—no full-blooded Exotic.

There had been a general feeling, an attitude to his mother, who of course had been full-blooded Exotic, that set her apart from other people. It was similar to but not the same thing as the overall impression given by people who have gone deeply into certain occupations, and who seem marked by that occupation—experienced teachers often had something about them that made them sound and look as if teaching was their lifework, long-time physicians to sound and look like medicians. This man did not seem to radiate the Exotic special aura.

He lacked that. Possibly he too was an Other, a second-generation mixture of Exotic and something else. But, whatever his antecedents, he did know a number of the Exotic-developed techniques in hypnosis and persuasion.

Particularly those of persuasion, since it had always been preached by Exotics, according to what Bleys had read and what his mother had confirmed one time when he had ventured to ask her, that hypnosis, except an individual's self-hypnosis as a memory aide, was a technique of last resort.

The instructor confined himself to ways of getting and holding attention; and to ways of further improving upon that attention so that it gradually developed into a susceptibility for persuasion. He stressed the necessity of referring to things that the one addressed would either find or already believe to be incontrovertible.

Without warning he suddenly addressed himself directly to Bleys.

"Now, do you have anything to say to that, Bleys Ahrens?" he asked, from the lecture platform.

Bleys felt the eyes of the class upon him. Now was not the time for him to begin showing any of his abilities or superiorities.

"No . . ." he said, thoughtfully, "no, I don't think so."

"You'll notice," the instructor once more addressed the class as a whole, "how I succeeded in focusing the attention of all of you upon Bleys Ahrens. Now, if he was as qualified as I hope all of you will be by the time you're ready to graduate, and he and I were working together as a team, that business of one partner directing general attention of everyone present to the other, could be very valuable. Stop and think about ways in which it could be used."

Bleys found himself intrigued. The directing of all the attention of the class upon him, this first time he was a part of it, had certainly been a good example of a point the instructor wanted to make. However, it was not lost upon him that so singling him out might have had another purpose as well. For one thing the question asked him—whether he had any comment—almost implied that he came to the class with something of a knowledge of what the instructor was talking about.

So his words had not only served the purpose of directing the attention upon Bleys, but establishing the fact that perhaps he might be differently equipped than the rest of them. The inevitable question which must occur to the minds of at least the brighter ones among the class must be—how much then did Bleys know that they did not?

It could be, for example, that the question, on Dahno's order, was designed to give Bleys a bit of a push toward an ultimate position of superiority over the rest of them.

"You're already familiar, from past classroom sessions," the instructor was going on, "with methods of both hypnosis and auto-hypnosis. Note that they all spring from capturing the attention of the one who is to be hypnotized, even when that one is yourself. That, of course, is only the first step. Then comes the focusing of attention. This becomes important when you're dealing with people whom you have not met before and whom you ultimately wish to persuade in some direction or another, possibly to get them to give you information that otherwise they might not give.

"Literally," he went on, "any method can be used to draw their attention. But note that it should be an attention that makes it pleasant to concentrate in that direction. You can certainly attract anyone's attention—man or woman—by saying something hostile or making a hostile move toward him or her. Or, simply by challenging them in some way." He paused for a moment, looking again at Bleys.

"However," he went on, "unless what you do leads to a desire on their part to pursue the matter from an interested viewpoint; and on the basis of regarding you in a friendly manner, even if they're not yet fully prepared to trust you, it's not the best method of making use of any kind of hypnotic reinforcement to what you want them to accept."

He lectured them on this subject for about another fifteen minutes and Bleys listened fascinated, hearing many of the things that he had picked up wordlessly from observing and imitating his mother, spelled out in words. Then the rest of the hour was given over to demonstrations and practice.

The instructor would call one of the class up on stage and quietly and privately explain a specific use of the hypnotic process in gaining information—all this out of hearing of the rest of the class.

He would then place an adhesive button behind the ear of the man to whom he had talked; and from offstage, through a hand-phone that hid his voice from everyone else, would coach him through the ear-button, step by step through an interview with another class member. One who had been given no instruction except to sit at a table and talk with the man being coached.

In this manner the instructor demonstrated three different

patterns of putting the uncoached member of the class into what he called a "communicative" state. None of these, he emphasized, was fully hypnotic, but only a heightened willingness to talk. Basically, it came from his planting the feeling in the other person that the one he was talking to was someone who could be confided in and trusted.

This instructor was followed by a woman who coached the class in a number of small differences in manners on the planet to which their class of trainees would be going as successful graduates.

"—Bear in mind," she said, "the differences in manners, alone, isn't going to make any large difference in attitude. But if your manners, your way of eating, talking, standing and so forth match those of the one you're talking to, it'll unconsciously foster the feeling that you're one of their own kind, and bring the two of you closer. Also to a certain extent, the idea that anyone is dealing with a person from the same family, clan, or society, relaxes the conscience about sharing essentially private information."

She paused.

"Not in all cases," she went on, "but for those met on a casual basis this hinting at a common background is normally a plus."

Following the hour with this instructor, they broke for lunch. This was served buffet style with the trainees filling their plates and taking them to small tables that held two or three together—at most four. Bleys, looking around the room, spotted the man who had trained with him in judo the day before, and was a little surprised to see him with one arm in a sling.

Bleys moved forward quickly, since the one arm was making it difficult for James to handle his plate and pick up things near the end of the line, like dessert and silverware.

Bleys moved forward and, smiling at the other, lent a hand in supporting the plate while the final things were gathered. He had expected almost any kind of reaction, but was rather surprised at the warmth of the return smile James turned on him. Bleys, carrying both his plates and one of James', led the way to a small table that could hardly hold more than the two of them and was at present deserted.

"What happened to you?" he asked James in his most friendly voice, once they were settled on the table with the plates set out. "There was nothing wrong with that arm of yours the last I saw of you yesterday."

James smiled again, this time a little ruefully.

"Punishment for my sins," he said lightly—but the phrase had an underlying seriousness of tone that betrayed a Friendly background—"It's only a pulled muscle. I ought to be all right in a day or two, but I'm going to miss at least a couple of days' practice. When the class was breaking up yesterday, *sensei* suggested I stay behind and the two of us work out a little further, together. Then he showed me how unfair it is to take advantage of someone with less experience than you. He didn't say a word and at first I didn't know why he was handling me the way he did; but at the end, after my arm had been hurt and he was helping me dress, he mentioned that there *'are always manners within the dojo—if nowhere else.'* I understood then. My apologies for what I did to you yesterday."

"They aren't necessary," said Bleys. Happily he was a quick thinker. This sudden development offered almost too many possibilities to consider at once. In the meantime he asked a question.

"You understood at once?" he said. "I don't follow that."

"Why, of course *sensei* saw what I did to you. He sees everything that happens in class—I should have thought of that," explained James, patiently. "I shouldn't have treated you that way, and he was pointing it out to me."

"You understood all that from a few words about manners?" Bleys persisted, still buying himself time in which to consider the situation. Looked at from all angles the whole affair did not seem something that could have been easily arranged by Dahno.

"Oh yes," said James, "but of course it wasn't just that he gave me a taste of the same sort of manners I used toward you. What he did and said had to do with something we all have to learn. There was also a hint there that I might have damaged my chance to graduate by doing it. If he did not pass me on my work in the *dojo*, then the fact I'd passed everything else wouldn't help. I'd be left behind when the others shipped out."

"Graduating means that much to you, then?" said Bleys.

"Doesn't it to all of us?" James stared at him in something like astonishment; then the astonishment went. "Your brother hasn't told you?"

"My brother tells me almost nothing," said Bleys, "that's part of *my* training."

"Why," James said, "none of us would want to turn our backs on the chance to build the future for all worlds."

"Ah," said Bleys, noncommittally.

"Your brother hasn't explained all that?" said James. "Why, what else are we mixed-breeds for? If not to give the inhabited worlds the best the Splinter Cultures have produced in specific individuals; to give them a government influenced by the fittest. What else were the Splinter Cultures for in the first place, if not to develop the things every one of us in this class combines inside ourselves, depending upon our particular heritage?"

"Put that way it does seem inevitable," said Bleys.

There was implied flattery in this statement. James clearly accepted it. He leaned forward over the table, resting his injured arm upon it.

"You and I won't live to see the end results of our organization, of course," he said, "but that doesn't mean we can't help get things started. The credit goes to your brother, who had the genius and foresight to start us moving toward that end."

"Yes," said Bleys, "Dahno always was a leader."

"Yes," James' eyes almost glowed, "he's the one Other who's absolutely essential. The information we gather has to center someplace, because that information eventually has to give us the power to take the rest of the race over bloodlessly; and lead them eventually all up to our own level. Our work would go for nothing if it wasn't for Dahno."

"It's good to hear you say that," said Bleys. "As I say, you'd be surprised at what I don't know about my brother."

CHAPTER

19

———

"BUT HOW DOES it happen that you know so little about your brother?" asked James.

"I've been with my mother all these years," answered Bleys. "My father was dead; and, as I say, my mother and I moved around a lot. We were on New Earth and Freiland and a couple of the other New Worlds and even on Old Earth itself for a while. I was on New Earth just before I came here. Neither my mother nor Dahno are great at keeping up a communication, so up until I came here to Association Dahno hadn't bulked very largely in my life."

"He's a remarkable man," said James. He went on to talk about Dahno at some length. But nothing he had to say provided Bleys with information of the importance of what Bleys had discovered in the first few words the other man had had to say.

After lunch they had a short hour more of classroom work, and then they moved into the gymnasium, for some more martial arts, then instruction by a swimming instructor.

As soon as Bleys was free he headed directly to the office. Once more Dahno was not there and he was free to work in what he now had dubbed in his mind the research room.

He went over some of the material he had read the day before, looking for new clues. What he found confirmed the rather astonishing thing he had learned from James. Dahno was deliberately enlisting mixed-breeds from the three main Splinter Cultures into an organization that was given the idea that it was to be the controlling influence on government for the New Worlds.

In the days that followed he continued his afternoon researches, and dug even deeper into the mass of available information. He discovered, however, very little beyond what he had found out from James originally. Whenever he got on an interesting track of developing information, it ended, blocked, up against the area Dahno had cued to be secret. Breaking the code that would let him into that secret part of this knowledge repository was beyond Bleys' ability. From what he now knew about his older brother, he doubted that anyone else besides Dahno had the ability to enter the secret area.

Nonetheless, by carefully applying what he had found out in the research room to the trainees themselves, and by gradually beginning to build a mental structure around what he did know, with what must be there to support it, Bleys finally got a picture of the organization. It was set up to be controlled by Dahno and spread out over at least eight of the New Worlds. It consisted, what with the recruits his trainees had brought into the organization, of something between ten and fifteen thousand people.

In theory, they were all Others, as Dahno had evidently named them. In actuality the only thing they had in common was a particular type of personality, very like that of the Friendlies, themselves, in that they had a fixed picture of the universe and followed without question. At the same time, they were both hardheaded and persuasive. The sort of profile that would ideally fit a lobbyist.

Unfortunately, it was at this point that he appeared to be blocked. It was frustrating. Undoubtedly there was more to be got from the files that were open to him, if he had only more background of information to knit them together. What was needed, he saw clearly, was time. While he had already decided that the days measured by his lifetime were precious, now some must be given to more studying and gathering of information.

Above all, he needed more information from the other trainees. It occurred to him suddenly that there could be no better time than now for conversation with those other trainees whom he had already made into friends. Since it was a weekend, undoubtedly they would be free to do what they wanted, and there would be time for conversation.

He went to the trainees' apartment building.

It was no different there than always before, although another old man was acting as guard on the desk inside the front door. But when he rode up on one of the disks of the elevator to the floor which housed the trainees and let himself into their quarters, he was startled to find no one there at all.

He smiled at his own stupidity. Of course, after being penned up here all week, they would find places outside to go to. And it had never occurred to him to check with any of those he knew as to what sort of place, if any, they gathered in on these, their two days off. He left and returned thoughtfully to the apartment he shared with Dahno.

The apartment was empty. Dahno, of course, was not there. He made himself something to eat and drink and lay down on his bed. He could have studied or simply read; but just at the moment he did not feel like either.

Lying there, he found himself slipping back into his image of himself as if he stood alone out in space, light-years from the nearest inhabited worlds, solitary, forever set apart from other humans.

He would never have a friend, a friend on his own level. He faced that fact squarely. That was the drawback to being what he was. The advantage was that from this lonely distance he could look and see the universe as a single and understandable whole.

He had half hoped that Dahno would turn out to be someone

with whom he could feel a closeness. But it was clear to him now that Dahno had found fullness of occupation in what he was building; and what he was building was far too small for Bleys.

Dahno thought only of the present and his immediate lifetime. Bleys thought of all time in the future. The means to help the race he had envisioned were still hidden; and would only be revealed as he learned more about his fellow humans and the situation on all the worlds. There was no question of the goal. It was to produce a humanity equal to any future challenge. A race of people gifted as he, himself, was gifted. His problem would be to start them on the route that it was his duty to put them on. Otherwise—why had he been born?

He could not yet understand it all, nor would he be able to in his lifetime. But nonetheless he knew what it was. And he saw a possibility for himself as a tool for the human race. It could be the one thing he could do that would save the race.

They would not know, they would not understand, they would never be able to grasp what he had done. Possibly at some time in the far future, they would have grown to the point where they could look back and see that it was he who took them off the dangerous path he saw them now on, and put them on a proper way to an unlimited future.

But for now—it occurred to him—he must make the best possible use of things immediately at hand to be learned and mastered. That meant gathering the skills and information to make himself a leader; and to understand Dahno's full network, together with Dahno's control of the people who made it up.

He could begin immediately by improving his own learning process. His work with the trainees was useful up to a point. But the abilities of his mind galloped ahead of them. It struck him that his greatest need was to be charismatic. Where he could not gain acceptance as an equal, he could as the superior he had been born to be. No more would he attempt to be accepted as one of them. Let them accept him as their director and commander.

It was so obvious he could not believe how simple and straightforward it would be. In every direction that involved book learning he was already far ahead of them all. Only in physical matters, like this study of judo, did he have to progress at a more normal pace—but even that normal pace could be improved as his understanding interpreted what he was told and fitted in into a whole pattern of action.

Meanwhile there were other things that he could be learning in the time he was now wasting in the classroom at the apartment building.

He must talk to Dahno about that.

He sat up on the edge of the bed and called Dahno's bed phone to leave a message on it.

I haven't seen you but I need to talk to you. Arrange your schedule so that we can get together for a short while at least. This is important.

Ironically, he was just completing this message when he heard the door of the apartment open.

He met his half-brother in the lounge; and Dahno smiled at him, but started to brush past him.

"I've got to dress for dinner," Dahno said. "How are things with you?"

"Things are such that I'm badly in need of a moment's talk with you," Bleys answered.

Dahno kept going.

"Not now if you don't mind," his voice floated back, as he disappeared into his own bedroom. "I've got just enough time to get dressed and get down to the restaurant."

"You can be fifteen minutes late, I think," said Bleys. He had quite boldly followed Dahno into the bedroom. His half-brother turned around and stared at him.

"What's this?" he said. "I told you I barely had time enough to get ready. As for being late—"

"If you'd kept in closer touch with me, I wouldn't have to delay you now," said Bleys, "but time's being wasted."

"Yes indeed," answered Dahno, "my time."

"Ultimately yours, but right now mine," answered Bleys. "Unless you can spare me fifteen minutes of your time now,

I'll walk out of this apartment and out of your plans for the future. I don't know how much you've counted on me, but it ought to be worth fifteen minutes."

"You'd walk out?" said Dahno, half-smiling. "You'd starve."

Bleys thought gratefully of the interstellar credit paper still in the secret compartment of the belt around his waist.

"That was taken care of before I left mother."

"Oh? Indeed!" said Dahno. "All right, let's go back to the lounge and talk."

They did so and sat down in facing chairs.

"Well, what's on your mind?" said Dahno in a mild tone. There was no sign that he had been at all disturbed by Bleys' interruption of his plans.

"It's very simple," said Bleys. "Some things like the judo classes are useful. For the rest of it, though, I'm as out of place among those people as I would have been in the little schoolhouse in Henry's district. I'll still keep going and joining them and working until I get to know all of them well, and I'll still take advantage of things where I need partners to work out with. But aside from that there are a number of specialized things in which I'd like to have instruction. A lot of that can be done with tutors or specialists that can come to me here. Unless that's more than you can afford."

Dahno laughed.

"The funds come when they're needed," he said, "haven't I mentioned that to you before? The thing to do is to have power, which lies in influence. If you have that not only credit, but everything else follows automatically."

"And on that theory, the more capable I am, the more useful I am, and the more influence I should be able to gather. So the more of everything else should follow," said Bleys. "Am I right?"

Asking that question was almost more bold a thing than following Dahno into his bedroom and insisting on talking to him. Hidden in it—and Bleys knew Dahno would recognize the fact—was a requirement of Dahno to state what he considered Bleys was worth to him. If he was not in favor of

hiring the special tutors and teachers and trainers that Bleys
had in mind, then obviously the future he had in mind for Bleys
was not one as lofty as he had always implied.

"That's a good point," said Dahno thoughtfully. "What do
you think you might want?"

"I'd better make you a written list," answered Bleys. "It'll
be quite a list, including special training with *sensei*, if that's
possible; a speech therapist to give me a larger range of voice;
and someone who teaches fencing to improve my balance. I
also want a tutor to begin the study of phase-shift mechanics
and phase physics. Then, as soon as I'm ready to go on to
studying those two things, I'll want tutors in them too. There's
at least a dozen other things. I'll make you a list, as I say."

"All right." Dahno smiled and got up. "I'm free to go dress
then, Mr. Vice-Chairman?"

"Absolutely," said Bleys, "but you might keep it in mind
that it would be a good thing if the two of us had time to talk
with each other at least once a week."

"It won't always be possible," said Dahno, "but—I'll make
it as possible as I can."

He went off to his bedroom. Bleys sat where he was, feeling
the beginnings of a glow of satisfaction. He had not only gotten
what he wanted, but he had plumbed the depths of Dahno's
interest in him. Clearly, Dahno was willing to do a great deal
rather than give him up. The reasons for that were something
that Bleys would have to discover somewhere along the line.
But for now, it was enough to realize that such an interest was
there.

In the next week he discovered where at least a good share
of the trainees were to be found on a weekend, as well as
making several new friendships among his fellow trainees. He
now was on good terms with close to a majority of the group;
and he expected—and was later proved right—that after a
certain number had been won over to him, the rest would come
almost automatically.

Rather like Dahno's rule about influence leading to power
and power leading to everything else.

At the same time, he was a little sadly amused at the way

they responded to what were essentially Exotic techniques—the same Exotic techniques on which they were lectured weekly, and some of which had already been explained to them. Such a discovery no longer made Bleys contemptuous of his fellow human beings, it only saddened him with the reminder of his own difference from them.

The place to which most of them went for their weekends was a particular hotel in town. Not all chose to go there, and in fact, he learned from James, from time to time they would drift to different hotels; but this information was unimportant compared to the fact that he discovered something else very interesting indeed. That was, that there was also a class of women trainees, who were evidently sent through much the same classes but differently and apart from the men. Not all, of course, but a good share of the men and women came together in their free time at the currently-used hotel.

Bleys had already come to understand that he was attractive to women. But he was still young and therefore still, to a certain extent, self-conscious. He was slow about making friends with the women; and he tended to shy away from those who seemed in any way aggressive. This reaction in him cropped out unexpectedly, to the surprise of all the rest, but to himself as well, when one of the women with whom he had had little to do came up and sat down on the arm of his chair.

"Just look at that hair," she said, and ran her fingers through Bleys' dark brown, slightly wavy, hair.

"No more of that, if you don't mind," said Bleys, instinctively pulling his head away from her hand.

Not so much the words, but the tone in which he spoke turned the heads of all the others within hearing toward him. The woman who had been about to say something teasing about his self-consciousness, on second thought said nothing. She got up from the arm of his chair and walked away.

Bleys suddenly realized he had spoken in a voice that he did not know he possessed. But he recognized whose voice it was. It was the voice of Henry, who was used to making no statements that were not orders, amplified and made even more potent by Bleys' recent training. At base was the fact that

Henry had never emphasized what he had to say, nor identified it as a command. But the absolute certainty that it would be understood and obeyed had always been clearly broadcast in the tone of it. As it had been just now—only more so—in Bleys' voice.

Unconsciously, Bleys had taken that tone and put it to use. A feeling of sudden guilt in him was overwhelmed by the feeling of surprise. He could hardly believe that an attitude of command had come to him that easily. With that understanding came another one, close on its heels: that it would be a mistake for him now to apologize, as he had just been about to do, to the woman who had run her fingers through his hair. At one stroke he had taken the attitude of someone to be obeyed by all the rest of them.

Immediately, he was concerned by the fact that by doing so, he might have made enemies of all of them, all over again. But, looking around at the faces around him, he did not see resentment on any of them. Just as he had assumed that they would do what he said, so they had assumed that he was in a position to tell them what to do.

It was a very large discovery indeed. He tucked it away in the back of his mind to be thought of when he had more time to himself.

In the weeks to come he tried to make some amends for any harshness the others might have felt in his words; and went so far as to make easy friendships with a number of the women. Affection he found. Love, he could not find; by consequence of the very fact he was committed to setting himself apart from all other humans.

So he could not talk to any of them about his plans for the future, his vision of a race purified and set right upon its way; and the result was to leave him feeling more isolated even than before.

Still, in other ways during the next weeks, months, and years, he made as much use of this situation as possible; gathering information almost as one might gather a bale of straw, a single straw at a time. Likewise, he did the same with the several new classes of trainees that succeeded his first one.

At the same time, his own private lessons were beginning to have their effect. The fencing instructor and the special sessions with the *sensei* developed him amazingly, not merely in the area of physical strength but also in the way in which he handled his body. Eventually, these instructors passed him on to those who could give him more advanced teaching in the same areas.

The same thing took place as well with most of those who came to give him special or private lessons. The speech therapist extended his vocal range a full octave and a half both upwards and downwards and a teacher of singing eventually brought his voice to a resonance that made the voice itself arresting; so that he discovered he could use the tone of it alone as a means of focusing the attention of someone on whom he wished to use his personal control of the Exotic techniques—in which he took further tutoring from a true expatriate Maran Exotic.

In the process, he stumbled upon a discovery. He had always studied what he had to, before. In the beginning, that had been those fields of information handed him by the caretakers; then, here on Association, it had become what he felt he required to reach the goal he had set for himself.

But now, he was free to learn anything he liked. Dahno was as good as his word. Bleys could spend whatever he wished on teachers and materials. For the first time he began to poke his intellectual nose into geology, archaeology . . . and other systems; ending finally with the arts—painting, sculpture, music and writing.

It was with these last that he made a marvelous discovery. He had never encountered any human, even Dahno or his mother, who had the power to stretch his own understanding to the limit. But in the arts, he found it—in the time-proven classics of brushwork, knife-work, and the mind-work that went into poetry and literature.

Why, he thought, *here they are, the people I could talk to and be friends with.*

What the makers had to say was to be found in the results of their efforts, in their carvings, their buildings, their words. *No,* he thought; it was not *in* these things, it was to be heard and understood *through* them. For that which came through, spoke to him as no human being ever had—on his own level of ability. It was as if a soundless chime was heard in his head whenever he encountered what was held in the living material of their work.

Sadly, those who had made these things might have proved as disappointing to him as all other humans—for he no longer believed that anywhere would he find his equal—but they had all possessed the capability of meeting him on a level in what they had created.

The result was that he pushed aside all the other attractive things that beckoned him after his important studies were found; and found himself losing himself in the culture of the total race, as exemplified by the best it had done for centuries.

He learned Classical Greek only to read the *Iliad*; but then he read it, and the original words rolled musically and thunderously in his mind. And the colors of the centuries stained him through.

He found himself thinking that, if only he did not have this higher, more important duty that held him in an unbreakable grip, he could live exclusively with these shining things; and maybe even try his hand at equaling some of them himself, forgetting all responsibilities to the civilized worlds and those who lived on them.

But the higher duty to move the race up—even one step—continued to hold him with a hand more powerful than the movement of the stars; and it was in the ordinary things and people such as the trainees themselves, that he finally learned what he needed to progress most surely to that end. Slowly, bit by bit from them, he picked up information with which he was able to build bridges of conjecture out over the void of that part of Dahno's organizational activities which Dahno had kept hidden from him.

Not one, but many such cantilevered bridges of logical theory, he built; until at last they all locked together and he became certain at last that he had a strong grasp on what he had set out to find.

It happened then, four years after his confrontation with Dahno over the special tutoring, that he was waiting in the lounge of the apartment late one afternoon when he knew Dahno was expected in.

When the door from the hall opened and Dahno finally entered, Bleys stood up to meet him and they met almost in the center of the lounge.

They stood eye to eye now. Bleys at last had the same height as his brother; but he was still slim, for all the hardness of his trained body. He had no illusions about becoming particularly dangerous physically. It was only that he conceived the work he would have to do with his mind needed a physical vehicle in the best possible shape. He had made it that way, accordingly; and he would work to keep it that way.

"Something on your mind?" asked Dahno.

"Yes," said Bleys, "why don't we both sit down?"

By custom they took the two chairs in which they usually sat facing each other in this room. As usual Dahno dwarfed the extra large size of his; but Bleys no longer seemed lost in its equally large partner. He sat easily, with his back straight, barely touching the back of the chair.

"It occurred to me right now there's something you might want to think about," Bleys said. "Also, I've got a suggestion about myself."

"Charge ahead," said Dahno, throwing himself back in his chair.

"The something you might want to consider," said Bleys, "is I think you've got a potentially explosive situation with those private gunmen of yours, or whatever they are, and wherever you've got them hidden; together with this newest political project you're involved in."

He delivered the bombshell of his words quite calmly, and ended looking at Dahno, waiting for his answer.

Dahno slowly sat upright in his chair.

"How did you get into the secret files?" he asked. "Neither the Hounds nor the project are in the open ones."

Bleys waved a hand dismissingly.

"I haven't," he said. "I'm only judging from deductions

made, from all the other information I've gathered over the past four years. There have to be many things in your secret files I don't know. But I know the general shape of a great many other things that have to be there. I've worked out only what I can; but it adds up to a pretty clear general picture of what you haven't been telling me."

He waited. Slowly a broad grin spread across Dahno's face.

"Well, well, Mr. Vice-Chairman," he said, "congratulations on your graduation. Those milk-teeth seem to be all gone finally; and I'd say that's a pretty serviceable set of tusks you've grown in their place."

CHAPTER

20

═══════

"I WOULDN'T CALL them tusks," said Bleys.

"I would," said Dahno, and there was no humor or mockery in his tone. "Knowledge is power, you know that as well as I do. Those are knowledge tusks."

"Whatever you want to call them," said Bleys, "they're at your service."

"Good," answered Dahno, "welcome to the firm, Mr. Number One Vice-Chairman. We'll put you to use. You'll begin by answering a question. Why do you think keeping Hounds is dangerous?"

"Because any loaded weapon in reach is always dangerous," said Bleys. "If it was an actual gun, and you couldn't lay hands on it at a moment's notice, you might end up thinking twice before using it. Otherwise, the time may come when you'll reach for it automatically—and later regret it."

"And you think that's a danger with me?" said Dahno. "Do you think with what I've done and what I am, I'd be the kind of person who'd go off half-cocked in a situation like that?"

"I think anybody would be in danger of going off half-cocked in a situation like that," said Bleys. "When you were young, did you ever use your strength to get what you wanted, without thinking out all the possible results and what might result from them?"

"Yes," said Dahno slowly. "But that was when I was young. I don't agree with you that the Hounds are any danger to anyone unless I want them to be. And I never intend to want them to be. They're there to be used as a threat, instead of as a weapon. Now, are you satisfied?"

"Yes, Mr. Chairman," said Bleys.

"Then that's settled," said Dahno. "Now, what do you know about this political project you referred to that I'm supposed to be involved in?"

"I only know there is one," said Bleys. "I'm fairly sure it has to do with all the talk I've heard about the building of another Core Tap to provide power to the planet. What I've had to do has been like figuring out the orbit of a star around some dark body, by the eccentricities of its orbit. I try to reason from result to facts. As a result, my facts are merely educated guesses. But I'll bet I'm right about the Core Tap."

"And why would you think I was involved with the decision in the Chamber whether or not to build it?" asked Dahno.

"Because it's such a huge, technical job to reach down into a world's hot core to generate power for the southwest of this continent. So, it's a question of spending so much credit that the very economic balance of the world will be affected," said Bleys. "The truth of the matter is, from what I'm able to judge of this planet, it can't afford that expense yet, badly as the energy from another Core Tap would be needed. Scientists would have to be hired from Newton, engineers from Cassida, and the cost of their salaries would be high, as well as the payments to the worlds they came from—all that in interstellar credit. Which must come hard to a world that is largely self-sufficient because it is so poor in materials it can export to gain that credit. About all Association, here, and Harmony, have to export is their young men as mercenary soldiers to the other worlds; and mercenary soldiers don't bring in a great deal of interstellar credit, except in quantity. At the same time, those young men are needed here."

"Right you are, in everything about the Core Tap," said Dahno, "but you didn't answer my question. Why would I be involved?"

"Simply because so many of your clients are representatives in the Chamber. Because they're involved, you'll get drawn into it. You could find yourself giving answers to opposite sides of the question."

"Good for you," said Dahno softly. "Suppose I say everything you tell me is true. Still, you tied that in with the question of the Hounds and my own personal safety. What I'm hearing is, I'll be involved too deeply for my own safety and the safety of our organization of Others. Be a little more specific, Mr. Vice-Chairman."

"Do I need to be?" said Bleys with a shrug. "Certainly the situation has to mean that kind of danger for you."

He paused, watching Dahno.

"Don't you think that could be part of my job?" Bleys went on. "Keeping my eyes on the general picture, while you're focusing on what specifically is to be done; and warning you if I think I see trouble?"

Dahno nodded slowly.

"Maybe that's a good suggestion," he said. "I have to keep my nose close to the grindstone, and it does limit my field of vision. Very good, Mr. Vice-Chairman. Your job can be to look around while I'm getting things done and make sure nothing creeps up on us from behind."

Dahno got up on his feet.

"Tell you what I'll do," he said. "I came home to change clothes before going to my regular table, but in honor of the occasion we'll stay away from that restaurant completely. I'm still going to change clothes; but we'll go have a private meal, just as we used to when I was bringing you in from Henry's place in the country. But first I'll take you by the office and I'll give you your key to open the secret files."

He was as good as his word. They stopped at the office first and Bleys was given a key to the secret files. Bleys' mind itched to be at them—for what he had been able to guess about them was only a fraction of what he knew he could discover from an actual look at them. But Dahno was there with him.

"I'm flattered," he said to Dahno. "Very flattered."

"You should be," said Dahno; "no one else has ever unlocked those files; and until you came to Association, I never thought anybody but me ever would."

He turned away.

"Now, for dinner," he said, "I know the place we want."

The place was all that two people could want who wished to keep their conversation private. The tables were enclosed in little alcoves so designed that sound did not carry from them, even to the most nearby of other tables and alcoves. Over the wine, which Bleys passed up, and of which Dahno drank copiously, his half-brother told him more about himself than Bleys had ever expected to hear.

Like Bleys, he had at first attracted their mother's hopes. Here, she had thought—as she had with Bleys—was someone she could show off; and who, in return could show her off. For if the child was that bright, people must think, how bright then must the mother be?

Dahno however, unlike Bleys, had never opposed her openly. He had pretended to go along with her while stealing more and more time for himself and his own activities; until she discovered this and—since by this time he was at an unlovely age and now looked entirely too old to be the wonder-child that she had first envisioned and in fact used him as—she locked him up. He broke out and ran away, trading on the fact he was already almost adult size. She had him recaptured and sent him on to Henry. Once again, this had been with the complaisant aid of Henry's brother, Ezekiel.

At Henry's, Dahno had worked his persuasiveness upon Henry, until he had Henry in a position to agree to the fact that for all Dahno's muscle, his mind and skills could be more help to the farm by putting them to use in the city.

Dahno was allowed to go, accordingly. Once there, by using his own natural ability to ingratiate himself with people, plus the Exotic techniques he had, like Bleys, picked up from their mother, he had soon climbed to a position in which he could find backers to start him in the business he was in now. He had made this a quite straightforward business deal; and had paid back all those who had lent him the funds originally to set him up. He was, in effect, a lobbyist-at-large—and not even restricted to politics at that.

To the astonishment and pleasure of those who first consulted him, his area of knowledge took in the whole scope of the economic situation on Association, and Harmony as well. Since then it had grown to where he could also take into account the situations on the other planets, the rest of the Younger Worlds as well.

From that point on he had begun to build his organization of Others. As Bleys had already discovered, there had been for some years a loose social group of the mixed-breeds on this planet, drawn together by the fact that they were different.

At the same time Dahno had been careful to pick from among them those who were strongly schooled in the Friendly attitude of mind. He wanted believers, people he could bring to a fierce adherence to his own plans and pattern; and who would find that more attractive than anything else.

Also, he had held up the chance of attractive rewards for their working with him. Following their training, which was indeed good training, not just make-believe, they felt themselves stronger and more capable—and even in the process of their learning they began to appreciate what Dahno was doing for them.

All this, aside from the fact that they would be going off, some of them even to their native worlds or at least to one of the worlds from which their parentage was derived, to set themselves up with the sort of rewards and power that Dahno enjoyed himself.

Also, Dahno made sure that in his dealing with them, what he let them see of him reflected the fact that his lot was indeed attractive as well as powerful. He had always paid his debts to those he had borrowed from; and first of all to Henry. He still made frequent gifts of money to the farm as well as the little gifts he brought, occasionally, for the building of Henry's tractor. He even made visits just to visit.

"—And how about you," he asked, at last, across the table to Bleys, "how do you like it here in Ecumeny?"

Bleys was touched, not merely by Dahno's unveiling of his personal past, but by a genuine reaching out of warmth from him to Bleys. It was something Bleys reciprocated, now; but with reservations, because he was aware how his brother—like their mother—was capable of changing attitudes completely at different times and different places. Dahno, like her, had the knack of being in his own mind completely truthful at any moment, believing he meant entirely what he said. But at another moment, somewhat removed in time, he could feel equally truthful with an attitude that was the exact opposite.

Nonetheless, for the time of this one dinner they were closer, and felt that closeness, more than they had ever been before.

Seeing the chance to get back to more immediate matters, Bleys ventured to say something of what he had in mind for himself.

"It'll take me some time to study those secret files," he told Dahno, "but if the situation warrants it, and you still think it's a good idea, maybe it wouldn't be a bad notion on my part to travel around to all the worlds on which we've got established organizations. That way I could not only get a firsthand picture of our people already there, and the organization they've built, but some idea of how they're developing. Also, how close they're following your overall plans for the Others as a whole."

Dahno nodded slowly again.

"Good idea," he said. "I'm not great for interstellar travel myself. I've got my hands full; and anyway, I'd rather stay here and mind the store. But this way you can do the two things at once. I'd like to know if any of them are drifting out of the pattern I tried to set them in, without having to take time off from things here, to find out."

Bleys found it interesting that his half-brother considered affairs on Association so demanding that he had been willing to risk the natural drift in attitude of those in his organization on other worlds. Dahno had to know, as well as Bleys did, what happens when people are removed from any outside source of attitude control. The next day Bleys opened up the secret files and went to work on them.

On the surface they did not seem to offer a great deal more than he had already guessed. The main difference was that in the secret files people were given names and assigned places. So that now he was able to get the list of the personnel in all of Dahno's organization.

Also there were details about Dahno's work with the people he advised; particularly those who were members of the Chamber.

Bleys was interested to note that his half-brother had been either consciously or unconsciously jockeying for a position of direct control over those within that Chamber from his beginning as an adviser. At the present time, on crucial legislation, the Five Sisters, whom he did not influence as a whole, had control; as long as they spoke and voted together.

The reason for this was that most of the church representatives in the Chamber were not necessarily the leaders of the church they represented. All five of the Sisters were charismatic. Eighty percent of the representatives were deputies appointed by leaders who felt it far more necessary to stay close to their flock, and give all their attention in that direction, than to sit off at a distance in the Chamber passing laws. Since the actual heads of churches tended to be charismatic, and their deputies tended to be less so, the Five Sisters were natural leaders of the rest.

Bleys also looked for—and found—evidence of those in the Others' suborganizations on other planets being less successful, and drifting away from Dahno's original purposes. Of this, he found no direct evidence, but some very convincing indirect evidence; which he printed off, and at his next talk with Dahno passed the pages to him to read, without comment.

It was a few days later, and they were in Dahno's office, together, on a bright, rainless winter morning. Bleys sat quietly while Dahno scanned through the sheets. Since Bleys' "graduation," he had given up most connections with the trainees, keeping only a few of his special tutors whom he considered necessary; and these were those training him in the physical area and on the subject of phase physics. The result was that he was free to meet with Dahno like this early in the day. Also, this was the best time for Dahno, when he was most free of people wishing to see him and ask his advice. The meetings had become a regular thing.

Dahno finished the sheets, put them down and looked at Bleys.

"You expected me to see what this indicates?" Dahno said.

"I knew you would," said Bleys. "And I thought it would be best you see the evidence first, without any comment from me."

"Right," said Dahno. "Quite right, Bleys. Have you got any comment now?"

"Why no," said Bleys, "I leave it up to you."

"I think we understand each other." Dahno smiled grimly. "It looks like your tour of our outworld organizations is overdue. It's high time you met our other groups."

He smiled again. But Bleys read anger behind the smile.

"Naturally, it'll officially be only a friendly get-acquainted tour; so you can get to know them and they, you."

"Of course," said Bleys.

"But it goes without saying," Dahno went on, "that if you find evidence of deviations, you'll let me know about it right away."

"I plan on sending letters by spaceship to you from each world, as often as ships from there leave for Association," said Bleys.

"Good," said Dahno. He slapped his enormous hand down on the stack of printout. "If changes are needed, make them—in my name."

"It might not be a bad idea," said Bleys, "if you gave me some sort of authorization to show them . . ."

"Of course," said Dahno. "You can count on it. No reason for your not leaving on the first ship out, is there?"

"None. But I've a list of the order in which I'd like to visit these worlds," said Bleys, "and it's not always the shortest way around. So I'll have to wait for the first vessel to Freiland. If you like, I can show you the list."

"Give me a copy of it," answered Dahno. He rose from behind his desk. "Well, I've got to get busy. I've appointments."

CHAPTER

21

========

"—Something to drink, sir?"

"No thank you." Bleys' low-pitched but resonant voice was polite but very definite. "Nothing at all. I've got a problem on my mind; and I'd appreciate not being disturbed."

"Of course, sir." The spaceship lounge attendant vanished.

Curiously, as in his last spaceship trip, years before, he was once more having to ward off lounge attendants; who offered to supply him with something to read, or something to drink or eat. Only now, it was for a different reason. It was not because one of them had felt a touch of pity for what she considered a lonely, inwardly lost, boy. Now, it was because of something that he almost radiated.

It was the effect for which he had used his life so far to prepare himself. Tall, now—far beyond the ordinary— handsome, straight, athletic and unforgettable, with his memorable voice and dark brown eyes that seemed to look deeply into people even when he gave them a casual glance, he was not easily ignored.

He was now someone whose attention people, including cabin attendants, instinctively found themselves wishing to draw upon themselves, in hopes he might find something in them as interesting as they found in him. It was an effect he had on everyone he met nowadays. He was conscious of it, but his realization of the full impact of it on other humans was yet to come.

In any case, the total effect was to cause him to be disturbed by attention he did not want. Courteously but firmly, he dismissed them; and, eventually, regretfully, they left him alone.

He needed privacy to contemplate this moment. For the first time in his life he was free to set about breaking loose on the path he had chosen. And there was something about gazing at the starscape from here in the spaceship, separate and solitary in its path through space, that reminded him of his own, familiar image of himself as someone isolated and alone, that made him able to look more clearly at the whole panorama of the race. Not merely at the point of time in which it lived now, but at its record up to this moment. All his study of art and history spread that record out before his mind's eye.

Against that panorama he saw the way he had picked out for himself more clearly.

It was now plain to him, the work that had laid itself upon him, to save humanity. It was something no one else had recognized, or there would have been mention of it and voices raised on its behalf before this. Over the years with Dahno he had come to see it with a clarity he could never have imagined earlier.

The duty was undeniable, correct, complete—part of the great evolutionary imperative he had found on Association. Humanity must obey it or dwindle and perish. Basically, the cause of all the race's troubles was the fact it had left the world of its origin before it was ready to do so. Now, it must go back, to start again.

What he foresaw he must do to make it return would mean doing many things personally repugnant to him. But that was the price. For the first time he felt the sort of peace and certainty that Henry MacLean had found in his smaller way. To Henry, God was the answer to all things.

But Bleys knew there was no God—except for the one that the human race had invented to fill the great hunger in them all for guidance. There were only the inexorable workings of a universe too big to be grasped just yet in its entirety. Even by him. But he could feel a corner of its completeness, the working of its inexorable laws.

It would be his job to do the God-work, bring the race back into synchrony with those laws, working inside them—instead of against them, as a human race drunk on technology had done, these past three hundred years. To correct that would require his gaining more power, and a far greater use of it, than Dahno had ever dreamed.

He smiled, a little sadly, at the stars. The race would not thank him for what he must do to it. They might well curse him . . . some of them now, all of them later. But finally they would come over generations to understand the benefit of what he had done.

There was no pride for him to feel, no credit, no feeling of personal reward as a result of the eventual success of what he would do. He had not invented, created, designed or plotted this task—he had only recognized it and submitted himself to the work. As many of the God-believers would say, he had been "called" to it. But not by any deity. By the necessity of the evolutionary imperative that required humanity to progress in accordance with the universe's laws, or be discarded.

Nor would it be important that others understand what he and they must do. It was only important that they, like him, submit to it.

He must not expect understanding—not even from Dahno. Had others understood, they might have tried to do before this what he would do now. But they had been blind and therefore could not be blamed for not understanding. He, who was gifted with the ability to see, must therefore turn and embrace the isolation that, as a child, he had hoped to escape from. Embrace it as his birthright.

But first, the power. One step at a time; and the first step was toward the beginning of his control of Dahno's organization of the Others. That done, he could move further to make the Others much greater as an instrument; and eventually, with them for leverage, gain control of all the worlds—even Old Earth.

He drifted into musing about what he must do on Freiland, first. Freiland—the oldest of Dahno's other-world organizations of the Others. The Vice-Chairman in charge there was Hammer Martin; and his file in Dahno's office had said he had all three—Dorsai, Exotic and Friendly—in his ancestry. But he had been raised a militant Friendly before he had broken with his family in his early twenties. The Vice-Chairmen in charge of the suborganizations were all ambitious or they would not have competed with the other trainees of their class to graduate first and lead part of the organization.

It seemed to Bleys that the combination of Friendly roots and ambition suggested a way to handle Hammer.

CHAPTER

22

"YOU'RE THE FIRST Dahno's ever sent out with a team to expand the organization to other worlds," Bleys said to Hammer Martin over the main course of their evening meal, that first day on Freiland. It was a simple enough statement, but the richness of Bleys' voice and the warmth in his steady brown gaze upon Hammer's own washed-out blue eyes, implied a strong compliment.

The restaurant that Hammer had taken Bleys to had a different decor than that of Dahno's favorite restaurant back on Association. It was somewhat more luxurious, but also more designed so that people there could view clearly more of the other tables with their occupants. It was plainly a place to see and be seen.

"Yes, I've always appreciated that," said Hammer. Like Bleys he was not taking wine, or any other type of drink or relaxant with his meal. So much of his Friendly sternness still showed. "It was a great opportunity for me; and I've tried to make the most of it. I flatter myself I have. The secret is subtlety, always subtlety, never force."

Bleys recognized the last sentence as part of the graduation speech that he had heard Dahno give three classes of trainees now. Hammer enunciated the words as if he had originated them; and—thought Bleys—at least in the surface of Hammer's mind, he probably felt he had.

"The situation's different here, of course, than on Association," Hammer went on, "it's bound to be in a more free society. So I've found even more scope for getting things done here on Freiland."

"I'm sure," murmured Bleys, "I'm looking forward to you showing me what you do; and how you make the differences work."

"You've got my time completely—well, almost completely," said Hammer, "until you leave. It'll be two weeks, you said?"

"Two weeks before I can get a ship direct to Cassida and Newton."

"While you're close here," said Hammer, "I'm a little puzzled you don't stop at New Earth first."

"I'll be stopping on my way back, first to Harmony and then Association," said Bleys, lightly. "The itinerary works out more conveniently that way. By the way, you were saying something about having to make adjustments in the local organization, because of the difference between Freiland and Association."

"Small adjustments. Small adjustments only," said Hammer. He had taken advantage of Bleys speaking to eat some of his entree and he had to hurry to get it swallowed and speak. "I'll be showing them all to you. Be sure to look them over and report to Dahno. If he disapproves of any of them—"

Hammer let the sentence hang in midair. Clearly he did not expect Dahno to disapprove. With part of his mind Bleys was considering the irony of this thin, hatchet-faced man with all the visible appearance of a Friendly, sounding and acting like a smooth-tongued Exotic.

"You saw the office today," went on Hammer, "nothing new there, of course. I'll show you the group of trainees we're working with right now tomorrow."

"There's still the file room at your office," demurred Bleys. "I'd like to go through the files there."

"Oh? Of course." Hammer waved a dismissing hand in a very non-Friendly gesture. "It's the same old information, most of which has been shipped on to your Association office in any case. But if you'd like to."

"I would, indeed," said Bleys courteously. "It's a matter of being able to go back to my brother and tell him I've covered everything."

"Of course." Hammer nodded.

"That ought to take me the next few days, even if I start early and work late. I might even drop over tonight and start looking at the files," said Bleys. The first thing he had done with the authority of Dahno's authorization was to get copies of all keys that Hammer said were connected with the organization and its activities. "I suppose you've early appointments in the morning, so I won't expect to see you until about midday, if then."

"Well," there was a note of relief in Hammer's voice, "if you don't mind, the schedule is pretty busy, just now. Freiland's a very open planet, as you know. That means that business interests are scattered all over, and there's a couple of out-of-town visits I should make in the next day or two. They could be put off, of course, but it'd be better if I didn't have to—"

"You won't have to," said Bleys. He smiled at the other man. "We'll make this visit of mine as pleasant and easy as possible."

Bleys could have gone directly from parting with Hammer after the meal to the man's office. He was not tired. But instead he chose to return to his hotel suite, to let the information, and what he had observed in Hammer, soak a little in his mind. Many things benefited by being put aside that way for a short while, to see if they did not then produce further information.

In the case of Hammer, Bleys was already certain that he might uncover something that would be both interesting and something Dahno might take strong objection to. He was also fairly sure that Hammer was making, or already had made, efforts to hide any such thing from him. But circumstantial evidence, in the form of implications and conclusions drawn from what the regular open files could tell him, would either back up or destroy that notion.

After all, the man was still seven-tenths a Friendly. What Bleys felt suspicious in him might be simply the result of his own unexpected appearance—a brother of Dahno's, whom Hammer had scarcely known existed. Particularly, a brother with such a sweeping letter of authority.

After a time of lying on his bed and thinking, a thought occurred to Bleys. He had visited Freiland, but only when very young, with his mother. It might be important to taste the flavor of the society from an adult point of view. He knew its history. Its first settlers had been some very rigid-minded groups from western and northern Europe. These, however, had not taken full advantage of the fact that the planet was self-sufficient in metals and power sources—there was no need for a Core Tap, anywhere on Freiland, for example. Its land masses had a sufficiency of mountains offering power sources in the form of water and sun-power collectors placed in the proper positions on them.

He got up and went downstairs to wander first through the bars and dining areas of the hotel, and then out into the immediate area of the city around the hotel to observe what else he could of the populace.

The natives he saw did not show anything like the self-discipline that was supposed to be the hallmark of the Dorsai, nor the inner calm and assurance of those from the Exotic worlds. Generally speaking, they were smaller, noisier and apparently less disciplined—in their hours of relaxation, at least.

He saw a great many more individuals either drunk or partially drunk than he had remembered seeing, even as a boy on New Earth and some of the other worlds. There was almost something of the frontier-town-grown-up about the Freiland city scene at night.

If this looseness and freedom were reflected in their politics, he would expect a lot more overt illegalities among the governing members of its three houses, though only one of those was a real power when it came to enacting laws and governing the country.

The other two represented established interests and—on paper at least—had little or no power. It had been interesting for him to note that business groups, as well as population sections, elected representatives to that one powerful governing body.

Bleys was at Hammer's office before dawn. It had been interesting to him when he had first seen it yesterday to notice that it was laid out and set up exactly the same as Dahno's. Even the desks for the two employees were in the same position in the same-shaped room; and the file and research room had a similar hidden door off Hammer's personal office, which opened to a touch of one of his keys.

He began his search through the files.

His study of Dahno's files had developed in him a quick ability to assess the value of a file he looked at. He went through them rapidly; and the greater majority of them were just as Hammer had implied—completely harmless and uninteresting.

But there were others that implied something else. What Bleys was looking for were patterns of organization or reportage which indicated things hidden. No human could do anything, day after day, without falling into habits that showed themselves in patterns in the way he or she did it. If part of that pattern was designed to hide something that the person writing the file did not want suspected, then comparison of enough files could find it cropping up often enough to waken suspicion.

There was nothing complicated about the process. Only, it required somebody with Bleys' ability to scan the files at remarkable speed, to identify the suspicious patterns and keep them in mind; ready to be triggered if a similar pattern showed up. When enough patterns had been gathered, it was then merely a matter of ordering the research machines to gather samples of the patterns, put them together and print them out.

Once with enough patterns in his hand, and remembering

their context, it was possible for him to begin making conjectures about what Hammer was attempting to hide. The more Bleys deduced, the more he knew what to look for in the way of other patterns; and the closer he came to what the other man had tried to conceal.

Still, capable as Bleys was, it took him a day and a half to gather any solid picture of what might have been obscured by these apparently complete, open files; and it was a long day and a half after that, before he was ready to talk to Hammer about it.

He chose to bring up the subject once more when the two of them were having dinner, after a certain amount of food and casual conversation had relaxed the other man. Then, with the main course dishes ready to be cleared away he reached into his pocket inside his jacket and brought out a paper which he handed to Hammer.

"I've seen that," said Hammer with a smile, "you showed it to me as soon as you landed."

"Yes," said Bleys quietly, but with his eyes very steadily on Hammer's eyes, "and you've obeyed it to the letter, haven't you?"

Hammer looked back at him puzzled, and as the silence continued and Bleys continued to hold his gaze, the smile slowly faded from the other man's face.

"I don't understand," Hammer said, "what are you getting at?"

Bleys took the letter back, rolled it up and put it inside his jacket pocket again.

"I'd hate to take that response of yours just now back to Dahno," he said.

For the first time, Bleys began to read minute, but undeniable, instinctive signals of alarm in Hammer. The general light of the restaurant reflected a little more brightly from his forehead, indicating moisture on the skin. His breathing accelerated—slightly but unmistakably—and his hands closed about items of tableware. One picked up a fork, the other clasped the stem of his water glass.

"I still don't understand," said Hammer, and his voice was beautifully controlled.

"All right, then," said Bleys, "we'll say no more about it."

"Good!" Relief was in Hammer's voice.

"Of course you know," said Bleys, "that I will have to tell Dahno when I get back to Association?"

"Whatever you think is right," said Hammer, tightly. He was no longer smiling.

"You see," said Bleys, quietly, "we've found that certain things are necessary in situations and organizations; or as part of an organization operating by itself; and one of those is that the person in charge necessarily has some things which must be kept secret—from everybody. On the other hand, very often they're things that he can't merely trust to memory. So, as a result, inevitably, there are secret files."

"I don't," said Hammer, "have any secret files."

"I think we should talk about them, anyway," protested Bleys, still mildly. "You see, one of the things that brings about a secret file is that anyone at all, in control or not, necessarily has a private life as well as an organizational one, and again it's inevitable that things from the private life will splash over and affect the organizational life. This is the sort of thing that needs to be kept secret. As I say, it always happens."

"You can tell Dahno," said Hammer between his teeth, "that this is one place where that rule's broken down. I never have had any need to keep anything secret from the organization; and I haven't. I repeat, there's nothing in the way of secret files here on Freiland."

"Good. I'll tell him exactly that," said Bleys. "Now, why don't we get off the subject? I'm sorry I had to bring it up in the first place; but you understand that it's something that is going to have to be asked at every stop I make?"

Hammer's tight jaw muscles stayed tense.

"Yes . . . ," he said, grudgingly moving toward a tone of better humor, "I can see that. Just as long as you make it perfectly clear to Dahno that there's nothing like that here."

"You can trust me," said Bleys, smiling at him. "I'll be

bringing him the exact facts on every Others' out-world organization we have."

With that apparently touchy subject behind them, both men made an apparent effort to smooth over the emotions it had aroused, and find more interesting and pleasant topics for conversation.

Hammer began to give Bleys a description of the various teachers and trainers he was using for his trainees, and how he intended to use the trainee class once they graduated—since those trainees that the out-world organizations produced were for their own use. The aim was eventually to have an effectively-trained person at every point where highly valuable information could be garnered.

Such talk took up most of the dinner, and after that Bleys made his excuses, although Hammer hinted that he might like to look at the recreational elements of night-life on Freiland. He was, Bleys said, a little more tired out from the trip here than he had thought. The first two days' excitement had carried him through, but now it was catching up with him. When this sort of thing happened, he told Hammer, he had a tendency to sleep straight through for ten or twelve hours.

Accordingly, with dinner finished, they parted and Bleys went upstairs to his suite in the hotel.

He sat down at the writing desk in the lounge of his suite and added to the log he carried the events of the day just past, including a verbatim account of his conversation about the secret files with Hammer.

This daily duty done, he put the log away in its carrying case in his suitcase and stepped out for a moment onto the balcony of his suite, that opened off both the living room and the bedroom.

He was on the thirty-fifth floor of a forty-two-story hotel, and the city sparkled with lights at his feet as far as he could see. He did note that, possibly something like a dozen blocks away, the dark spire of an office building rose directly in line with his hotel, such that someone with a window or a balcony like this one could look directly in the direction of his room.

It would do no good, of course, to run a picture recorder

from the vantage point of a floor in the other building that was on a level with his own. The flimsiest of inner drapes would be like an opaque wall to such a camera, at such a distance. But a sound-pickup gun could easily catch the slightest noise he made during the night. Of course, if he slept clear through, as he had told Hammer he might, the listening would be rather uninteresting.

It was a relief to feel safe about a long-distance camera, at least, being focused on his two rooms to see everything that might happen there.

Bleys normally locked such balcony doors as a matter of course. But tonight, when he went into the bedroom to get ready for bed, he opened wide one of the two french doors to the balcony, locked the other, and merely pulled the inner, net drapes. Then he took off his shoes and put on a robe, tying the cord at the waist. He lay down on the bed on his back, turned the light out and clasped his hands behind his head.

He lay, staring at the dark ceiling overhead in the room, that was just barely lighted by the glow of the city lights outside—so that it was a place of darkness to anyone whose eyes were not adjusted to it, but dimly visible to Bleys as his eyes adjusted to the gloom.

Shortly after midnight, two dark human bodies descended silently onto his balcony. They could only have come here by being lowered from the roof. Bleys, as silently, rose from his bed and moved over to a corner of the room where the wall met the glass that fronted on the balcony. He untied the cord which belted his robe and held it loosely in both his hands, before him. In slightly deeper shadow of the corner, he waited.

Cautiously the two intruders peered through the open door of the french window. With the outside light still enlarging their pupils, they would not be able to see from out there whether there was a body in the bed or not.

After a moment, they tried the one french door that was closed. Finding it locked, they entered in single file through the other door, pushing silently through the parting in the gauze curtains behind the open doorway and into the room. They were both carrying handguns that Bleys recognized, by their long barrels, grotesquely bulging toward the end from the wire shielding wrapped around them, as void pistols.

Assassins' weapons. The military had no use for them, because of their extremely short range and doubtful accuracy at more than ten meters. But they were absolutely silent, and they left no mark whatsoever upon the body they struck with their pulses of energy. Only the electrical activity in that part of the body that was touched, was canceled out for several minutes. A heart shot meant instant death, which could not be distinguished from simple heart failure, even in this day and age.

As the second one stepped clear of the doorway, Bleys moved into position behind him, the cord in both hands, held a little apart, so that a section of it draped between the two hands.

He threw the cord over the head of the second man and pulled it tight with a jerk around his neck, snapping it tight with all the strength of the arm muscles he had developed over the past five years. The man froze for a second, then dropped as shock and the cutoff of fresh blood to his brain hit him at the same time.

Bleys broke the fall of his body with an encircling left arm and with his right arm scooped up the void pistol that was starting to drop from the man's hand. The assassin hit the floor; and the one in front of him, alerted by the small noise, spun around to find, several inches before his nose, his partner's void gun aimed directly at him.

"Drop the pistol!"

It was Bleys' voice, with all the strength and resonance built into it during the last years of lessons, together with the note of absolute command he had learned from Henry.

"Back off to the foot of the bed."

The second assassin did so. Keeping the first weapon trained on him Bleys stooped briefly to scoop up the one that had just been dropped. He stepped wide of the bed, still keeping both the conscious and the unconscious man covered with the weapons.

"Pull your friend to the foot of the bed. Then lie down

beside him—both of you on your stomachs. And stay there. I'll have a pistol on you all the time."

He obeyed.

Bleys walked around to the head of the bed, snapped on the lights, and switched on the bedside hotel phone.

With one finger he coded in Hammer's private nighttime number. Wherever the other man would be, the call would be automatically relayed from this phone to him.

The call was slow enough in being answered to indicate a reluctance to answer it. Finally, however, Hammer's voice came on, thickened as if he had just been roused from sleep.

"What is it?" his voice said.

"Who is it—I think you mean," said Bleys. "This is Bleys. I've run into a rather troublesome little situation here. I'd like you to come over to my hotel suite immediately."

There was a second of unintelligible mutter at the other end and then Hammer's voice came through, still thick with sleep but clear enough.

"I'm sorry, I can't come now, Bleys," he said. "I'll see you in the morning—"

"Hammer," interrupted Bleys softly, "do you remember the signed paper that was the first thing I showed you when I met you at the spaceport terminal here?"

There was a pause. Then Hammer's voice came, no longer thick with sleep, but angry.

"I remember it!"

"Then you can come over right away. Good," said Bleys, "how soon can you. get here?"

"It's not easy," growled Hammer, "I'm in bed. The best I could do would be half an hour."

"Half an hour?" said Bleys. "I don't think—" He broke off to turn his head from the phone to speak to the one would-be assassin who had been choked unconscious and had come to and was instinctively beginning to try to get to his feet.

"Stay down there!" said Bleys, but without undue emphasis, knowing his voice would also carry over the phone. "I'm afraid I can't wait half an hour, Hammer. Twenty minutes."

He broke the connection.

"Did you hear that, both of you?" he asked, stepping to the foot of the bed to stand over the two on the floor there. "You'll have to stay where you are for another twenty minutes. Just relax. If either of you tries to get up, he'll be shot."

The two neither moved nor spoke.

It was a little more than twenty minutes, but only by a minute or two, before the doorbell to Bleys' suite rang. He depressed the button that allowed him to speak to whoever was on the outside.

"Who is it?"

"You know—Hammer!"

Bleys triggered the bedside control stud that unlocked the door. He heard Hammer enter and the door close behind him; and a moment later the other had come through the entrance from the lounge to the bedroom. He stopped abruptly at the sight of the two young men on the floor and the void pistol in each of Bleys' hands.

"You know these two, of course," Bleys said.

"I? I never saw them before in my life!" said Hammer. He smiled. "You seem to be getting all sorts of strange notions tonight, Bleys."

"All right, you two on the floor," said Bleys, "you've heard his voice, now you can lift your head from the floor for a moment long enough to look at him. Go ahead."

They lifted their heads briefly and put them down again.

"You know him, of course," Bleys said.

Both of those on the floor muttered negatives.

"And you're sure you don't know them, Hammer?" said Bleys. "That's a pity. I thought this whole business could be taken care of quietly and easily. It looks like I'll have to kill them; and then you'll have to take care of disposing of their bodies; and then see to it that I'm not bothered by the police or hear any more of this . . . though I might be discharged by court, anyway," Bleys went on thoughtfully; "they're obviously intruders. They made a point of dressing up all in close-fitting black suits. And planetary customs didn't find any void pistols in my baggage when I landed. Yes, I might just get off at that but—"

He smiled at Hammer.

"—I'd rather have you take care of it."

"What do you think I can do if you kill them?" Hammer demanded. "What makes you think I can keep the law off you?"

"You don't think you can?" said Bleys. "Well, that's interesting. You're the first of the Others' world organizations to be set up outside of Association. You're the oldest group in terms of being in place the longest. You mean to tell me that after all this time here, you don't have the kind of influence to take care of something like this, even if it does get to be a matter of police and courts? I don't really believe you, you know. I think you're just being modest. I know Dahno would be very surprised to hear that you didn't have that kind of influence. In fact I'm sure you could take care of this if I killed them. I just thought it would be less trouble for you if I didn't have to kill them. You see, I was sure you knew them. Are you absolutely positive you don't?"

There was a long pause, while Bleys' gaze moved back and forth from the two on the floor to Hammer and back to the two again—and then back to Hammer.

"All right, I know them!" said Hammer. "They're mine, the clumsy idiots!"

"Now it's them you're being hard on," said Bleys. "I'm sure somewhere along the line the members of your class were told that it's the one in charge who's always the one responsible. If they were clumsy, you were responsible. Now, how about disposing of them?"

"Let them go—" said Hammer.

"In your custody, certainly," said Bleys. He spoke to the two on the floor. "You can get up now and go with this man here, or do what he tells you."

Bleys kept the pistols trained on them while they got to their feet, looked at him, looked at Hammer, and stood undecided.

"There'll be a rope or something outside," Hammer told them. "Get out there, have whoever's on the roof pull you back up again; and the two of you try to get out of here without leaving any sign of having been here—if you can!"

Somewhat sullenly, they left. They were both remarkably alike, except for a slight difference in hair color; so that if the hair had only matched they could have passed for twins in their black suits. They left without looking further at either Hammer or Bleys; simply turned around and went back out through the opening in the curtain onto the balcony.

Bleys waited until he heard the sound of what was apparently a piece of scaffolding being pulled back up toward the floors overhead. Then he put down one of the void pistols, reached out to the controls by his bed and turned on all the balcony lights. Meanwhile, the void pistol in his other hand casually pointed more or less in Hammer's direction.

Outside the lights sprang on; and showed the balcony empty.

"Now you see why I said a little earlier this evening that under certain conditions certain things are inevitable. Weren't there some secret files you were going to show me?"

"You'll see them tomorrow," said Hammer.

"And you know what?" Bleys said. "By tomorrow when I see them, they might just be a little bit different. Strange how that can happen to files sometimes. But certain things will go missing and other things will be altered so that their meaning is different. Suppose we go look at them now."

"Now?" said Hammer. "It's the middle of the night—or later!"

"That's quite all right," said Bleys, "I'm not the least tired."

CHAPTER

23

HAMMER'S OUTER OFFICE had the same garish appearance such offices always do at such a time of night, under such conditions. The seemingly too-bright lights, the naked surface of the night-clean desks, seemed to reject any daytime sense of life about the place.

Even Hammer's inner office, with its carpeted floor and paneled walls, had something of the same look about it. As they were about to go through the door into the file room Bleys placed a friendly hand on the shorter man's shoulder, feeling the muscles under the jacket tense at his touch.

Friendlies as an ordinary rule were careful to avoid physical contact; and enough of Hammer's raising had stayed with him to make him still that way. Bleys spoke to him in a soothing, friendly tone.

"Now," he said, "you know, and I don't, how much reading there is to do in these files I'm about to look at. I'll want you in the file room with me while I'm going through them. So why don't you bring a chair in if you think you'll need it?"

"No thanks," said Hammer tightly, "I'll sit in the desk chair there."

"I may want to use that myself," said Bleys. "In fact, I'll probably be viewing the files on the desk screen."

Without a further word Hammer picked up one of the slimmer floats in his office and carried it through the relatively narrow door of the file room to set it down at the room's far end.

He took his seat in it, crossed his legs, sat with his arms on the armrests of the float and stared at Bleys.

"How do I get into these files?" Bleys asked.

Hammer reached in a pocket and tossed him a key ring.

"It's the number seven key, there," said Hammer, "I mean, the one marked with the number seven."

Bleys used the key in the slot of the desk control pad, and saw the screen light up with, in large letters, the word PERSONAL. He tossed the keys back to Hammer and seated himself before the screen.

He began to summon up the files in alphabetical order, scanning them briefly, and moving on.

"Are you actually reading those?" asked Hammer after a few minutes.

"Yes," said Bleys, without looking up from the screen, "I'm a fast reader."

He continued through the files. It took him a little over an hour and a half to read them all completely. Then he shut off the screen and swung his desk chair around to face Hammer.

"Very interesting," he said to the other man. "Now, suppose you take me someplace quiet where we can talk—we can even go back to my suite, if you think it's safe. But I imagine it's bugged, isn't it?"

"It was," said Hammer briefly; "as you know, hotels sweep the rooms in suites for listening devices daily. We hadn't had time to set in a new microphone yet. But I can take you to a private club, where we ought to be free from interruption at this time of night, and as comfortable as you like."

"Good," said Bleys.

The private club, it seemed, was only a few minutes' drive

away. Hammer unlocked its front door with another of the keys on his key ring and stepped inside. A man almost as large as Bleys, and a good deal heavier, rose from a chair behind a small desk and stepped in their way.

"Is this gentleman a guest of yours, Hammer Martin?" he asked.

"Of course," said Hammer.

"One minute," said the man. He stepped back to his desk, sat down and wrote on the window of a small, discreet badge, "Guest of Hammer Martin." He stood up, stepped back around to Bleys and pressed the badge against the lapel of Bleys' jacket. It adhered. He went back to his seat; and Hammer led Bleys on into what seemed to be a very large lounge, completely empty except for overstuffed float-armchairs, with a little wing table attached to one padded arm of each, holding a control pad and space for a drink or a plate.

"Wherever you like," said Hammer, waving at the empty room.

Bleys led the way over to a couple of chairs seated around a small round table in a corner.

"I actually don't have to ask you if this is bugged," he said to Hammer as they sat down, "because it'd be more to your disadvantage than mine to have what's said here overheard."

"It's not bugged," Hammer retorted.

Bleys leaned toward him, smiling engagingly. With voice and body he was able to command attention and sometimes automatically produce compliance, from someone who did not even know him. But he did not have Dahno's almost magical talent for making firm, warm friendships at what seemed hardly a glance and a word.

As a result, Bleys had concluded that he never would be able to match Dahno in this. The reason for Dahno's success was that with him, as with their mother, at any given moment everything he did and said was honest and true. He believed utterly in each word he spoke, as he spoke it. Bleys, who had come to see the universe in absolute and inflexible terms, could not hoodwink himself that way—blowing true one moment and false the next.

Here, however, was where the charisma he had worked to develop would pay off, if at all. With voice and eyes compelling, now, with his body leaning slightly, confidentially forward in the chair, and with a smile on his face, he spoke to Hammer.

"I wouldn't say there's anything in those files of yours that's beyond mending," he said in a warm, friendly voice, low-toned enough to be confidential.

Hammer said nothing.

"You've set up your own private corps of assassins," Bleys continued, in the same gentle voice. "That's not permissible. You've been taking personal payments, bribes and kickbacks, in addition to contributions to the organizational fund. *That*, you know, is also not permissible."

He paused, letting his words sink into the other man. Then he smiled. "On the other hand, anyone in charge of one of our organizations needs his own discretionary fund, and is allowed to set one up—with due understanding that it doesn't reach an unreasonable size—from the income that comes the way of the organization in the ordinary way of business. Only records have to be kept. Third, you've got a number of contacts here in important posts, governmental, military, legal and business, that aren't mentioned in your regular files. These are perhaps the most serious faults, of the ones I've mentioned so far. There are a few other smaller ones—call them peccadilloes—"

"Let's not waste time rehearsing what we both know you just read," said Hammer. "What do you want?"

"That's something we'll talk about in a moment," said Bleys, "and it's not something I want as much as something I can offer you. I'd make the same offer to anyone in your shoes right now."

He paused, to let this register on the other.

"As far as my listing your errors," he went on, "that was mainly to give you some evidence I actually did read through those files closely. Well now, you asked me what I want. Actually, that isn't the question you ought to be asking, in any case."

"No?" said Hammer. "What question should I be asking?"

"How can the two of us put things properly on their way here?" said Bleys. "You see, your organization is part of our total organization. It follows that anything you do affects the whole of our Others group. Just to clear our decks, have you anything at all to say as justification for these things?"

"Certainly," said Hammer. "Dahno is nearly superhuman. We all know that. You seem to have a great deal of capacity yourself. But the point is, something could happen to Dahno. Something could break the structure of the total organization you talk about, so that each group like mine, on its world, is alone. If that happens, things should be set up so that it can survive by itself."

"Now," said Bleys, "that leads very nicely into the general plans which are part of what I came here to tell you. But I couldn't in conscience tell them to someone who wasn't organized to accept them."

"All right," said Hammer stubbornly. "Our only sure hope of survival has to be having only one man here—the person in charge—holding the ultimate reins of power; and able to make his own decisions about handling things. This isn't Association, you know. Those secret files you looked at were simply part of my attempt to protect this organization, if it ever should be cut off and we had to operate on our own."

"I hardly think that Dahno would be satisfied with that answer," said Bleys mildly.

"I know he won't!" said Hammer, doggedly. "You know he won't. It's still *the* answer. I'll ask you again—what is it you want?"

"What do I want?" Bleys echoed. He leaned back into his chair and steepled his long fingers together before him. "What is it Dahno wants? What is it any of us want, including you? You see, Hammer, those are all meaningless questions. It assumes we're only concerned with ourselves. But we aren't. Now you certainly knew that when you left Association. I'm sure you know it now as well."

"Of course," said Hammer, "we want the full organization to grow and gain in power. But—"

"Quite right," Bleys' voice overrode his, "*the full organi-*

zation, Hammer. I'm sure you remember Dahno talking about its ultimate future. Well, the time to begin work on that future is now. It affects everybody."

"Everybody?" Hammer said. "You mean Dahno—and maybe you, too, as well?"

"I mean *Us*—every Other alive," said Bleys patiently. "Think for a moment. We're an organization because we're a people. A different people. We have the advantage of the fresh and better thinking of the cross-breed. Whatever improvement or refinement humanity's discovered in one special Splinter Culture, joined to whatever advantage another Splinter Culture may have."

"Not all cross-breeds have that," said Hammer.

"No," said Bleys, "not all. But it's important that the general public on all the worlds come to think of all Splinter Culture cross-breeds as specially talented. That way, there's enough of us to form a people. We may be scattered, and are; many cross-breeds don't even know us who're in the Organization. But we want to convince them, as well as the general public, that we're all a special people—born to be leaders of the ordinary human race."

"How're we supposed to do that?" asked Hammer. Some of the tension had gone out of his voice, and Bleys knew that he was beginning to have his effect on the man. "And what's that got to do with me if we do?"

"To answer your first question—by recruiting all cross-breeds into the organization and calling them all 'Others,' just like us. That was always the plan and the time's finally come to put it to work. To answer the second question—can't you see that doing so would make you a kingpin in a very large and powerful organization indeed?"

He paused to let Hammer absorb that idea. He began to feel that he was beginning to capture the man. It was not only that Hammer had hesitated, and was sitting absorbing the notion. His very posture was different. A great deal of the muscle tension hewed by his recent antagonism to Bleys, had gone from him on seeing in what Bleys was telling him *his* personal future.

"Yes," said Hammer slowly, at last; and Bleys could see the attractiveness of the idea had caught him. "It'd make us much more of a power among the stars."

"*The* power," said Bleys.

"That's something that wasn't talked about when I was in training," said Hammer, still thoughtful.

"The time wasn't ready, then, to mention it," said Bleys.

"And I don't remember Dahno talking about it in his graduation address to us, either," said Hammer.

"No, you wouldn't have," said Bleys. He leaned back in his chair. "But you see now that while the organization is concerned with the care and feeding and propagation of its own units, in a larger sense we'd be tarred with the same brush, if the news got out that cross-breeds in general had secret corps of assassins."

Hammer was silent for a long moment.

"I see what you mean," he said at last.

"Just suppose something went wrong; and you—or one of the Other organization heads—couldn't stop it in time," said Bleys. "If someone of our organization had an assassin get caught and the connection with the name 'Others' became known, there'd be the danger of triggering off a situation in which the great majority of ordinary people—and they still outnumber us thousands to one—could start to look suspiciously on anyone calling himself an Other."

Once more he paused to let his last words ring in Hammer's ears.

"That," he went on, "we can't afford. We have to make the name something to aspire to, not something to try to exterminate. It's not only that such a pogrom would put us all in danger; but it would make absolutely impossible the workings of our organization. And the organization's our only hope of being recognized for what we are. You follow me?"

Hammer sat for a moment. His eyes were abstract and his whole demeanor was thoughtful. After a few moments, he roused himself from this and looked directly at Bleys.

"And you really see a time when the Others could be a large

enough organization to be a power among the stars—generally?" he asked.

"We will own at least the New Worlds," Bleys said; "eventually—maybe eventually Old Earth as well. But it means in addition to supplying Dahno with local information, your major effort from now on will be to recruit any and all cross-breeds on this world into the organization."

Hammer made a wry face.

"What'll we do with them all?" he asked.

"In the long run, find each of them some job for the organization—in the short term, simply make them up in groups and keep them in training until you've got a spot for each," said Bleys.

"Yes . . ." said Hammer, drawing the word out thoughtfully. Then he looked up at Bleys. "But you, what're you going to do now?"

Bleys pushed back his chair. "Well, I've got several more days before I leave. I've already thoroughly read up on this world, but I want to check what I read against some personal observation. I'll be spending the rest of my time here looking around. You can get me a pass to the visitors' gallery of the Second House of government, can't you?"

The Second House was the powerful one.

"Oh, certainly," said Hammer, getting to his own feet. But ever since Bleys' argument seemed to have reached him, he had begun to change back from the bristly, antagonistic opponent he had been for most of the time since Bleys started asking to look at his secret files. With this change, his reawakened sense of duty as host to Bleys was brought back to life again. "Wouldn't you rather have me show you around? You ought to be able to enjoy at least part of this trip; and there's a good many things here in the city, or a short flight outside, I think you'd enjoy."

"No. No thank you," said Bleys, "I'd rather get to know the world, as I say. That's the best you can do for me between now and when I leave."

"Well, do you want me to show you around wherever it is you want to look?" Hammer asked.

"No. Specifically no," said Bleys. "I want to see what I want to see with my own eyes and without any influence, no matter how well meant, from anyone with me."

"Well, all right," said Hammer, as the two of them went out. "But I'll want to talk to you at least one more time before you leave."

"Certainly," said Bleys, "just before I leave, on the day I leave. If the ship goes at the right time, we could have lunch and you could put me on it."

"It'd be a pleasure," said Hammer.

Bleys smiled broadly at him; and after a moment Hammer smiled back.

In the next few days Bleys did exactly what he had said he would do. He sat in the visitors' gallery above the floor of the Second House and noted that it was not all that different from the single Chamber on Association. Probably it was not different from most governing bodies everywhere else.

This, however, was a light and airy place, with huge skylights in its domed top that not only made what went on on the floor, Bleys thought, much more pleasant for the people on it, but was a boon to visitors in the gallery. He did note that the representatives he observed did not seem the sort of group that could be led by a few strong, charismatic minds, as was the case with Association.

With this established, he ignored all else to do with government. He turned his attention instead to the business community, and the general state of the city, and even the countryside around it. His general conclusion was that this was even a richer world than he had expected. None of the Younger Worlds, of course, could hold a candle to Old Earth, not only in natural resources still available to modern methods, but in accumulated wealth of different kinds, including a lot which reflected the history of the Mother World.

Bleys' final decision was that Freiland was a planet that could be called upon for a great deal quickly, industrialized as it was, but would exhaust itself in a much shorter time than someplace like Association, which would find trouble giving much, except human bodies. But being mainly an agricultural world, even though there were only a few rich farming areas, it would be slower to fall apart than someplace like the world he was on.

On the other hand, Association belonged to one of the three major Splinter Cultures, all of which were self-doomed; simply because, while the best of the Splinter Cultures had produced the greatest in human development, for that very reason they were less viable in the long run, than a mixed-culture world like Freiland, New Earth, or—again, the ultimate example— Old Earth, itself.

Bleys had told Hammer he wanted to be left alone these last days until just before he took off. But the night before his ship was to leave he got a call from Hammer inviting him to a dinner at which he could meet other members of the original class of trainees who had settled down on this planet. It was not the sort of invitation he could turn down; so he went, but left early on the plea that the spaceship's leaving tomorrow was earlier in the afternoon than he had expected, and he would need his rest.

He did not mention getting together with Hammer personally before he left.

Hammer, however, had not forgotten. He called Bleys the next morning, as soon as he could decently expect Bleys to be up and about—though actually Bleys had been up for a good two hours by that time.

"How about a very early lunch, after which I can take you out to the spaceport?" he asked.

"Fine," said Bleys. They disconnected.

Bleys could almost imagine the words in which Hammer would express the ideas that must have been bubbling inside him, these last few days. He turned out to be very close in his guess. Across the lunch table, after the first few polite exchanges of conversation in which Hammer asked about how satisfying his last few days had been, he dived directly into what was on his mind.

"This whole business of the Others eventually being a power—no, that's right, you said *the* power among the Younger Worlds," Hammer said, "I've been giving it a good deal of thought. It suggests a number of things. One is we've always made a point not to display the name of Others openly, although we've never denied we called ourselves that. Maybe now we should start talking ourselves up and the name up, to the rest of the planets."

"It might be a bit early for that," answered Bleys. "Here on Freiland, why don't you simply publicize—not extensively, but noticeably—when your organization makes a charitable donation to something needed."

"Yes, that's a thought," said Hammer.

"You might also make a point of looking up cross-breeds who might be in personal or financial difficulties or even in bad health, and doing what you can for them," Bleys went on; "that, you wouldn't even need to publicize. You'd accomplish two things. The cross-breeds not connected with the organization who are nonetheless treated kindly by it, would draw closer to the organization themselves. Instinctively they'd feel a kinship to what knows itself to be an elite group, and they'd also spread the word of what you'd done for them to those like them."

He paused to let this sink in on Hammer. Hammer nodded.

"Granted," said Bleys, "they'd only spread it among those they knew. But there's no rush about having the general public here notice us, until we really are in a position of strength; and, with all due respect to what you've done here, I'll be telling Dahno that with the exceptions you already know about, you've been a good manager of the local organization. But you're still not really a power in Freiland politics. Moreover, I don't expect to find any of the organizations on other Younger Worlds to be powers where they are—yet."

Hammer thought about it for a moment.

"Yes, that makes sense," he said. "Of course there's no reason for us not to begin to be a little more aggressive in getting into positions where we have a finger in the pie of everything of importance around the planet."

He glanced at Bleys.

"You don't object to that, do you?" he asked.

"No, not at all," said Bleys. "In fact it's the sort of thing I'd like to see you all doing; but be very unobtrusive about it. If I were you I'd mention that kind of aim only casually; and even then to one at a time of your own classmates. Also, warn them not to mention it yet to your own recruits who are still learning."

Hammer nodded.

"I understand," he said. "You can trust me, Bleys Ahrens. We won't claim anything we don't already have firmly in our grasp. And then we'll mention it just as an incidental matter."

"I think you'll find, as you establish strong bonds of friendship with planetary politicians—nothing but friendship, mind—" said Bleys, "if they're such good friends that they want to loan you or give you funds or anything like that, that's fine. I know you were exposed to the rule we never ask for anything. But I predict once you've formed strong bonds of friendship with a majority of those in power on this planet, the rest will come quickly to you, on their own."

"You think so?" said Hammer.

"I do," answered Bleys, "once you have the whole planet firmly in your grasp, you can begin being open about your superiority; and the superiority of our organization, over anything else locally. But that's still going to be a ways off yet. It'll take a few years, even if things move fairly fast for all of us, to get individual organizations into that sort of position of control."

"Oh, I understand perfectly," said Hammer. "Now, how much of this should I clear with Dahno, or you, before we do it?"

"Try clearing it with me, first," said Bleys. "You know, Dahno has his hands full managing Association himself and our organization there. If I can deal with it, then we've saved him that much of a drain on his time and attention. If not, I can always pass it on to him."

"Excellent," said Hammer. "Then I'll address all information dealing with this to you, first."

Bleys looked at his wrist monitor. It was almost time for him to leave. They had covered everything that he had wanted to cover, and he had done successfully all he had set out to do. He let Hammer drive him to the spaceport, making general talk about Freiland and the diversity he had noticed, of its peoples, even with common customs. Hammer endorsed the comments and even threw in a few of his own.

An hour and a half later Bleys was in space, in the lounge of the ship that would carry him to Cassida; and watching the starscape, while his mind processed everything of the past week to set it in context with his continually growing picture of the human race and what he must do, when the time came.

CHAPTER

24

"AH, BLEYS AHRENS! Honored to meet you! Honored!" said a voice rather closer to the floor of the Cassidan terminal than Bleys had expected, as he felt his hand grasped by the hand of a short, slightly rotund man, with his round face wreathed in smiles. "I'm Himandi Messer. You were expecting me to be here, I think?"

"More or less, yes," said Bleys as Himandi pressed his hand warmly and came very close to pumping it up and down in a way that had been customary centuries ago.

He had indeed been expecting Himandi, who was the leader of the local Others association. Bleys looked down now at a man who was clearly in his forties.

Bleys, who had had some contact by letter with Himandi before his coming, had looked for clues in the letter to Himandi's background, but it had been impossible for him to say what kind of a cross-breed he was, and which Splinter Cultures had come together to produce him—usually a situation that indicated the man did not know who his parents were. He had tested out as pure Exotic.

Bleys would have guessed a certain amount of Exotic parentage, but that was as far as supposition could take him. In any case, he was undeniably capable.

"But you came direct from Freiland!" said Himandi, finally releasing his hand. "I rather thought you'd stop at Newton first?"

"Why? asked Bleys.

Himandi chuckled deeply.

"Oh," he said, "it's just that I thought as long as you were this far you might want to spend some time looking at Newton. It's a remarkable place—" His voice trailed off. At the moment he even looked almost uncomfortable.

"No," said Bleys, "as I've been telling people along the way, this isn't in any sense a recreational trip. I'm making these visits purely for business reasons."

"Oh, I see. Well, certainly . . ." Himandi babbled on as he drew Bleys deeper into the terminal. Bleys understood what was behind that question of his about Newton. It was very nearly a reflex in most Cassidans.

Cassida was a technological world, where technicians were taught, put to work and exported when profitable to other planets like Association for difficult projects like putting in a Core Tap.

It was a world that had an almost symbiotic relationship with Newton; and Newton was a world primarily of research scientists, who were supported in this labor of pure research by the occasional licensing of some discovery that was useful and marketable to the technicians on Cassida.

Cassida had the people and the facilities to turn such things into concrete realities that could be sold on other worlds, including even Old Earth.

The relationship, however, extended even to the social areas of both planets. In spite of several hundred years of association there was still a covert tendency on the part of the Newtonian scientists to look down their nose slightly at Cassidans—and a sneaking tendency on the part of the Cassidans, which they would never admit but which showed itself in questions like the one Himandi had asked just now—to look up to and imitate Newton.

It was an influence which reached into every branch of Cassidan life. It even affected their governmental structure. Newton was ruled by a twelve-man Board of Governors. Beneath that Board there was a large unwieldy body that consisted of scientists of enough seniority and repute to qualify as members of it—like top members of a teaching staff at a college or university—but of whom there were so many that it was difficult to find a place to get them all gathered together for any kind of lawmaking.

The result was that the lower body, which called itself the House of Representatives, could actually meet only once a year in a large underground stadium. Except in some very rare instances, it simply went through the motions of rubber-stamping the decisions that had already been made by the Board of Governors during that year.

All this information, Bleys had absorbed in the process of studying these two worlds before his trip here. The awkward type of government set up on Newton had inevitably had its effect, if on a more practical level, on Cassida. Here, they also had upper and lower houses of government. The lower one had only about double the numbers of the upper, however, so that the lawmaking process could go on most of the year around.

Also, on Cassida the lower house was much more ready on occasion to override the upper house. This would all be something that Bleys would have to take into account—this business of Newton's influence—when he came to seeing what kind of work the local organization was doing. His own conclusion from studying the matter back on Association was that in spite of everything, Cassida's upper house was still the one with the power. Theoretically, the organization should have concentrated its attention quite strongly on that.

Aside from that, Cassida was a business-oriented world and they should also have their connections and their influence reaching out into the area of business and commerce.

He had been listening to, without hearing, Himandi Messer. But now the other man, almost trotting beside him as they went toward the front of the terminal, was asking him questions which required some answer.

". . . What would you like first, now?" Himandi was saying, "a chance to rest? A meal? Or should we just go someplace and sit where we can have some light refreshment, while you tell me in more detail what your plans are for the days you're here?"

"The last, I think," said Bleys.

"Fine, fine!" said Himandi, coding away at his wrist monitor, "I've sent your luggage to the Elysium. I think you'll like it. It's the best hotel we've got here. Now, the place we'll be going to is right close to the hotel. Come along with me."

Bleys continued with him to the basement parking area where an auto-call had already brought Himandi's magnetic car into the waiting line of those already summoned by people who were leaving the terminal. It was actually the first time he had ridden in a magnetic car, which instead of riding on an air cushion like Dahno's hovercar, rode on magnets that worked against the ones in the road bed to keep the vehicle floating above the ground. Dahno, Bleys knew, could easily have had one of these, rather than his lesser, unimpressive hovercar that traveled on its air cushion, but he was far too wise to attract attention in that way.

Bleys wondered how wise Himandi was to drive what he did.

However, once out on the highways, Bleys noticed Himandi's type of car was far in the majority of the vehicles he saw. Cassida was, of course, a much more wealthy planet than Association; perhaps Himandi's car was unremarkable here.

The lounge Himandi took Bleys to seemed to be part of a hotel that was not the Elysium, to which his baggage had already been sent. Nonetheless, the room they sat down in was a very pleasant room with a number of little conversational circles and padded floats within them. About half the seating areas were occupied by groups; but Bleys noticed as they walked past these that even within a few feet it was impossible to hear any sound of voices from the people talking less than a few feet away. Apparently some invisible sound-blocks were in place.

It was not to be wondered at on a technologically-oriented planet like this.

Once seated, they ordered drinks to which Himandi added a small order of hors d'oeuvre—like finger food. Fruit juice varied in taste from planet to planet, even when it was the juice of the same fruit, because of differences in soil and environment. Therefore, Bleys stayed away from the fruit juices and instead settled for a dry ginger ale, that was a common and uniform thing on all the spaceships and all the worlds, being specifically made for travelers like himself who might have trouble with a change in food tastes every couple of weeks. Himandi ordered some kind of alcoholic drink, and drank it with as much gusto as Dahno, although not with Dahno's gargantuan capacity.

"Now tell me," said Himandi, "what would you like first? You probably want to rest the rest of today. But this evening or tomorrow we could have a general meal at which all the original members of the organization here could be present and you could meet them. Or would you rather look over the city first?"

"I think I might as well start at the top," said Bleys. "I'd like to see your offices, both the general office and your own private office and anything connected with it in the way of a file room."

"Certainly! Certainly!" said Himandi. "And you'll want to go through the files. Very good. Very good, indeed. And of course you'll want to see the secret files too?"

An alarm bell went off in the back of Bleys' head. It was just barely possible that news of the fact that he had insisted on seeing Hammer's secret files could have reached Himandi here before him. It might barely have been arranged by mailing a letter ahead on a ship that made a connection to Cassida, before Bleys' direct flight had left Freiland. There were two or three days lead time that might have made this possible.

But besides being unlikely, it would require that Hammer had written directly to Himandi himself. That was hardly to be considered. There was no reason for the heads of the Other separate world organizations to be secretly in correspondence. A more likely possibility—unless the offer had been completely innocent—was that the free offering of secret files was an attempt to divert Bleys' attention from something that might be hidden somewhere else in the organization.

"I'll want to see everything, of course," said Bleys pleasantly. "And I'm not at all tired from my trip. After we finish here, why don't we simply go straight to your office?"

"Yes! Absolutely!" said Himandi.

Himandi's outer office, with two people—men in this instance—working busily at a couple of desks with piles of messages in code, had no essential difference from the outer office of Hammer—or Dahno's, for that matter. Himandi introduced Bleys to the two men working there; and then led the way into his own office, which was almost spartan by comparison with Hammer's and Dahno's, but at the same time had a touch of elegance about it that was almost oriental.

Without hesitation, Himandi led the way further into a file room opening off this inner office, and settled Bleys in a float-chair before a large screen.

"Where would you like to start first?" Himandi asked.

"I generally go alphabetically," murmured Bleys. "I'll work through your files that way. These are the secret files or the general files?"

"The general files!" said Himandi. "I thought you'd like to see those first."

"Quite right, I would," answered Bleys. He activated the screen, the controls of which were the same—in fact all such controls were universal on most of the Younger Worlds—and began examining the files.

"I'll be getting some work of my own done in my personal office," said Himandi, "—unless, that is, you want me here with you?"

"It's not necessary," said Bleys. "By all means do what you want; but stay close in case I have questions for you."

"Oh, of course," said Himandi, and went out, gently closing the door of the file room behind him.

Bleys went through the considerable number of open files he could find. They were similar enough to the ones that Hammer and Dahno kept, so that he could go through these even more swiftly than he had gone through Hammer's. Essentially, he was looking for references that left question marks in his mind.

It was at times like this that he felt a small, pleasurable feeling of excitement. It was one of the few opportunities that came to him to open himself up, so to speak, and put his whole ability to a job, even as simple a job as this one. It was like being in a low-flying airship, racing at low altitude at top speed, over a terrain with which he was fully familiar, his vision keyed to pick up anything unusual or different.

In this particular case, the one thing that struck him most strongly, was that the contacts of all the Other members of the Cassida organization were almost completely with members of the lower house. He could find no reason in the rest of the information on file as to why they should be restricting themselves unduly. He tucked the information away for future consideration.

Less than two hours after he had begun he went back to the outer office, where Himandi was at work at his desk. The other looked up, then jumped to his feet as he recognized Bleys.

"Yes?" Himandi said. "There's something I can help you with?"

"Not directly," said Bleys. "I've simply finished going through the general files. I'm ready to look at those secret ones of yours now."

Himandi stared at him in disbelief.

"You've finished with the general files?" he asked.

"Yes," said Bleys, "as I just said, I'm ready for the secret files now."

"But—" Himandi almost stammered, "you couldn't go through all those files in just this much time. I was assuming it'd take you days—maybe a week—to do anything like that."

"As I told Hammer Martin, who heads the organization for us on Freiland," said Bleys, "I'm a fast reader. Now about those secret files—"

"Why, right away. Right away," said Himandi. But his face

was darkened by a puzzled frown as he went past Bleys into the file room and sat down himself before the screen.

As Bleys stood and watched him Himandi carefully set up a code on the screen, which dissolved into a picture of large letters saying: TOP SECRET. AVAILABLE ONLY TO THOSE WITH CLEARANCE.

He put in another code, the screen cleared and the word READY appeared. Himandi reached into his pocket for a bunch of keys, selected one and stuck it in the slot beside the control pad. The screen cleared again and once more the words TOP SECRET appeared on the screen.

Bleys watched with interest. Everything that Himandi had done, except use the key, was sheer flummery. No code input to a machine like this could keep out those who knew and understood such devices.

Himandi got up from the seat before the screen, his smile back on him and apparently all puzzlement and surprise forgotten.

"Just punch the open key for A, and you can go through these files, just like you did the others. They're much shorter."

"Thanks," Bleys sat down before the screen, "in that case, it shouldn't take long."

He did not turn his head, but he heard the file room door click softly closed again behind him as Himandi went back out.

He began to go through the secret files. They seemed to consist mainly of dossiers; those on a number of governmental and business and even some militia people, but also complete dossiers on all the members of the Others group in the Cassida organization. It seemed that a good deal of work had been put into compiling as much information as necessary about the people working under Himandi.

But that was not what riveted Bleys' attention particularly. It was the fact that a great many of the political figures, on whom there were files, were from the upper house. There seemed only one conclusion; and that was that Himandi was personally almost exclusively in contact with those known friends and associates of the organization in the more powerful branch of the government. That meant his subordinate classmates handled the less important people.

Bleys reached the end of the secret files, and switched off the screen. He sat for a few seconds, thinking, then got up and went back out into Himandi's office. The other man was once more at his desk and at work. Just as before, however, he jumped to his feet and came around the desk, leaving the work behind at the sight of Bleys.

"You're really through with the secret files, too?" he asked incredulously.

"Yes," said Bleys. "Now I think I'd better go to my hotel and sleep on what I've read. Perhaps you could set up passes for me tomorrow to the visitors' gallery of both the government houses."

"Oh, absolutely!" said Himandi, leading the way to the door to the outer office.

In his suite at the Elysium Hotel, which was a good deal larger than Bleys needed and luxurious to the point of ostentation, Bleys ordered up a light dinner. Himandi had already left. Outside, the day was beginning to fade into the planet's early twilight. It was his intention to do exactly what he had told Himandi he would do—sleep on the material he had scanned this afternoon. It was one thing to put the information into his mind, another thing to fully consider it. He had discovered that this was best done during sleep hours.

But, just at that moment, the phone on the control pad at the end of the sofa, only a few feet from his elbow, rang. He swung around on his seat float, and keyed on the phone.

"Hello?" he said.

"Bleys Ahrens?" said an anonymous male voice at the other end.

"Speaking," said Bleys.

"We have some interplanetary mail for you that evidently just caught up with you, down here at the desk. It just came in. Should I send it up?"

"Where's it from?" Bleys asked.

"The superscript on one piece of mail says Association," answered the voice, "the other says Ceta. Shall I send them up?"

"Yes," said Bleys.

CHAPTER

25

═══════════

It took a little under five minutes for the uniformed attendant to ring the lounge doorbell of the suite and be admitted with the letters. Bleys, unsure whether to tip the man, played safe and did so. Customs differed from planet to planet. On some planets tips were practically demanded. On others they were an insult. Here, it appeared, a tip was not an insult. The attendant smiled broadly, thanked him and went out.

Bleys looked at the travel envelopes of both letters. They were both hand-addressed to him, in different but similar handwriting. The one from Ceta had been written a good two interstellar months previously. The one from Association was barely a week and a half old.

Bleys ripped open the older envelope first. He found inside a regulation military envelope, once again addressed to him with a return address that was merely a military code number. He opened it and glanced at the last page. It was a letter from Henry's youngest son, Will, its two pages covered with close handwriting on both sides—probably the military limit imposed upon Will. He must somehow have ended up in the militia. Bleys read it:

Dear Bleys,

I'm not allowed to tell you where we are, and it really doesn't matter anyway. There was a draft from our area just a couple of months ago, and now it seems in no time at all I've been through training and am already here on Ceta as part of a force that may be seeing combat soon. On the other hand, we may not. They tell us very little.

I've written Joshua and Father; but I wanted to write you too—simply because I don't know what may be the next chance I get to write, or what may happen to us.

I just wanted to tell you that I missed you, after you left the farm and your visits from time to time brightened all our days. Joshua was always the strong one—after Father, that is—but you were strong too, in a different way. As I remember being young, I remember how safe I used to feel with the two of you and Father. I was always the weak one. And I'm afraid I still am.

I do not feel safe now. I know that it is my duty to the Lord to be chosen for one of the expeditionary units; and that what our services earn will help everyone back home. But I'm not particularly close to anyone else in my Group; and without Father, Joshua, and particularly you, I feel very exposed, sometimes.

I can place my dependence in God and do, but somehow what I miss, even in a way I don't miss Joshua and Father not being close, I miss your understanding of things. I think that somehow if I understood more why God should arrange it that I was sent here, I would be a better soldier for Him.

You would understand this situation if you were in it; and if you were here you could explain it to me, so that I would feel less alone. Somehow, it is even a comfort to write you like this. Not as good, but something like having you here in person. Because, as I say, I know if you were

*here you would understand and you would show me how
to understand.*

*There's not much space to write on these pieces of note
paper they issue us, so I'll close now.*

God and my prayers be with you, Bleys.

All my love,
Will

At total variance with his usual habits, Bleys read the letter
through several times, trying to reach through its words to a
picture of Will sitting in his black expeditionary uniform,
somewhere on Ceta; with a piece of paper on some kind of
makeshift desk, like a board across his knees, writing it. Will
would be nearly eighteen now, but his letter showed him still very
young inside; as he had always been young for his years.

Finally, Bleys put that letter down on a table and opened the
other one. This one, from only about ten days ago and in
bolder handwriting, was from Joshua.

Dear Bleys,

*I tried to call you in Ecumeny from the store, because
I thought you would want to know, but they say you're
off-planet at the moment. So I've written this letter, asking
your organization and Dahno's to forward it on to you
wherever you are.*

*I'm writing you, because I know it would be difficult for
Father to do so. He hasn't told me that, but when I
volunteered first to phone, and then to write he did not
object. I think I could tell he was relieved that I had taken
this on me, because of course he says and shows
nothing—at least to any other eyes than my own.*

*Father and I have always felt the strong, comforting
hand of the Lord firmly upon us. It has not been Will's
fault that maybe at times he did not feel it so strongly.
Perhaps if our mother had not died when he was so
young, he might have been better armored in his Faith.
But he was not; and therefore I know that this business of
being chosen by the militia for draft, probably on contin-*

gent to be rented out offworld—as indeed it turned out he was—was hard on him.

I spoke to the selection committee for our district and tried hard to get them to take me in his place, since it would be much easier for me to go. But their decision was that I was of more importance to the farm and the farm of more importance to feeding our people; and so I must stay at home. They were in the seats of judgment in which the Lord had put them, and I could not quarrel with their decision, any more than Will could.

I was going to wait until you returned from offworld so that perhaps you could come out to the farm and I could simply tell you about his leaving. But today, we got news that Will, with all of his Group, was taken into the Lord's bosom as part of an action that took place on Ceta in a principality there, the name of which was censored in the letter that informed us of Will's death.

I knew you would want to know as soon as possible, and therefore I'm writing this letter. You must know that Will was very fond of you, as we all were, though it was sadness to all of us that you had never succeeded in giving yourself to God. But you know Father has always said that every man and woman belongs to the Lord in his or her own way, whether they know it or not. For that reason he would never join any of the volunteer evangelistic groups that our church sent into cities and other areas, where the beliefs of the people were either lacking or gone astray. I must rejoice that Will is now with God, even though I mourn him silently as Father does. When you return to Association and Ecumeny, we'll both be very happy if you could make a short visit to us out here. We have not seen you in some time.

> *God's blessing be on you,*
> *Joshua*

Bleys laid Joshua's letter down on top of Will's. He stood for a moment, looking at nothing; then picked up both letters and carried them into the bedroom to put them in his personal luggage case. He stood looking at the luggage case after he had relocked it.

Suddenly he shouted with all the force of his lungs. In a lightning movement he spun on one foot, bent over almost parallel to the ground and with the other leg lashed out at the bedroom wall beside him.

There was a crashing sound and an explosion of plaster. The wall, which was only a dividing wall with wooden studs beneath the plaster, suddenly showed a hole big enough for him to put both fists through.

He straightened up, looked at what he had done and after a moment laughed a little, angrily, at himself. He stepped to the phone and signaled the desk.

"I've just made a hole in my wall here," he said. "Send up whoever you have on duty at night and get it repaired."

There was a moment of confusion at the far end and then the voice of the man who had answered got himself under control. "Would you like us to move you to another suite while repairs are being made, Bleys Ahrens?"

"No," said Bleys, "just get them to fix this wall."

He went into the living room and from there onto the balcony. He stood with his hands on the stone-textured upper railing of the balcony, looking at the lights of the Cassidan city below and around him.

He did not see the lights, however, as much as he saw in memory an image of Will throwing himself forward to hug him, in that last moment, when Dahno had taken him from the farm permanently. For the moment he let the memory hold him; then, with an effort of will, he banished it.

If he accomplished the work he would set out to do, it well might be that he, himself, should yet be the cause of the death of both Joshua and Henry, or possibly, Josh's descendants, among millions of others. There was no point in dwelling on the chance that had killed Will.

With an effort he put the matter away. He was concerned that it should touch him at all.

He must not let this sort of thing get in his way. He had never experienced the loss of anyone he cared for. Mainly because, with the exception of his mother, he had been careful never to become close to anyone. He remembered now how instinct had kept him at arm's length from the women trainees of the first class that he had encountered in Ecumeny.

He had not thought that there was in him the capacity to be ensnared by an affection for another being. Not even Dahno— because he knew that Dahno could prove false, as their mother had to them. But, evidently, unknown in him all this time, there was still in him a potential weakness. He could see no cure for it, except to be sure that he stayed at a cautious distance from all other human beings. That was best in any case. It would leave his vision of what must be done, unimpeded.

Behind him, the doorchime rang; and the two cover-suited men outside identified themselves as the night repair crew sent up to work on the wall. He let them in; and then went to the phone in the far end of the living room.

"I've changed my mind," he told the desk. "You can move me to another suite, after all."

Within ten minutes a uniformed attendant was there to move his luggage and guide him to new quarters.

Once settled in his new suite, he went to bed and—after a while—slept soundly.

He was up, dressed and ready to have breakfast sent up, when his phone rang and Himandi's voice spoke in his ear when he keyed it in.

"I thought you might like to have breakfast with me," said Himandi.

"Fine," said Bleys.

They broke the connection and Bleys went down to the breakfast room of the hotel, where he found Himandi already at a table, waiting for him. Bleys sat down, and they ordered.

"I understand you had a small accident with one of the walls of your suite last night," said Himandi, after the morning greetings had been exchanged.

"Yes," replied Bleys in a perfectly level voice, "I had a small accident with one of the walls in my suite."

His eyes were directly upon Himandi's as he spoke; and he continued to hold them there after he finished speaking.

Himandi looked away.

"Well, of course," he said, "the local organization wants you comfortable while you're here. If you have any problems, just get in touch with me."

"I don't expect problems," answered Bleys.

Himandi fished in his pockets and came up with two self-adhering badges, which he passed over the table to Bleys.

"One for the lower house, one for the upper," he said. "The minute you step in the front door of the building that encloses both of them, directories will show you the way to either one of the visitors' galleries."

"Thank you," said Bleys.

He put the badges away in his own pocket. They talked about the weather and various minor matters. Once or twice Himandi ventured to veer in the direction of the business part of Bleys' visit. But Bleys was apparently deaf to any such things. He went on talking of inconsequential subjects.

Himandi finally saw him off in an autocar which took him directly to the Government building.

As Himandi had said, once he reached the building that held the two parts of the legislature, Bleys had no trouble finding his way to both the visitors' galleries. The building was open, pleasant and well lit; and directions were frequent and explicit, on plaques on the wall.

He spent a relatively small amount of time in the gallery of the lower house, which was perhaps a quarter filled, with a debate of some kind going on. In the visitors' gallery of the upper house he spent a little bit more time. This particular chamber was almost empty. Only four or five people occupied seats at the individual desks on its floor, listening to one man on his feet, who was making a speech; apparently as much for the record as for those listening. After a while, Bleys left this gallery too and went out to find a phone.

He called Himandi, and found him at his office.

"I'd like to talk to Director Albert Chin," Bleys said. "He's one of your clients. Can you arrange for me to see him for perhaps fifteen minutes, right now?"

"If he's in his office," said Himandi, "I can try. Do you want to call me back in about half an hour? There's a very good restaurant on the ground floor. You might want to go down there and put in the time having something to drink."

"Yes," said Bleys. "Call me there. I'll leave word when I go in that I'm expecting a phone call."

He broke the connection and went down to find the restaurant. As Himandi had said it was both a pleasant and a comfortable restaurant. He ordered the same ginger ale he had ordered after getting off the spaceship from Freiland, and sat with it, examining what the back of his mind had picked out of the wealth of material he had absorbed yesterday that seemed worthy of attention.

He had counted over forty Directors, as members of the upper house were known—probably in imitation of the Newton Board of Directors—who had been in the files as consulting with Himandi at one time or another.

That was very close to being two-thirds of the total membership of the upper house. He had picked Chin's name at random from the rest; simply because his appointment with Himandi had been only three weeks before, according to the secret file on Chin. This was time enough for whatever he had consulted about to show some results; and also time enough to raise a further question about the relationship between Chin and Himandi.

The meeting had been briefly labeled "a discussion of investments" and this enigmatic subject had also caught at Bleys' interest.

He had been sitting there sometime longer than half an hour, perhaps as much as forty-five minutes, when a speaker on his table came to life.

"Bleys Ahrens?" said the voice from the table speaker. "There's a call for you. You can take it at your table if you like, if you'll just punch the outside phone stud. Bleys Ahrens, have you received this message?"

"I hear you," said Bleys. He pressed the outside phone stud and spoke into the voice grille of the table.

"This is Bleys Ahrens. Did you want to reach me?"

"Bleys Ahrens," came back a female voice, "Director Chin will see you right away. Are you in the building?"

"Yes, down in the restaurant," said Bleys.

"If you'll come up right away then," said the voice at the other end.

"I'll be there immediately," Bleys said.

Director Albert Chin was indeed close. He turned out to be only several floors up and a short walk down a corridor. Three secretaries, two women and a man, were in his outer office. It was one of the women, in something more like a dark green robe than a dress, but which however fitted her dark hair and aquiline face, who let him into the inner office.

"Bleys Ahrens!" the Director said, rising from behind his desk. He was a tall man, almost as tall as Bleys, and had been good-looking in his own way at one time. But a certain amount of extra weight had softened the line of his jaw and produced a slight potbelly. He was possibly in his mid-forties.

"Yes indeed, Director," said Bleys, coming up to the desk. They clasped hands and the Director immediately sat down, motioning Bleys to an armchair float opposite.

"I understand you're something of a traveling inspector for your organization," said Albert Chin. "Himandi mentioned you'd probably only want a word or two with me."

"That's right," said Bleys. "Himandi's Vice-Chairman of the branch of the organization here, as you know. I'm Senior Vice-Chairman for all our organization. I wanted to talk to one of his clients, simply to round out the picture before I leave."

"You're leaving so soon then?" asked Chin.

"Yes, at the end of the week," said Bleys. "I go next to Ste. Marie."

"I see," said Chin. "Now, what can I tell you?"

"First I wanted your confirmation that you're one of the personal clients of Himandi," Bleys said.

"Yes," said Chin. He smiled a little, "as a matter of fact I wouldn't feel satisfied, dealing with anyone but the top member of your organization. You understand. After all, R.H.I.P. Rank Has Its Privileges, Bleys Ahrens. As you undoubtedly know."

Bleys nodded.

"I take it you're quite happy with him, then?" said Bleys.

"Absolutely. In fact," said Chin, "Himandi's become something of an old friend. I'd be tempted to stick with him, even if for some reason he ceased to be the ranking member of your organization, here."

"I'm glad to hear that," said Bleys. "That's the sort of thing I'll be reporting on to our Chairman when I get back to our headquarters. Let's see now, you see Himandi fairly frequently then?"

"Oh, I wouldn't say frequently," answered Chin. "Several times a year."

"And I think the last time the two of you talked was the twenty-fourth of last month?"

"Was it? I don't always remember these things offhand," said Chin, "I could have one of the secretaries look it up—oh yes, I remember—it was just when we were passing Bill K410 of this season."

"And you haven't seen him since?"

"Since?" There was surprise and a little touch of defensiveness in Chin's voice. But then he smiled and his voice was easy again. "No. No, I'm sure about that."

Bleys stood up. Behind the desk Chin rose also.

"Well, I'm happy to have had a chance to talk to you on such short notice," said Bleys. "It was very good of you to make time for me."

"Not at all, not at all," said Chin. "Your organization—well, that is, Himandi, at least—certainly fills a useful purpose as far as I'm concerned."

They clasped hands again and Bleys went out; Chin reseating himself behind Bleys before he had completely left the room and becoming engrossed in some papers on his desk.

Bleys closed the door to Chin's private office behind him and nodded at the secretaries as he left. He went downstairs again and called for an autocar. As he stepped into it, he phoned Himandi's office. Himandi himself answered the phone.

"I had a very pleasant talk with Director Albert Chin," Bleys said into his phone as the cab was taking him toward Himandi's office. "I'm on my way over to see you now."

"Now? Right now?" said Himandi.

"Yes. Why?" asked Bleys. "Is there any reason I can't talk to you now?"

"No, no, not at all," said Himandi, "in fact why don't I meet you at the door and we'll take your autocar on to someplace where we can have lunch?"

"Excellent," said Bleys, and broke the connection.

They ended up at a two-person table in a small, but very comfortable, restaurant that reminded Bleys of the ones that Dahno had used to take him to on Bleys' visits to Ecumeny. Bleys opened the conversation.

"I don't suppose," he said to Himandi, once their drinks had been placed before them, "you've ever thought of doing a survey to find out how many Others there are on Cassida?"

Himandi looked startled.

"There aren't any Others outside of those in our organization," he said.

"No, no, you've got to think beyond that," said Bleys gently. "Where do you draw your local trainees from?"

"Why, from the local mixed-breeds—" Himandi's eyes had just narrowed. "You mean I should consider anyone who's a genetic mix from Splinter Cultures, from the Dorsai, the Exotics or the Friendlies—as an Other?"

"That's exactly what I mean," said Bleys. "You have to look into the future of the organization. I suggest you do a survey and note any mixed-breeds currently on Cassida who fill the qualifications. In the general sense they're all Others. They just aren't part of the organization yet."

"Yet?" Himandi stared at him.

"Yes," said Bleys, "you've got to see that with an organization like ours, we either go up or go down. Either we gain more and more influence; or we reach a point of stasis, from which the only way is down in importance and influence. That way, eventually we disappear. We have to look beyond our present lifetimes, you and I, Himandi."

"But—" Himandi shrugged, staring. "Why should we look beyond our lifetimes? The upcoming members of the organization can take care of themselves when the time comes. Also, just how far do you expect an organization like we have here on Cassida to grow? How far do you expect all our branches, on all the worlds, to grow?"

"Until they control all the Worlds," said Bleys.

His eyes were fastened on Himandi; but it was not those that were emphasizing what he was saying. It was his deep-toned, trained voice, which had Himandi focused completely now; and within that focus Bleys thought he should now be able to handle the other man.

"Would you want to stop at less?" he asked. "If you look at it closely, we're as different from the ordinary run of mankind as another species of *Homo sapiens*. Potentially—at least. It isn't a question of our being able to gain control eventually, it's an inevitability; unless some of us fall by the wayside and don't keep pushing in that direction. In which case, as I said, we dwindle and disappear."

"But you're talking about thousands of mixed-breeds," said Himandi. "I can't give you the population of Cassida, offhand, but perhaps as much as half of one percent of it, maybe even a bit more, could be Others under that definition."

"*Are* Others," Bleys corrected. "Stop and think, Himandi. We've gone from where we had no influence to where we are now. Here on Cassida you and your classmates have gone from a handful of unknown men and women to a position of relative influence and authority."

He paused.

"Otherwise, would you have taken it so easily, having to pay for the repair of a wall in a hotel room? If you can come from zero to this point, why not continue?"

He paused again. He had Himandi's whole attention now. For the other man the dining room around him had ceased to exist.

"Think of it for a moment, Himandi. The possibility wasn't

mentioned in the early days to trainees; or even to organization heads like yourself on other planets, once you were set up and thriving. But the time's come now to recognize a goal. We're inevitably going to end up leading the rest of the human race, as an elite. We've been bound from the start to rise to the top, as cream rises in milk. And now it's time for at least our senior members to see and understand this. You can see and understand it, now that I've mentioned it, can't you?"

He stopped and waited.

Himandi sat where he was, not moving, not even picking up his glass. Finally he sighed.

"You're right," he said, "it's been inevitable from the start."

"Exactly," said Bleys. "Now that you use it you've got to begin to operate on it, as a basis, starting with a survey and census of the Others on this world; who don't yet recognize themselves as Others, except for perhaps feeling alone and apart from the general run of humanity. You do follow me?"

Himandi picked up his glass and drank deeply of it.

"Yes. Yes," he said, "I see it now, very clearly."

"It'll mean a change in the organization itself, to handle and employ many more individuals; and to do that there'll have to be changes in the organization structure. I won't give you any suggestions or directions about what you might do here, outside of taking that survey, but you ought to be thinking of how you'd handle an organization of thousands."

"I will," said Himandi, "beginning now."

"Good," said Bleys, "that's why I'm going to see if I can plead your case with Dahno, to let you stay in charge, here."

CHAPTER

26

═══════════

It took a moment for the shock of what Bleys had just said to bring Himandi out of the state of light hypnosis into which Bleys had led him; and make him realize what Bleys' words had implied.

"I—don't understand," he said.

"You're an excellent manager," said Bleys, "and as far as I can see you've done many things right here, considering the conditions with which you had to work. I thought at first that you might have some personal ambition or interest in corralling all the Directors of the upper house as your personal clients—"

"No, no," began Himandi. "You don't understand how it is—"

Bleys smiled and held up a hand to stop him.

"Then I found out today," he went on, "that as the situation exists, the members of that group would almost require to be handled by the head of our organization with his or her personal attention. On the other hand, you've made some classic mistakes. However, I'm beginning to think that I'll find these same mistakes made by nearly all the heads of all our out-world suborganizations. It's possible to tell a lot from the files you made accessible to me, cross-connecting information from one file to another and from one situation to another. For one thing, when was the last time you had a meeting with Albert Chin?"

"Why—I don't know offhand," Himandi said. "It'll be in the files—"

"What's in the files is the date of the twenty-fourth of last month. You haven't met with him at least once since then?"

"What gives you the idea I might have?" asked Himandi, "I'm sure—"

"Himandi," interrupted Bleys gently, "remember what I was just talking about? I'll do what I can to persuade Dahno to keep you here in your present position; but beginning right now you'll have to tell me the truth. Also, make available to me the things you've had hidden. Now, again—when was the last time you saw Albert Chin?"

"A week ago, Wednesday," said Himandi, looking down at his plate.

"Exactly," said Bleys. "I'm glad you decided against any more evasions and false answers. Now, that last meeting didn't happen to have to do with some kind of payment to you personally, did it? Let's say, some kind of gift to you personally?"

"It was in the way of a . . . retainer," said Himandi, still looking down at his plate. "I get it quarterly from everyone in the upper house who's a client."

"I thought so," said Bleys. "It brought up the immediate question of whether you were merely trying to line your pockets, or what kind of use you had for this income. However, after studying the available files, I'm sure that you weren't thinking of making yourself rich. What you wanted was to set up a fund that nobody would know about; against any sudden emergency, such as finding yourself cut off permanently from Dahno and with the ultimate control of the organization in your hands only. Am I right?"

Himandi looked at him, lifting his eyes from the plate and the table with a surprised look on his face.

"How did you guess that?" he asked.

"I didn't guess it," said Bleys. "For someone who's able to study and understand the files you let me see, it was obvious your heart and soul were in the organization here. But you were operating it defensively; and that's not the way it'll need to be handled from now on."

He paused to give the other a chance to speak. Himandi said nothing. Bleys went on.

"Since we face a period of expansion, possibly even within the next few years, you're going to have to stop being protective and become aggressive. In short, you're going to have to take more chances and not rely so much on being able to take care of yourself if you're left alone, but on being part of an inevitable movement toward a larger future. I've no direct evidence of any of this—but then I don't need it for Dahno. He'll take my word for it. But I can see clearly enough to recognize some other things. First, I want you to disband whatever kind of armed or strong-arm organization you've set up."

Himandi's eyes widened.

"You're a clairvoyant!" he said. "How did you tell that from the files I showed you?"

Bleys smiled.

"It was a guess," he answered, "but a solid one."

"I . . . didn't set it up," Himandi said. "I just have an agreement with one of the local military leaders to have the use of certain specially trained troops, if I should need them."

"I'd like you to sever that connection," said Bleys. "Anything like that is like a loaded gun around the house. Someone who otherwise might not shoot anyone else in an argument, just might if the weapon was handy. Now, and finally—will you show me your actual, top-secret files?"

"Yes," said Himandi. "Any time you want."

Bleys pushed his chair float back from the table.

"Right now," he said.

Half an hour later, in Himandi's office, he was deep into a

brief, but very revealing, set of records. The information these contained would have been enough to make Dahno react, if Bleys had even needed to show his half-brother.

"Actually," said Bleys, closing off the final secret files and handing the key to them back to Himandi, who had sat in the file room with him, waiting while he went through them, "what I've seen now confirms a belief that you're far and away the best person to run the organization on Cassida. I want you to send me word when you've put the existence of these tapes on open record, and made them available to anyone like myself who's qualified to see them. Also, I want to hear you've ended your agreement with the military; just as I'd like to hear you've started the survey and the census. As you let me know these things are done, I'll present them to Dahno in the best possible light."

"Do you think—?" Himandi did not finish.

"As I said—I think I can persuade him to keep you," said Bleys, "yes.

"Now," he went on, "I'll spend the rest of the days I have here before leaving, by getting to know as much of certain areas of government and business as I can. The last world I stopped at, I met the rest of the members of the original class of trainees who were sent out there at a dinner the night before I left. I'd like to do that again."

"It's an excellent idea," said Himandi, "excellent. But you won't fall out of touch with me the rest of the time you're here, will you?"

"No," said Bleys, "nothing could please me more than seeing you make a start on those things I asked you to do, so I could tell Dahno that they were already underway at the time I left."

In the next few days before his ship took him off to Ste. Marie, he spent his time as he had on Freiland, taking the pulse of the business climate of the planet and the structure and operation of the government. These were things he would need to know in the future and were not connected with the purpose of his present trip—which in itself was not exactly what he had given Dahno to understand it to be.

Far from his making this trip to acquaint himself with the organizations, he had made it to begin his contacts with those same organizations and if possible to point them in the right direction. On both Freiland and Cassida he had been able to do just that.

Such good fortune could not go on without some kind of an interruption. Ste. Marie was a small but relatively rich world under the same sun of Procyon A as Kultis, Mara and the mining world of Coby. Coby had no organization and Kultis and Mara of course were the Exotic worlds where an organization would be useless.

The organization on Ste. Marie was correspondingly small and slightly more relaxed. Nonetheless, because it had been involved in a great deal of use of off-world mercenary military, the planet had a fair number of cross-breeds that could be brought into the organization. As a mainly pastoral planet, it would be useful but not remarkable.

However, it was on Ste. Marie that the organization was run by a lady named Kim Wallech. Like the organizations on Freiland and Cassida, she had some very private files that she was not eager to make available to Bleys.

At the same time she had a disconcerting tendency to agree with everything he suggested and predicted for the future, and yet balked at opening up the private areas of her command.

She was obviously the kind of person who fights to the last ditch and then disconcertingly finds one ditch more behind that one she has been finally forced to abandon.

However, at last she gave in; and agreed to modify the organization, eliminating those things that Bleys suggested should be eliminated or changed. Bleys' private opinion of her, as a matter of fact, was that of the three leaders of suborganizations he had spoken to so far, she was probably the most capable and steadfast.

His next stop was at Ceta, a large planet which had a surface gravity no greater than that of Old Earth. Old Earth's gravity had always been one of the measures by which other worlds had been chosen for settlement.

The last two stops were on New Earth and finally Harmony;

and on each one, Bleys encountered roughly similar situations with the head of the local organizations; and used roughly similar methods of persuasion.

This, with the aim of not only getting the organizations themselves to prepare for change, but to bind them to himself; ostensibly—to begin with—merely as channels through which official business could be transacted between them and Dahno. Some three months after leaving, according to the interstellar calendar, he was standing once more back on the surface of Association.

He checked in by phone with Dahno, from the terminal, to explain that he would like to go out and visit Henry and Joshua first, even before meeting with Dahno, to let them know that he shared in their loss of Will.

Dahno was quick in agreeing. His ready emotions had apparently responded almost immediately to the news of Will's death. He had already made visits to the farm and used all his untouchable persuasive skill to lift the spirits of the two of the family that were left.

This, Bleys thought, must have been a remarkable effort, even for Dahno; since Henry would probably not discuss his dead youngest son at all; and Joshua would find it painful to discuss Will, limiting his talk about his brother as much as possible.

Nonetheless, there were ways of being comforting simply by being there—overflowing the one chair that could hold Dahno's weight, in their front room; lending a hand about the farm, which he had done for a large number of years; and generally radiating sympathy.

Accordingly, Bleys was not too surprised when Dahno told him to take as much time as he wanted with Henry and Joshua.

It was after dark when Bleys pulled a rental hovercar into the yard of the farm. The lights were on inside the house. By this time, he knew, both Henry and Joshua would have had their dinner. Also they could not have failed to hear the roar of the air cushion of his hovercar and driving jets coming up the farm road.

Consequently, it was Joshua—not Henry—just as Bleys had

expected, who came bursting out of the door of the farmhouse, as Bleys stepped out of the hovercar, now settled down on the ground.

Joshua was now in his mid-twenties, but he ran to the car almost as Will had run in that one moment when Bleys had left for the city. He did not throw his arms around Bleys, though, as Will had done, but merely put out his hand, which Bleys took; and they grasped each other strongly for an emotional moment.

"I knew you'd be here as soon as you could be, Bleys!" said Joshua. "Oh, but it's good to see you!"

"It's good to be here," said Bleys; and found he meant it.

"Bleys—" said Joshua as together they both headed for the house, "you won't bring up the subject of Will until Father does, will you?"

"No, I wasn't going to," answered Bleys.

They went inside.

Henry was seated at his table, at his paperwork for the sale of the goat milk. He looked up with that brief smile of his.

"Welcome, Bleys," he said.

"How you've stretched up!" said Joshua, staring at him in the sudden light of the room. "You're a giant!"

Bleys laughed.

"Dahno's still the giant," he said, "not me."

"Are you taller than he is?" asked Henry.

"We're exactly the same height," Bleys said. "But he outweighs me by anywhere from forty to eighty pounds. And none of it's fat."

Joshua had evidently been mending one of the cart harnesses for the goats. It was draped over the chair he had been sitting in. He ducked into what had been the bedroom he had shared with Bleys and Will; and came out again, carrying the oversized chair that Dahno had been used to using on his visits.

"Sit," he said to Bleys. Bleys did so and Joshua went back and retook his own chair, draping the harness over his knees and picking up the awl and the heavily threaded needle he had been using to make holes and sew on a place that needed mending in the leather of the harness. Like Henry, he continued working as they talked. With anyone else, this would have seemed like a disturbing element to Bleys. But he knew that the two of them had to use every available hour to get all the work done on the farm; and he remembered them this way, always busy, even in the evenings. Here, it was a comfortable, almost a homey thing to sit with them, so occupied.

"You've been off-planet?" Henry asked, without looking up from his papers.

"Yes," said Bleys. He was finding the chair more comfortable than he had expected—not surprising since it had been built for Dahno; and for the past few months, Bleys had been sitting in furniture that was scaled for people a good deal shorter than himself. "I've been on all the worlds where there're extensions of Dahno's organization."

"But not on Ceta?" said Henry, still not raising his head.

"No," Bleys lied, "not on Ceta."

Henry did not say anything and Joshua stepped into the gap in the conversation.

"What were these other worlds like, Bleys?" he asked. It was not just an idle question. Joshua was interested.

Bleys smiled.

"The cities were pretty much all like Ecumeny. The people—the people were pretty much like the people who live in Ecumeny here, when you got right down to it. The same things, business and politics went on."

"Still, it must have been an interesting trip," said Joshua; and there was—for him—almost a wistful note in his voice.

"It wasn't uninteresting," said Bleys, "but nothing I ran into was mind-shaking. You haven't missed a lot by not seeing the places I saw."

"Our work is here, Joshua," said Henry.

"Yes, I know, Father," answered Joshua; in just the same way that Bleys could remember him answering many times when he had lived with them.

It was taken for granted that Bleys would stay the night at least; and hopefully for several days and nights. Joshua had torn out Bleys' old bunk in the boys' room, which in any case would have been too small for Bleys nowadays, and replaced it with a bedframe also made for Dahno, with a couple of mattresses.

This bed had been left in place, in hopes that Bleys would come by soon. So he found himself, after all, at what was now for him the relatively early hour of nine o'clock at night, going to bed in the same room across from Joshua, just as he had when they were boys.

The next day and the next, during the daylight hours, he was out with the two of them working at one thing or another. The alternative to doing so would have been to sit in the farmhouse alone by himself, which was foolish as well as uncomfortable—since he had never taken to killing time very well.

He began by working mostly alongside Joshua. As they worked, Joshua filled him in on many things previously unmentioned, from the years between the time when he had left the farm and the present; and even ventured a few opinions about his father.

"Father would never speak of it," he said, "and as far as he can he'll never show it; but the loss of Will on top of the loss of Mother some years back has left him feeling very alone."

They were mending one of the fences by stringing new wire.

"That's one of the reasons I've hesitated to go ahead and get married," he went on. "Right now this is still his farm. If I bring in a wife and eventually we have a family, little by little he'll feel that he's being pushed into the background, into the chimney corner. I hate to do that to him. On the other hand, Ruth—I can't ask her to wait indefinitely."

"Ruth?" asked Bleys.

Joshua stapled a top strand of wire to the fence post, nodding at the stretcher in Bleys' hands. "Take a strain on that."

Bleys' large hands closed the jaws of the stretcher on the wire, pivoting the tool's head against the fence post to draw the wire taut. Joshua drove a second staple, fastening it with the maximum degree of tightness and, using the puller, lifted the staple he had put in originally. They walked on down to the next post.

"Ruth McIntyre," Joshua said, "you'd remember her from school here—no, that's right, you didn't go to our local school. In any case she'd have been a little bit older than you and you probably wouldn't have seen much of her. But you must remember the family of the McIntyres."

"Yes," said Bleys, "I do."

He tried to summon up the picture of the Ruth whom Joshua was talking about, but no memory would come. If he had seen her, it would have been on a Sunday, at the time of the church service to which every family went.

"Tell me what she looks like," Bleys said.

"Oh, she's tall, almost as tall as I am, with very black hair and sort of a round face," said Joshua. "I think I love her, Bleys."

"Perhaps you should get married, then, in spite of Uncle Henry. I know if you asked him, he'd be the first to tell you to do that."

"That's why I've got no intention of asking him," said Joshua, "at least not for a while yet."

"Perhaps, I—" Bleys was beginning. Joshua shook his head and stopped him in mid-sentence.

"I'll handle it myself when the time comes," he said.

They talked about the weather, the animals, farm prices and other things. Then, there were other times, in which he found himself working with Henry, usually in construction, since Henry was enlarging the barn that held his herd of goats, intending to add numbers to the herd itself. Henry, by contrast, talked about the work and about a number of day-by-day things of merely passing importance. It was not until the third day that he paused after finishing a part of the roofing and, having come down the ladder and wiped his brow, looked squarely at Bleys.

"Will thought a lot of you, Bleys," he said.

"I know," said Bleys, "he told me so." It occurred to him that perhaps this was the ideal time. He reached in his pocket for the letter Will had sent him from Ceta. "He said so in the last letter he wrote me. Would you like to read it?"

"If it's not an intrusion on your private correspondence, or Will's—" Henry said. But his eyes were fixed almost yearningly on the letter.

Bleys passed it over. Henry took it and read it, standing there. Clearly, he read it several times before at last he reverently folded it and held it out once again to Bleys.

"Why don't you keep it?" said Bleys. "This was Will's home and the rest of his things are here. This last letter probably should be with them."

Henry shook his head.

"It was a letter he wrote you," he said. "If you want to keep it, that's your decision."

"Be sure I will," said Bleys, reluctantly taking it. "If you ever change your mind and want it back—"

"No, the matter's settled," said Henry, picking up a new roll of roofing material and beginning to climb the ladder again.

Later on that afternoon, however, Joshua managed to get Bleys alone.

"Showing Father that letter," said Joshua, "was the best thing you could have done. He reads it to mean that Will found solace in the Lord before his death. You've no idea how that thought comforts him. Could I also see the letter?"

"Of course!" said Bleys, pulling it out of a pocket and passing it to him. "I should've thought of showing it to you right away. I tried to make your father take it to keep it here; but he wouldn't hear of it."

"I know," said Joshua, reading the letter as hungrily as his father had done, "he told me not to let you give it to me, either."

He interrupted his reading to look up at Bleys.

"But if you're willing to, I'll take it," Joshua said. "Later on, he'll be glad I did, no matter what he says to me about it."

A few hours later, that afternoon, a message came from the store via one of the local people passing by, that Dahno had phoned for Bleys. Bleys took his hovercar down to the store. It was faster than taking the goat-cart, although Henry offered it to him. He reversed the charges and got Dahno on the phone.

"Sorry to interrupt your visit," said Dahno, "but I think it's time I had you here and heard from you about your trip. Have you got transportation?"

"Yes, I rented a hovercar," answered Bleys.

"If you'll come right away then," said Dahno, "we can talk over dinner. Henry and Joshua had to come first, but it's time you and I talked."

CHAPTER

27

BLEYS HAD READ an urgency into the phone call from Dahno. But now, sitting in a small, private restaurant with his half-brother, right after having left the farm and Henry and Joshua, the relaxed attitude of Dahno took Bleys back in memory to the days when he used to be brought into Ecumeny on visits.

Dahno was talking about everything under the sun, interesting talk, humorous talk, but about nothing important except the city and some of the goings-on in it; and only a few things that were a matter of business or politics, but none of them particularly important.

Bleys waited.

After they finished the main course of the meal, Dahno ordered and got another drink and sat back in the private quarter circle of padded booth in which they had eaten. Bleys suspected the restaurant of knowing Dahno well and catering to him, for as it also was in the large restaurant where he usually held court nights, the seat and seat-backs offered leg room not only for Dahno, but for himself.

"Now," said Dahno, "if you want to tell me about how your trip went . . ."

So, thought Bleys. The long comfortable beginning of the meeting was over.

"Absolutely," Bleys answered. "There may be a few surprises in it for you. If so, I'll appreciate your waiting until I'm done with the whole story before we talk about it. All right?"

Dahno nodded.

"Just fine," he said, taking a large swallow from his drink, "charge ahead."

"You know, I went first to Freiland," said Bleys, "and the important man I saw there was Hammer Martin—"

"Good man, Hammer," said Dahno.

Bleys held up a finger in protest. Dahno nodded an apology and waved him on.

Bleys began the recital of everything that had happened to him on Freiland, not giving his deductions or conclusions as he went along, but simply making a bald account of events. He reported what he had said and done; and what Hammer had said.

However, when he came to his final, long heart-to-heart talk with Hammer, he gave this to Dahno word for word, quoting from his trained memory.

Dahno had ordered several more drinks and drunk them before Bleys had finished talking. His expression did not change as Bleys told about painting a future in which the Others would consist of all the qualified mixed-breeds.

In the face of Dahno's silence, he went on to describe going through Hammer's secret files; and what he found there; as well as what he deduced—and later told Hammer he would have to report to Dahno. At the same time he repeated his own recommendation that Hammer stay in place.

It was a bald recital. His telling was as poker-faced in its own way as the face of Dahno, opposite him; still perfectly relaxed, and with the glint of humor that was always there unless something had specifically happened to drive all humor from him.

Bleys continued his story to Cassida and Himandi, with the story still told just as it had happened. After that, he gave his experiences on Ste. Marie, Ceta, New Earth, and finally Harmony. Only on Harmony, he told Dahno, were there no hidden files, no secret armed enforcers, kept by the head of the organization there himself. Kinkaka Goodfellow, the leader of the organization on Harmony, had followed the rules explicitly.

"But I told him the same thing about the mixed-breeds and the future," said Bleys calmly, "and came back here. Ordinarily, he's the one leader I'd recommend replacing. But the way matters work, Harmony's almost an extension of your own command, here on Association. It's a little too close—you could appear on his doorstep any time."

Dahno nodded.

"—And while none of them," Bleys went on, "at least to begin with, suspected I could ferret out what they were doing that had not been original orders; *he* suspected from the first that I was a sort of Inspector-General."

"Did he?" said Dahno, showing a first sign of surprise.

"Yes," said Bleys, "he went deliberately to work to show me that nothing was hidden. The only reason I say this might disqualify him would be that so much suspicion could stand in the way of his accepting the future I suggested for the Others—that I offered him, too."

Dahno nodded again, but this time with his expression unreadable.

"On the other hand," Bleys said, "I think, given time, he'd be able to see it. If he did, there'd be the great advantage that he'd probably adopt it with all his heart and soul. So, even him, I'd suggest we leave in place."

There was a moment of silence between them in the padded little enclosure around the table.

"You know," said Dahno, mildly after a moment, "you weren't sent out to do anything like this with all these people of ours. That paper I gave you was only supposed to make sure you had their cooperation. Not to use as a lever to threaten them with me, and make them take on a notion of all Others eventually ruling all the planets. I know I've talked about this to the trainees. But I thought you understood it was that—just talk."

"I did," answered Bleys levelly. "Mine wasn't. I think it's a perfectly desirable and reachable goal."

"Do you?" said Dahno. "Then I'll put off hearing your answer to what you thought we—and that means I—could possibly gain from it. Suppose you tell me, instead, what reasons you might have for believing in a future like that. You've got to have realized, long ago, that my success and theirs depends on personal, one-on-one contact."

"That's why such a future's inevitable," said Bleys. "You're like anyone who succeeds in any field. The more success you have, the more work you make for yourself to do. In spite of sending outfits out to a number of the other planets, you and your organization here—but particularly you, yourself—long ago reached the point where you put in a good eighteen-hour day, seven days a week. That's why you're on-call by phone twenty-four hours a day. Being you, you're able to do it without seeming to be frantically busy. The flaw is—the other members aren't Dahnos. But isn't it a fact that what I've said about your schedule is right?"

"Mr. Vice-Chairman," said Dahno. He emptied his glass and pressed the stud on the table's control pad to order a refill. "You're right. I take it the implication is that I myself will soon have to take on extra help."

"Isn't that one of the reasons that you wanted me as your Senior Vice-Chairman?" asked Bleys. "You could see a long time back you were moving towards a time when there'd be too much to do. You wanted to be able to pass some of that off eventually, to at least one person you could trust?"

"Correct again, Mr. Vice-Chairman," said Dahno. The glass with his drink rose, brimming but steady, through the hole that opened before him on his table; then closed again, once the filled glass was at table level. Dahno watched it, as if it were some kind of clever performer.

"Still," he said, "the sort of growth you suggested in what you told the heads of the suborganizations; and—as I gather—

convinced them of, is a little hard to swallow. I don't see it myself."

"I think you would if you had time to study the matter; the way I have, these last few years," answered Bleys. "You're unique. I could almost bet on you to convince an Exotic, which I think no one but another Exotic could do."

"No, not an Exotic," murmured Dahno, gazing at his full glass. "But go on."

"Take the time to study it," said Bleys. "I think you'll see, as a future, it's definitely there. All it needs is a conscious intention by you and me to have it."

"Wrong," said Dahno, lifting his eyes from the glass to look at Bleys, "you mean it's there to be acquired, but only I've got the ability to acquire it?"

"Yes," said Bleys, "but it would come faster—in our lifetimes—only if I'm there beside you."

Dahno chuckled good-heartedly.

"You wouldn't be my baby brother—let alone being Mr. Vice-Chairman now," he said to Bleys, "if I hadn't seen that any attempt to make you useful at all would have to accept the fact that you'd become useful to the point of being someone I couldn't do without."

"But you don't see a reachable future, as I outlined it just now?" asked Bleys.

"No. No, I don't," answered Dahno. He emptied the glass before him in one large, easy swallow; and stretched his massive arms in a gargantuan gesture of relaxation. "I can imagine it, of course. But whether I'll agree to it, or not, I think that's something I'll need to think over."

"Can I ask how long you think it'll take to think about it, Mr. Chairman?" asked Bleys.

"I don't honestly know, Mr. Vice-Chairman," said Dahno. "Maybe overnight. Maybe, a matter of months. I'm not like one of the heads of the suborganizations you talked to. I've got to take what you suggest and put it against what I see as possible. I may even want to see whether events, over a little period of time, tend to confirm it or not."

He stretched again, enormously.

enough from Ecumeny not to be considered usually as having any connection with the governmental city. But Moseville was also large enough so that it could satisfy the recreational needs of any such group of armed retainers. Either the resort area or the surrounding farmland would be practical as a place to set up a training school and permanent camp.

The possibility that their address was in the farmlands occurred suddenly to Bleys, now.

The name *"Circle Drive"* implied a road that went nowhere. *"Box 149"* indicated that perhaps it was simply a circular post office drop-off spot, lined with rural mailboxes to which the locals came to collect their mail.

His mind, having made that jump, made another. *"hs"* suggested the word *"Hounds";* and the *"hs"* suddenly connected in Bleys' mind with the thought that the legalist, who might be Dahno's shadow lieutenant, could make all the personal contacts with them. Dahno need never go near the place.

Also if *"hs"* could stand for *"Hounds,"* *"1d"* could stand for *"first dog."* It was the sort of thing to tickle Dahno's particular sense of humor. Together, the two codes fitted a pattern: the second-in-command was to seem to operate within the law and the retainers outside it.

Bleys' mind ran swiftly through the secret files once more, picking up tiny little scraps and bits of possible evidence that shored up this pattern of interpretation and indicated that his translation of the shorthand in both cases was correct.

The pattern seemed to hold. Bleys checked the monitor on his wrist to find out if the legalist who had signed Dahno's will was in town, in Ecumeny itself. Norton Brawley had a legal office less than thirty blocks away.

CHAPTER

30

BLEYS NEEDED TO find out about the shadow lieutenant and the Hounds as quickly as possible, so that no surprises came out of anywhere to trip him up while Dahno was gone. Norton Brawley was closer; but he preferred to confront the man—after all, it was only a suspicion—with as much information in hand as possible; and that included all that could immediately be known about the Hounds.

So, it should be the Hounds first.

Bleys flew to Moseville, in a self-drive atmosphere craft, with an auto-pilot to back up his own knowledge of handling such craft. He parked the aircraft at the local airport and rented a hovercar.

A phone call to the local postal department established the fact that 15 Circle Drive was one of many such places as he had imagined—drop-off spots for rural mail—merely a circular stretch of road with postal boxes side by side all along it. The 15, apparently, did not refer to a point on the circle drive, but that it was the fifteenth of such Circle Drives, in the southwest country just beyond Moseville.

It was late afternoon when he got there. This turned out to be fortunate because it was a time of day when a number of the boxes were being emptied by people who lived in the rural area but worked in the city, and were now on their way home and had stopped to pick up their mail.

He got back in his hovercar and drove on around the circle until he came to someone at a box who could not have seen him when he got out of the car to look at Box 149. Seated within the car, his unusual height was not so noticeable.

He stopped the car, put down the window and leaned out to speak to a man with a long narrow face under a receding hairline of brown hair, with a wart on his chin, who was just turning away from the box from which he had collected his own mail.

"My apologies," Bleys said to him, "my brother's been at whatever place that's connected with Box 149. I've been writing him at that address. I didn't realize it was a drop-off address, like this. I thought I'd surprise him. I've got some unexpected time off from the business that brought me into Moseville. Do you know the area around here? How would I find the place which gets its mail from Box 149?"

Rural people on both Association and Harmony tended to be generally friendly and helpful to strangers, as long as the prickly matter of religion did not come up between them. This man was no different. He rubbed his chin with the wart on it, thoughtfully.

"Yes, I know it," he said; "it'd be easier for me to show you the way there than give you directions, though. Do you want to follow my car and I'll lead you to it?"

"Thank you," said Bleys.

He rolled the window up. The other man got back into his own maroon-colored hovercar and led the way off the circle onto the road; on which it turned left and drove some little distance, making right- and left-hand turns which Bleys stored in his memory, noting something at each turn that could be used as an identification point later on. The other car stopped at last before a long and high stone fence, with a pair of heavy steel gates set across the entrance road through it.

The maroon hovercar driver rolled his window down, stuck his head out, and called back to Bleys, who had also put his window down and looked outside.

"This is it!" called the guide. "Punch the button under the screen in the wall to the right of the gate and you can talk to them up at the house. They can open the gates from there for you."

"Thanks!" called Bleys. The other waved a dismissive hand and drove off.

Bleys turned his attention to the seat beside him and went through the motions of gathering things together, until his guide might not look back through his rear-viewer, and wonder why he had not gotten out to press the gate button.

Finally the other car turned off on a crossroad and disappeared behind some trees.

Bleys stayed where he was, looking out through the window on the passenger's side of the car at the gate and the screen with the annunciator stud below it. Gate and wall itself were built with extraordinary sturdiness. There was no sign of special protection about the wall, but Bleys suspected that there would be a variety of alarms there.

He started up his car and drove along until he found the same crossroad that his guide's car had turned off on. That vehicle was only a maroon speck in the distance, now.

Bleys got out; and, using a pair of compensating binoculars in the growing dusk, looked up and down the wall. It continued across in front of him, turning a corner visibly at last to his right and apparently went back from the road. But on his left, it stretched out for quite a ways, until it disappeared in some trees.

Bleys drove up as far as the trees and found, as he had rather thought there might be, an unpaved road leading in among them. He drove his hovercar far enough down this to hide it from anyone passing on the road, got out and walked on through the trees until he came out on their far side and could once more examine the wall. It had turned from the road already and was headed back at a right angle.

Now that he was beyond the trees, he could see that the wall ran back from the road only about a hundred yards further, then took a sharp right angle to wall the back of the estate, or whatever it was. Clearly, it was not an ordinary farm.

He went back to his car. He had come prepared for the fact that he might have to take some kind of action right away. It might be safer to leave now and come back at another time; but the chances of getting in and out of Moseville without attracting attention were greatest if he did everything on this first trip.

Back at the car he opened a suitcase and changed completely into black clothing, including a tight hood over his head, covering all but his face; black gloves and a pigment to black out the skin of his face. Finally, he put night lenses into his eyes. The lenses were made to gather available light whenever the level of outside illumination dropped below a certain level—as the daylight already had—but not interfere in the case of normal levels of lighting.

He took with him a number of small devices, some small sensing equipment; as well as a couple of throwing knives—one inside his boot, with its handle hidden by his pantleg over the top of the boot; and the other in a sheath on a cord around his neck, and hanging down under his black jumper beside his upper spine.

He also took with him a vial of specially prepared scent for any guard dogs that should be within. At last, ready to go, he approached the stone wall opposite his woods.

By this time it was quite dark. However, his lenses were picking up as much vision as a pair of night glasses held to his eyes would have done. One of the things that Bleys had included in his studies was just such burglar-type work as he was now engaged in. As with a great many other of the things he quietly studied, this had not been one he had had any particular immediate plans for using; but had only felt might come in useful, in later years. Now, he found himself putting to use his sneak-thief techniques earlier than expected.

He reached the wall but was careful not to touch it. Examining it with his sensors, he found nothing until he climbed a nearby tree and was able to aim one of them at the top of the wall itself.

He had expected some kind of alarm system; and sure enough, there it was. The mortar between the stones at the very top of the fence was sensitized.

There was an answer to this type of situation. Bleys' instructors in this type of activity had taught him what to do; and made access for him to the equipment he needed. From a hip pocket of the suit he was wearing he took something that looked no larger than a folded handkerchief; but when unfolded appeared to be a very thin sheet of black plastic, perhaps five feet long and four feet across.

He went up close to the wall and quickly threw this blanket with one move over the top of the wall.

It was what was known as a mirror-image transmitter. Now it blanketed out the mortar that had been sensitized to transmit a picture of anything crossing it, for the distance of the covering itself. But what it showed to the sensors reading the length of mortar it had covered, was an image of the sky-scene the mortar had been transmitting just before it was covered. Bleys could, and did now, climb over it while beneath him the mortar continued to transmit a picture of the night's emerging stars.

His sensing equipment, operated from the top of the wall, reported that the ground on the inside of the wall was in no way equipped with man-traps of any kind. He dropped down lightly from the top of the wall onto the ground and looked about. Before him were more trees, although these were carefully planted, trimmed and tended trees, with an almost lawn-like ground inside them.

Dimly beyond the trees he could see illumination of some kind, as it might be the windows of a building further on.

He went toward the light. After several minutes one of the sensors on the belt around his waist began to beep, and he lifted up a small dial-faced instrument to see an arrow pointing slightly off to his right. Below this was a reading of two hundred. As he looked at it, it clicked down to one-ninety. Guard dogs, to be coming at that speed and in that silence.

They would be less than a couple of hundred feet from him by now. To the right of the number a small dot of red light had been lit. To check, he picked up another of the sensing instruments from his belt and punched for an identification read-out. The words appearing on the back-lighted screen were *"dogs 2."*

That last bit of information was all he needed for the moment. He found and unstoppered the vial. The stopper ended in a small device which sprayed a narrow band of almost invisible droplets. In fact the droplets were so fine that it was essentially a mist. But its effect was to lay down a strip on the ground that gave off certain odors.

He waited. Dogs like this were an expensive investment.

He could just begin to see them now with the night vision of his lenses—two large black dogs running side by side silently and eagerly. They looked like dobermans. To get such animals, it was necessary to buy frozen embryos shipped in from Earth and rear them under special laboratory conditions to the birth stage; and thereafter continue to handle them carefully until they were grown.

Bleys waited.

So far the dogs seemed to be paying no attention to the scent barrier. But their noses might already have caught it. For a moment, Bleys was afraid that after all the stuff did not work. He took the knife from his boot in one hand and the knife from his back sling in the other and stood ready in case the dogs reached him.

But now, suddenly, they were slowing as they approached the barrier. At about six meters out they came almost to a halt, their noses sniffing eagerly before them. Their heads dropped almost to the ground and they moved forward gradually, increasing a little in speed until they came actually to the scent strip, where they stopped to sniff directly at the spray on the ground.

The odor in this case was an artificial copy of the phero-mones from the urine of a female dog in heat, with a methyl-ester drug added that would trigger off a nerve collapse when sniffed at closely, as the two dogs were doing now.

Abruptly, it worked. Both animals collapsed, twitching, completely conscious but having lost all nervous control of their bodies. Bleys walked out to where they lay and gave each a spray-injection that would render them completely unconscious for the next three hours. By the time they came to, all trace of the other chemicals he had sprayed on the ground would have evaporated.

He went on toward the lights in the distance.

As he came out of the trees and got closer to the building which was now fully visible with most of its lights lit, he was able to clearly see areas for outdoor exercise and training. He passed a running track, an exercise maze, and patches of ground that looked as if they were laid out for types of exercise which could be anything from fencing to martial arts.

He got close to the building and these gave way to lawn. He came up against the building and began to circle it, examining for ways of entry.

He came finally to a ground-level door, black against the shingle wall of the house, the color of which his lenses were not capable of aiding him to make out. He stopped and held one of the sensing devices against it. It whirred for a second and then clicked. He stood back, tilted it up from its connection to his belt and looked at its face.

Zero 4. No other, he read on the face.

"No other" would mean that there was nothing required other than one of the versions of ordinary keys to open the door. This was remarkably light security, but on the other hand, Dahno had been probably counting on its isolated position to protect it, more than anything else.

From a ring of key blanks Bleys selected a number 4 key blank, and slid it into a slot on one side of the sensor itself—which was barely large enough to take it. There was a moment's wait; and then the former blank came out a slot on the far side of the sensor, cut into key shape.

He took it. It was a little warm in his fingers but not uncomfortably so. He found the lock slot of the door, pressed the key and turned the handle below it. The door swung silently open. He withdrew the key and stepped inside, closing the door as silently behind him.

Within there was nothing much more than a night light, but with his lenses this made it as bright as he could wish. He seemed to have stepped into a place of lockers and shower rooms. He went through them, found some stairs and mounted them, setting his sensors as he went for any information on people nearby or approaching.

It was, however, remarkably quiet. He climbed several levels and explored several corridors, looking into lounges, recreation rooms, one practice firing range, an indoor swimming pool; and then up to another story where the rooms were obviously bedrooms. It was exactly the sort of place in which a group such as he believed Dahno to have would be set up, with all that was needed to train and keep them; but there was a remarkable emptiness to the place. No one seemed to be around.

The unusual makes anyone wary; and in this case Bleys was doubly so. He continued his explorations and accumulated evidence that proved this was the home of a corps of anywhere from thirty to a hundred men devoted to physical training and training in combat, with or without arms. He ran into no sign of life, however, until he approached one end of the building and his sensor alerted him to a large gathering of people up ahead.

He went more slowly and carefully. After a while, he could hear chanting. A little farther and he was able to understand it. It was simply two words repeated in unison over and over again.

"Dahno Ahrens, Dahno Ahrens, Dahno Ahrens . . . "

The chanting was from the floor below, he realized, now that he was almost on top of it. Instead of going down there, he searched around the floor he was on for some entry that might let him into a higher level of the room in which all these people were gathered and chanting where he could observe without being observed.

He found it with remarkably little difficulty. It was a door without even a lock on it, and it let him into a small

gallery—the kind of a gallery that might have held a choir at a
religious service.

In fact, the choir stalls image was a good one, he decided.
He moved forward past several rows of fixed wooden seats to
a balcony from which he could look down on a floor where a
good fifty individuals, robed in black, were apparently squatting on their knees and chanting in unison; with one individual
up on a slight stage at the far end of the room, who also
squatted in his black robe, facing them. Behind the single
individual was a wall with a large, three-dimensional image of
Dahno—ordinarily dressed, but seated like Buddha—smiling
down on them.

The walls, the arched ceiling of the room and the floor, as
far as Bleys could make out, were of highly polished wood,
and the acoustics were excellent. He could almost make out
individual voices from those who chanted.

Observing them, he came to the conclusion they were in
something like a hysteric trance. The room itself was like
nothing so much as a chapel, except that there were no signs of
what type of worship was involved, unless it was worship of
Dahno himself—which to a great extent it resembled.

Bleys went quietly out again and set about finding his way
back outside. On the way he stumbled across a door which
opened into what was obviously their armory. Not only void
pistols but needle guns, power pistols and—surprisingly, for
they were effective only under very specialized conditions—
power rifles. Like the pistols, they were devastating, but their
range was relatively short. Still, they had a tremendous
potential for destruction at short range.

Bleys finally found a way out. Once he had gotten outside he
discovered his exit had been through the main entrance to the
building. Over the wide double doors were carved the words:

Isonian Prayer and Retreat Center

The word "Isonian" rang with no familiarity in Bleys' mind,
and he knew his own vocabulary to be extremely extensive. He
suspected it of being a made-up word.

Certainly, what was inside was not a prayer and retreat establishment. He went down the steps and around the building again until he came to the small door by which he had entered originally; and, following the directions of his sensors, retraced his steps.

He passed the dogs, which were just beginning to come out of their bewilderment and lift their heads from the grass, but were still in no condition to be a threat to anyone. He continued to the wall, then up and over it where the mirror-blanket waited for him; took the blanket off from the far side, returned to his hovercar, and drove to the airport.

On the very verge of flying back to Ecumeny that night, Bleys changed his mind. He made some inquiries at the all-night desk of the terminal, and followed the directions he was given to a very good hotel in Moseville—one that could have held its head up with the better hotels of Ecumeny.

The next morning he went out after breakfast, stopped in front of the gates, pressed the annunciator button and spoke to the face that appeared on the screen.

"I'm Bleys Ahrens," he said, "Dahno's brother and second in command. Let me in."

He had guessed they would react more promptly and compliantly to something that was almost a command, than to any kind of a polite request. It was so. Within seconds the gates swung open for him and he drove up the winding driveway to park in front of the doorway by which he had left the building the night before.

The two doors, of what he now saw to be a dark wood, highly polished to bring out its grain, were opened for him as he walked up the steps. Inside, on each door, was a young man wearing the same black robes he had seen on those in the chapel the night before.

Bleys was wearing his ordinary, everyday business clothing. As he stepped inside, the man on the right-hand door bowed slightly, with his head only and spoke.

"The Kennel-Master," he said, "will be honored to see you in his office, Bleys Ahrens."

They were in small, dark wood-paneled lobby. The man

who had just spoken crossed it in front of Bleys and opened another black door to his left. Bleys walked past him and inside the room beyond. The door softly closed behind him.

A man in his late thirties or early forties with a lean, brown-eyed face that spoke of high physical conditioning, and wearing a robe like those of the two who had greeted Bleys at the door, came out from behind his desk. He inclined his head slightly in a bow to Bleys.

"Honored to meet you, Bleys Ahrens," he said. "Shall we sit down?"

His arm indicated a couple of over-stuffed chairs half-facing each other and half-facing a fireplace in which some aromatic logs were burning. "My name is Ahram Moro."

"Thank you, Ahram Moro," said Bleys. He took one of the chairs and Ahram took the other.

"I assume you've been fully briefed on what my appearance here means?" Bleys said.

Once more Ahram inclined his head slightly.

"We received instructions early from Dahno Ahrens that if you appeared, you would be for the moment in authority over us, as Dahno would be. We were not to inquire as to the reasons for this, or anything else about it, but simply accept you as our leader. We are proud to do so. What can I do for you, Bleys Ahrens? Would you like a drink? Something to eat?"

"Neither," said Bleys, "my time here is necessarily short. I want to see your files."

"Of course," said Ahram; "which files in particular?"

"All of them," answered Bleys.

Ahram's face showed a faint puzzlement.

"Forgive me, Bleys Ahrens," he said, "but you just now said your time was short—"

"It is," Bleys interrupted him; "nonetheless I want all the files brought to me."

"As you wish, it shall be done," said Ahram. He pressed a stud in the control pad among the padding of the right arm of his chair, and spoke to whatever sensor there was equipped to pick up his voice.

"Bring in all our files, also a reading table for Bleys Ahrens," he said, and turned back to Bleys. "They'll be here in just a few minutes. It'll take a little time to get them all together and bring them in. Meanwhile, are you sure you won't have something to eat or drink?"

It probably would do no harm to unbend a little at this point, thought Bleys. They could have hardly behaved more obediently and agreeably.

"Yes, I might as well have a drink, while I'm waiting," said Bleys, "if you'll have one with me, of course."

"I'd be honored, Bleys Ahrens," said Ahram. He got to his feet and opened the door of a large wooden cabinet, jammed with bottles and glasses. "Would you prefer beer or something distilled?"

"Beer will be fine," said Bleys.

Ahram selected two tall tumblers, and filled them from a tap with a dark brown liquid giving a surprisingly white, thick head. He took one to Bleys and sat down with one himself.

"This particular brew was Dahno Ahrens' favorite," he said to Bleys, "I hope you like it as well."

Bleys had already lightly tasted what was in his glass.

"It's fine," he said. He put the filled glass aside on a table near his chair as the door behind him opened and a cart wheeled in, bearing a screen and control board with a memory unit attached. A small square table that fitted comfortably across the thick arms of his chair followed and the memory unit was placed before him and turned on.

"Thank you," said Bleys to the young men who had brought it. They bowed their heads and backed out, closing the door behind them.

Bleys checked the control board, and it had its buttons and studs in standard position. He began to work through the files, not category by category, but simply alphabetically, file by file, flashing the equivalent of a page on the screen, reading it at a glance, and passing on to the next. Ahram watched him for some little time.

"Forgive an impertinent question, Bleys Ahrens," he said,

"but are you merely looking for something or are you actually reading parts of those pages?"

"I'm reading the complete page in each case," answered Bleys without looking at him.

Ahram sat silently after that, merely watching as Bleys went through the total extent of the files. He finished his first glass but did not refill it. Bleys' glass continued to sit, practically untouched, where he had left it.

The files, not extensive in Bleys' experience, took him a little over an hour to go through. When he was done he got to his feet and Ahram rose immediately with him.

"Now, what else can I do for you, Bleys Ahrens?" Ahram asked. "Would you like to see our men in competition? As Dahno has possibly told you we have here the finest body of modern *ninjas*—"

He broke off.

"You recognize the name?" he said. "The original *ninjas* were assassins."

"I know," said Bleys, dryly. He was about to refuse, when it struck him that there might be some knowledge to be picked up here that he could be overlooking.

"Yes," he said, "but merely a sample of their unarmed combat and a sample of them with the weapons, plus watching some fifteen or twenty of them run an exercise course, will have to do. As I may have said earlier, I don't have a great deal of time. I need to get back to the airport."

"Whatever you wish, Bleys Ahrens," said Ahram. "If you'll come with me?"

He led the way out and Bleys followed him. Ahram went on a little bit ahead when they came to a room that apparently housed the leaders of groups or divisions within the general body of the Hounds. He spoke briefly to these leaders and then came back to join Bleys.

"If you'll follow me," he said, "the unarmed exercise can be set up quickest."

CHAPTER

31

═══════════

BLEYS SAT BACK with the atmosphere craft on autopilot, on the flight back to Ecumeny. The files he had just looked at and stored in his mind had not yet claimed his attention. He was still thinking of what he had seen in the demonstrations of the Hounds in practice.

On the surface, the young men were quite good. But after watching the first couple in action against each other, he began to suspect something, which was confirmed by the next two pairs he saw. Eventually he asked Ahram's permission to step onto the mat with one of the ones who had just finished demonstrating, and Ahram of course gave it. He knew the *katas* they were working with; they were the same ultimately-derived karate-type *katas* his earliest instructor had taught. Bleys entered into competition, and after a few moments, more or less because he assumed it was expected of him, he finished things by stretching the other man breathless on the mat, and stepped off himself.

"Thank you," he said to Ahram, "that was exactly what I wanted."

Looking into the eyes of Ahram, he could see that not even the leader had picked up on what had disturbed Bleys.

He said nothing more, accordingly, as they went on to the weapons demonstration. Again, he said nothing during the section in which a small group of them ran one of the exercise courses before his eyes.

Done with these demonstrations, he thanked Ahram; and accepted a driver to take him back to the airport. Meanwhile, two of the other members, both of them dressed in ordinary clothes for stepping outside the precincts of their own private area, took his rented car back to where he had picked it up.

Now, he sat thoughtfully with the session in his mind. What had leaped to his eye in the encounter of the first two demonstrating their unarmed martial art, was that they fought strictly at a fixed distance and in a straight line.

When he had stepped onto the mat, consequently, he had made a point of circling and either standing back beyond the distance to which they were accustomed, or moving inside it. Once he had done either of these things, he found them close to helpless and at his mercy.

What all this added up to was that they would be very successful against someone who fought under the same limitations that they had learned and imposed upon themselves. They might also be successful against someone who knew nothing at all of the unarmed martial arts. But they would be essentially useless in attacking anyone who was skilled outside the field of their training.

Later on, watching the weapons-use demonstration, he had found the same dangerous sort of limitations. A great many of them handled their weapons more by rote, than from the standpoint of having the kind of almost family-like familiarity with their weapon that a good, a really good, handler of that weapon would have had. Against a self-trained rifleman for example, who had spent his growing up years like Joshua, teaching himself how to use a needle gun to get small game, they could not hope to compete.

Finally, over the exercise course, he had seen them clearing each barrier the same way, all running in the same pattern. If this was ordinary competition with competitors a long distance apart, extreme individualism would have been shown in the way they acted.

In short, against someone who was an all-around athlete—self-trained or otherwise—but who thought as an athlete and who reacted instinctively as an athlete, they would be at a remarkable disadvantage. The thoroughly-seasoned, fully self-trained athlete would notice their weaknesses at once, and exploit them.

Well, thought Bleys, at any rate it probably did not matter. Barring the unexpected, he would be seeing that neither during Dahno's absence, nor eventually, would they be used. He put that element of the Hounds out of his mind and began to run through his memory and examine the files he had read.

The history of the Hounds ran back a little less than eleven years. That would be some five years after Dahno had left the farm and gone to live and find his own occupation in Ecumeny. Individual Hounds had been recruited when they were ten to twelve years old—an unlikely thing to happen on almost any of the settled worlds nowadays, but oddly enough not on Harmony or Association, where over-large families and under-sized or non-productive farms often caused those who considered themselves old enough to strike off on their own, usually with family and community approval.

These young Friendlies, Bleys told himself, would have been particularly susceptible to being attracted and captured by the sort of organization that Dahno's Hounds offered. It had, obviously, its aspect of near-religion, in its concentration on the person of Dahno himself; and Dahno, in person, had undoubtedly been able to reinforce that by visits to these youngsters; and by doing what he could do so well, which was win them as friends and supporters.

It was in the setup for their training, including their instructors and all else, that Dahno had made his most serious error.

Uninterested in martial arts and weapons himself because of the natural advantage of his unusual size and strength—and in fact, very probably having enough of an inheritance from his and Bleys' Exotic mother, of feeling against the use of force, he had accepted too readily the first form of training organization he discovered; and the first teachers and trainers who had presented themselves for his use in educating the Hounds.

If he had studied across a spectrum of a number of schools of unarmed combat, and an equal spectrum of weapon types and uses, as Bleys had deliberately done, he would have seen what was lacking in the training they had been given.

Happily, as Bleys had suspected, and the files had confirmed, the Hounds had never been used. They had, however, been trained in one respect that made them dangerous; and had absorbed it well.

This was the same kind of training that was more often used with guard dogs. They were given the impression that they could never lose. That they would always win. The files, now that Bleys could read them, reflected a few occasions on which the Hounds had been secretly turned loose in situations in Moseville where they could encounter physically someone who was either untrained, or whose training was not equal to matching them in the area they worked.

The result had been that every one of them now believed himself invincible. They were given vacations and days off to go into Moseville for recreation, now that they were older; but always in ordinary civilian clothes, and under the condition that they in no way betrayed what they really were. The Hounds took eagerly to this idea; but just to make these days off safe, Bleys had read in the files, Dahno had had each one on his first few trips observed by hired private observers from cities that were neither Ecumeny nor Moseville, to see if in any way they gave away what they were, or boasted about their background.

None of them had.

On the other hand, unfortunately, as Bleys had said, they were now essentially a loaded weapon itching to be used. Just lately, Ahram had said, they had been training for a specific assassination exercise, although he volunteered no information as to whether this was merely an in-house training exercise, or if they were actually going to be given a live subject, as they had been when they were sent in to reinforce their training against civilians in Moseville.

By and large, most of the files concerned themselves with merely the cost and record keeping of the organization.

Having squeezed most of the juice of important information out of the files, Bleys closed his eyes, tilted his seat back and dropped into a light doze, which was not broken until his ship sat down at Ecumeny. He paid off pilot and airship, and took an autocab back to the apartment; where he climbed into bed and abandoned himself to serious sleep.

He woke later than his usual hour the following morning, but with his mind in that sudden state of crystal clarity that sometimes follows a good night's sleep, once body and mind together have fully come to.

The most immediate item on his program now was to deal with Norton Brawley.

He called the man's office while he was making breakfast. His call was answered by a female voice who turned out to be a receptionist; and who passed him on to a male voice.

"Norton Brawley's office," said the male voice, "how can I help you?"

"This is Bleys Ahrens," said Bleys, "tell him I want to see him here at the apartment in fifteen minutes."

There was a moment of astonished silence at the other end.

"Who did you say you are? What did you say?" said the male voice.

"Bleys Ahrens. He's to be here at the apartment in fifteen minutes. Just get the word to him," said Bleys.

The male voice, when it spoke again, seemed to have recovered some of its composure.

"I'm afraid legalist Norton Brawley wouldn't be able to see you within fifteen minutes under any circumstances, let alone out of his own office—"

"That's up to you," said Bleys; "whether it's your doing or his, if he isn't here in fifteen minutes I'll have to assume that he no longer wishes to maintain his former connection with us. Good-bye."

"—Wait a minute. Wait a minute," said the male voice, "who did you say you were?"

"Bleys," said Bleys, enunciating very clearly, "Ahrens."

"And where did you say you were, at a place called the Apartment?"

"The apartment I share with Dahno Ahrens," said Bleys. "He'll know where it is."

"I don't see—it's completely impossible, of course—" the male voice at the other end stopped suddenly, "*Dahno Ahrens?* But you're not Dahno Ahrens."

"I'm sorry," said Bleys, "but I can't waste any more time talking to you. He's either here in the next fifteen minutes or not. Good-bye."

He hung up.

He went back to making his breakfast.

He was sitting down to eat it when the annunciator chimed.

"Yes?" he said, raising his voice slightly, but not leaving the table.

"Norton Brawley."

Bleys pressed the door release on the nearest control pad, which happened to be the one on the sideboard, without getting out of his chair. Every once in a while he was a little amused at the length of reach of his own adult arms. This was one of those times. He went back to eating as the door opened and a man in his late thirties or early forties and wearing dark business clothes, tall by ordinary standards but not by Bleys', came in.

His face was oval, his eyebrows and hair jet black and straight, and his skin was a dark olive color which made him look Mediterranean in ancestry.

It was a bit unusual, in that most of the European immigrants to the Friendlies had been northern rather than southern Europeans. He had a dapper look, somewhat marred by a slight sheen of sweat on his brow and a slightly flustered look.

"Norton Brawley!" said Bleys, without getting up from the table. "You made it in good time. I'm just about through here. Will you have a cup of coffee with me in the lounge?"

"I—I—" Norton Brawley pulled himself together visibly and stood even straighter. "Certainly, Bleys Ahrens."

"Black?"

"If you don't mind," said Norton Brawley.

Bleys stood up, and saw the other man's eyes widen a little at the sight of his height. Bleys smiled inwardly. It was always very shocking for a man who considered himself generally taller than most other men to run into someone who over-topped him not by a little but by a great deal.

"Take a seat in the lounge, then," said Bleys. "I'll bring the coffee in, in a second."

Norton went out of sight out of the dining area into the lounge. Bleys disposed of his tray and everything on it and drew two cups of black coffee, which he took around the corner into the lounge.

He handed one of these to Norton, and, with the other, sat down himself in a facing chair.

"Sorry to break you away from your work so suddenly," said Bleys genially, "but I've got a small crisis I wanted to talk to you about."

"If you mean Dahno's leaving and being off-planet now, I already knew that," said Norton, somewhat stiffly; "he phoned me as soon as he made the decision."

"Not as soon as he made the decision, Norton," Bleys corrected him gently. "He made the decision when he was with me."

"Ah . . . oh," said Norton. He reached for his cup, which so far he had not touched, and drank from it. "I didn't know that."

"How could you?" said Bleys. "However, since he left me in charge I've had to make a quick review of things, just to make sure I had all the strings in my hand, so to speak. I find myself a little concerned about this assassination exercise, after seeing the Hounds themselves yesterday."

Norton drank from his cup again, holding it so tightly that his hand almost trembled.

"Why don't you give me your opinion of it?" went on Bleys.

He had nothing more than a guess that the Hounds might be

put shortly to active use. But he had already read enough from Norton in the way of reaction and body signals, to know that this guess might have some basis in reality.

"I don't know how much Dahno told you about this . . ." Norton hesitated. His fishing for more information from Bleys himself was obvious.

"Don't concern yourself about that," said Bleys, waving the question aside with a hand, "just talk about it on the assumption that I, of course, know everything about it. Give me your opinion as if you were telling me about it for the first time. You see, I know Dahno's opinion, I know what's in the files and his secret files; and I'm sure the Hounds to be engaged in it haven't any idea whether it's simply another practice, or the real thing. Let's not waste any time now. Your opinion?"

For the first time since Norton had walked in, there was a hardening of Bleys' voice on the last question; a bit of a whip-crack, demanding an instant answer rather than asking for one.

"I'm sorry," said Norton hastily. "I didn't understand you'd have anything to do with it."

"Who else?" said Bleys. "Go on, now."

"Well, I don't see how there can be any problem to it," said Norton, falling back into what were obviously something like his ordinary office tones of judicious judgment. "Leaving the speech, any guards McKae's got are going to be relaxed. Also, with our men wearing ordinary clothes as well as whatever badges or emblem the *Arise!* people have handed out to their own ranking members, the odds have to be overwhelming that everybody will assume that McKae was the victim of enemies in his own church."

"That's providing," said Bleys, "that all our Hounds get away without being caught, questioned and revealed as belonging to our organization."

"Well, they don't belong to our organization," said Norton; "actually they know nothing about it—even Ahram. They know about Dahno's public face, that's all. But even Dahno's safely off-world now."

"Are you positive," asked Bleys, "that the Hounds are fully

prepared? It looked to me as if they could use some more time in practice when I was out at their place yesterday."

"What gave you that idea?" said Brawley. "They looked perfectly all right both to Dahno and myself even a week or more ago, when we last saw them. Also, McKae's speech itself is still three weeks off. If there's something you want sharpened up on their training, I'm sure that can be done."

"What's been done about getting them to where the speech is going to be held?" Bleys asked.

"Why," said Brawley, "of course, they'll be flown in, in private atmosphere ships with our own men driving them—the ships, that is. Then they change to five cars, six Hounds to a car, and move down into the area of the main auditorium here, a good hour ahead of time. Particularly with the badges, they ought to be able to get inside the building, so that they're behind McKae when he leaves. If they shoot him down on the steps it can't help but look like a fight of factions within his church itself. That sort of thing happens all the time. Church members get definitely lined up on one side or another."

"And then the Hounds just slip away to the cars, correct?" Bleys said.

"Exactly," answered Norton, smiling.

"And what if the police have any reason to investigate the ground cars on their way in, or what if any of our Hounds are caught, trying to get away from the scene after the shooting?" Bleys said.

"Surely, Bleys Ahrens," said Norton, "you must know all that. As far as the police are concerned, we've arranged through our connections on the city force, that the cars are to be let through no matter what the situation is. As far as other police at the scene, or the church members, or McKae's own guards—I believe our intelligence tells us that he'll only have guards who're simply self-trained individuals. Men who've perhaps had a little experience in wars between the churches. He'll be counting on the mass of people in his church for his main protection; and his so-called 'security' people'd be no match, man on man, for our Hounds, anyway."

"It does sound excellent," said Bleys, in a thoughtful tone of voice, "provided nothing unexpected goes wrong. I still think the Hounds involved in that could stand a little more practice, though."

"Well, that's easy enough to arrange, Bleys Ahrens." said Norton. "Do you want me to take care of it?"

"Yes," said Bleys, still thoughtfully, "perhaps you'd better do that rather than I, since they've had more contact with you than with me and they probably only know you and Dahno at all well."

"Certainly, absolutely. I'll take care of it the moment I get back to my office," said Norton. "I'll phone out there."

"Better go in person," said Bleys; "I'd like you to impress on them the urgency that I feel about their being in top training."

"If that's what you want," said Norton, rising, "but I do think you may be concerning yourself a little more over this than is necessary."

"Better safe than sorry," said Bleys.

"But what I don't see," said Norton as Bleys walked with him to the door of the apartment, "is why you consider this something of a crisis. You could simply have called me and given me the message to take out to them."

Bleys smiled down at him.

"I thought perhaps I ought to impress you, too, with my own feeling of concern and urgency," said Bleys. "I hope I've done that."

"Indeed you have, indeed you have," said Norton. He offered his hand to Bleys and they clasped. "Yes, it probably was wise for you to see me now as soon as possible, if you're feeling this way about it. But I do promise you there'll be nothing to it when the time comes."

Bleys let him out and closed the door behind him; then went back to sit down in the chair he had been occupying when they were talking. What was facing him was obvious. He would have to look into McKae's church and at McKae's top people, somehow. He had to get a much clearer picture of McKae's vulnerability.

He had fished for most of the information he wanted from

Norton Brawley and got it. But it had been information he was not particularly happy to have. Norton, clearly, was no more able to plan and put together the kind of thing the Hounds were to be sent on, than anyone in the Hounds, themselves.

In short, the necessity was to avoid the risk of bringing the name of the Others into newsprint exposure as assassins. The militia would not be long in making that connection, once Ahram had pointed Norton Brawley out to them. The publicity would bring the name to total and utter ruin—which he, Bleys, could not afford now or in the future. Particularly, with the plans he had for it on a much more advanced scale.

Clearly he would have to do something about the situation, himself. He got up and went down to the exercise room in the apartment building, to give his body something to do, while his mind had time to work out the situation.

The answers he wanted were buried in the back of his head, and took time to surface, as he had expected they would. He had been under a great temptation today, with Norton, to plunge into an investigation of McKae's church, trusting that his mind would sort out what needed to be done as he went along.

However, experience with his own ways of thinking had taught him better than that. He was always best when he had a chance to let his unconscious ponder the situation until it began to come up with all the answers on it.

Two days after his talk with Brawley, it had.

CHAPTER

32

THE NEW AND small, but active Arise! congregation in an old Ecumeny church, abandoned and outgrown by whatever other church had owned it originally, paid little attention at first to one of the newest worshipers, except to remark on his exceeding height. Tall as he was, his clothes were still a little too big on him; and were old and shabby, giving the impression that he had not perhaps eaten as regularly lately as he should.

Eventually, at his second meeting, when some of the other members of the congregation ventured to make his acquaintance, he admitted that he was out of work at the moment. He had grown up on a farm not too far from Ecumeny and was taking his time trying to find something in the city that he thought he would like to stay with. His name, he said, was Bleys MacLean.

Bleys had given some thought to what name to call himself. Sooner or later, if he got close to McKae, he would be checked back on. To a large extent, he intended to tell the truth, using Henry's farm as his background and with only the small difference that Henry was his father, rather than his uncle. He felt fairly safe with this. The members of a congregation of a country church were very clannish toward any outsider—particularly an outside investigator.

They might not have liked Bleys, and might still not like him, but that did not mean that they would correct someone who was inquiring about him under an altered name. They would simply go along with the fact that Bleys' last name was MacLean and if necessary direct the person to Henry.

Henry, who was even more protective of his family than the congregation was of one of its former members, would give away nothing. So, Bleys felt fairly sure that his background as a country boy growing up on Henry's farm would hold up under any investigation McKae's people might give his background.

"And what brought you to our Church?" another member of the congregation asked.

"I heard our Great Teacher Darrel McKae speak; and I realized at once that it was him I should be listening to," said Bleys.

"Oh, you heard Darrel McKae himself?" said the man who had just spoken. "What church of ours was that at?"

Bleys swayed a little, uncomfortably, and looked down at his large, worn boots as if embarrassed. He seemed to have a permanent stoop to his shoulders; as if he was continually and apologetically trying to get down to the level of the people to whom he talked. Outside of this, he gave the impression of not being too bright.

"Actually," he said, "it wasn't a church. It was on the floor of the Chamber. I was in the visitors' gallery, there."

They stared at him a little.

"The visitors' gallery?" said the man who had been doing all the talking so far. "What were you doing in the visitors' gallery? You need a special pass even to get into the Chamber building."

Bleys looked even more embarrassed.

"I found a pass in the street," he said; "it was only for one day, and someone must have thrown it away; but the pass was for the same date as that day, so I put it on and went inside, just to see what I could see. The guard on the door of the gallery wasn't too happy about someone like me visiting"—Bleys smiled awkwardly—"but he let me in. Our Great Teacher was talking about the Core Tap and how the people who worked on it had to be Godly people, people who were steady church attendants, no matter what world they came from."

"Quite right, too," said a woman who was part of the group, "he really told them! Read it in the newsprint."

"And that made you go looking for one of his churches?" asked the same man who had been asking so many of the questions.

"Yes," said Bleys, "I saw one church, but it was pretty grand. I thought I'd look for something a little more . . . homey. Like the church we used to have out near the farm."

"So you came to our church. Quite right," said the woman. "God and the truly religious have little use for mere size and ornament!"

There was a general agreement from those in the group standing around Bleys.

"And I like it here very well," added Bleys.

"And we're happy to have you, Bleys MacLean," said the same man. "You'll find friends here. You'll find True Faith-holders, every one of us!"

"Thank you, thank you," murmured Bleys, "I try hard to be a True Faith-holder myself."

"Have you met our Teacher, yet?" said the man.

Bleys shook his head.

"Well, come meet him, then," said the man, taking Bleys by the arm and literally pulling him forward. Bleys hung back for a second, then followed. The other church members with them tagged along.

They went up to the front of the church and around a small corner. Behind a fretted wooden screen there, they found a middle-aged, rather plump man with, by contrast, a remarkably thin face, washing his hands. He had evidently just taken off and hung up the black robe he had put on for the service.

"Teacher," said the man who still had his hand on Bleys' arm, "I want you to meet a new member of our congregation. Bleys MacLean. He saw the bright light of our Arise! Church as a result of listening to our Great Teacher Darrel McKae, himself, speak. Teacher, this is Bleys MacLean. Bleys, this is Teacher Samuel Godsarm."

With his hand on Bleys' arm he literally pulled Bleys forward to confront the church-leader.

"I'm very honored to make your acquaintance, Bleys MacLean," said Samuel Godsarm. He offered his hand to Bleys' clasp, and Bleys took it briefly, hesitantly, as if he did not want to hold the other's hand too long in his long-fingered grasp, or press too hard. "This is your first time here?"

"No, no," put in the woman, who was still among the group behind Bleys. "He's been here once before, but he sat in the back, by himself; and he's been a little bit shy about coming forward to make friends. We thought the best thing was for him to meet you, and know that this Arise! Church is his religious home."

"Well said, Martha Aino," replied Samuel Godsarm. He smiled up at Bleys. "We're all your friends here, Bleys MacLean. Just take that for granted."

"Thanks. Thanks a lot," mumbled Bleys.

"What is your occupation, Brother Bleys?"

Before Bleys could answer, the people he had just been talking to in the group around him began to answer for him, telling the church-leader of how Bleys had found a pass, wandered into the visitors' gallery of the Chamber, and heard Darrel McKae speak about the Core Tap.

"Well, well, well," said Godsarm, "you may not believe it, Brother Bleys, being new among us, but many of us have not had the good fortune you've had of hearing the Great Leader directly. I have, myself, of course. It was the reason I was inspired to found this particular church. But many of our people who've come to us from other, false, churches, have merely heard the message of the Leader, and at once known that they wanted to follow him."

"Have you preached?" asked the woman who had followed them up to this point.

Bleys had considered the chance of being asked this, but only briefly. He was familiar with the fact that most of the sects on both Friendly Worlds expected all their members to be ready to preach at a moment's notice. It was assumed that if they were truly in touch with the Lord, that the words would come to them from the Lord, as needed. This was a matter of belief and not to be set aside.

"I have . . ." said Bleys, sounding only a little more unwilling than he actually felt. It was not that he could not preach if he had to. It merely went against his grain to do something for which he had not prepared.

"Most of the members are still in the church yet, Samuel," said the woman who had come along and spoken up before. "Do you suppose that our new Brother Bleys here could preach us a short sermon; and perhaps tell us about his experience in listening to the Great Leader from the visitors' gallery?"

"A very good idea, Martha," answered Godsarm. He stepped back from the sink, turning to Bleys. "If you will oblige us, Bleys?" he asked.

"Of course," said Bleys, a little hesitantly. In truth, he was not hesitant. He had no doubt of his own capability to give them a short sermon or tell them about McKae's speech.

Seeing that Godsarm was still standing back from the sink, obviously inviting Bleys to use it, Bleys realized that the Arise! Church must be one of those in which the practice of the preacher washing his hands before his sermon and again afterwards was adhered to. He stepped to the sink, laved his long hands in the stream of water from the tap, rubbed on some of the rough homemade soap from the soap shelf, and rinsed the hands off. Turning off the tap he dried his hands on the loop of toweling that hung nearby, and turned back to Godsarm.

"I'm ready," he said.

Everyone else except Godsarm, Bleys saw, had left; undoubtedly they had gone back into the body of the church.

"Come with me then, Bleys," said Godsarm. "I'll introduce you to our members."

Bleys followed him around to the front of the screen and up to the lectern that stood on the platform three steps above the general floor of the church. Buzzing with interest, the people still there after the regular service, who must have numbered forty or fifty, were sorting themselves out and taking seats in preparation for what they had probably already heard was going to happen. It was quite common for church members to linger in a church like this, not merely for minutes but sometimes for hours. For many of these people it was the one social occasion of the week available. Godsarm stepped up to the lectern.

"Quiet, everybody," he said.

The congregation quieted and those who were still on their feet sat down. They sat in expectant silence.

"I have to introduce to you today," said Godsarm in the rolling tones of a practiced preacher, "a new member of our church, Bleys MacLean. He saw the light of our way, when by chance he found himself in the gallery overlooking the floor of the Chamber; and heard our Great Leader speak words of fire about those from off-world who should work on our new Core Tap, if indeed the Core Tap is voted into being."

He turned to Bleys.

"Brother Bleys," he said, "our Brothers and Sisters wait to hear from you."

Bleys stepped up to the lectern, which came barely to his waist. He had been an actor almost from the time he could toddle, thanks to his life with his mother, and he saw instant advantages in what was happening. For one thing, he could let himself go in the sermon and the telling. The audience would credit it, not to him, but to inspiration by the Lord.

He gripped the outer edge of the lectern with his hands so that the long, powerful fingers were visible. It was a gesture of strong theatrical effect, and it worked on the congregation. The people in the body of the church were already silent, but now the hush about them became one in which everyone seemed to hold their breaths at the same moment.

"Brothers and Sisters," he said, with all the power and command of his trained voice; which, following closely on

Godsarm's announcement, was like the carrying notes of a trumpet, after the notes of a flute.

"I speak to you with the words the Lord gives me to speak. First, let me remind you of one of the laws of the Lord. When I was a boy, on our farm we had a neighbor. This neighbor had many goats, but after a while they began to sicken, one by one and die; and finally he came to ask my father if he would come and look at these sick goats; and tell him perhaps what was wrong with them, why he could not keep them in good health.

"My father went and saw the goats. They were in clean quarters, they were warm—for it was wintertime and they liked the shelter of their barn better than the outside and the chilling winds. There was food in front of them but they were not eating.

"My father turned to his neighbor and said, *'Do you talk to these goats?'*

"*'What do you mean, talk to them?'* asked the neighbor.

"*'Do you know them by name? Do you call them by name? Do you spend a few moments each day perhaps in brushing their coats and speaking to them?'*

"*'I do not,'* said the neighbor, *'I have never heard of such a thing.'*

"*'Do so,'* said my father, *'then, after a week come and ask me to see them again.'*

"A week later the neighbor came over and his face was lit as a lantern is lit from inside by a candle.

"*'Come and see my goats now!'* he said.

"My father went over with him and saw the goats. They were still in the shelter of their shed, but they were entirely changed. Their coats shone, their ears stood up and most of them were eating from the mangers in front of them.

"*'Tell me,'* the neighbor asked my father, *'how did you know that what you told me to do would have such a marvelous effect on them?'*

"*'It is one of the laws of the Lord with all his creatures,'* said my father. *'They will sicken and die if they receive no attention from he who controls and directs every moment of their lives. Even as you would not ignore your children, if you had some'*—for the neighbor was unmarried and had no progeny—*'you must give your beasts some attention, some care and even some love. Do that and your flock will flourish.'*

"Members of this congregation, I have never forgotten that," went on Bleys, "and it is so, what my father said. I have looked all my life for leaders who cared for their flock as my father had said it should be done. The other day, sitting in seats high above the floor of the Chamber where laws are made for all our world, I listened to just such a leader, enunciating just such a law.

"That leader was our Great Teacher, Darrel McKae. He was speaking about the Core Tap, which we hope to add to those two that already provide power to this hard and hungry planet of ours. His words were better than any I could use to tell you of what I heard, so I will repeat now to you what he said then—word for word—for, from the time I could first talk, I have been blessed with a memory that loses nothing of value in God's eyes."

Bleys began to repeat from memory, for his verbal memory was as good as his visual memory, McKae's speech on the floor of the Chamber. When he had at last ended and stepped back from the platform, there was a long moment of almost frozen silence from his audience. And then everyone began to call out at once, blessing McKae and blessing Bleys.

"Your memory is a true gift of the Lord," said Godsarm, when he and Bleys were together behind the screen and Bleys was washing his hands again. This time no one had ventured to come up from the floor. They had looked at Bleys, at the end of his speech, in fact, with awe and almost disbelief.

"Yes," said Bleys, returning to the uncertain voice with which he had talked to everyone before he stepped up to the lectern. "I am indeed thankful to God that I have been so blessed."

"I think, Brother Bleys," said Godsarm, judiciously, "that perhaps it would not be the Lord's will for you to be wasted here in this small congregation, when our Great Leader might have better uses for you. Accordingly, with your approval, I will send you to him, with a letter—which will be sealed, for it is for his eyes alone—telling him of what you did here and leaving it to him to make such decision as God would want."

Bleys looked at him.

"Thank you," he said. When he left the church, some twenty minutes later, after being thronged about by the members, most of whom would have liked him to stop and talk to them, he headed not for the hotel that was McKae's headquarters in the city and to which Samuel Godsarm had directed him; but only far enough to make sure he had thrown off any secret pursuers. After that, he called on his monitor for an autocab and rode back to his apartment.

Back at the apartment, he skillfully, with a heated knife, lifted the wax seal of the envelope with its imprint of a lion bowing its head before a cross and took the paper out and unfolded it.

The message on it was very brief.

To: Our Great Leader
From: Samuel Godsarm of the Thirty-second Church of Arise!
Dear Leader:
    I am sending to you one of our new members, Bleys MacLean, whom you may, in your greater wisdom, see better ways to make use of than our poor, small church deserves.
    He has a perfect memory and has been brought up in a lifetime of hard work, on his father's farm. So both his strength and his memory may prove to be of use. If this is not so, perhaps you, or one of those with you can send him back to us.
                    With praise to God, who directs us all,
                                    Samuel Godsarm

Bleys resealed the letter, and took it into his bedroom, where he put it in a small bedside file drawer.

Returning to the living room, he sat thoughtfully in one of the overstuffed chairs for a long moment; then turned to the phone beside him and punched the stud.

The screen lit up with the cheerful face of a young man with neatly combed, straight brown hair. He looked almost too young to be working as an information operator.

"At your service," he said.

"Your equipment there should show you my address," said Bleys.

"Yes," answered the operator, glancing down briefly, "it does."

"Could you find me the number of the nearest college to my address, and the number in particular of their athletic department?"

"Just a moment," said the operator.

The screen blanked out. A moment later it lit up with an eight-digit number in large numerals. Behind the numerals the voice of the operator went on.

"There it is if you wish to copy it down," it said; "would you prefer that I simply connect you with it?"

"I have it, now," said Bleys, "but why don't you connect me anyway?"

"It'll be my pleasure."

The screen blanked out, the soft chime of a phone bell at the far end was heard. After four chimes, the screen lit up again, this time with the white-haired, capable face of a woman in her late fifties or early sixties.

"This is the Athletic Department," she said. "Can I be of assistance?"

"Yes," said Bleys, "I'd like to talk to your wrestling instructor, if you have one and he's there at this time."

"Did you particularly want a male instructor?" asked the woman.

"It makes no difference," answered Bleys.

"Well, let me see." She glanced aside from the screen for several seconds. "Professor Antonia Lu is here at the moment. Do you want me to ring her office?"

"Please," said Bleys.

Once more the screen blanked, the phone-chime was heard. And another young male face, looking remarkably like the telephone operator in some way, even though his hair was black and his face was long and rather thin, appeared on the screen.

"Professor Lu's office," he said, "can I be of assistance?"

"I'm Bleys Ahrens," said Bleys, "and it will be most kind of you if you could ask the Professor if she could take a few moments to speak with me on the phone right now."

"May I ask—does she know you, Bleys Ahrens?" asked the face. "She's out on the gym floor right now; if she doesn't know you, could I ask the reason for your calling?"

"She doesn't know me, as a matter of fact," said Bleys. "You might tell her, though, I've had quite a broad grounding in a number of the traditional Japanese disciplines, particularly judo and the judo-based arts. I need to know about the differences between the kind of wrestling you do there at the college and what I studied."

"I'll take her that message," said the young man at the other end. "It'll probably be a little while yet before she can get back to you. Will you leave your number?"

Bleys pressed a stud on the control board below the screen, which automatically transmitted his phone number to the screen of the party he was talking to.

"Thank you, Bleys Ahrens," said the man at the other end; and the screen went blank.

Bleys resigned himself to waiting several hours, if necessary. But it was actually only a little over ten minutes before his own phone chimed; and when he answered, it lit up with the face of a woman in her late twenties or early thirties, with blue eyes, remarkably matched to nearly black hair; and facial boning that made her, Bleys thought, the most beautiful woman he had ever seen. Her voice was light and cheerful.

"Bleys Ahrens?" she said. "This is Antonia Lu. Did you have something you wanted to talk to me about?"

"Yes, I've got a favor to ask," said Bleys.

She looked puzzled.

"I believe I know you," she said, "—by reputation, anyway. Bleys Ahrens, aren't you the brother of Dahno Ahrens?"

"Yes, as a matter of fact I am," said Bleys, "but I don't think we've ever met."

"No, of course not," she said, "but my brother was James Lu, who was one of the trainees in one of the classes for Others put on by you and your brother. We're both mixed-breeds you know, Friendly and Dorsai. And I always thought what you and your brother are doing is the beginning of a great future. What can I do to help you?"

"If I could come over and simply watch some of your students wrestling and perhaps even try wrestling one of them myself . . ." He let the sentence trail off.

"Well, we don't ordinarily let the general public rubberneck around here, let alone get on the mat with one of our students," she said, "but I know from what James has told me that you're not the usual sort of rubbernecker. I've just finished one class and my students are all practicing; it's an ideal time for you to see them at it. How long will it take you to get here?"

"By autocar," said Bleys, "perhaps : . . fifteen minutes?"

"That's fine. We usually spend at least a couple of hours in free practice after class," she said. "If you've got gym clothes bring them along. I'll have to decide after you get here just who you might have a chance to wrestle."

"Of course. I'll be right over," said Bleys.

He did not, in fact, own the kind of gym clothes she was talking about. The *do-gi* he wore for martial arts was not appropriate in this situation. But he could easily stop the autocar at an athletic equipment shop along the way, and buy what he needed.

He did just that. The best gym pants they could find for him were too large in the waist and short in the legs. The body top was far too narrow-shouldered to wear. However, he had anticipated that; and had brought along an undershirt which would do for the top. The pants would be all right even if they did ride a bit high on his legs. They were more than roomy enough in the crotch.

Luckily, she had given him explicit directions for finding the gym where she held her classes. He arrived only a little late—perhaps eighteen minutes instead of fifteen. He had changed in the autocar on the way over, and came in wearing the athletic pants which reached just below mid-calf on his legs, and his own, short-sleeved undershirt above it.

He left the autocar now and went up the stairs into what seemed to be an office; where he identified himself to a small, bright-eyed female student with an aureole of blond hair, sitting behind a counter and working away at a keyboard, with some papers beside her.

"Bleys Ahrens?" the student said. "Dr. Lu said you were to go right in."

She got up, opened a flap in the counter and let him through, then pointed to an open doorway through which he could see a gym. He went in. Inside, he saw a glassed-in office to his left, with Antonia Lu sitting behind it. Looking up and seeing him coming, she rose to meet him.

She looked at him with a small, ironic grin, as they clasped hands.

"I must admit," she said, "I wasn't expecting anyone as tall as you. Well, come with me, and I'll show you around."

He followed her to one of the mats where a pair of students were down on the mat itself, and grappling. Just as Bleys and Antonia got to them, they broke loose, both got to their feet and they started over again.

"Any match is decided on points," Antonia said to Bleys, as they watched. The two ended up on the mat again. "For example, the student with his back to us now would get a certain number of points for that take-down; since he initiated it and ended up on top of Dick, his opponent. Of course, the match can also be won by pinning your opponent's shoulders to the mat and holding him there for five seconds. Otherwise they wrestle for three three-minute rounds with a one-minute rest in between, and the match is decided on points."

The two in front of them had once more broken loose from each other and gotten back to their feet. Bleys watched, fascinated, as the same man took his partner down.

"I think I'd like to see as many take-downs as possible," said Bleys.

"In that case," answered Antonia, "as soon as any pair are

down on the mat look around for another pair that's on their feet and watch. I'll leave you to it for the moment."

Bleys took her advice and she went back into her office.

After about ten minutes she came out again, to find him watching now a pair of wrestlers that were on the mat and working steadily there to achieve a position on top from which a pin could result.

"I see you're not watching take-downs exclusively any-more," said Lu.

"No," answered Bleys, with his eyes still on the two on the mat in front of him, "these two are the best, here."

"You can tell that, can you?" said Antonia. "Yes, they're both seniors and my star pupils. They'll be wrestling on the varsity team in a couple of months when the colleges start competing against each other for this year."

She looked up at him curiously.

"Have you decided that you might like to try getting on the mat with one of my students, now?"

"One of these two, if you don't mind," said Bleys.

She hesitated, but only for a second.

"All right," said Antonia; "you'll have to wait until their current bout is over, then I'll ask for you. And you'll have to take those shoes off."

Bleys had been wearing a pair of running shoes, which were not exactly appropriate for the gym, but at least could do its wooden surface no harm. He bent down, untied them and kicked them off.

When the break came and the bout ended between the two who had been wrestling, he was ready to step on the mat. Antonia put a restraining hand on his arm.

"Let them catch their breath first. I suggest you try Anton, the blond-haired one there. Anton, will you come over here, please?"

The young man she had spoken to came to them.

"Anton, this is Bleys Ahrens. As soon as you feel ready for it, he'd like at least a three-minute round with you; if that's agreeable to you. He's never done our kind of wrestling before, although he's had training in the martial arts—"

She looked up at Bleys.

"—Which of course he won't be allowed to use here. Bleys Ahrens, note that points are taken from you if you use any of the blows or throws that you may have been taught. In our wrestling you mustn't take your opponent's feet off the ground."

"I'd guessed that," said Bleys. "I think I know what the limitations are. But if I make a mistake Anton can simply tell me—won't you, Anton—?" He let Anton's unknown name hang on a note of query.

"Oh, I'm sorry," said Antonia. "Anton Lupescu, this is Bleys Ahrens, as I said. Bleys is merely a student of martial arts generally, Anton, he's not connected with the college here."

"That's true," said Bleys. He clasped hands with Anton. "Honored."

"And I likewise." Anton grinned. "I'm honored to make your acquaintance. Also I'd be glad to wrestle Bleys Ahrens."

"Thank you," said Bleys.

He could see Anton's eyes measuring his height advantage and considering how to deal with it.

After a few moments, they faced each other on the mat. In imitation of what he had seen, Bleys put his right hand on Anton's shoulder and grasped the other's elbow with his left. Anton reciprocated.

It was, Bleys thought, even as he was doing it, absurdly easy and almost unfair. He took Anton down right away, with himself on top, and pushed his stomach out as Anton exhaled for a moment, so that the pressure of his lower body against Anton's diaphragm made it almost impossible for Anton to breathe.

After struggling breathlessly for about twenty seconds, Anton gave up and made an attempt to break loose, which Bleys let him do.

They got back to their feet, took hold of each other's shoulders and elbows again; and once more Bleys immediately took Anton down and tied him up with legs and arms so that the other was once again immobilized and forced to break loose to get a new start.

By the time the first three minutes of the round was up, they had gone through this process five times.

"I think that'll be enough," said Antonia, who had stayed to watch, with Anton's former opponent standing fascinated beside her. "You'll have learned as much as you needed to know, haven't you, Bleys Ahrens?"

"Yes," said Bleys.

"No!" protested Anton. "Let me go the full distance with him, Toni. I'm sure I can get him."

"I don't think so," said Antonia Lu decisively. "Go back to your regular practice with Dick, there. Bleys Ahrens, will you come with me?"

She led him into her office and closed the door so that they could not be overheard outside. She turned to Bleys.

"You know," she said, "I don't know whether to describe what you did as cheating or not. There's nothing in the rule book against it; but effectively you're giving Anton something he had no hope of handling. Those were restrained *katas* you were using to take him down, weren't they? And you were holding back so that he went down with his feet on the floor, rather than being thrown down. Weren't you?"

"You're right," said Bleys.

"I won't ask you any personal questions about your background," said Antonia, "but you've evidently had a good deal of rather high-level training in your martial arts. I think if you're going to practice on anyone, you'd better find someone besides my pupils. Would you mind telling me what you wanted this experience for?"

"It's a personal and somewhat secret matter," said Bleys; "effectively, I may have to appear like a country kid who learned to wrestle the way it was done in the countryside, as he was growing up."

"Hmm," said Antonia. "I won't ask you any more; but I will say that you're almost doubly unfair, both with your height and reach and being experienced in the fighting methods you know. You're sure you don't want to tell me any more than that?"

Bleys shook his head.

"But thank you very much for letting me learn what I did today," said Bleys.

"Not at all," said Antonia. She offered her hand once more, and he clasped it. "I have to admit that you've got my curiosity roused."

"Maybe someday I can satisfy it," said Bleys.

Her hand felt very warm and pleasant in his and he was conscious of a desire to hold it longer. Then he remembered how his path led forward in life; and how it could never be other than a solitary path. If he had ever encountered any woman he had wanted to see again it was the woman before him. But that was the dangerous part of it. He dare not.

"—Though," he added, a little belatedly, "I'm afraid the odds are against being able to do so."

Their hands parted, they smiled at each other; and Bleys went out, back to his autocar, leaving both her and the gym behind.

CHAPTER

33

═══════════

HE PROGRAMMED HIS autocar to take him, not directly back to the apartment, but to the office. There, he spent a little over an hour going through all the messages from off-world that had come for him since he had last been there. There was no word from Dahno on Earth. But there were a number of messages from each of the leaders in charge of Other organizations on all the worlds he had visited.

Uniformly, they reported the beginning of a recruitment of Other cross-breeds, and, with growing astonishment, reported also how many other things now were possible to them, now that they were getting the extra personnel. Of course, those other things were still in the planning stage.

The newly-recruited mixed-breeds would have to be trained; and Bleys was pleased to see that they had not picked any beyond the age of forty, since it would be hard to put people that old or older into a new way of life. The time might come when they would be able to use the older ones too; but that time would have to wait until they were more firmly in control, on the various worlds.

As for the original leaders, the very fact that they had worked this wholeheartedly proved his original belief that they were ambitious. Bleys had shown them the way to greater positions of power, and barring the unforeseen, they were his now.

He coded messages to all of them now, alerting them to a meeting of the Vice-Chairmen on a world other than their own. They would be notified which world in due time. Meanwhile, they should be ready to leave at a moment's notice; and he encouraged them to keep on with what they were doing.

This much done, he sat back for a moment in his chair. He had bet a great deal on the fact that the first and most senior trainees that Dahno had sent out had all been recruited on Association. Either by birth and upbringing, or by upbringing alone, they very much had a Friendly attitude toward humanity in general and society at large.

It was that, and their obvious ambition, he had been counting on when he had recommended that all of them stay in the positions of authority in which he found them. There might, in fact, be better leaders than they among those they were recruiting now.

But he wanted these firmly indoctrinated with the new life to which he intended to put all of them.

It was, after all, something that rang very close to the Friendly attitude in all their churches, that anticipated an eventual time when all humanity would be worshipers. They were on a new track now; and anyone, even Dahno, would find it hard to switch them back off it, onto his original aims for them.

He left the office and went back to the apartment. The day was darkening into twilight outside when he left the autocar at his apartment building, and went up to the apartment itself.

He made himself a light dinner, then gave his mind a holiday, letting it roam through a number of the books on poetry and prose he was always accumulating. Books that contained no information in any way connected with what he was faced with at the moment; but which were full of the magic of art that fascinated him.

Eventually he went to bed. As he lay there, he found himself thinking of Antonia Lu; and to put her from his mind he deliberately envisioned once more his original familiar image of himself as far out in space, isolated, looking at all the worlds and all humanity over a great span of space and time.

There was a cold sort of comfort in this lonely image. It took him away from all other things and reminded him that the minutes of his life were ticking away, and nothing must be wasted.

Somewhere along about this time he drifted off into sleep, and the image of himself apart and dedicated in a finite and understandable universe became a dream of that same image.

Only, in the dream, there was a difference. Dreaming, he could not pin it down, but somewhere on the edge of his dream there was something unclear. Something unknown that did not seem important in itself, yet somehow concerned him. Unless he had made some kind of mistake, nothing should threaten to mar the image of the future to which he had committed himself. In his dream, he told himself that what bothered him was an illusion; but still it seemed to maintain its place, until at last he fell into deeper slumber and forgot about it.

When he woke the next morning, he had breakfast, and dressed himself very much as he had been dressed when he had gone to visit the church run by Samuel Godsarm. But he made slight differences. His clothes were not quite so ill-fitting, his shoes were not quite so cracked and old. They showed a certain amount of care, in spite of their age; so that, over all, he gave the impression of not being quite at such loose ends as he had been when he had gone to the church.

He took an autocar to within a few blocks of the hotel that was the headquarters of Darrel McKae and his organization, and walked the rest of the way.

At the door of the hotel itself the doorman looked warily at him, but let him in. He noted a couple of men in city clothes, but with the suntans of those who had lived most of their life in rural areas, lounging about the steps. These considered him closely as he went in.

Within he went up to the desk, produced the letter Samuel Godsarm had given him and explained why he was there.

The clerk behind the desk sent him over to sit and wait in the lobby lounge, and he did so, refusing the voice that spoke to him over the annunciator in his small chairside table, that offered him something to eat or drink. A moment later, the clerk came over and handed him a work application blank; which he filled out under the name of Bleys MacLean, with Henry listed as his father, Joshua and Will as his brothers. After about an hour, the clerk called him from behind the desk, took the filled-out form and handed him a badge and a key.

"The key is for the special tower elevators," the clerk said. "Take one of them to the top floor and show your badge to whoever you meet when you step off the elevator."

"Thank you," Bleys said to him. But the clerk had turned away and did not bother to answer. Bleys crossed the lobby, conscious of a number of other men and women lounging around in seats and at the small tables where late breakfasts were being eaten, who looked closely at him as he passed. He put his key in the elevator, its doors opened and he stepped inside.

The silent elevator whisked him up some forty stories. When he stepped out of the elevator he was confronted by two men almost as tall as he, and outweighing him by anywhere from twenty to forty pounds apiece. Without a word, Bleys handed over Godsarm's letter.

One of the two took it wordlessly. He carried it off while the other stood with his arms folded, facing Bleys. He showed no animosity, only alertness.

He stood squarely and his balance was good, thought Bleys. But folded arms were not the most sensible position to be in, if you really had to defend yourself against a skilled opponent. That, and a general feeling that he got from the other man, made Bleys feel that he would have no trouble with this particular guard, if it was a situation in which just the two of them were concerned. After a few minutes the other guard returned and beckoned with his head. Neither of the two men had yet said a word to Bleys.

Bleys followed the guard who had beckoned with his head, and the other stayed at the elevator. Bleys made no attempt to look as if he was in any way dangerous; but, at the same time, he also made no attempt to look particularly impressed by what was around him.

Bleys was led from the lobby in front of the elevators into a typical hotel corridor, and at the end of it they stopped before a door that was also typical; but Bleys noticed that it was at the very end of the corridor; and deduced that beyond it there was not simply a single room, but a suite, since the large luxury suites were normally found in the position where they could have at least two windowed walls.

"Boris," said his guide to the door, after knocking lightly at it.

There was a second or two of delay, then the door swung open. Boris put his hand on Bleys' back, lightly directing him through the doorway.

They stepped, as Bleys had expected, into the spacious lounge of what must be one of the hotel's most luxurious suites. The furniture, however, had obviously been altered from what was customary. There were several armchairs along the side walls. But the main piece of furniture in the room was a large desk, behind which sat Darrel McKae.

He was wearing ordinary gray trousers and a light blue shirt. A black cape was thrown over the high back of his chair.

"All right, Boris," said McKae. Close up, his voice had a curious ringing quality that might have something to do with the effectiveness of it when he had been making the speech Bleys had heard. "Stand over there by the door. Just wait."

Boris disappeared from Bleys' field of vision. Bleys himself stood alone on the far side of the desk looking across it at McKae. The desk itself was covered with paper; but on top of everything there, and right in front of McKae, was Samuel Godsarm's letter that Bleys had carried. Its seal was broken and it had been unfolded for reading.

"Bleys MacLean," said McKae, looking up at him.

"Yes, Great Leader."

"I've just been talking to Samuel Godsarm on the phone,"

said McKae. "I see he didn't exaggerate your size. But I'm a little at a loss as to why he thinks you might be particularly valuable to me here. Suppose you tell me all about going into his church, from the time you first entered until he sent you off to me."

Bleys did so, using simple but straightforward language.

"And it was after you preached and told the congregation what I had said on the floor of the Chamber," said McKae, after Bleys was through, "that he decided to write this letter?"

"Yes, I think he made up his mind then," said Bleys; "he could see how deeply I'd been moved by you, watching from the visitors' gallery and listening to you."

"Tell me," said McKae, "I take it your sermon was well received by the congregation?"

"I think so, Great Leader," said Bleys, "but it was my repeating to them the words of your speech on the floor that moved them most deeply. I don't believe they'd been so moved in their lives."

"You must have rendered it well," said McKae, smiling a little. Unexpectedly the smile became a friendly one, only for Bleys. "I suspect Samuel of worrying you might be a better preacher than he. Perhaps he was more interested in getting rid of you, than sending me someone who might be of use. On the phone he told me you'd grown up on a farm and that your father kept goats. Where was this?"

"It's Green Pastures District," said Bleys, "maybe ninety miles from Ecumeny here."

"Yes. I see," said McKae.

There was a shrewdness in the man, Bleys noted, that was at odds with his religious appearance. If this had been any world but a Friendly one, he would have suspected McKae's religiousness to be merely a front behind which his ambition worked.

However, since this was one of the Friendly Worlds and McKae had grown up on it, it was highly unlikely that he would be a charlatan in any sense of the word. In short, thought Bleys, McKae was in somewhat the same position as Bleys himself. He wished to gain control, but only in order to direct what he controlled in the path that he believed was right.

McKae had obviously been taking a few moments out to think. But now he spoke up again.

"What can you do, then?" he asked Bleys.

"Any farm work, Great Leader," said Bleys, "and I can handle goats of course, harness them to a cart or a plow and care for them. Outside of that, not really anything. I was hoping there'd be work to be done with my hands, here in the city, because we need the money back on the farm. So far I haven't found any."

"Have you ever handled a gun?" asked McKae.

Bleys hesitated, as he knew that someone who was what he was pretending to be would do, in case of a question like this. It was normal for all but the poorest of farmers to own some sort of weapon, both for hunting rabbits as well as for defense against raids from an opposing church group. But McKae's question also hinted that Bleys might be involved in such raiding himself.

McKae would be unlikely to be concerned over such, but the man Bleys was pretending to be would be cautious about admitting it.

"I've done a little shooting with a needle gun," he said. "We had our land posted to keep foreign rabbit hunters off. But they come anyway, you know. One of them must've left his gun behind, because I found it in the tall grass. It was pretty dirty, but I got it working and we used to use it ourselves, to hunt rabbits."

McKae, who was clearly country-bred himself, let these words of Bleys' story about how he came to have a needle gun pass without comment. Of course, thought Bleys, he knew better.

"How good a shot are you?" he asked Bleys.

"Pretty good," said Bleys, "usually I always came back with some rabbits when I took the gun out. And—I'm a powerful wrestler."

"Powerful wrestler, you say," said McKae with another sudden smile, broader than he had given Bleys before. "Now that's interesting. With your size, and if you're any good with a needle gun and as good a wrestler as you say, there might be a way you could serve our church and me."

He got up unexpectedly and came around from behind the desk. He was about four inches shorter than Bleys, but his shoulders were nearly as broad and he tapered down to a slim waist. "I'm a fairly powerful wrestler myself. Do you think you could throw me?"

"Oh, Great Leader," said Bleys, "I wouldn't want to hurt you."

"Don't worry about that," said McKae. He stood with his body perfectly balanced, one foot a little behind the other and apart, his elbows bent and his hands out and half curled, ready to grab. It was the typical country wrestling style that Bleys had seen a number of times during the years he had been at Henry's. "You see, I don't think you can throw me. Do you think you can?"

"Great Leader," said Bleys in a distressed voice, "I really don't want—"

"Do as you're told," said McKae. "Now, you better throw me or I'm going to throw you."

He began circling Bleys.

"If you say so, Great Leader," said Bleys with a sigh. There were very few rules in country wrestling, Bleys knew. He would have known more about it if he had gone to the local school near Henry's, since wrestling was one of the primary recreations for rural males of all ages.

He took a step toward McKae, his forearms half upraised; and with very creditable speed, McKae seized his left arm, stepped in and attempted a hip throw. Bleys dropped to one knee however, and with one arm holding McKae's arm and the other grasping his collar, levered him over the bent leg and onto the carpet. He let go immediately and stood back. McKae bounced back to his feet.

"Very interesting," said McKae, looking at him. "I've done more than a little wrestling and I never ran into that before. Boris!"

The last word was a summons to the man by the door. He came over to them.

"No, no, Boris," McKae's voice stopped the other man before he could lay hands on Bleys himself, "I don't want you to try him out. Take him off, run him through Weapons and Unarmed Combat; and then come back and tell me how he did."

He turned to Bleys.

"I'll hope to see you again, Bleys MacLean," he said.

"Thank you, Great Leader," said Bleys. He followed Boris out the door.

They went down several floors to one whose long central corridor had been turned into a practice range for shooting with needle guns. The door at the far end of it that led to whatever room or suite was beyond it—probably a suite—had been blocked and heavily padded to stop any of the fired needles from going through and doing damage. When they got there Boris turned him over to another man who was easily into his fifties. A lean, dried, brown man with a sharp nose and a narrow mouth, but with a pair of very bright, brown eyes under his thinning brown hair on a brown skull.

"Bleys MacLean," said Boris, "this is Seth Tremunde. He'll tell you what to do."

Bleys offered his hand but Tremunde merely waved it aside.

"We don't waste time in courtesies here," he said. "What are you down here for?"

"He's to be tested with a needle gun and anything else you're set up to test with. Great Leader's orders."

"All right," said Tremunde.

He turned to a large cupboard set up along the wall of the corridor, slid its door back a little and brought out a transparent case holding a needle gun in its two parts. He stripped the case off the two parts and handed them separately to Bleys.

Bleys grinned. It was an old trick. Someone who was well used to needle guns could snap the stock and trigger assembly part to the barrel-section in half a second. Anyone who had not handled a needle gun repeatedly over a period of time would have to fumble, getting the two to lock together. Bleys snapped them into one piece in the blink of an eye.

Tremunde did not look impressed; although, Bleys knew, he had scored on the other man.

"All right," said Tremunde, waving at the far end of the corridor, "there's a target pinned up down there. Let's see what you can do with it."

Bleys looked down the corridor and lifted the needle gun to his shoulder, pressing the *target-read* button with his thumb as he brought the sights in line with the white square of the target.

This, he knew, was a second test. One of the things that was important about shooting a needle gun was to adjust your pattern of needles to the size you wanted at the distance the target was from you. The needles spread in a ring-pattern as they went out, and if distance was not known, or misjudged, then the pattern might well be so wide when it at last reached the target, that it simply encircled it without doing any real harm. At the same time as Bleys set the pattern size for the distance he got off the *target-read* dial—for the *target-read* went by light reflected off the surface it was aimed at and had to be adjusted for the ambient lighting—he blinked twice, very quickly together with both eyes.

An invisible, transparent telescopic contact lens dropped down into his right eye, his sighting eye.

Bleys was a good shot without any artificial aids; but in this case he wanted to make no mistake in impressing them with his marksmanship. The lens that he had kept tucked up under his lid and practiced with until he could put it either up or down with the proper blinking move of his eyelid, was adjusted in rings from its outer circle inward so that he was able to focus not only on the target but on both the rear and front sights of the needle gun.

He fired a very brief burst. That, he knew, was a test also. Anyone without experience with a needle gun tended to fire long bursts. The briefest touch on the trigger was all that was necessary if the aim was correct. He blinked the lens back up into hiding under his lid and lowered the needle gun.

"Sure you don't want to take a second shot?" said Tremunde. But the sarcastic tone of his voice indicated that Bleys had scored on all tests so far. In the meantime Tremunde had pressed a button on the wall and the white target was off the backing and being slid along a runner rail up to them.

Three pairs of eyes looked at it as Tremunde took it off. The pattern of hits was no larger than Bleys' thumbprint, and in the very center of the bull's-eye of the target.

CHAPTER

34

"YOU'RE TOO GOOD to be true," said Tremunde, filling out a form and writing several lines near the bottom in a box that was obviously there for comments. Bleys could sympathize with him.

Bleys had done very well with a power pistol on one-tenth charge in an adjoining room, which had obviously been several hotel rooms before it had been opened out to make another, shorter range for the power weapons; and he had done exceptionally well, without any need at all for the hidden lens over his right eye, on the range in another such room with the pop-up targets.

In this final exercise, Bleys had held a needle rifle in one hand at his belt level and walked through the range, firing from that position. He was, both by inclination and training, a superb hip-shooter; and he suspected it was mainly this to which Tremunde was referring as he filled out the form.

The form filled out, Tremunde folded it and passed it to Boris, without giving Bleys a chance to read it.

"You've been a Soldier of God?" he asked.

"No," said Bleys.

"Well, we're most of us former Soldiers, here," said Tremunde. He turned to Boris. "We'll take him on, anyway."

Bleys and Boris left the shooting gallery area and went down another floor, which turned out to have been remodeled into one huge gym. In charge down here was a little, brown man, no taller than the average twelve- or thirteen-year-old on Association, almost bald, but very brisk and gray-eyed and obviously in superb physical condition.

"He claims to be a wrestler," Boris said, jerking his thumb at Bleys. "The Great Leader tried him out and this man threw him. The Great Leader wants him checked out."

"Right," said the small man, sharply, in an accent that Bleys recognized as being Old Earth of some kind or another.

He made a wild guess that it might be Australian.

"I'm Jimmy Howe," said the little man, extending his hand to Bleys, "since Boris didn't think to introduce us. And you're—?"

"Bleys MacLean," said Bleys.

"Pleased to meet you, Bleys," said Howe. "This way, then." He led the way off about thirty feet to a wrestling mat, and stepped up on it. He was wearing high-laced gym shoes, Bleys noticed. Bleys had already begun to take his shoes off.

"That's right," said Jimmy Howe, approvingly.

Bleys stepped onto the mat and faced him a little more than reaching distance away.

"All right," said Howe, "see if you can throw me."

Bleys took a step toward him, reaching out, and clutched empty air. A moment later he was caught in almost the same hip throw that Darrel McKae had tried on him, but from his left side, when he had been expecting contact on his right. He went down. Howe was already back on his feet, fists on hips and looking down at him.

"Want to try again?" Howe asked. Bleys got to his feet, made a feint with his long, left arm to the little man's left and then caught him deftly behind the neck with his cupped right hand. The little man was obviously greased lightning, very much faster than Bleys. But Bleys' length of limb was something that almost everybody underestimated, and—probably just this one time—Howe had underestimated it too.

He stepped forward to get away from Bleys' hand cupped on his neck and Bleys spun himself in toward the little man, who was now off-balance, and flung his now released left arm about the other's waist. Howe was forced to move to keep from falling; and Bleys began to rotate them both, with himself as the center of a pivot and Howe on the periphery of the circle around it.

This was, in fact, one of Bleys' favorite throws. When it had first been demonstrated on him, he could not believe that simply a loose grasp and the continual circular movement could keep the other man captive and moving in the circular path, whether he wanted to or not. But the fact was it could. It was instinctive to try to keep from falling, and the result was to keep him running in a circle. Bleys spun Howe around a couple of times and suddenly reversed direction. Howe flew off at an angle from him like a stone off from a string that breaks as a boy swings it around his head.

He skidded across the mat onto the floor, was back up on his feet in a moment and back on the mat facing Bleys; but he held up a hand as Bleys was about to move toward him again once more.

"That's enough," said Howe. "You've had training. Want to tell me about it?"

"Oh, there was a neighbor of ours, back when I was on the farm and growing up," said Bleys. "He'd never wrestle himself, but he had a reputation of being able to beat anyone around with no trouble at all. Some of us, if he took a liking to us, he'd show a few things to. I was one of the lucky ones."

"I'll bet," said Howe, and grinned unexpectedly. "Kind of a tall tale, that. But if it suits you it suits me."

He turned to Boris.

"I don't need to see any more," he said. "Take Bleys Ahrens here back to the Great Leader and tell him this is the best man he ever sent me. As far as wrestling goes."

Boris nodded, a little sourly it seemed to Bleys, who was

now sitting down on the mat and putting his shoes back on. He got to his feet and went off with Boris.

"Drop by any time, Bleys MacLean!" Howe called from behind him. Bleys looked back and nodded.

Boris took him back up to McKae's office, tapped on the door and said his name, as before. This time a voice that was not McKae's answered back, telling him to wait another ten minutes, then knock again. Boris led Bleys off to the lounge and picked two chairs facing each other. He pointed wordlessly to one that Bleys took, and sat down opposite him, still without saying anything.

Ten minutes passed without Boris venturing on any conversation. At the end of that time he got to his feet, jerked his head to summon Bleys to follow him and went back to the door of McKae's office. This time when he rapped and gave his name it was opened to him. He and Bleys went inside. The room was empty except for McKae behind his desk. Boris went up to his desk and put down on it the unfolded form that Tremunde had filled out.

"Jimmy Howe says to tell you that this man is the best you've ever sent him."

"Does he indeed?" murmured McKae. He was busy running his eyes over the form. "I see he did well at the shooting, too."

He looked up at Bleys.

"Suppose we try something else. Boris, you can stand back." He handed Bleys a piece of paper from his desk, on which there was a list of numbers, totaled up at the bottom.

"Run your eye over that," McKae said.

Bleys did so.

"Now, hand it back," said McKae. He received the paper, put it down in front of him and looked up at Bleys once more.

"Now," said McKae, "repeat the numbers back to me in the order they are in the column and give me the total."

Bleys had been able to scan the column and total it the moment he had had it and it was all firmly in his memory. But for his purposes this was one test he decided to fail.

"The first number in the column," he said slowly, "is 49.20.

The second number is 13.00, the next number is 87.84, the next number is—"

He hesitated.

"—The next number—" he hesitated again, "is 87.84—no, I just gave you that number, Great Leader. The one after that is—is—"

He stopped and looked helplessly across the table at McKae.

"I'm sorry, Great Leader," he said, "I just didn't have enough time to learn them all. I don't know what comes after 87.84."

"That's all right," said McKae, almost absently. "I wonder what gave Samuel the idea that you have what he calls 'a perfect memory.'"

"I think," said Bleys diffidently, "it was because I remembered your words of fire on the floor of the Chamber that day. I was able to tell the congregation word-for-word what you said."

"But you can't do it with numbers?" McKae said, looking back up at him.

"I remember only what the Lord bids me to remember. It comes with no effort when it comes, being the Lord's doing rather than my own," said Bleys. "In all other things I am no more than most people as far as memory goes."

"Is that so?" said McKae. He sat thinking for a second. "Have you read the Bible?"

"Of course, Great Leader," said Bleys.

"All of it?"

"Oh yes. All of it," said Bleys.

"And that's the sort of thing that the Lord would bid you remember, isn't it?" said McKae.

"Oh yes. Absolutely," said Bleys.

"Very well, then," said McKae, throwing himself back in his chair, "begin at the beginning of the First Book of Samuel and tell me what it says. Keep telling me until I tell you to stop."

"Yes, Great Leader," said Bleys.

He let enthusiasm flow into him and radiate from his face and the way he stood, the way an actor might, in the wings before stepping out onto the stage in the character he was playing.

"Now there was a certain man of Ramathaim-zophim, of Mount Ephraim, and his name was Elkanah, the son of Jeroham, the son of Elihu, the son of Tohu, the son of Zuph, an Ephrathite:

"And he had two wives; the name of the one was Hannah, and the name of the other Peninnah: and Peninnah had children, but Hannah had no children.

"And this man went up out of his city yearly to worship and to sacrifice unto the Lord of hosts in Shiloh. And the two sons of Eli, Hophni and Phinehas, the priests of the Lord—"

"All right," said McKae, holding up a finger to stop him, "that'll do. It's a useful gift of the Lord but I think we'll regard it as something to be called upon only if needed. Meanwhile, there are Soldiers of God who've joined the Arise! Church. They've formed a special body of Defenders to protect me, so that I can safely continue to preach—for there are those who'd stop me. Would you like to be one of my Defenders?"

"I could think of nothing greater," said Bleys, with enthusiasm.

"All right," said McKae, "Boris'll take you down to the Leader of those men; and you can begin following his orders. You'll be in training. In spite of your skills with weapons and the fact that you're such a powerful wrestler"—McKae smiled just a little—"there'll be things you'll have to learn in order to work with the others. If you feel after some days that it isn't the work for you, simply tell the Leader, and you'll be given a chance to talk to me once more, when I have the time to spare you. Also, if the Leader should decide that you're not proper material, then he'll tell you you're not to be one of them; and again, you'll be given a chance to speak to me, before you leave us and go back to Godsarm's church."

"Thank you, Great Leader," said Bleys, "I don't know how to thank you enough."

"See how the training agrees with you," said McKae, waving his hand in dismissal.

Bleys and Boris went out and this time they went down only one floor and into another suite that had also been turned into an office; but one that was nowhere near as large as the one where McKae sat.

Behind the desk there was a man who also was very different from McKae. He wore a heavy, old, checked shirt and work pants stuffed into work boots. At first glance, Bleys had taken him for a farmer right off the farm; but a second look had told him the man was something more.

He obviously, however, had a background in the out-of-doors. Bleys was introduced to him by Boris, who after that immediately left them. The man's name was Herkimer Shone. And he was plainly a very informal sort.

"Pull up a chair." He indicated a straight-backed chair that was not far from the desk. "Sit down and I'll get the details on you."

"Well, that should take care of it," said Herkimer at last, having questioned Bleys about Henry's farm and church, and written down all the details. He put them in a file. He frowned at the file folder drawer, which was jammed, before closing it.

"Ordinarily, we'd want you in the hotel here," he said, "but we're overcrowded for space, and a lot of the churches are so new, so their tithes aren't yet much use to us. So we've got a financial problem, too. I'd like to keep you here for three days while you run through some of the group maneuvers with the rest of us. After that, if you're married, or even if you have someplace to stay elsewhere in town, at your own expense, we'll be satisfied if you'll drop in at the designated hours to practice with the rest of the guardians. Do you have such a place in Ecumeny?"

"Yes I have," answered Bleys, "you see I met this friend—"

"Never mind the details, give me an address."

Bleys gave him the address of the apartment. He was a little fearful that the other might recognize it as being a building in a part of the city that contained a number of luxury apartments; but evidently the man was either not acquainted with the city that much, or did not care. He put down the address and phone number.

The next three days Bleys slept in a temporary cot set up in the on-duty guard's room; and had nothing to do but kill time these days. He assumed what he had said on the application was being checked out. The third morning, he was awakened at five A.M. and hustled by the duty guard through a quick shower, a rather slim breakfast, and conducted to a meeting room at six.

"Just go on in," said the duty guard, and left him.

Bleys pushed through the door and stepped into a room that was already filled with people. They were of all shapes, sizes and ages. They had in common the deeply tanned, outdoor look Bleys had remarked on the men in the lobby when he had first entered the hotel yesterday; and which, thanks to the fierceness of the sunlight from Epsilon Eridani, he still had, also.

They were dressed, like Herkimer, in all sorts of comfortable work clothes, no two alike. He searched around, found a chair and sat down; while the lean-faced man in his fifties, up on the platform, dressed and looking very much like the rest of them, was still speaking. Needless to say, he drew the attention of more than a few of the audience while he was doing this.

He sat and waited for the man on the platform to finish what he was saying, which had something to do with the plans for the day. But shortly he came to the end of what he was saying. He looked out over the audience.

"I see the last of our recruits has shown up, finally," he said.

There was a small mutter of laughter, but it did not sound to Bleys at all derisive or antagonistic.

"All right," said the man on the platform, "all three of you stand up and tell us about yourselves."

Bleys, with the others, stood up.

"We'd use that one for a flagpole," someone said and there was a little more laughter.

The man on the platform let it die down.

"We'll start with you," he said to Bleys. "Your name?"

"Bleys MacLean," Bleys answered, "don't you have that up there?"

"I have it," said the man on the platform, "but everybody else needs to hear it too. For the benefit of the rest of you, Bleys MacLean here ran up some very good figures indeed, on the weapons range, on the exercise, and in the hand-to-hand. Bleys MacLean, how many wars have you been in?"

"None," said Bleys.

There was an interested muttering from the audience.

"Interesting, that," commented the man on the platform to the room full of people at large. "Well, we'll start trying him out. Anyone want to volunteer to be coach?"

"I'll take it on, Charlie," said the man seated on Bleys' left. He was at least in his forties, and slightly heavy. None of them there looked at all overweight, but this man came as close to it as any. But his face was square, weathered and not unkind.

"Come to think of it," said the man on the platform, "in this case we'd better have two. Anybody else want to volunteer?"

"I'll take on that chore, Charlie," came a voice from across the room.

Bleys could not see exactly who had spoken.

"You three can go, then," said the man on the platform. "Now, about you other two new recruits—"

But the man beside Bleys had already risen and was nudging Bleys ahead of him past the two other occupied seats out the end of the row, and out the door of the room.

"I didn't hear your name," said Bleys, as the first coach who had been assigned to him started off down the corridor. Bleys fell into step beside him. "Where are we headed?"

"Armory," answered the coach, briefly. "As for my name—"

He glanced sideways and up at Bleys and smiled. "It's Sam Chen. Not short for anything—just Sam."

Bleys looked over his shoulder, but he did not see anyone else who might have emerged from the room behind them.

"What's the name of my other coach?" he asked.

"I'll let him tell you, when he gets around to it," answered Sam. He was now looking straight ahead again.

"I thought he'd be with us," Bleys said.

"He will," said Sam.

With that rather uninformative answer, Sam led the way silently down to the Armory, where they were both given what were known as "poacher's" versions of the needle gun. These were needle guns that were still in two sections disassembled, each section shortened to make a smaller version of the weapon. Each part fitted into one of two narrow, vertical pockets inside whatever jacket you were wearing. It was possible normally to button the jacket quite tightly, and still not betray the fact that you were carrying a weapon. Sam already had such pockets in his jacket, and the Armory supplied Bleys with a jacket equipped with pockets in his turn.

Sam led them out of the hotel into the streets. Four blocks away, he came to a battered old gray hovercraft, which he unlocked and slid into, beckoning Bleys to take the seat beside him. Once the doors were closed and the engine had lifted the craft on its cushion of air, he headed out into the countryside.

They went clear out into the open fields, where city began to give way to farmland. He stopped at last at a large area of either abandoned or unused land; and to Bleys' surprise they practiced creeping and crawling along with their assembled weapons cradled in the crooks of their elbows. The rocky earth beneath Bleys' elbows was not kind on them. Also, the exercise made use of muscles that Bleys was not in the habit of using. Nonetheless, they stayed at it for a couple of hours, until Sam suddenly gave a disgusted grunt and began to get to his feet. Bleys rose with him.

"What is it?" Bleys asked.

"We were spotted," said Sam, with a resigned tone of voice.

Bleys looked around him. He had seen no one else on the horizon in any direction from the time they had started and he saw no one now. Yet, Sam was already headed back toward their hovercar. It occurred to him that his other "coach" was actually an observer to see and report on how well he did.

They returned to the city and had lunch at a sidewalk cafe, where to Bleys' surprise, Sam idled over cup after cup of local coffee. Bleys felt fortunate that he had learned early to wait patiently. They made occasional conversation, Sam occasionally asking some general questions about Bleys' background on the farm and his father, Henry.

Sam was interested as to whether he had ever known Henry MacLean at the time he was a Soldier of God; and it turned out that as far as Bleys could tell him, he hadn't. In turn, Bleys probed Sam for details of his past; and Sam made it clear that he didn't want to give these or indeed talk about himself at all.

From time to time however, he threw in a sentence of advice, which startled Bleys with its usefulness.

"Look at the legs," Sam said, after they had been sitting with their coffee for a little over an hour, "watch the legs."

"The legs?" Bleys asked—instinctively, at the same time taking note of the legs of the few people passing around the street before them and the intersection a third of a block away.

"Why the legs?" Bleys asked.

"Suppose we're here to watch for people who may be moving in to try an assassination attempt on the Great Leader," said Sam. "They try to move in as inconspicuously as possible, one by one, and then join together; or sort themselves out in positions from which they can all attack at once. We try to get here well ahead of time, and watch for them moving in."

He glanced at Bleys.

"What we watch are the legs," he went on. "Take a close look. A man or woman can't change their walk. They can be identified by that, even after they've changed their body shapes and their faces completely. A Soldier walks differently from a civilian. City people walk differently from country people. Likewise they give away the way they feel by the way they walk. Look closely at a man or woman moving into a position where they're going to try to kill someone; and hoping not to be spotted as anything but simply someone going down the street. He or she walks with their body weight forward and neck extended, a sort of walking-on-billiard-balls look. Watch for it. You won't see it right away, but after a while you'll begin to pick it up. You'll notice anything different right away."

"You can pick out differences like that, right away, yourself?" asked Bleys.

"That's right," said Sam, toying with his cup but with his eyes on the street. "After several wars it becomes automatic. You learn to read people by the way they walk, as if they were carrying banners. See that short, rather fat man down near the end of the block in the pink jacket?"

"Yes," said Bleys.

"He's running away from something," Sam said, "what, I don't know. It could be some person, it could be just something in his own mind; but his body's reacting by trying to run. Look at how he kicks his leg out as if he was going to take a longer stride, and then deliberately shortens the step when his foot comes down, so it'll look like he's walking ordinarily. Watch him for a bit."

Bleys did.

He was fascinated by this new bit of insight, as by all new knowledge. He concentrated closely on everyone whose legs were to be seen in motion on the street, and from time to time tried out his interpretations on Sam. Sam corrected most of them at first—then gradually Bleys began to come up more and more with interpretations the other man agreed with.

"You pick it up fast," said Sam.

This made the time move swiftly for Bleys. Still and all, they must have sat for two or three hours, until Sam pushed his cup away and shook his head disgustedly.

"Spotted again," he said. "No fault of yours, but you stand out like a distress rocket on a dark night with all that height."

By this time it was into afternoon. Sam led him through a shopping area, and up one of the buildings onto an observation tower, very windy and cool enough so that Bleys was happy to have the protection of the jacket. At this last place they killed another hour. This was the one time where Sam ended up the afternoon smiling.

"All right," he said, "Nicky didn't pick us out at all. That's better. We'll head back and you can turn in your needle gun; then you're free for the rest of the day."

"I don't have any idea what we did all day," said Bleys. "I mean, I don't see what we were supposed to be doing."

"Trying not to be seen," said Sam. "No, let me change that. We were trying to be seen, but not have any attention paid to us. Tomorrow, we'll try something different. I'll meet you at the Armory at six-thirty A.M., all right?"

"I'll be there," said Bleys.

They went back to the hotel and turned in their needle guns; but on Sam's advice Bleys kept the jacket. Free to do what he wanted for the rest of the day, Bleys left the hotel and returned with some relief to his own apartment, got out of his clothes and had a pleasant soak in the agitated water of the stimulant bathtub of their apartment. This had purposely been built extra large for Dahno, and therefore was comfortable for Bleys as well.

Through with the bath, and resting on his bed in his favorite thinking position, Bleys decided that two things needed to be done. He must somehow manage to do both of them without endangering his appearance of wholehearted devotion to guarding McKae.

The first was to visit the Hounds' Kennel and discover whether his orders to sharpen them up, which he had passed on through Norton Brawley, had been obeyed; and, secondly, find out whether they had, if obeyed, produced any change in the ability of the Hounds to carry through their assassination attempt. This last, he doubted. He was now convinced, not only that that assassination attempt was to be aimed at McKae; but that the Hounds did not stand one chance in a thousand of bringing it off.

By killing McKae, Dahno would at once remove all threat to the Five Sisters, and put himself, particularly, back in good order with those five Members of the Chamber. That had been the reason behind his ready agreement to Bleys' picture of the future. It made a good excuse for him to be off-world when the assassination was attempted.

The clerks in the office had reported that they had been hammered at for days now, by both representatives of the Five Sisters, and the Five Sisters themselves, demanding to know where Dahno was and how they could get in touch with him.

The clerks had repeatedly responded that they did not know. They had also, on Bleys' orders, not mentioned him at all; and the few times his name had come up they had claimed to know nothing about his whereabouts, either.

In a sense, both answers were perfectly truthful. They did not know where Dahno or Bleys was at any given moment. Possibly, Bleys was the only one who knew that Dahno had headed toward Earth rather than to one of the other worlds. Norton Brawley could know that he was off-Association, but probably not his destination. In Dahno's eyes, Norton would have had no need to know.

Meanwhile, Bleys had told the office staff nothing about what he was doing; so that while they knew he was in the city, and might on rare occasions be at the apartment, they had no idea of where or when.

All this, they dutifully reported to him, when he appeared at the office to look at his off-world mail and ask them questions. He told them to continue stonewalling any attempt by any of Dahno's clients to reach either Dahno or himself and, out of their deep loyalty to Dahno and their budding loyalty to Bleys, they were quite cheerful about accepting the assignment. They were, surprisingly, almost fierce in their determination to protect both brothers.

CHAPTER

35

═══════════

BLEYS REPORTED FAITHFULLY at six in the morning on the next
five days.

On each day he and Sam worked more closely with other
Defenders, as McKae's security force called themselves, until
by the end of the five days he was engaged in general
movements of large numbers of them in a single exercise.

In the process he learned a great deal about his fellow
Defenders; and also about the way they operated. Their manner
of defense and attack was entirely different from that of the
"modern *ninjas*" that Ahram Moro had trained for Dahno.

In a sense this did not surprise Bleys. He had been
suspicious right from the start of the contempt with which
Ahram and Norton Brawley both seemed to dismiss those who
would be guarding the charismatic young church leader. To go
way back, it did not fit with what he had seen of Henry; either
in his day-to-day life, or in that moment in which he had faced
down the rest of the congregation when Bleys had been in
danger of being mobbed by them.

He could not picture Henry as a bumbling farmer engaged in a completely untrained firefight with other bumbling farmers. Nor did it make sense, on a world where armed disputes between churches were common, that men who had ended up fighting in these disputes all of their life by matter of choice should remain essentially inept and unorganized.

Furthermore, he had gathered the impression that when the militia moved in on one of these disputes, it was not an easy time for the militia at all; sometimes the churches combined against them, and then the casualties among the militia were high—and in any case they were considerable.

Also, Bleys learned something of the in-group language of the Defenders. The second day out he heard Sam speaking to one of the other Defenders with whom they were engaged in some kind of practice exercise that Bleys did not completely understand, but which involved working through the city streets in groups of no more than two and then joining up at a certain place. Among the words that were bandied back and forth, was one that struck Bleys oddly. The other Defender made a reference to "Bodies."

"What did he mean by 'Bodies'?" asked Bleys, when he and Sam were off by themselves again.

Sam looked at him with an unusually sober expression on his face.

"He was talking about those who were willing to give their lives, to make sure that their Great Leader was not hurt," said Sam.

"I thought that was our job?" asked Bleys.

"Our job is different," said Sam. "The 'Bodies' are simply the volunteers who offer to cluster tightly about our Great Teacher, so that their living flesh becomes a shield against any needle, power blast, or void bolt aimed at him. Our job is to stop people from firing those blasts and bolts before they start."

"The Bodies aren't really Defenders, then?" asked Bleys.

"They're entitled to the name, but most of them don't use it," said Sam.

Bleys tucked that away in the back of his mind for future reference. He was learning a great deal. Gradually the orga-

nization, and something of the tactics and strategy of the
Defenders, were becoming clear to him as the days progressed.
The Bodies made a living shield wall of their bodies around
McKae at all times when he was moving about in public. The
Defenders spread out ahead almost as skirmishers, ready to
come together in force against any enemy, before these had the
chance to do anything lethal.

It became more and more apparent to Bleys that the
Defenders operated more like old pros, like veterans, in doing
their job. He learned that most of them had had actual battle
experience, as well, in militia drafts off-world. They operated
like an army unit. They were in contact with each other at all
times and their aim was to face the enemy not one-on-one, but
as a unit; firing and operating together, and able to call
reinforcements to their aid to outnumber an enemy.

Their working together this way was helped by the fact that
so many of them had been through this before, and like old
experienced hands at any business, most of them needed only
a minimum of commands. From the way things would be
developing, they could see what was best for each of them to
do.

Bleys was reminded of examples out of history. The Greek
phalanx, against the Persian king's so-called Immortals, at
Marathon. The Roman phalanx against the Transalpine
Gauls—the Germans of their time. Caesar had written something in one of his campaign messages back to Rome, to the
effect that the Transalpine Gauls were one-on-one, superb
fighters, noticeably superior to the Roman legionary, in this.
But the organization, discipline, purpose and strategy of the
legions caused them to win battle after battle against the
northerners.

These so-called barbarians had even had superior weapons.
A lot of them were working with steel at a time when the
legionary's weapons, like his armor, were still only of iron.
The Gauls were larger on the average, and stronger. They were
extremely fierce fighters. But the Legionary stayed tightly in
his phalanx, obeyed his orders, and conquered, nonetheless.

The more he compared the two, the more Bleys became

convinced that the *ninjas,* for all their training in all departments, could not begin to deal with the superior experience, battle-tested tactics—and, above all, unity—of these rough-clad Defenders.

If this was so, then, finally, the pattern of things to come fell into place, like a tipped-over row of dominoes. But it would be wise to double-check that conclusion first.

On the eighth day of his employment, which happened to be a Monday, Bleys asked to speak to Herkimer, and was given permission to do so.

He stepped into the office, in which everything, including Herkimer's clothes, looked as if nothing had changed since he had first met the man a week before.

"Yes, Bleys," said Herkimer, looking up at him as he came in. "Your coaches tell me they're pleased with you. What did you want to talk to me about?"

"It's a little problem with time," Bleys said. "I've got a cousin out in the country who's being married tonight; and he'd like me to be best man. The whole thing is likely to run rather late; and I'd have trouble getting back here by six in the morning. I just might be a little worn out tomorrow. I was wondering if I could come in late, the day after tomorrow?"

Herkimer laughed.

"You haven't been with us long," he said, "but you've struck everybody as being a pretty steady hand. I think you can come in late the day after tomorrow. If you really feel too rocky after the night before, simply call in and I'll let you have off until the following morning. In fact, why don't you just take off when you're free until the second day after that?"

"That's real good of you," said Bleys, "that's *real* good of you. I know my cousin is going to be happy to hear that."

"Call him up now and tell him," said Herkimer, waving at the control pad on his desk.

"Thanks," said Bleys, "but he hasn't got a phone."

He hesitated, and went on.

"My section leader said there was nothing really important for me to do the rest of today . . ."

Herkimer laughed again.

"Oh, go on!" he said. "You can take off from now until the time I told you."

"Thanks a lot," said Bleys, "I appreciate that."

"We'll make you work for it after you come back," said Herkimer, still with a smile. "Now go along and let me get back to work. Oh, by the way, be sure to tell Sam on the way out about the time off I've given you."

"I will," said Bleys.

He left, after passing word of Herkimer's permission to Sam, who merely nodded. Once outside the hotel, he walked for several blocks and turned several corners. Sure at last that he had not been followed from the hotel, intentionally or otherwise, he used a street corner call-box to get himself an autocar and rode back to his apartment.

He stopped there only long enough to change clothes into the ordinary, rather expensive business wear Dahno had insisted he outfit himself in after his move to Ecumeny.

He walked down to the street instead of calling from his apartment; and from a nearby corner-box, once more called an autocar to take him to the office. There he used one of the office phones in his room to call the Hounds' Kennel and speak to the Kennel Master, Ahram Moro. The other's voice answered him within seconds.

"This is Bleys Ahrens," Bleys said.

"Yes, the officer of the day recognized your voice and keyed me in immediately to your call. What can we do for you, Bleys Ahrens?"

"Well, I thought I'd drop out this afternoon and see how the Hounds are doing on this latest exercise of theirs. I'm going to be in Moseville overnight, so it struck me that I could take care of two things at once. Suppose I take them all out to dinner in Moseville tonight—unless you have some objection, of course?"

"I . . . oh, no objection at all," said Ahram. "When'll you get here?"

"I should fly into the local airport about one o'clock. It'll be a private plane, of course, and I don't know just to the minute when we'll get off from here."

"That's just fine," said Ahram; "there'll be a couple of our Hounds with a car there waiting for you when you get in, Bleys Ahrens."

"Good," said Bleys, "I'll see you all later today then."

"We'll look forward to it."

"Good-bye," said Bleys.

"Good-bye," answered Ahram.

Bleys switched off. He called the airport and arranged for the plane and a pilot, explaining that he would be staying overnight; and that he would want the pilot and the plane to do the same.

It was about a half an hour after one, when he sat down finally at the Moseville airport. The Hounds were there with a large, luxurious car as promised. They brought him to the Hounds' Kennel in about twenty more minutes.

There, Ahram insisted on Bleys having a glass of wine with him, then himself drove Bleys out to the practice ground and parked on a hill from which they could see a complete mock-up of the streets and buildings, which Bleys recognized as those of the building holding the Chamber from which McKae would emerge after his speech, eight days from now.

Bleys watched with an almost sardonic interest as the exercise was run. It took them no more than forty minutes, from the time they first began to move into place until those playing the part of McKae and his party were all down on the ground, playing dead. Everything had happened like a well-rehearsed play.

Ahram drove Bleys back to the Hounds' Den.

"What time were you thinking of taking the Hounds into Moseville for dinner?" Ahram asked, once they were seated back in his office.

"I've got to go into Moseville just about now," said Bleys. "Send them to the restaurant of The White Horse in the Triumph Hotel. Have them there about five P.M."

"All of them?" asked Ahram.

"All who aren't on duty or needed here," said Bleys.

"That means at least eighty of them—possibly ninety.

Almost our full complement," said Ahram. "You'll want a private dining room, of course?"

"No, I don't think so," said Bleys. "Between you and me I'd like to see them out among other people. Going to a dinner in a private dining room is simply transferring their usual dinner to a different set of walls, floor and ceiling. Just make a reservation for a half or three-quarters, or whatever section is necessary, in The White Horse's best dining room and add extra waiters. Our men should get used to being waited on. Don't you think?"

"Well . . . I've never really thought of it," said Ahram, "but I suppose you're right. After all, in the long run, they'll all be recognized as important and be dining themselves in the best places."

"Yes, indeed," said Bleys. He stood up. "Now, if you'll get those two Hounds with the car around in front, they can take me into the city."

Half an hour later Bleys was registering at the Triumph Hotel. He had checked by phone from Ecumeny before coming, and with the aid of the local Civics Responsibility Bureau in Moseville, had found the kind of place he wanted.

He had specified a hotel that was off a busy indoor plaza or concourse, with a balcony from which he could stand and look down to see the Hounds as they came in, and then with a dining room that could handle a special party up to a hundred people and still be open to the public.

Now, he stood at the balcony after taking a look at the suite they had assigned him, and saw that the choice had been a good one. The balcony looked down on a busy floor with little kiosks, restaurants and shops, running all around the outside of it, except on two sides where huge revolving doors allowed people in and out. An escalator led from the bottom floor up to the floor that was the entrance to the hotel.

He smiled a little to himself. The question he had been expecting—in fact that he had been sure he would hear—had come from Ahram only diffidently, just before Bleys had stepped into the car.

"Oh, by the way," Ahram had said, "you'll be wanting the

staff and myself—so on and so forth—as well as the Hounds?"

Bleys stopped with the door open in his hand.

"No, I don't think so," he said judiciously. "Let's give them a complete evening off without the eye of authority upon them. I'd like to make the evening as informal as possible. Oh, yes—and tell them they needn't come back till something like, say, three in the morning. I want them to have some free time to do what they want in the city, after the dinner is over."

"If you say so, Bleys Ahrens," said Ahram. His tone was perfectly agreeable, but Bleys could feel, almost as if it was radiating from the man, a very strong dislike of the freedom Bleys was demanding.

Now, here at last, Bleys gave over his inspection of the concourse below him and went back up to his hotel suite to lie down on the bed and plan.

There had been no appreciable difference between the exercise he had seen run today, and what he had seen on his last visit. Theoretically, this could mean that the Hounds were at the peak of their training.

Bleys did not believe it. Either Norton Brawley had not passed along his order that the Hounds be sharpened up, or else it had been disregarded by Ahram. The Kennel Master had stood beside him today, perhaps counting on Bleys' expertise in such armed actions as the assassination to be so slight that he would not notice that there had been no difference.

Furthermore, the full force that Ahram had detailed to the assassination was a little under thirty of the Hounds. These would be going up against well over a hundred of McKae's Defenders—and would be outclassed, in every way, by a large margin.

The whole situation spoke of deep ignorance in Ahram's and Norton Brawley's cases. Moreover, one or both of them had deliberately disregarded his order. This was exactly the situation he had envisioned when he had suggested to the heads of the Other organizations on the other worlds that armed retainers could be more of a danger than a benefit. The risk that was run was to give the Others a bad name—one which painted them as advocates of force, rather than reason. And an attempt to assassinate Darrel McKae would be entirely too large to be kept out of the press.

Bleys had pointed out the disparity in numbers alone to Ahram once they were back in his office.

"You know," he had said to Ahram, "McKae has a good two hundred of what he calls his Defenders. And you're sending a little over two dozen Hounds against them."

Ahram had laughed.

"Yes, Dahno found out their numbers and passed it on to us," Ahram said. "But you know they're nothing but a bunch of farmers and such, with weapons that in some cases probably haven't been used for years. They'll have no real idea of how to defend McKae. Whereas, our Hounds are trained like Dorsai, to be just the opposite—and armed with the best."

Bleys had forborne to argue. In his eyes the Hounds going through the exercises had looked exactly as they had before—unthinking, uncaring, and more than a little bored.

He rolled over on the bed and keyed his phone in, putting a call through to his office back in Ecumeny.

CHAPTER

36

THE DAY BEFORE a message in special code had come to him from Dahno on Old Earth, setting a date two weeks, interstellar time, from now for the meeting there and specifying a rendezvous location.

"This is Bleys," he said as soon as he was connected with the office. Arah's face looked back at him from the screen, looking almost annoyed.

"You don't have to tell me that, Bleys Ahrens," she said. "It's good you phoned right now, though. We were both going to leave the office a little early this afternoon. You caught us just before we went out the door."

"I'm glad," said Bleys, "because I want you to do something for me right away; and it's urgent. Send coded messages to all the Vice-Chairmen on other worlds with the following message:—ready—?"

"I've turned the recorder on," said Arah.

Bleys dictated:

> *"Concerning that matter about which I informed you recently, you will be personally ready to travel so as to arrive at the destination in twelve days. The destination will be Old Earth, in a hotel called The Shadow, which is in the main Denver area of the North American continent. I want you all assembled there no later than noon, twelve days from the date of this message.*
>
> *Bleys Ahrens*

"Did you get that all, Arah?"

"Yes, Bleys Ahrens," answered Arah.

"It's important that those messages go out on the first vessels possible to get them to the various Vice-Chairmen in the quickest time. You'll see to that?"

"Right this minute," said Arah.

Bleys cut the phone connection and rolled back to lie on the bed, once more staring at the ceiling.

There was no longer time to make sure before he acted. It was necessary to gamble that things would fall out as he had planned. True, the odds were overwhelming that they would. But the difference between the best possible gamble, and certainty, could be wide and deep enough to bury anyone.

He was out on the balcony, looking down at the concourse, fifteen minutes before the first of the Hounds could arrive; lounging on the railing there as if he was simply waiting for someone to meet him.

In due time, the Hounds did start coming in through the street-level doors. He watched them with a keen interest, noting how they walked, how they reacted to the strangers around them, and everything else about them which would indicate their response to the general public.

It was very much as he had feared. They were all in ordinary civilian clothes; the black robes and their other uniforms and special clothing had been laid aside. That much, at least, was as Bleys had expected.

But in spite of the change of clothes, they carried themselves with an air almost of arrogance, as if those around them should have already recognized that they were people of authority, and different.

Bleys faded back from the balcony, before the first of them emerged at the head of the escalator to the level he was on. He went back into the hotel, and directly down to the dining room, which he had already checked out.

The maître d' there, recognizing him, insisted on escorting him to a table, one of twenty which had been set up to allow five each of the Hounds to dine together. The maître d', and the hotel management itself, had been a little surprised that he had not simply wanted one large table for his whole group, plus a sight-and-sound barrier, projected between them and the other ordinary diners.

However, Bleys had been insistent. It was the Hounds' reaction to the rest of society he wanted to observe. He sat at his table, watching the Hounds come in, watching their reaction to the maître d' and to the other diners, and was not at all surprised when the four top-ranking members of the Hounds came to join him at his table.

During the dinner, Bleys chatted with those who had joined him and listened as best he could to the Hounds at the adjoining tables. They all sat ramrod-straight at first; and their chatter became louder, as the wine he had ordered began to take effect on them.

From all the accounts he had read, they were acting exactly the way soldiers on pass had always acted, when turned loose to their own devices. Only at his table was a certain amount of protocol preserved, with the Hounds who had joined him speaking only when he spoke to them; until the alcohol began to work on them and, little by little, the conversation became general.

They finally reached the end of the meal, which had been a sumptuous affair with ten courses and different wines for each. A good number of the Hounds were obviously half, if not more than half, drunk. However, they managed to remain sober enough so that none of them did what Bleys had told Ahram must not be done—which was for any of them to stand up and offer some kind of toast to him, their organization, Dahno or anything else.

After the meal, as ordered, they took their leave. Some came by his table to thank him for the meal, but there were not as many of these as he had feared might do so. Certainly it singled his table out, but it did not really lift the meal to the level of a formal affair—which Bleys had wanted to avoid at all costs. He had wanted to see the Hounds on their natural behavior; and that was largely what he was doing.

He, himself, finally made his excuses to the Hounds still at his table, aware that they would not venture to leave until he made some move to do so himself, even though the rest of those who had made up their party had already left the dining room.

They would all have some celebration in mind beyond the meal. A celebration which, in most cases, they would just as soon that neither Bleys nor Ahram knew about. Bleys returned to his room.

He had left word with his pilot to be ready for a five A.M. takeoff. And so, once back in his suite, he went to bed himself, and fell almost instantly asleep. The next day he was in his office at six in the morning, and phoned to wake a Norton Brawley who was still groggy from sleep, and order him down to the office immediately.

Brawley showed up within the time limit of forty minutes that Bleys had given him, with the mixed look of someone who is thoroughly outraged at being gotten out of bed unexpectedly and at the same time trying to show a polite exterior to the situation.

"Sit down, sit down, Norton," said Bleys from behind his desk, as Brawley came in through the door.

Brawley took a chair across the desk from Bleys. He was wearing a brown business suit that looked somewhat rumpled, as if it was one that he had worn yesterday, or possibly even a couple of days before. And his thin, graying hair was awry. He tried to smile at Bleys.

"Well," he said, "we're up this morning early, aren't we, Bleys Ahrens?"

"Yes, I think so," said Bleys, "but not too early considering the seriousness of the situation."

"Do we have a serious situation?" asked Brawley.

"Yes," said Bleys. "I was out at the Hounds' Kennel yesterday and watched them run through a rehearsal of their plan to handle the McKae affair. I didn't see any improvement at all. Meanwhile, I've been investigating McKae's security, and it's plain to me, at least, that any such attempt by us would be nothing but a disaster. So, I'm calling the whole thing off. We may look at it again sometime in the future."

"Have you told Ahram Moro about this yet—calling it off, I mean?" asked Brawley.

"No," answered Bleys, "I'm just about to. But I wanted you to know first, just in case you might be speaking to him yourself on the phone today."

"I see," Brawley's face had gone quite pale—whether it was the paleness of anger or shock, Bleys could not tell. His voice remained calm—in fact, if anything it was calmer than it had been since he had walked in through the door and sat down.

"In that case," said Brawley, getting to his feet, "Dahno left a paper with me, in case of just such an instance as this. It's in a folder down in my car which is parked in the basement garage of your building here. If you'll wait just a minute I'll bring it up to you."

Bleys looked at him narrowly.

"A paper Dahno gave you, but didn't tell me about? One you were to show me as you said—in an instance like this?" he said slowly, his eyes on Brawley's eyes.

"Exactly," said the legalist. "I'll be right back."

He went out the door. Bleys sat back in his chair with a sigh. He had expected, not specifically what Brawley had said to him, but an objection of some kind.

The man was acting almost exactly as Bleys had thought he would act; once he was confronted with the fact that he was indeed Bleys' subordinate, and had no power over anyone including the Hounds, except with Bleys' authority behind him. This meeting would have to continue to its inevitable and unhappy conclusion. But it was a conclusion he could not dodge. It was part of his commitment to the plan of his life and the future he dreamed of for the whole race.

Within a matter of minutes Brawley was back. But he was followed through the door by two large men, neither of them as tall as Bleys, but heavily built, and showing signs of past fights. The name of "musclemen" fitted them as neatly as their clothing, which was almost incongruously expensive in comparison with their physical appearance.

They came through the door and stood on either side of Brawley.

"Bleys," said the legalist—he held a folder in his hand but made no attempt to open it—"are you sure you won't change your mind about canceling the exercise by the Hounds?"

"Absolutely certain," said Bleys. He had pushed his float a little back from the desk so that his knees were out from under the desk.

Brawley reached into the folder. What he brought out, however, was not a piece of paper, but a void pistol, which he pointed at Bleys from a distance of no more than ten feet.

"Don't move," he said to Bleys. Then he spoke to the two men alongside him without looking at them. "Go get him. Don't damage him. We want to throw him unhurt off the roof."

The two produced short, bulge-ended blackjacks from their pockets and moved around, one on each side of the desk.

Bleys stayed where he was until they were both level with him and moving in toward him. His hands were grasping the edge of his float and he literally pushed it out from under him so he fell in a sitting position onto the floor, swiveling himself around so that his head was to one man, his legs another.

Just as people tended to underestimate the reach of his arms, they always very much underestimated the reach of his legs. The flat soles of his shoes lashed out in a kick that literally lifted the blackjack-carrier on that side of him off the floor, and slammed him against the wall. He doubled up and lay still.

The other man's blackjack whistled through the air where Bleys' head would have been if he had still been at the desk in his chair.

Meanwhile, Bleys was pivoting once more so that now his

feet faced in the opposite direction. One toe caught the blackjack and sent it flying, the other lashed into the man's crotch. He, too, folded.

So swiftly had everything happened that Brawley got off his first shot only as the second man went down. But by now the desktop was between Bleys and the void pistol, which could not penetrate any sort of shield. The charge spent itself harmlessly against that thick and varnished surface.

Bleys rolled around the desk and threw the blackjack he had picked up at Brawley's face. The man's hands instinctively went up but it slammed against his right upper temple hard enough to send him staggering back against the door, not unconscious but dazed.

Then Bleys was on his feet and with two long strides reached him and ripped the void pistol from his hand.

Bleys felt as if his heart moved in his chest. Brawley's eyes were directly on the void pistol, which was now pointing straight at him.

"No—" he began. Bleys pressed the trigger button and Brawley crumpled, his eyes open and his face still fixed in a look of terrified reproach. Bleys drew a deep breath, looking at the dead man.

He had expected a deep inner shock when this moment of killing came—but strangely, there was none.

A part of him felt deep regret over Brawley; but a greater part told him that there had been no choice. Norton's death had been a necessity to cut all connections between the Hounds and himself. He turned back to find the two musclemen were now climbing groggily to their feet.

"Both of you go around that side of the desk," said Bleys, pointing toward the back corner farthest from him. He kept the void pistol aimed at them and walked the other desk-side as they came around and backed up toward Brawley. They looked at the body and then looked back at the void pistol.

"I assume now, he's the one that you better throw off a roof, someplace. Preferably not this roof," said Bleys. "What he planned for me will work equally well for him and as long as he goes off some other roof at this hour of the morning, preferably into an alley where his body won't be noticed for a few hours—the greater security you, as well as I, are going to have. He probably has the keys to his car in his pocket. In any case, carry him down to his car, get in it, drive out of here, and find some other place to throw him down from at least ten stories."

He looked at them for a long second.

"Oh," he said, still keeping the void pistol aimed at them. "And I hope never to see you again. If I do, something will have to be done about you, as well."

They looked at him numbly for a second; then, still without a word, bent down and picked up the body of Norton Brawley between them and went out with it. From beginning to end, neither of them had said a word.

Left alone, Bleys sat once more at the desk and leaned with his head in his hands and elbows on the desk. He was trembling inside. But he told himself that it was something that could not have been avoided. Now he must phone and cancel the assassination attempt.

The void pistol still dangled loosely from his right finger, hooked in its trigger-button guard. He laid the weapon on the desk; and noticed that his hands were visibly trembling as well. If the two musclemen came back through the door right now, he thought, he might not have the will to defend himself against them.

Looking again at the pistol, he saw it lay upon an unopened off-planet message, which must have come after he had talked to Arah on the phone yesterday. It was from Old Earth, which meant it had to be from Dahno. He picked it up and ripped it open. It was in code, but he had long since passed the point where he needed to actually decode such messages, letter by letter. He read it off as if it was written in plain Basic.

Dear Mr. Vice-Chairman,
    Meet me at the hotel I mentioned in my last letter, in the Denver metropolitan area. I think, for business reasons you better bring along five of our tame Hounds. They may be needed.

*I'll look forward to seeing you in about thirteen days,
on the interstellar calendar.*

The Chairman

He put the letter aside and picked up the phone. He called
through to Ahram Moro at the Kennel. At that end there was
a small wait, while one of the Hounds currently on duty sent
for the Hound Master.

"Bleys Ahrens!" said Ahram, when he came on the line.
"My Hounds are most grateful, most grateful indeed—I should
say, your Hounds and Dahno's. But that dinner was a real treat
for them."

"I'm glad they liked it," said Bleys, "because I've some
unfortunate news for them. We're going to hold off indefinitely
using the maneuver your men have been working on. I got an
interstellar message from Dahno."

"Oh," said Ahram. There was a slight pause. Then his voice
came on again, more cheerfully. "Yes, of course they'll be
disappointed. But with your dinner to balance it off, I don't
think any of them will be too upset."

"Five of them needn't be," said Bleys. "You've got the
address of our office in Ecumeny?"

"In Ecumeny? Yes, Bleys Ahrens. I know it well."

"All right. Send five of your best Hounds to me there
immediately. You'll probably have to hire a private plane so
they can leave without delay. Tell them I want them here
within three hours. I've got to leave the office now. But I'll be
back in three hours."

"Three hours, Bleys Ahrens?"

"Three hours," said Bleys, "or they'll be left behind. Tell
them pack—lightly—for an off-world trip."

"An off-world trip?" echoed Ahram, with a new note in his
voice. "The ones who go will be the envy of all the rest!"

"I need them here in three hours, remember. Rent a car,
aircraft, anything you need, buy anything you need. You'll be
reimbursed."

"No need to worry about that, Bleys Ahrens," said Ahram.

"We have more than adequate funds on hand. This is a red-letter day."

"We'll hope so," said Bleys. "But—in any case, keep your mind on business. As I say, if those five Hounds aren't with me at the end of three hours, they'll be left behind. I'm going off-world myself and they're going with me."

"You're leaving too?" asked Ahram, incredulously.

"Only temporarily," said Bleys.

He noticed that the other man had not mentioned Norton as a source of interim orders. No doubt he was counting on hearing as usual from the legalist.

"But who will we get our orders from if you and Dahno are gone?"

"The office will let you know," said Bleys. "Otherwise, just continue as usual. Good-bye for now, then."

He hung up, not waiting for Ahram's answering good-bye.

He got heavily to his feet. Then he remembered there was another phone call he had to make. He called the agency through which he had booked passage several days ago. The day staff not yet being there, he told the nightline that he required shipspace for five more travelers who would be going with him.

There was some confusion, some delay, and finally the voice of a man he had not spoken to before came over the phone to him.

"I'm sorry, Bleys Ahrens," the voice said regretfully, "but all space is booked. We couldn't find room for even one additional passenger, let alone five."

"For five thousand interstellar—note, *interstellar*—credits," said Bleys, "could you find space for five more?"

"I—" The voice broke off. "I'll have to call you back in a few minutes, Bleys Ahrens. What's your phone number at the moment?"

Bleys gave him the number of his office. But it was less than two minutes before the phone rang again and the same voice spoke to him, almost jubilantly.

"Five more spaces have been found, Bleys Ahrens," he said. "It seems that we overbooked, and I hadn't noticed it until just recently. So I had to tell five of the people who already had passage—the last five, that is—that we couldn't take them. Then I found out I'd miscounted. There's cabins available for five who are traveling with you."

"Thank you," said Bleys.

"Not at all, Bleys Ahrens, our pleasure."

Bleys broke the connection and gave a short, bitter laugh in the silence of his office. He was about to leave for his own apartment to do what little packing he meant to do, when he noticed Dahno's message, again.

His laugh came again; and it was only when he realized there was a slightly bitter note to it, that he forced himself to stop laughing abruptly. He went out the door.

CHAPTER

37

THESE DAYS, WITH modern spaceship travel, what the passenger subjectively experienced was simply a going up into the star-filled darkness of space; then, to all the limits of perception, seeming to stand still there for a number of days, until finally descending at the world of their destination.

Consequently, the spaceships carried as much as possible by way of entertainment, so long as it did not use up too much valuable space, since the cost of carriage was so high.

There were approximately five meals available every day, all fixed by the best of chefs, and tailored to the tastes of whatever world the individual passenger had come from. There were unlimited alcoholic drinks. There was a small game room and a small gambling room, both jammed with almost every device people might want.

Unfortunately, Bleys had never been greatly interested in food, except as a necessary fuel when his stomach felt empty; he could drink but intoxication was only an irritation to him—he wanted his mind clear to think at all times. Gambling bored him. He could imagine an addiction to alcohol more easily than he could imagine an addiction to games of chance.

This caused no particular hardship for him, however, because his mind was always hungry, always busy; and he was perfectly content to sit for several days and simply work with what he knew. One reason for this was the fact that planning what he would need to do, to bring about the startling upheaval and change in the human race that he had originally dreamed of, was an immensely complicated arrangement of events. And there was no end to the planning that had to go into that, simply because he worked with a continually-shifting situation on the part of the human race.

On the other hand, he could not see how he could fail if he simply decided to remain steadfast and committed to his goal. Things would have to be done that were repugnant. But they must be done when the time came.

Norton Brawley had needed to be taken out of the picture. He would have needed to be taken out of it eventually, no matter what else had happened. McKae's upcoming speech had simply precipitated matters.

In the ship's lounge, he looked at the starscreen and once more felt the cold but peaceful comfort of being firmly on the outside of the race and its worlds, working toward an end that the human race must come to, or perish, in the long run. His killing of Brawley had finally put him, he felt, outside all other human society. Now where there had been the nerve-endings of ethics in him, there was nothing. No more uncertainties, only the never-ending test of his will.

With this thought, he felt ready to go on. The next uncomfortable point would be acquainting Dahno with Brawley's death. But, that too must be done.

His confidence about this did not waver, even when at last they landed on Old Earth. For, unlike Dahno, he had been fortunate enough to get a ship that was going directly from Association to the Mother World.

He was also pleased to find that the prospect of his seeing Dahno again did not cause him to worry about that meeting, but simply made him more eager to reach it.

The Shadow Hotel turned out to be about eighty miles west of the original site of the city of Denver. It was in some ways no more luxurious than some of the hotels he had been in before. But there was a difference there, a difference that it was hard to put your finger on. It was just a little taller and had, somehow, a more permanent feeling than any of the buildings he had been in on the New Worlds, including those that were the heart of governments, such as the Chamber on Association.

Old Earth was not only the cradle of the human race; but the fact that those alive on it now knew this, made them—Bleys found the word a little odd, but it was the only one that described it—more *solid* in their own estimation, in what they built and what they did.

It was something that should have put a slight chip on Bleys' shoulder, child as he was of one of the newer worlds. But curiously, it did not. Instead, it was reassuring.

With his five Hounds in tow he paused in the lobby of the soaring building to call up to Dahno's suite; and heard his half-brother's voice tell them all to come up right away.

They did.

"Come in, come in," boomed Dahno's voice cheerfully from the annunciator over the door, when they pressed the door button. They stepped into a long, large room that seemed to be almost all window; and even had some of its ceiling slanted backwards, with a skylight in it. Either this room projected from the body of the hotel or the hotel narrowed as it got to its higher levels, where they were now. Bleys rather thought the second.

Dahno waved toward a buffet with food and drink on it.

"Help yourselves," he said.

He was on his feet to clasp hands with Bleys; and Bleys found a curious pleasure in talking again to somebody whose eyes were on a level with his own. The five Hounds had taken Dahno's invitation at its face value and were busy at the buffet. But Bleys ignored it.

"Let's sit down," said Bleys. "I've got a lot to tell you."

"Oh?" Dahno said. His brown eyes were penetrating on

Bleys. "Come over here then. I've got a little side room we can step into."

The side room was not all that little, but it had been built to give an effect of coziness, with the walls covered with a bas-relief tapestry, the carpet deep, mounting partway up the walls of the room; and the chairs, Bleys was interested to see, tailored to his and Dahno's proportions.

Dahno led him to a facing pair of such armchairs by a window, and waved Bleys into one, while he took the other.

"Go ahead," he said, "bring me up to date."

"Norton Brawley is dead," said Bleys, bluntly. "He had plans to take over the organization for his own use."

"Oh?" said Dahno, but his voice did not echo the surprise that the word might have indicated. "Who killed him?"

"I did," said Bleys, "when he came to kill me."

Dahno nodded slowly.

"I'd had my eye on him for a little while, I must admit," said Dahno, thoughtfully. "One of the problems was that while he was a mixed-breed, he wasn't one of our trainees; just someone I got to know after I moved into Ecumeny. He was already in practice as a legalist. But the man was clearly ambitious—in fact if he hadn't been, he wouldn't have been that useful to me. Any danger of his death being traced back to the organization?"

"I don't really think so," said Bleys. Briefly, he told exactly what had happened when Brawley had come to his office that early morning, with the two men.

"Yes," said Dahno, when he had finished listening. He nodded. "Probably better now than later as far as Norton went. But I'm interested in why you thought that the attempt to knock out McKae should be canceled. I don't remember saying anything about your doing that, even if things looked unlikely, before I left."

"No," said Bleys, "of course you didn't. But then you left in rather a hurry. What made up my mind for me was that I infiltrated McKae's own security force—"

He told Dahno about his experiences with the individuals of the McKae camp.

"What it wound up being," Bleys said, "was a lopsided situation in which I didn't see any real chance of the Hounds pulling it off; and it would have been too open a gun battle to keep out of the papers. So . . . it was a situation that called for a decision at the moment. I decided."

"Yes," said Dahno, "I can't fault you for making the decision. Also, it sounds like the kind of decision I'd have had to make if I'd been there at the time. I was a little bit concerned about things, which was one reason that I decided to buy your idea of a larger and more ambitious future."

He slapped his knee, as if dismissing everything that had happened.

"Now, about the meeting," he said. "After looking at the situation here, I've come to the conclusion that Earth's security system is so large and fast that we couldn't even rent a place, or use hotel space for our meeting, without having the authorities around asking questions before our chairs were warm. Crazy as it sounds, our best chance to meet undisturbed will be to simply take over a private estate, rather than trying to rent, or even buy, one to meet in. It'll leave fewer tracks for us to be traced by—particularly if we make a swift move in, a quick meeting, a swift move out—and an immediate departure from Earth. That leaves no time for anyone to catch on to us. And if there is any fuss, we'll already be off-planet as well as unidentifiable. So whatever happens here, Earth won't be shut off to us after this. The ship of your new plans can still be launched."

Bleys noted, with an inner interest, that Dahno was already referring to Old Earth simply as Earth. It might mean nothing. On the other hand, it might mean an immediate response on Dahno's part to Old Earth's importance.

"Now, the place I've picked out," said Dahno, "is a bit further west from here, fairly high in the mountains and isolated. It's got a strange reason for existence. It seems about fourteen years ago an empty small spacecraft was found drifting near Earth, with a two-year old boy named Hal Mayne aboard. No adults at all."

"*No* adults?" echoed Bleys.. "But was the boy alive?"

"Yes, and there were instructions left for how he was to be taken care of," said Dahno, "and saying that the ship and its contents could be sold to finance that care. You know what any kind of deep-space craft is worth, even though this was somewhat out of date."

"Much out of date?" asked Bleys.

Dahno smiled.

"They figured that its design went back to the kind of spacecraft they were building eighty years ago," he answered. "A puzzle, eh? At any rate, sold, the craft brought in enough Old Earth currency to buy the land, put up the building and hire three tutors for the boy."

"How old's he now?" asked Bleys.

"Sixteen," said Dahno.

Sixteen, thought Bleys—only three years younger than Will MacLean when he had died on Ceta. But Dahno was going on.

"The isolation's perfect for our use," he was saying. "I'll give you an air map and complete details; and I want you and the five Hounds to go there tomorrow and take it over. I'll come in late tomorrow myself, and I'll expect to find you have the place under control. Don't hurt anyone. Just lock them up in a room where they can't alert the local law, and you and I'll simply persuade them to host us for a couple of days."

He paused to smile at Bleys. "With our talents, we should have no trouble making them glad to have us."

Bleys kept silence, and after a moment Dahno continued, "I've left word for the other Vice-Chairmen, when they get to the hotel here tomorrow, how to find their way out for the meeting. We'll have an afternoon meeting, and either turn the people loose again or make it possible for them to get loose from whatever room we've penned them up in within a few hours. Then we'll head right for Denver spaceport. I already have passage for all the Vice-Chairmen, you, I and the Hounds. So we'll take off, at the latest, the morning after we have our get-together."

"How many people are there at this place?" asked Bleys.

"Just the boy"—Dahno waved one hand to indicate the unimportance of the numbers—"and the three old men who are his tutors, one Dorsai, one from Harmony, I believe, and one Exotic. All very old men. The house itself is completely automated."

He grinned at Bleys.

"The boy's an orphan—like you and me, Mr. Vice-Chairman," he said.

He got to his feet.

"I'll show you a layout of the house and tell you more about the people there, after we've got the Hounds settled," he said. "I've already got rooms reserved for them. We'll put them in, two to a room here. That should be good enough for them, under campaign conditions; and this is hardly an uncomfortable hotel, even its smallest guest rooms."

Bleys found himself wondering about the boy, Hal Mayne.

CHAPTER

38

As HE RETURNED to his own suite in the same hotel, the idea of the orphan boy found in the spaceship continued to nag at Bleys. The coincidences involved were almost too much to swallow.

Those with the child would have had to have deserted someone that young only very shortly before the ship was found. How could they be sure the ship would be found, if they deserted it? Secondly, in a small courier ship like that, that would not have been exactly childproofed, how could they possibly be sure that the baby boy, left alone, would not start pulling levers he shouldn't and punching buttons that he was ordinarily not allowed to touch? At almost three years of age, he was just at the point where he would rush for the chance to experiment, the minute Authority was out of the way.

Thirdly, thought Bleys, having floated down on one of the elevator disks and stepped onto his own floor, what had caused them to abandon Hal Mayne in the first place? Presumably, the adult or adults had been perfectly healthy and all right, otherwise they could not have brought the ship into the kind of close proximity with Earth's immediate space, so that its being found was likely.

Most people did not realize the mind-baffling immensity of space. Just as, for hundreds of years, people on Old Earth had not really appreciated the enormous volume of water involved in the seas of that world. So little had they understood it, that he had read once that very often people could not believe, when someone was lost overboard from a ship at sea, why he could not be searched for and found, even if he had sunk below the surface.

Finally, he thought, unlocking the door of his suite and stepping into it and having the lights go on all around him, was the curious upbringing that those with the boy had specified for him. A Dorsai, a Friendly, and an Exotic as tutors. It was quite obviously an intention to have the child brought up exposed to all three of the major Splinter Cultures at once. Why? There must have been some reason why the boy was to grow up knowing those three, very disparate points of view.

It was as if those who had left him had had some special future in mind for the boy, once he had grown up. And if they had such a special future in mind, what could it be? To possibly preach the virtues of those three chief Splinter Cultures to the population of Earth? It was an answer, but Bleys' mind was uncomfortable with it. The arrangements were too elaborate for such a straightforward goal.

Obviously, what he needed was more data on the boy himself, and on everything connected with him.

Bleys sat down in one of the overstuffed floats with armrests, hardly noticing that, like the ones in Dahno's suite, they had been tailored to his size.

If it was information he wanted, nothing was easier. The hotel's communication system would link him with the twenty-four-hour network of libraries and reference sources all over Old Earth. The only place he would not be able to access for information would be The Final Encyclopedia, in orbit somewhere overhead right now.

An odd thought struck him and he sat up straight in his chair.

The Final Encyclopedia was supposed to be in a special fixed orbit, and kept there by its own drive engines, when gravity threatened to change its position. Just exactly where was that spot? It would be interesting to know where it hung in relation to the surface of Earth, below.

He keyed the library service and asked the question. The answer came back immediately.

He checked the coordinates he was given with the location of the estate that Dahno had told him to take over the next day. It could not be a coincidence. The Final Encyclopedia hung directly over the estate, even though it was miles out from the surface.

This was more than merely interesting, thought Bleys, since to hold a fixed orbital position over Earth this far above the equator, the satellite—which was what The Final Encyclopedia essentially was—would have to have its drive engines working steadily to hold it there. Normal geosynchronous orbits, as such fixed positions were called, had to be over the equator. He called the library again. Yes, the Encyclopedia had been deliberately put in that position ninety-two years before. It was the only case, the voice told him, of a satellite of Earth in a state of "dynamic geosynchronicity."

So, why was that? —Unless someone in the Encyclopedia wanted to keep a viewer steadily fixed on young Hal Mayne as he went through the process of growing up?

That too, was a farfetched supposition.

By this time, Bleys' instinctive curiosity was at full heat. He dived into everything that could be found about the background of the boy's rescue, the selling of the cruiser ship in which he had been found, and his raising since.

His raising since had been curiously unnewsworthy. There had been no information to speak of logged on it at all. The estate sat out by itself, deep in the Rockies, in a place that was neither convenient nor attractive to anyone else, and included a fair amount of territory, ranging widely from mountain lake, through forest, to the bare rock of vertical mountain peaks.

At the end of two hours, he ended up in a state that was unusual for him—extraordinarily frustrated. There was little

more information available about the boy or his tutors, who
seemed to have simply appeared at the right time to be hired,
than he had been given by Dahno, originally.

He was now more than ordinarily interested in the estate he
would see tomorrow and the people he would meet. He
deliberately forced thought of them to the back of his mind, so
he could deal with the more mundane matters of getting the
Hounds together, getting a craft to take them in, and getting the
maps that would allow them to land a little distance away and
slip up on the estate buildings. Thankfully, the one thing that
these *ninja*-trained young men did possess was the ability to
move quietly and without attracting attention.

He arranged for everything and turned in for the night. They
left the following morning, at dawn in a craft that Bleys
himself piloted. As he approached the estate—which was
indeed isolated—he indulged his curiosity to the point of
gaining altitude and reaching a point where he could look at it
from a long angle high in the atmosphere. But his viewing
screen gave him a closeup picture of the estate and its
surrounding territory.

It lay in a shallow bowl-shaped valley in the mountain rock,
facing south and slightly east. It was surrounded by lodgepole
pines, which went off from it to reach partway up the sides of
the neighboring heights and cliffs, for they were completely
surrounded by peaks.

It was at least twenty miles, a little over thirty kilometers,
from the nearest habitation. But the house itself was large, and
looked to be luxurious. It nestled in a flat part of the bowl
looking directly southeast, with a little lake before it and a
walking path around the lake. Other paths led off into the pines
and were lost to sight behind their branches.

Bleys could feel the impatience, almost like a sort of rising
heat from the bodies of the five Hounds in the back of the
aircraft, behind him. It was, as Dahno had said, an ideal place
for the Others to hold the meeting of the heads of their various
world organizations; and if there were really only four people
there—the three old tutors and the boy—in a completely

automated house, it was not likely that anyone would bother them during their meeting.

At the same time, Bleys continued to have an uneasy feeling about the whole thing. He disliked loose ends on general principle; and it was simply the fact that the boy and his tutors had not existed in his mental universe until Dahno had told him about them. There was nothing remarkable in this, since there were uncounted millions of people he did not know. But most of those uncounted millions did not have this kind of a puzzle attached to them.

How could a two-year-old remain alive in a spaceship, adrift in space and from which any adults who had been with him had disappeared? Add to that the remarkable fact that the ship was old-fashioned—although eighty years back, ships were not all that different from the way they were now. Only, when the older ships were phase-shifted, it had been a matter of temporary discomfort to the passengers, which was not true in the present-day spaceships.

And finally, what a curiously fortunate coincidence that the ship with this near-baby aboard had been found adrift almost in Earth orbit. The chances of anything being found in space, even close to Earth, were so small that the odds against finding this one while the child was still alive must have been astronomical.

The fact was—he finally admitted to himself—this boy was an exception to the whole pattern for the future with which he had been working; a potential rock down among the cogwheels and gears of his plans.

Why this should be so, he was unsure. But the very existence of Hal Mayne troubled him.

However, these questions were ones he could only pay attention to later on when he had more time. The thing now was to take over the house and its inhabitants.

He turned the ship away until he dipped below the horizon of the valley top, and then came back in at low altitude, stopping about two kilometers from the edge of the bowl and the house itself. Here he set the ship down quietly, and turned to the five Hounds behind him.

"All right," he said, "now we go. Stay with me. Do exactly as I say. And under no circumstances shoot anyone unless I tell you to."

They left the ship and headed toward the house, from a direction that would bring them up against the side that faced toward the mountains and away from the lake. From the layout of the windows in the house, it seemed that this side was the one which was least likely to have people looking out and seeing them approach. In spite of this, at Bleys' directions they all took advantage of cover and tried to approach unseen.

When the house itself at last became visible through the trees Bleys called the five Hounds to him and instructed them in a whisper.

"You two and you two," he said, pointing out a pair of them in each case, "come in from behind the bushes at the back and sides of the patio. You two from the left. You other two from the right; and remember you come in, not to the house, but to the patio behind it, overlooking the lake, which is where I could see a couple of people standing just before the trees hid the view, as we landed."

He turned to the one remaining Hound.

"You," he said, "will follow me. I'm going directly in the door on the back side of the house in front of us, here, and you're to follow me at about one room's distance behind me. Stay out of sight, but watch me to see if I'm caught, or trapped in any way. Then it'll be up to you to step out and help me. Have you got that straight?"

The fifth Hound nodded.

Bleys looked at their faces. They were all different. About the only similarity between the five of them, was that they were all brunettes. Aside from that they had no real similarities. Their faces in particular were all individually different, ranging from round to angular. Nonetheless, he could not escape the feeling that they were all identical, all as closely like each other as brothers, all cut from the same piece of cloth.

"All right," he said, "if you have any questions, ask them now."

He waited. But none of them asked him anything.

"Very well. Remember, those of you who are coming in from the ends are to stay behind the bushes and out of sight until you see me on the patio. You, the one who is going to follow me, also stay out of sight until I'm out on the patio. All right, here we go."

He turned, for all practical purposes putting the other five out of his mind. There was really only one person he could depend on here; and that was himself. This, in spite of the fact that he was not armed and they were. It had been impossible, of course, for them to bring weapons onto Earth. All the planets had very strict laws about any attempt to carry weapons onto them from another planet. Anyone found trying to do that was immediately deported back to the planet he had come from.

To make sure the deportation occurred, the planets had jointly made the spaceship companies themselves responsible. The spaceship companies, in turn and in self-protection, had required that all passengers—such as Bleys and these five had been—pay double fares when they left Association. Double fares were the rule. The one-way passenger got back the unused part of his fare from the spaceship company, in whatever currency it had originally been paid, after the passenger had passed all custom checks on the world of destination.

Dahno, however, had produced five void pistols for the Hounds in the Shadow Hotel. He had not explained, to them or to Bleys, where he got them; and Bleys had not been interested in asking. If it had been up to him, the Hounds would have carried either no weapons, or else imitation or unloaded ones. It made no difference. He wanted to handle this without anyone getting hurt.

Once the Hounds had vanished noiselessly right and left among the trees, he went forward himself to the back of the house; and, standing a little to one side, glanced in the window next to the door there. He saw that the room the door opened into was empty. Still, he was cautious as he turned the knob and opened it with as little noise as possible.

He had stepped into what was evidently a sort of mud

room—a place where outdoor clothes that would track dirt into the house were taken off, hung up, put on racks, or otherwise left while the person involved changed into something that would bring less dirt further inside. There was nothing on Bleys' shoes, however, but pine needles, he noted.

He peered through the partially-opened door within, to a sort of corridor that led to the right to a kitchen and to the left to several closed doors, which could be bedrooms or something else. Guessing that with the two outside that he had seen from the air, the chances were that the house was not over-full, he went silently in the direction of the kitchen, found it empty as well, and passed through it into a dining room.

From the dining room he moved into a large lounge; and, still moving in the same direction as when he had entered the back door, into a room that was obviously a library. Its walls were twelve feet high and its shelves were loaded with books. Overwhelmingly, not modern books which required being stuck into a player to read, but ancient artifacts of covers and printed pages.

In spite of himself Bleys took time out to wander up and down the shelves and see what was there. He ran into innumerable classics in a number of different languages, and found himself becoming half-intoxicated by the scent of leather and paper. This was the kind of room which touched off the fascination he had found in the arts of literature. He found himself caught up in elegance and perfection that were between the stiff old covers on the shelves. He could have spent a great deal of time here, if it had been reasonable to do so. He would, he thought, probably have spent most of his time in this room until he had read everything that was here.

By the time he had approached the french windows on the far side of the wall, which could be opened out into the patio, he had come to the section on poetry. In a padded armchair float, closed, but with a bookmark marking a place in it, was a thick, brown leather-covered book. Out of sheer curiosity he picked it up and opened it to the bookmark to see what it was.

It was apparently an anthology of poetry by Alfred Noyes, in twentieth-century English. Noyes, a poet with his roots in the nineteenth century, had fallen almost completely out of sight, but had been rehabilitated in the twenty-first century and recognized for the artist that he was. A brown leather bookmark lay against a page of the poetic play of *Robin Hood*. The central diamond of the bookmark touched a speech that Oberon, King of the Fairies, was making to one of his retainers, telling them about Robin, who had once rescued one of them.

Bleys was about to lay it down again where he had found it, when, through the glass of the patio, he saw two old men, one very white and sturdy, the other wearing the robes of an Exotic, but also very old and with the almost lineless, but ancient, face that was common in some very aged Exotics.

Recognizing the Exotic made the connection in his brain. The other must be a Dorsai; in fact, looking at him now through the french window, Bleys told himself that he should have recognized him as a Dorsai at first glance, though the man was well past the age of any military usefulness. These must be two of the three tutors for the boy. He moved close to the french windows on that side of the room. He could hear them speaking now, if he listened closely.

CHAPTER

39

===

"I DON'T KNOW," the Exotic was saying. He lifted what looked like a two-inch-square cube from his robe and showed it. "All I know is I've had this warning."

"More of your Exotic hocus-pocus," growled the Dorsai. But the growl was only half disdainful. "I'll go warn Obadiah."

"There's no time." The Exotic's slim and slightly knobby hand reached out and stopped the other. "Obadiah's been ready to meet that personal God of his for years now, and any minute we're liable to have eyes watching what we do. The less we seem to be expecting anything, the better Hal's chance to get away."

Hal Mayne, thought Bleys; of course they would think of the boy first.

The Dorsai looked about in silence for a moment, and then the Exotic said something softly, which Bleys did not catch.

"He'll stay," said the Dorsai grimly. "He's not a lad now, but a man. You and Obadiah keep forgetting that."

"A man, at sixteen?" said the Exotic. "So soon?"

"Man enough," grunted the Dorsai. "Who's coming? Or what?"

"I don't know," answered the Exotic. "What I showed you was just a device to warn of a sharp pressure increase of the ontogenetic energies moving in on us. You remember I told you one of the last things I was able to have them do on Mara was run calculations on the boy; and the calculations indicated high probability of his intersection with a pressure-climax of the current historical forces before his seventeenth year."

The words *historical forces* jolted Bleys almost like a solid thing. It was the historical forces that were his concern in the long run. He had thought his understanding of them to be something unique and personal. He had known—as everyone did—that the Exotics at one time had a remarkable interstellar information service; but he assumed it had ceased to be anything important long ago. How could they be so informed on the historical forces, which he, himself, had deduced only from bits and pieces of information in his reading?

He turned his attention once more to the patio. He had missed part of what the Dorsai had just said.

"Don't fool yourself!" the Exotic was answering him, almost sharply for one of his birth and upbringing. "There'll be men or things to manifest its effect when it gets here, just as a tornado manifests a sudden drop in air pressure. Perhaps—" He broke off. The Dorsai's gaze had moved away from the Exotic. "What is it?"

"*Others*, perhaps," said the Dorsai, quietly.

Bleys was once again jolted. Dahno's practice had been not to hide the name of the Others, but to make no particular show of them. There had been no branch of the organization attempted on either Kultis or Mara, the two Exotic worlds, for the simple reason that it would not have worked there. Why, then, should this Dorsai even mention them, now, let alone be concerned about them? His face raised, as if he were testing the cooling air of the late afternoon.

"Why do you say that?" The Exotic glanced around him as if he expected to see Others rise up around them out of the patio pavement.

"I'm not sure. A hunch," said the Dorsai.

The Exotic's face crumpled.

He murmured something in so low a voice that Bleys could not hear it.

"Why?" snapped the Dorsai.

The response was also so low Bleys could not hear it. He moved forward toward the windows.

"The Others aren't 'devils'!" snapped the Dorsai in answer, not bothering to keep his voice down. "Mix your blood and mine, and Obadiah's in with it—mix together blood of all the Splinter Cultures if you want to and you still get men and women. Men make men—nothing else. You don't get anything out of a pot you don't put into it."

"Other men and women. Hybrids," the Exotic said. "People with half a dozen talents in one skin."

Bleys let the words echo sardonically in his own mind. If only the trainees that Dahno had turned out had anything like two or three, let alone half a dozen, talents in them. The potential for those talents was there, but few of them had begun to show themselves.

He grew suddenly thoughtful. Perhaps when these trainees had moved into suborganizations on other worlds, some of the capabilities within them had begun to flourish. He would have to look into it. If so—

"What of it?" the Dorsai was growling beyond the patio door. "A man lives, a man dies. If he lives well and dies well, what difference does it make what kills him?"

"But this is our Hal—"

"Who has to die someday, like everyone else. Straighten up!" muttered the Dorsai. "Don't they grow any backbones on the Exotics?"

The Exotic took a deep breath and straightened up. He stood tall, breathed deeply and in a way that Bleys had only seen one Exotic do before in his life, put on an air of peace that could almost be seen.

"You're right," he said. "At least Hal's had all we could

give him, the three of us, in skill and knowledge. And he's got the creativity to be a great poet, if he lives."

"Poet!" said the Dorsai. "There's a few thousand more useful things he could do with his life. Poets—"

He broke off suddenly; and in a moment the Exotic folded his hands in the wide sleeves of his blue robe.

"But poets are men, too," the Exotic went on, as if in the middle of some cheerful academic discussion. "That's why, for example, I think so highly of Alfred Noyes, among the nineteenth-century poets. You know Noyes, don't you?"

Bleys was instantly alert. The Exotic, somehow, had sensed the presence of Bleys and the Hounds.

"Should I?" The Dorsai was saying now.

"I think so," said the Exotic. "Of course, I grant you no one remembers anything but *The Highwayman*, out of all his poems, nowadays. But *Tales of a Mermaid Tavern*, and that other long poem of his—*Sherwood*—they've both got genius in them. You know, there's that part where Oberon, the king of elves and fairies, is telling his retainers about the fact Robin Hood is going to die, and explaining why the fairies owe Robin a debt—"

"Never read it," grunted the Dorsai.

"Then I'll quote it for you," said the Exotic. "Oberon is talking to his own kind and he tells about one of them whom Robin once rescued from what he thought was nothing worse than a spider's web. And what Noyes had Oberon say is—listen to this now—

" '. . . He saved her from the clutches of that Wizard,
'That Cruel Thing, that dark old Mystery,
'Whom ye all know and shrink from . . . !' "

The Exotic broke off. Through the french window Bleys saw him looking at a Hound, in his dark business suit and holding his void pistol, who had stepped from the lilac bushes behind the Dorsai. A moment later the other Hound emerged to stand beside the first; and then two more appeared from the bushes at the far end of the terrace. Four pistols covered the two old men.

Through the patio windows Bleys had seen them, too, and a cold anger was suddenly born in him. It was too late now to overhear any more; but perhaps he could salvage something of what could have been a civilized capture. He stepped through the french window, speaking:

"'. . . *Plucked her forth, so gently that not one bright rainbow gleam upon her wings was clouded . . .*'" He finished the Exotic's quotation in his most vibrant, impressive voice. He was still carrying the book he had found, with one finger lodged in the pages.

". . . But you see," he continued, addressing the Exotic, "how it goes downhill, gets to be merely pretty and ornate, after that first burst of strength you quoted? Now, if you'd chosen instead the song of Blondin the Minstrel, from that same poem—"

He raised his voice and pitched it upward, almost singing.

> *"Knight on the narrow way,*
> *Where wouldst thou ride?*
> *'Onward,' I heard him say,*
> *'Love, to thy side!'*

". . . then I'd have had to agree with you," he finished.

The Exotic bent his head a little, politely; and Bleys thought he had touched the other. An Exotic, trained through a lifetime to respond to every subtlety, must surely feel as much or more than Bleys himself did, of the genius behind the words. And Bleys knew he, himself, was creating, with words and voice—with his very appearance—high drama.

"I don't think we know you," was all the other said, however.

"Ahrens is my name. Bleys Ahrens," he answered. "And you needn't be worried. No one's going to be hurt. We'd just like to use this estate of yours for a short meeting during the next day or two."

He smiled at the Exotic. He was focusing all his power to be likable on the two old men; in voice and smile and body language. Neither showed any response; but the pale-faced young Hounds watched him worshipfully.

"We?" asked the Exotic.

"Oh, a club of sorts. To tell you the truth, you'd do better not to worry about the matter at all." He looked about at the lake and the woods near it.

"There ought to be two more of you here, shouldn't there?" he said, turning back again. "Another tutor your own age; and your ward, the boy named Hal Mayne? Where would they be, now?"

The Exotic shook his head, looking baffled. Bleys turned to the Dorsai, who looked indifferently back at him.

"Well, we'll find them," said Bleys in a confident tone. He looked once more at the Exotic.

"You know," he went on, and though his voice did not betray it, there was a wistfulness in him behind the question, "I'd like to meet that boy. He'd be . . . what? Sixteen now?"

The Exotic nodded.

"Fourteen years since he was found . . ." Bleys paused. "He must have some unusual qualities. He'd have had to have them—to stay alive, as a child barely able to walk, alone on a wrecked ship, drifting in space for who-knows-how-long. Who were his parents—did they ever find out?"

"No," said the Exotic. "The log aboard showed only the boy's name."

"A remarkable boy . . ." said Bleys. He looked about beyond the terrace. "You say you're sure you don't know where he is now?"

"No," answered the Exotic.

Bleys glanced at the Dorsai, inquiringly.

"Commandant?"

The Dorsai snorted contemptuously.

Bleys smiled, but the Dorsai remained unchanged, unchangeable, before him. Bleys dropped the attempt.

"You don't approve of Other Men like me, do you?" he said. "But times have changed, Commandant."

"Too bad," said the Dorsai; and Bleys felt the dry contempt behind the words like a sharp point.

"But too true," he said. "Did it ever occur to you your boy might be one of us? No? Well, suppose we talk about other things, if that suggestion bothers you. I don't suppose you share your fellow tutor's taste for poetry? Say, for something like Tennyson's *Idylls of the King*—a piece of poetry about men and war?"

"I know it," said the Dorsai. "It's good enough."

"Then you ought to remember what King Arthur has to say in it about changing times," said Bleys. "You remember—when Arthur and Sir Bedivere are left alone at the end and Sir Bedivere asks the King what will happen now, with all the companionship of the Round Table dissolved, and Arthur himself leaving for Avalon. Do you remember how Arthur answers, then?"

"No," the Dorsai said.

"He answers—" and he made his voice ring with its power again, "*The old order changeth, giving place to new . . .*" Bleys paused and looked at the old ex-soldier to see if he had made his point.

"*—And God fulfills himself in many ways—lest one good custom should corrupt the world,*" interrupted a harsh voice from the side.

All of them turned, to see a thin, elderly—even ancient—Friendly being herded out through the french window at the point of a void pistol held by the fifth young gunman.

"You forgot to finish the quotation," he rasped at Bleys. "And it applies to your kind too, Other Man. In God's eye you, also, are no more than a drift of smoke and the lost note of a cymbal. You, too, are doomed at His will—like that!"

He had come on while they all watched, until suddenly he snapped his bony fingers with that last word, under Bleys' nose. Bleys found himself laughing, and realized that he was on the edge of losing control. The knowledge startled him.

"Posts!" he snapped.

The Hounds read their error in his voice—of the four already there, three had left off covering the Exotic and the Dorsai to aim at the Friendly, as he snapped his fingers; only one still covered the Dorsai. Almost cowering at the tone of Bleys' voice, they pulled their weapons back to their original targets.

"Oh, you fools, you young fools!" Bleys said softly to them. "Look at me!"

Guiltily, their dog-like glances came back to him.

"The Maran"—Bleys pointed—"is harmless. His people taught him that violence—any violence—would cripple his thinking processes. And the Fanatic here is worth perhaps one gun. But you see that old man there?"

He pointed at the silent Dorsai.

"I wouldn't lock one of you, armed as you are, with him, unarmed, in an unlighted room, and give a second's hope to the chance of seeing you alive again."

He paused, as the Hounds' attitudes begged his forgiveness.

"Three of you cover the Commandant," Bleys said, finally sure of having made his point. "And the other two watch our religious friend here. I'll undertake to try to defend myself against the Exotic." He smiled, encouraging them to relax from the tension with his touch of humor.

The aim of the pistols shifted, leaving the Exotic uncovered. Bleys had looked back at the Friendly.

"You're not exactly a lovable sort of man, you know," he said.

The old man stood, the very picture of a Friendly; and that picture stirred in Bleys his old response from the years with Henry. His mind brought before him the image of Henry's solidness, of Gregg's bent-backed calmness.

The old man before him—Obadiah Testator, the library information had said—seemed the proverbial Fanatic. He was stick-thin, mere weathered black skin stretched over his bones, as if shrunken in death years ago to a leather-wrapped skull. But that skull seemed to be lit from the inside, and Bleys recognized that those fierce, hawk-like eyes were burning with a kind of joy.

Bleys stared back at the old man for a moment, once more. It had been the face of such a faith as this he had been unable, either to touch or understand. And the sure old eyes looked back at him, knowing that difference between them.

"Woe to you," the Friendly said, in utter calmness, "to you, Other Man, and all of your breed. And again I say, woe unto you!"

For a second Bleys continued to stare into those eyes. Then he shook himself, mentally. His gaze turned from the Friendly to one of the gunmen covering him.

"The boy?" Bleys asked.

"We looked . . ." The answer was almost whispered. "He's nowhere . . . nowhere around the house."

Bleys turned abruptly to the Dorsai and the Exotic, feeling a need for quick action.

"If he was off the grounds one of you'd know it?"

"No. He . . ." The Exotic hesitated. " . . . might have gone for a hike, or a climb in the mountains . . ."

Bleys focused himself on the eyes in that unlined face. He poured his energies into his eyes, seeking to capture the Exotic's attention and mold it into a state of light hypnosis from which perhaps he could get an answer.

"Now, that's foolish of you," said the Exotic, quietly, simply returning the gaze blandly. "Hypnotic dominance of any form needs at least the unconscious cooperation of the subject. And I am a Maran Exotic."

The truth in the words cut the legs out from under Bleys' effort; and as he realized that he had again lost control of the situation, alarm bells began to ring within him.

"There's something going on here . . ." he said, but found himself interrupted by the Exotic.

"All that's different," the Maran said, "is that you've been underestimating me. The unexpected, I think some general once said, is worth an army—"

—And he jumped across the few feet between them, at Bleys' throat.

The attack was a clumsy thing, made by an untrained body and mind. But it was the last thing Bleys had been expecting; and his mind, thrown off-balance by the last few minutes, stood by in a kind of paralysis even as his trained reflexes brushed the Exotic to one side.

At the same time one of the Hounds guarding the Friendly fired at the Exotic, sprawled on the terrace.

In that split second of distraction, the Friendly hurled himself—not at either of the gunmen guarding him, but at one of those covering the Dorsai.

The Dorsai himself had been in movement from the first fractional motion of the Exotic's move. He had one of the two still holding pistols on him, before the first man could fire. And the other's shot missed his rapid movement.

The Dorsai chopped down the gunman he had reached with one hand, as if it was some sort of killing wand. Almost in the same motion he turned and threw the second gunman into the discharge from the pistols of the two Hounds who had been covering Obadiah; just as the remaining armed man, caught in the Friendly's grasp, managed to fire twice.

In that same moment, the Dorsai reached him; and they went down together, the gunman rolling on top of the old man. It was over.

It had taken longer for the bodies to fall than for the action that killed them, Bleys thought. The Exotic lay to his side, across from the Friendly, who seemed to be staring at his friend in death.

Once more he seemed to feel his very heart move in his chest, as he looked over the scene before him. He had well and truly lost control of the situation here, he thought.

Two of his Hounds were down, dead, and one was badly hurt, lying half on his side. The Friendly also lay fallen, with his head twisted around so that his open and unmoving eyes stared blankly in the Exotic's direction. He did not move. No more did the man the Dorsai had chopped down, nor the other gunman the ex-soldier had thrown into the fire from his companion's pistols. One other Hound, knocked down by the thrown man, was twitching and moaning strangely on the terrace.

Of the two gunmen remaining, one was still lying on top of

the Dorsai; the other, still on his feet, cringed before Bleys' fury.

"You fools!" he said again, softly but fiercely. "Didn't I just get through telling you to concentrate on the Dorsai?"

The only response was silence.

"All right," he said, sighing, "pick him up," and pointed to the wounded man. He turned to the gunman on top of the Dorsai.

"Wake up." He prodded the man with his toe. "It's all over."

The man prodded rolled off the Dorsai's body and sprawled on the stones. Bleys looked at him for a moment, wondering if he had ever been in control in this place at all. He felt no fear of that, though, but only his usual cold sense of isolation.

"Three of ours dead—and one hurt," he said. "Just to destroy three unarmed old teachers. What a waste." He shook his head and turned away.

He held open the french window so that the wounded Hound could be helped into the library by his companion. Bleys followed, still holding the volume of Noyes' poetry the Exotic had been reading. He closed the french doors on the dying light of day.

CHAPTER

40

═══════════

Night closed in swiftly behind the twilight. Outside the french windows, now, it was dark. In the library a fire had lit itself automatically in the fireplace and its flames threw a ruddy, comforting light upon the heavy furniture, the thousands of books and the ceiling. Dahno had arrived; and he with Bleys was standing before the fire, talking.

"—So," said Dahno, "what did you do with the bodies?"

"I helped the one uninjured Hound I had left," said Bleys. "This house has a walk-in freezer. We put the bodies there."

"The freezer?" said Dahno, lifting his head suddenly, "why didn't you bury them?"

Bleys shrugged.

"Eventually, this place is going to be checked on," he said. "Eventually the local police will come. When they do they'd find any bodies we had buried within any distance that we could reasonably carry them from this house. The freezer will do just as well. Besides, the boy might prefer it, knowing eventually that his three tutors had a decent burial. They were gallant old men."

"Gallant!" Dahno exploded. "This isn't a storybook matter, Mr. Vice-Chairman."

Bleys sighed and faced him.

"No, it isn't," he said, "not for you and not for me."

"Yes, you can say that," said Dahno. He was still angry. "Your dogs made something of a mess taking over here."

"Your *Hounds*, Dahno," said Bleys.

The thick-bodied giant brushed the answer away.

"The Hounds I lent you. It was your job to set up the conference here, Mr. Vice-Chairman."

"Your Hounds aren't properly trained, Mr. Chairman. They like killing because they think it proves their value in our eyes. That makes them unreliable with void pistols."

Dahno had recovered his good humor. He chuckled. But his eyes were hard and bright.

"All the Vice-Chairmen should be here on schedule, then?"

"They'll be here," said Bleys. "I don't worry about them."

"Who do you worry about then, Bleys?" asked Dahno looking at him narrowly.

"The boy," said Bleys, "the one we didn't catch."

"Boy?"

"The ward these three were raising and tutoring."

Dahno snorted faintly.

"You're worried about a boy?" he said.

"I thought you were the one who valued neatness, Dahno. I wasn't able to find out about him from the three old men before they died. Courtesy of your Hounds."

Dahno moved a massive hand through the air—a little impatiently dismissing the matter.

"Why would the Hounds think it was necessary to keep them alive, anyway?"

"Because I didn't tell them to kill!" Bleys' voice was not raised, but it came with a particularly penetrating tone. Dahno cocked his head, looking at his half-brother.

"Why all this concern about the boy?" he said. "What can a boy do?"

"That's what I think it might be necessary to know," Bleys said. "Do you remember what you found out about this estate?

This place was set up under a trust established from the sale of an unregistered interstellar courier-class ship which was found drifting near Earth, with a boy in it as a two-year-old child. No one else was aboard. I don't like mysteries and you shouldn't either."

"What makes him any different from any other boy?"

"There are no other boys that I know of on any of the worlds who were discovered as orphans, in space, near Earth—with the odds of discovery at hundreds of thousands to one—who were raised by three tutors, an Exotic, a Dorsai and a Friendly. All as laid down for in instructions that they found in the ship with the boy. He's a very unusual youngster. I don't like mysteries; and you shouldn't either."

This was not the whole truth. There was something more than the mystery surrounding Hal Mayne that was concerning Bleys. There was that deep-buried, uneasy feeling in him that Mayne's very existence in some way seemed to threaten all his plans.

"It's all that Exotic blood in you that doesn't like mysteries," said Dahno. "I've got control of mine, thankfully. Where would we be if we took the time to understand every mystery we came across? Our game is controlling the machinery on all the worlds, not understanding it. Tell me another way that a few thousand or a few hundred thousand of us can hope to run all the worlds, in the way you've been talking up lately."

Bleys felt a weariness. A strange weariness, as if he were a very old man, rather than a very young one. The burden of what he had to do lay heavily upon him. But the time had come.

"Let me explain that more fully when the other Vice-Chairmen get here," said Bleys.

"I don't want to wait for my explanation until tomorrow," said Dahno.

"You mean tonight," said Bleys.

"Tonight? It was scheduled for tomorrow—our meeting," said Dahno.

"I know," the weariness still held Bleys, "that's one of the many orders of yours I've changed recently. They'll be here in the next hour or so. That was another reason for putting the bodies in the freezer."

There was a second of silence.

"Bleys," said Dahno slowly, looking hard at him, "you'd better tell me what you're talking about."

"It's just," said Bleys, "that I have larger plans than you had—for the organization. I have a reason for wanting to control all the worlds. I plan to change history; and for that I need a great many people and eventually enough to swing the whole population on all the worlds except the Dorsai and the Exotics."

He paused.

"Go on," Dahno continued in that quiet voice. "I've only heard part of an explanation so far; and I'll reserve judgment until I've heard it all. Why do you need to control all those planets and all the people on them?"

"Because the people out there are going to die anyway. Die out," said Bleys, "in somewhere between the next three hundred and a thousand years."

"What makes you think that?"

"Humanity went into space too early," Bleys said. "We Others are the proof of it. Cross-breeding—a last-ditch measure by the race to save itself. The penalty for going out too early is death for the race, unless I can stop it. But I can stop it, using the combined production power and fighting power of all the Newer Worlds."

"To do what?"

"To conquer Old Earth—and particularly its brain and heart together, which are the Final Encyclopedia," said Bleys. "That's the only way we'll at last get Earth. And it's only on Earth that all the mixed-breeds, we Others, we who have out on the Newer Worlds developed things that the main, full spectrum race can use, can bring them fully back into Old Earth's bloodstream. So at last we can mature, to be ready finally at last to go out safely, to go out armed, ready, and capable of establishing a place in the universe the way we should."

"Bleys," said Dahno, "I think you've gone a little bit

insane. Or maybe you were insane from the start. What you're talking about is nonsense. It'd take generations. It'd take literally hundreds of years. Our bones will be turned to dust, yours and mine, before anything like that could be completed."

"That's right," said Bleys, "our bones will be. But the race itself will end up being what it should be; what it was headed toward being, before its technology went to its head and it stampeded out to settle the New Worlds too soon. It'll end up with a full race of people like you and me."

"Bleys," said Dahno gently, "I think you're no longer my Vice-Chairman. What you've got in mind is psychotic. But, more than that, it's not what I have in mind. And I made this organization. I made it, I run it, and I'm going to keep on running it. I don't know how much you've done to infect the other Vice-Chairmen who will be coming here; but none of them can seriously have bought the future you're talking about. They're out for payment in their own lifetime, not in some wild future hundreds of years down the line."

"They don't know about it," answered Bleys. "You're the only person I've told and this is the first time I've ever said it to anyone. But I've said it because I need you."

"I don't think you heard me, Bleys," said Dahno. "I said you were no longer my senior Vice-Chairman. You're more a danger than a help. I don't need you."

"It isn't your choice anymore," said Bleys. "When I toured the worlds I sowed the seed of the beginnings of the future that can save us—in fertile ground. The ambition of the men you'd already put in charge of the organizations was already set up. They've been dealing with you, they think, through me. Actually, they've been dealing directly with me. They've already expanded their organizations more than you know; and they're ready to move into a situation where we dominate all government and other powers on all the New Worlds, except the Dorsai and the Exotics."

"*You* sowed the seed?" Dahno said, and smiled, "just as *you* arranged for them to come earlier than I planned? Well, when they do get here, watch me kill that seed and put them back on the path I want for them."

"You won't be able to," said Bleys. "If you look closely at how you trained your people, you trained them to gain ever greater authority in their lifetime. I've shown them a way to do that. I even showed you a way to do that back on Association—enough, so that you were half-willing to entertain it."

"Half-willing is the word," said Dahno. "I went along with you on an if-basis. I'm not happy with you canceling the assassination. Different plans will have to be made now. But also, now that I know what you really have in mind for this expansion, I can't let it happen. And you know when I talk to the other Vice-Chairmen I can bring them around to my way of thinking."

"Perhaps you could, Dahno," said Bleys, "but you won't."

Dahno looked at him.

"I won't?" he said.

"No," said Bleys, "you won't. You won't because I never should have gotten here from Association."

"I don't understand what you mean," said Dahno.

He was suddenly very large and very dangerous in the warm and quiet library. In the moment before Bleys spoke again, a piece of wood exploded with a sudden loud crack in the fire that seemed a noise ten times larger than it was because of the silence.

"No," said Bleys sadly, "I don't think you even consciously planned it this way, but it was the only way things could have worked out. Your Hounds didn't stand a chance against McKae's Defenders. Those were veterans, trained experienced veterans of many church wars, used to working together like part of an army. You had a handful of young men who had been fed full of their skill in the gymnasium and on the firing range. They would have walked into a bears' den and been chewed up. But really, it didn't matter, even if the Hounds had won. You realized that, late in the day."

"And why wouldn't it matter?" demanded Dahno.

"Because even if they won, the conflict between them and

the Defenders couldn't have been kept quiet, not even with all the influence you have. Most of that influence stemmed through the power of the Five Sisters and the rest of your clients in the Chamber. The Five Sisters have already lost most of their influence; while your other Chamber clients are rushing to sever connections with them—and therefore you—like refugees running from a disaster too big to handle."

He paused.

"I don't know—you may even have looked into the kind of people McKae had to defend himself with, and realized—subconsciously, as I say, even if not consciously—that your Hounds didn't stand a chance," Bleys went on. "In any case, you realized there had to end up being a public and political scandal. In a situation like this on Association, the top man rides out the storm; the underneath man goes down. McKae was already on top, before you left; so you had to see what was coming. But your only hope to save the Five Sisters, and therefore yourself, politically, was still to kill McKae and take him out of the picture completely. So you had to try it, regardless."

"That was the idea from the start," said Dahno.

"But not with the odds as they were when you knew you were likely to lose, one way or another," said Bleys; "not with the idea that there'd have to be someone to take the blame, if your Hounds failed."

He paused again. This time Dahno said nothing, only stared at him with eyes that almost glittered.

"Once the militia started investigating, they'd find the training center of your Hounds," said Bleys; "they'd make the connection with Norton Brawley. But you didn't trust Norton if they began to question him the way the Friendly militia do. You knew he'd come apart, like a piece of plastic paper with acid poured on it. So you had to prevent that. And that prevention was living right there in your apartment, had an office in your office, someone at whom Norton could point the finger and say, 'I didn't realize but it must have been him.' Him—*me*."

"I didn't mean—" began Dahno, and stopped abruptly.

"No," said Bleys, "Big Brother, consciously you never look in any direction where you don't like the view of things. You look someplace else. With your eyes turned the other way, you left Association early; and left me in line to take the blame for the whole thing if the Hounds tried the assassination and failed. And you could have known what was going to happen ahead of time—you may have known much earlier than I did. Maybe you knew that McKae already had strong backing in the rest of the Chamber. So you made sure you took off first, for Earth and alone. If I could survive to reach you, well and good. If I didn't, at least McKae would be dead, you thought; and you could go back to Association."

He stopped and waited for Dahno to speak. But Dahno just looked at him and shook his head.

"No. I know," said Bleys, "you deliberately didn't look far enough to see the worst that could happen, if I took the blame. If you had, you'd have seen that, because of our relationship, Association would be closed to you. The Five Sisters and the other Chamber members would never trust you again. Now, tonight, the Vice-Chairmen are meeting here. They've been dealing with me, not you—though they thought they were merely dealing with you through me. But in any case they want the future I offered them. You knew what they were when you set them up as the leading Vice-Chairmen of each out-world unit. They're ambitious on their own, as well as for anyone else. I showed them a greater future. By this time the changes are already under way. They're recruiting Others all over their individual planets. They can't wait to get started getting solid chokeholds on the government of their particular planet. And what about you, Dahno?"

He waited a moment and then asked the question again.

"What about you?"

Dahno stood where he was. But the dangerousness had gone out of him. Instead there was an incredible weariness.

"All right," he said finally. "All right—once I was here, I saw the dangers back there. But it was too late to change things then. In any case, I'll just have to start on some new world, fresh."

"If that's what you want, fine," said Bleys. "But you're tired, Dahno. You're dead tired, if you'll only admit it. Your personal involvement in Chamber politics carried you too deep into it. You ended being the doctor on twenty-four-hour call for all of your clients."

He looked at Dahno with sympathy.

"Let me offer you something better than starting again on a world that hasn't had an Other organization on it yet. Though, as I say, you can have that if you want."

Dahno looked at him and for a moment the old smile came back. He chuckled, if still wearily.

"What could you offer me, Little Brother?" he asked. "What is there for you to offer me? Nothing."

"No, I think I've got something you'll like," said Bleys.

Dahno chuckled again, sadly, shaking his head.

"I'm not trying to talk you into anything you don't freely want," said Bleys. "Remember how you told me you wanted me to choose to work with you, if I was going to, of my own free will?"

"I remember," said Dahno.

"Well, I'm saying the same thing to you now. You see, I believe you've got a real affection for me," said Bleys, "in spite of the situation you left me in on Association. You've got more of a kinship feeling with me than with anyone else. You like me. But also—under certain circumstances, to survive— you'll always put yourself first. I understand that. You can't help it. It's the way you're built. Remember our mother?"

Dahno's face showed sudden anger.

"Don't tell me I'm like her!" he said. "Never tell me that!"

"Of course you are," said Bleys. "So am I. But I found something large enough to lose the similarity in. You might too, if you go along with me."

"I won't take that, Bleys," said Dahno. He was dangerous again. "I'm not like her."

"You needn't be," said Bleys. "As I say, listen to me. Listen tonight, and see if you want to join me of your own free will. See if it doesn't suit you, if it doesn't free you and you don't like it!"

"All right," said Dahno, "let's hear it again now, then."

"I'm going to do what I told you earlier I was going to do," said Bleys. "I'm going to use the New Worlds to move the human race back to Earth and start it out once more to grow into what it should be—the kind of society where you and I'd be the norm, instead of the exception. It can be done."

"And you're that sure?" said Dahno.

"I'm sure," said Bleys, "I've got the vision and the plan. Also I know the opposite side of the coin. The Others can offer improvements to the race. But one-by-one and even in our organization, they aren't that superior to other people. But as a united force to influence politics scattered on the various planets, we can triumph. Only, though, if you and I lead them. Together, we can show them the way to take over Earth; and return to Earth those who belong there. The other new planets will be left to die in their own way."

"And how does this help me any?" asked Dahno.

"We'd work together—as I just told you," said Bleys, "you'll be what you always have. More so. We'll let the Vice-Chairmen know that it's you that's running this new organization of Others, and I'm simply your executive. Only, gradually, I'll come to be more and more present to them, and they'll come to think of you and I together, as equal parts."

"What you're really offering me," said Dahno, "is the chance to be your second-in-command."

"No," said Bleys, "the plan's mine; but what I'm offering is the chance for you to build the organization and control it—so it'll succeed."

"It won't work," said Dahno. "The two of us trying to operate together that way."

"Yes, it will," Bleys said, "the fact is, I need freedom to operate quietly. With you in visible charge, I would be. We just have to stick to my plan. That's all I ask."

"That's all!" said Dahno bitterly. "You still haven't told me why you need me, except to get things started. Once they're started, you won't have any use for me, and you'll get rid of me."

"No, I won't," said Bleys, urgently. He took a step toward

Dahno and put one hand on a massive forearm. "The need for you will always be there. You can convince anyone of anything. I can't do that. I trained myself to stand up on a platform and impress people. I can juggle events to force a peg into a hole. But you can charm it into that same hole; and your way of doing it causes no one to pay attention; while my way often attracts too much attention. I need you and I want you, Dahno. I want you also because you're my brother. I feel the same closeness to you, you felt to me. The only difference between us is, you can always count on me. I won't suddenly leave you out on a limb. I won't, because that's what I am. That's what I was to begin with; and that's what's been made in me by what I've become. If I say anything, you can trust it."

He stopped speaking. Dahno said nothing.

"Well?" asked Bleys. "*Do* you trust me?"

For a moment Dahno did not move, then he nodded slowly. He glanced at his wrist monitor.

"The other Vice-Chairmen will be arriving here anytime in the next half hour or so," Bleys said. "Time is short. But I want you to tell me if you're going along with me. If you say it, I'll know you mean it. Or, tell me if you can't. If you do, I'll still take care of you, the way you would have taken care of Henry and Joshua—but in the style you're accustomed to, rather than in their style. Remember, you can always change your mind. Dahno, I need an answer!"

Dahno looked at him and slowly his face lit up again. The twinkle was back in his eyes.

"I trust you, Bleys," he said. "You know I trust you. I trusted you the first time I drove into Henry's farmyard; and never stopped after that. If what you say proves out, maybe we'll do all right together with this wild, enormous plan of yours. If it doesn't work, then I'm no worse off than if I tried starting up something new on some new world. Yes, I'll go along with you. I was up to my ears in Association. There was too much to handle; and you're quite right. I'm tired. If I have to—can I lean on you then, Brother?"

"Always," said Bleys; and laughed. "So you're with me—at

least unless the other Vice-Chairmen give you reason not to be. Right?"

"Other Vice-Chairmen, hell!" said Dahno. "I'll even help you convince them tonight, if you want. We'll debut our new act together."

Their eyes met.

"You know," said Bleys, smiling himself, "I think it'll work like a phase-shift!"

Dahno opened his mouth to answer, but before any words came out a doorbell chimed all through the house.

"One of our lesser Vice-Chairmen is early," he said, as they both lifted their heads at the sound. "Shall I go meet him for you, Mr. Co-Chairman, or shall we wait for him here?"

"Let's wait for him here," said Bleys, "both of us."

SCIENCE FICTION FROM
GORDON R. DICKSON

☐ ☐	53577-4	ALIEN ART	$2.95 Canada $3.95
☐ ☐	53546-4	ARCTURUS LANDING	$3.50 Canada $4.50
☐ ☐	53550-2	BEYOND THE DAR AL-HARB	$2.95 Canada $3.50
☐ ☐	53544-8	THE FAR CALL	$4.95 Canada $5.95
☐ ☐	53589-8	GUIDED TOUR	$3.50 Canada $4.50
☐ ☐	53068-3	HOKA! with Poul Anderson	$2.95 Canada $3.50
☐ ☐	53592-8	HOME FROM THE SHORE	$3.50 Canada $4.50
☐ ☐	53562-6	THE LAST MASTER	$2.95 Canada $3.50
☐ ☐	53554-5	LOVE NOT HUMAN	$2.95 Canada $3.95
☐ ☐	53581-2	THE MAN FROM EARTH	$2.95 Canada $3.95
☐ ☐	53572-3	THE MAN THE WORLDS REJECTED	$2.95 Canada $3.75

THE BEST IN
SCIENCE FICTION